I0645606

THE WHARF RAT GUILD

ELIZABETH FOREST

ARBORI BOOKS

The Wharf Rat Guild

Copyright © 2021 Elizabeth Forest

All rights reserved.

https://www.elizabethsforest.com

No part of this book may be reproduced in any form or by any electronic or mechanical means, including information storage and retrieval systems, without written permission from the author, except for the use of brief quotations in a book review.

Arbori Books

https://www.arboribooks.com

Print ISBN: 978-0-9996894-4-8

E-ISBN: 978-0-9996894-5-5

LCCN: 2021916410

1
———

SPIRITS

LONDON, *September 4, 1660*

Whereas the Houses of Parliament are informed, that divers lewd Persons do go up and down the City of London and elsewhere and in a most barbarous and wicked Manner steal away many little children... (*Tudor and Stuart Proclamations, no. 2613a*)

If I'd known that was our last day together, I would've dragged Daniel out of the city to sleep in the fields, to hide from anyone who came near. But I didn't know, and we needed to eat.

The day was soft and damp, the sun a glowing white pearl behind the clouds layered above the Thames. Mist obscured the water, and the rumbling of carts from across the river sounded close at hand. On the Custom House wharf, ships bobbed gently on the slack tide. It was too damp a day to be loitering on the wharves with no obvious work on offer, and few people were about so early. Even the gulls drowsed on the spars and rigging, feathers fluffed against the damp.

On the foreshore below the wharf, the Mud Men were out with their long poles, picking through the flotsam left in the mud by the receding tide. Always sent to do the dirtiest jobs, they were searching for lost goods, coal fallen from boats, or bodies.

I'd taken shelter from the drizzle inside the deserted watermen's hut. Water dripped from the roof onto the glistening planks. Mist drifted across the river. I'd just turned fourteen, and my skirt was becoming too short. My brother was a few feet down the wharf, his sharp, pointed face like my own, but instead of freckles and toffee-colored eyes, tilting up at the corners, his eyes were dark, deep set, and often solemn.

They weren't solemn now; he and Penny were laughing. She ruffled his dark curls and he smirked.

Seeing how pale and thin he was, I felt the familiar ache in my chest. I'd done my best, but trying to keep him alive and out of trouble hadn't been easy, never mind feeding him, since Da died.

Penny saw me watching them and winked. I smiled at her. That we'd survived at all was largely due to Penny; without her help we would've starved. A year younger she might be, but she'd survived two years on the wharves before we met her and knew more about how things worked than most. She found us wandering the quays, turned out of our lodgings after Da died. Somehow she knew what Daniel was without a word spoken, and brought us to live with the wharf rats, saying it was the safest place for us.

She was pretty, with long red hair and plump cheeks that belied her lack of regular meals. Not that I cared about her looks; I mostly envied her having someone to rely on. Her older brother Jimmy watched out for her, and she, in turn, watched out for us. Well, Daniel, really. She was the one who convinced the group of wharf rats who slept together for safety to let us join them. I confess I didn't figure it out, not right away, but they were different from the other orphans who banded together to steal or do the tricky jobs like chimney sweeping. They stayed together because of that difference, and it was the reason she'd invited Daniel to live with them. I was there on sufferance because Daniel insisted.

We learned how to earn our coin, Daniel and I, and though

never far from hunger, we weren't as badly off as some. We earned enough to stay alive, running errands and carrying messages for the sailors and merchants.

And strangely enough, Daniel was happy.

"Penny!" someone called from down the wharf.

I turned to look. A girl of about ten, with a halo of straw-colored hair, threaded her way through the crowd of wharfies and street sellers, followed by a limping little boy, his shiny brown hair cut in a bowl. I recognized them as belonging to our gang of children who slept together in the same alley, but I didn't know their names.

Penny and Daniel went to meet her on the quay where a fat-bellied merchantman was in the final stages of preparing to sail.

Beside the boarding ramp, a well-dressed, handsome young man, his dark hair in a queue, watched them with a bored expression.

Penny and the girl huddled together, whispering.

My brother glanced behind him, then placed his hand on the boy's head. Daniel's face had a faraway expression.

He's at it again. I pelted down the river road, hoping to stop my sly brother before anyone saw what he was doing. Daniel saw me coming and quickly knelt beside the boy, hiding from me behind Penny's skirts.

Before I reached them, Daniel was already on his feet. "Should be right as rain now," he said cheerily to the boy. The boy looked startled, then slowly smiled, revealing a missing front tooth.

"What's going on?" I asked sternly.

Penny waved toward the ship. "There'll be a cargo of servants coming. Be careful."

"You know that's not what I meant." I knelt beside the boy. "My name's Lizzie. What's yours?"

He smiled shyly. "Ben'hamin."

"Hullo, Benjamin."

The girl with the straw-colored hair took hold of my arm and yanked me to my feet with surprising strength. "And *I'm* Mattie, his sister. Who are you, Mistress Bold-as-Brass, to interfere in our business, I'd like to know?"

I shook my arm free and glared at her. "What *my* brother does is my business."

"Lizzie's my guardian angel," Daniel murmured apologetically. "Don't worry, Lizzie. No one saw."

Penny touched my arm. "We should go. The cart is coming. And the agent's watching." She nodded toward the dark-haired young man who stared openly.

The rumbling sound of metal-shod wheels drew closer, and then the cart, packed with men and women, appeared at the end of the wharf.

I'd seen such carts before and knew the drill. The captain waited until the last minute to load his most valuable cargo: men, women, and children, bound for the colonies as indentured labor. Their hands were tied to the cart rail to prevent escape, in case they changed their minds.

The rats knew to stay away from such carts and the agents who recruited for them. The poor, the desperate, and the drunk signed contracts trading years of labor for a passage across the sea in hopes of a better life, or at least an escape from whatever threatened them in this one. The promise of food, lodging, and new clothes, paid for by the agent, was often incentive enough. He had to keep them safe until they boarded ship, or he'd lose his investment. That's why they were imprisoned, closely guarded, and tied to the cart rail. No slyboots could run away with new clobber and full bellies. Voluntary or not, they were prisoners, bound for an unknown fate.

The cart drew near to the ship. Mattie grabbed Benjamin's hand. "We're off. Thanks for your help, Daniel. Penny." Me, she scowled at as she walked past.

I scarcely noticed. My eyes were on a girl my age, hands tied to the cart railing. She was crying, and in between her hoarse, racking sobs, she called, "Won't someone help me? I'm being spirited! I never said I'd go!" My own stomach clenched in sympathy, imagining her helplessness.

"Come away, Lizzie," Penny urged, pulling on my arm. "It's not safe."

Daniel nodded at the young man, now chatting with the captain on deck. "Who's that?"

"That's the agent, James Muldaur."

The captain handed him a drawstring purse. James counted the coins before tucking it in the purse on his belt; then he shook the captain's hand, turned on his heel, and walked away without a glance at the folk in the cart. Others besides the girl were crying, but most were grim-faced.

"What will happen to them?" Daniel asked quietly.

"The captain owns their contracts now," Penny said. "When the ship reaches Barbados or Virginia, he'll sell them again, to the local planters. He'll make a lot more money than he paid James, if none of them die. The poor souls have no say in who buys them, or even in how long they have to work till they're free. The sailors say those contracts are changed all the time, once they're over the sea."

"So perhaps the girl *is* being spirited," Daniel said.

Penny shrugged. "Perhaps. Or she's changed her mind, now that it's come to it. Perhaps she signed the contract to get away from a bad master or mistress and regrets it now. We've no way to know. Besides, what constable would listen to us?"

Some agents did kidnap, or spirit away children to the plantations, to the grief of their parents or masters if they had them. If they didn't, no one cared. "Fatherless" children were fair game. The Crown was happy to send surplus mouths across the sea.

On the other hand, an accusation of spiriting could be deadly for the accused. I'd been on the street when a mob attacked a woman accused of being a spirit, and in the confusion several people were hurt. Becoming an agent was a good way to make a great deal of money in a short amount of time, but there was always the danger they'd be accused of kidnapping. If it was a small child stolen, they might even be killed by an angry crowd.

It was past time to leave, but I lingered to watch the girl being dragged aboard ship and hustled below. *That could be me, or Daniel someday.* We were "fatherless" now, along with the rest of the wharf rats.

We'd lingered too long. "Come away, Daniel. See you later, Penny."

Penny bent down and murmured something in Daniel's ear. "I know," he said sullenly. "But I don't see why I should."

"Don't argue. Do this for your sister's sake at least." Penny nodded to me, and then walked away.

"What was that about?" I asked.

He pointed at the watermen's hut. "Tell you inside."

Once we were inside the bare little hut, its benches empty, Daniel whispered, "I'm not supposed to tell you, on account of you're not one of us." He bit his lip. "But I think I have to."

I'd come up against that hesitation more frequently lately. The rats warned Daniel, but I was on my own.

"At least tell me what you're stubbornly refusing to do? You're being a looby, I can tell that much."

He smiled. "She wants me to go into hiding for a few days."

The back of my neck prickled as though someone had breathed on it. "Why?"

"It's been three months since the last child was nobbled by the river. Everyone says we're due."

"I don't understand. Children are spirited away all the time."

He met my eyes. "Penny says it's not a spirit, but a tracker."

And that's why they don't warn me. "How could she possibly know?"

"It's a guess." He frowned. "But a *gifted* child disappears from the wharves every three months. The sailors say so too. No one knows who's responsible. Not even Kat, I asked her."

My younger brother sounded far too knowing about such things. It surprised me Kat would even speak to him. Kat Jenkins seemed to know more than any wharf rat should, but she was secretive and solitary. More went on behind those clever dark eyes than she ever revealed, but that wouldn't stop Daniel. He'd talk to anyone. "What did she say?"

"She said there's no knowing who it is, but she believes they're taken aboard a ship that calls every three months."

"I've never heard a word of this before."

"We've only been here two months," he said reasonably. "No one's been nobbled since we came. But don't you remember? Penny told you about the last girl. She was an Elizabeth, just like you."

Of course I remembered. She was nobbled right in front of the Fish Street Tavern, Penny said. Had that been three months ago? The timing was most likely a coincidence, everyone hoping there was a pattern so the kidnappings would be predictable. Plenty of agents stored their human cargo in "depots" in Saint Katharine's parish near the Tower, barely a few steps away. Whatever the rats thought, any disappearance was likely due to an agent. Like that James fellow. Pity such a good-looking cove sold people for a living.

I remembered my wayward brother was taking risks again. "I thought we agreed you wouldn't use your gift where folk can see?"

He shrugged, hands in his pockets, unconcerned. "His foot was badly infected, Lizzie. He was getting sicker. It only took a moment. No one saw. Where's the harm?"

"You don't know who saw."

His mouth set in a stubborn line. "I just touched his head is all. Why are you so cross when I help people? It's the right thing to do, and you know it."

I was silent. That was *exactly* what Da would say. "If Penny thinks you should hide, then we should."

"You'll notice she's still here," he pointed out. "So's Mattie. Most of our gang's still here. I can't earn anything if I hide."

"I can earn, while *you* hide. No tracker will be after me. That's why she didn't warn me." That, and the fact that she didn't trust me completely.

"We can't be certain. Maybe it *is* a spirit, and they like girls your age: strong enough to survive the voyage, but easier to control than the boys. None of those planters have womenfolk. They need someone to cook and clean." He grinned at my disgusted expression.

I refused to be diverted. "Tomorrow we'll find a place for you to hole up for a few days. Those old smugglers' tunnels Penny showed us, perhaps. I'll bring you food."

"All right, Lizzie," he said. "Whatever you say. But remember, smugglers would cut my throat as soon as look at me. At least a tracker would keep me alive."

2

BRIDEWELL

London, *September 4–5, 1660*

Dusk deepened to evening and the mist rose from the river once more, filling the streets and slicking the cobbles. The smell of garbage and cesspits came with it.

Daniel and I joined our gang of wharf rats in the damp, narrow alley. We crawled beneath my old blue blanket, the only possession I'd salvaged when the bailiff turned us out. A tattered piece of scrounged canvas hung over a rope to keep the rain off. The wharf rats lay curled around us, lying on rags, beneath their own bits of canvas.

In the grey, predawn light, I woke to the sound of a cart rumbling over cobblestones. It was too early for work on the wharves. The sound drew nearer. I poked my head out of our makeshift tent just as the Mud Men's carts came to a halt, blocking both ends of our alley. Someone cried a warning. "'Tis the bum bailiffs!"

I shook Daniel. "We have to run." But it was already too late.

Hand in hand, we ran for the far end of the alley. A fat-bellied man in a greasy coat, reeking of sour wine, grabbed Daniel and dropped him into the wagon bed. Once his hands were tied, it was too late for me. I couldn't leave him behind. Another man picked me up and carried me to the cart; my hands were tied to the rail, just like the indentured servants'.

The others tried to run, but the Mud Men threw nets or struck out with their staves, aiming for legs and knees. The kinchin were scooped up and dumped into the wagons like so many sacks of barley. Some fought, and the Mud Men beat them. Others were too sleepy to make a sound, and stared in bewilderment.

Once it was full, our wagon moved off, swaying from side to side, to plunge into the fog on the river road. It began to climb up the hill, wheels creaking loudly. The smell of mud, tar, and rotting things drifted to us from the dirty Mud Men seated on the driving bench.

"Where are you taking us?" Mattie called. They didn't answer.

A thin band of apricot-colored sky appeared in the east. By the time the cart came to a halt beside a building of dirty yellow bricks, sunlight was gilding the ship masts and roofs below us. But there was nothing golden about the entrance to Bridewell jail.

They dragged or carried us each in turn into the main cell, where the beggars, drunkards, thieves, and the mad were brought after the streets had been scoured. The noise of our arrival woke the other inmates. They stirred, muttering curses. Most turned their backs and went back to sleep.

I'd never been there before. The sprawled bodies and vacant stares of the mad frightened me. Footpads and foists exchanged knowing smiles before closing their eyes to drift back to sleep. Damp sweated from the stone walls, and the light falling from high windows gleamed in puddles on the floor. The jailer came in after us to throw more straw on the mud, but it quickly sank. The place stank of overflowing pisspots and despair.

"Lizzie? Where are we?" Daniel whispered, his mouth to my ear.

"Bridewell. Don't wake the others."

Someone moaned, a pitiful sound.

I recognized the voice, and searched the huddled bodies for her.

Beneath her red hair, Penny's face was grey and twisted with pain. I stepped carefully over the sleeping bodies to kneel beside her. Her brother Jimmy was trying to comfort her, his normally cheerful face pale with anxiety. "What's the matter?" I whispered.

"My leg," she said. "One of the brutes hit me and now I can't walk."

She drew up her skirt. A large green and purple bruise was spreading across her shin, but worse, something sharp pressed oddly beneath the skin. It looked wrong. "I think it's broken," I said, finding no words of comfort.

She looked stricken, her mouth trembling. In this stinking, filthy place a broken bone could be a death sentence. "What can I do?" she asked desperately. "That jailer won't help unless I pay him."

I bit my lip. If Daniel helped her, someone would see.

Then he was beside me, his hands on her leg. "Are you in pain?"

I wanted to tell him to stop, but I couldn't. It was Penny, who had saved *us*. And arguing would draw more attention. I glanced at the barred door.

The jailer was chatting to someone I couldn't see, just beyond the door. Above all, he mustn't see. An old woman in the corner was watching us, and another rat, Potts, the boy with an old man's face and dirty fair hair, stared vacantly in our direction. Most of the rats had fallen asleep. Mattie met my eyes and looked away. Daniel was Penny's only hope. I stood, holding my skirt wide, to block the view from the door.

"Be quick," I whispered.

Daniel nodded, running his hands over her leg. Sweat shone on his face, and his eyes unfocused for a moment. Then he nodded as though satisfied and wiped his forehead on his sleeve. "How do you feel?"

Penny gasped. "'Tis much better," she said.

"Come away now. Penny, Jimmy—not a word." I gave them a sharp look.

Penny lay down, her eyes closing in relief. Jimmy whispered, "Thank you."

I led Daniel to the corner near the pisspots. No one would fight us for that piece of wall because of the stench, and I wanted our backs protected. We were in even greater danger now.

I glanced at the door. The jailer was gone.

The day wore on. Daniel and I slept fitfully, huddling close in the foul straw.

I woke to the sound of loud voices, a shadow falling across my face.

I opened my eyes in a moment of nameless fear. Nothing looked familiar. Bodies lay everywhere and the stench hit me again. Daniel lay curled beside me, one arm over me, his breath on my face. Even in sleep his brows were drawn together. The straw stank of vomit, but the room was closely packed and there was nowhere better.

A loud argument between a group of men and a woman had woken me.

"Under Cromwell we had our liberty."

"Liberty." A barefoot man spat into the straw. "Liberty ain't for the like o' us. Only the nobs and the merchants can afford it. An' he took away Christmas and May Day. Folk like us need their holidays."

"We've lost our chance now, with the king's party back," a man with a kerchief over his head said. "Now the only free men are in the colonies, though there's plenty o' petty tyrants ruling there too. We should've kept the Republic. If that foul traitor Monk hadn't betrayed us, we wouldn't be in this fix."

Another man waved his hand dismissively. "That old chestnut.

The people wanted an end to the riots, man. Besides, there's not much to choose between kings and Republics, I'm thinking." The man looked respectable, with lace above good broadcloth, but his face was blotched and red, as though he drank too much and too often. "Which would ye have, kings and the bishops blackmailing you with taxes and courts, or the ranting preachers who tell you what to believe and forbid plays and festivals?"

"Why worry about it now? The king's back, what's done is done, and there's worse than kings to fear," an old woman said, her cap strings untied, her wiry grey hair falling around her face. "What about that corpse the Mud Men found on the foreshore a few days ago, eh? Folk say *he's* back."

"Shut your gob," the barefoot man growled.

"Why should I? 'Cause you're scairt o' him? I've the same right to speak as you. And these kinchin should know." To my horror, I saw she was nodding at *me.* "They're the ones he'll nobble."

"Who do you mean, mistress?" Daniel asked. He'd been listening too.

"He collects children," she said darkly. "You'll know what I mean, I expect. Kinchin stolen for him are never seen again. Not just children, o' course. They say he'll kill anyone who stands in his way, like swatting a fly. Like that poor fool they found on the mud yesterday."

"That's enough, jade. These kinchin have done you no harm, and you're scaring 'em."

"I'm helping 'em, is what. Otherwise they're easy pickings."

"So who killed the man on the foreshore?" Daniel asked.

"I dunno, do I?" the woman said coyly. "But it's Hazelton's name on everyone's lips when a body is found and no one knows why."

"But that's no proof," Penny scoffed. She had hitched herself closer to the woman to listen, with her leg out straight before her. "It coulda been robbers, or a jealous husband, or a brawl, so how could you possibly know—"

"Lord Hazelton," the woman interrupted, dropping her voice so that only those closest would hear, "got his title by blackmail and his estates by murder. And them's just the stories everyone believes. Some lord or other petitioned the House o' Lords to have him removed, and that lord disappeared soon after. Naught was ever proved, o' course. Folk say he wants more power than the king. Collecting children is his hobby. Enthusiastic about it, he is."

A skinny woman with her cap askew, reeking of alcohol, had stared unseeing for hours. Now she had a stricken look on her face. She rose to her feet, staring at the old woman in horror. Crossing herself, she muttered a prayer, and stumbled across the room to get away from her.

The barefoot man and the man in the red kerchief had gone pale. They too rose and went to stand by the door, throwing dark looks at the old woman.

Daniel and I looked at each other but said nothing.

The middle-class drunkard smiled condescendingly. "What nonsense. Folk who have nowt else to blame use him as their bugbear. 'Tis evil Lord Hazelton!' they cry, giving him credit for the work of spirits or robbers."

The old woman leaned back and nodded. "Believe what you like. I know what I've heard and what I've seen. It's the kinchin who need to know. No child is safe from him."

"How can we protect ourselves, then?" Penny asked in a low voice.

"That's enough, woman. You'll get us all murdered if you keep on like this." One of the men across the room nodded at the jailer who stood watching at the door. "Anyone could be listening."

The old woman glared at the door and the shadow behind it. "Oh, informers are always about. Anyway, I'm done." She looked directly at Daniel. "Be careful, dearie. If you hear word old Hazelton's about, go into hiding."

Daniel looked wordlessly at me. We were probably thinking

the same thing: Maybe *he* owned the ship that came every three months.

SHAFTS OF SUNLIGHT fell from the high, barred windows, moving across the floor. A madwoman staggered about the room muttering and whining. Daniel dozed beside me, but I couldn't sleep again. The beggars and foists were up and about, shuffling in the confined space, and I kept an eye on them. An old man crouched beside me, speaking urgently. It sounded like a warning, but he had no teeth. All I understood was "beware" and what sounded like "boy." He shambled off and my stomach rumbled. It was past suppertime.

A shadow appeared at the door. "You, boy. Come here." The jailer leaned forward, his eyes on Daniel.

Daniel and I exchanged a look and then approached the door together.

The jailer smiled broadly, revealing missing teeth. He spoke softly, forcing us to lean close to the bars to hear him. "You're a likely looking lad. I've a proposition for you. How'd you like a *real* job, with coins to jingle in your pocket? I've a captain friend, looking for a cabin boy for his ship."

My heart beat painfully. Someone told him about Daniel healing Penny. Or he'd seen. "He already has work," I said shortly. "He's not interested."

"And who are you to interfere?"

"She's my sister."

"Ah. Don't you want to *help* your sister?"

I was sure he'd seen. Or someone had told him. "No," I said. "He's too young. We stay together."

The jailer ignored me, giving Daniel a lopsided grin, reminding me of a yawning cat with a mouse in its paw. "Well, boy?"

Daniel looked uncertain. "Well, but a cabin boy, Lizzie. I could make a steady living."

I pulled him close and whispered, "He knows. Don't listen."

The jailer shook his head. "Don't you *want* to help your sister? You could be earning a man's wage, near enough, not skulking in jail." He turned to me and his smile disappeared. "Be sensible, wench. Your brother could learn a sailor's trade while earning coin. It's a good apprenticeship. Ain't no trackers at sea and sailors don't peach gifted children—they need 'em too badly."

So he did know. He might have a tracker already waiting.

"And I'll earn a wage too?"

My God, Daniel was considering it.

"That you will, son, that you will. So will you do it?"

I whispered, "He knows, Daniel. He's selling you. There's no ship." Or if there was, it wasn't a cabin boy they were after, but more cargo to sell. A lump of ice formed in the pit of my stomach. There was a third possibility: The three months were up. Whoever was nobbling the wharf rats might have found their next child right here.

The jailer narrowed his eyes. "I've found the lad a good berth; where's the harm if I earn a tiny commission? It's a lucky chance I'm offering, maybe the best one you'll get. Think on, wench—if I don't get a commission this way, I can earn it another, from someone who doesn't care what happens to the boy. But I have a conscience, me. I'd rather the boy went to sea. Be sensible. 'Tis a fair bargain."

There was the threat. I'd been about to pull my brother away, but I was light-headed, my hand trembling on Daniel's shoulder. If we didn't do as the jailer said, he'd be off to find a tracker to earn the bounty.

Daniel's expression didn't change. "He's right, Lizzie. A ship is the safest place for me. You won't have to worry anymore."

Won't have to worry? The jailer was twisty as a corkscrew. If there was a ship, it was the best bargain we could make. But all the jailer had to do was put the word about in any tavern that he was looking for a tracker and Daniel would be gone forever.

I repeated, "We have to stick together."

He shook his head and said, "I want to go."

The jailer grinned and rattled his keys, unlocking the door.

"Wait! What's the captain's name?" I pleaded. "And the name of the ship?" I wanted to be convinced there was one, or if it was Hazelton's, to know the name.

The jailer's ratlike faced wrinkled as though he'd smelled something worse than the stench around us. "The captain isn't one to bandy his name in the streets, girl. He's a quiet one, see? And it's lucky for your brother I picked him, for the captain wouldn't give just any boy a chance. It's a lucky berth, son."

"My name's Daniel," he said quietly. "Daniel Nelson."

"Well, Daniel, you'll make your sister proud. Are you ready to have adventures, see foreign lands, and learn the mysteries of the sea? Why, I'm jealous of your opportunity, so I am."

I'd stopped listening to the man's nonsense. I only had eyes for Daniel. He was excited, ready to leave the constant fear behind. He believed he'd be safe from trackers and earning a wage too. The jailer had known the right things to say. Daniel was the only family I had left and I was going to lose him.

"Tell me the name of the ship," I pleaded. "I need to know where my brother is. That's fair, isn't it?"

Doubt flickered, finally, in Daniel's eyes.

The jailer smiled shrewdly. "O' course. But she'll have sailed before I let you out, so don't think you can make the deal yourself. She's the *Bright Hope*. A good omen, eh boy? She'll make your fortune."

I wanted to grab Daniel's hand and run as far as we could from that stinking cell the moment the door opened. "Promise me he'll be safe."

"O' course. Safe as houses, 'cept o'course for storms and such as happen at sea. He's a good cap'n and it's a good ship. Come, boy." He swung the barred door open. "Time to go."

The rusty hinges squealed and every head turned to look.

I hugged my brother, tears running down my face. "Be careful. Be safe. Come and find me when you get back. Don't take risks and come back to me. I'm counting on you."

He smiled and kissed me on the cheek. "Don't worry, Lizzie. I'll be back, with coin in my pocket. I promise."

He stepped through the door. Quick as a snake the jailer's arm darted out to clamp him to his side. He locked the door, the rattling keys like the sound of chains.

They walked away, Daniel looking small and helpless.

I spent the rest of the night pacing, tears running down my face. A man with a scarred face cursed and threatened me, then pulled a knife and said he'd cut my throat if I didn't stop, so I sank down, drew my knees up and muffled my sobs in my skirt. No one else came near. There was nothing they could do.

The next morning we straggled out, bleary-eyed and blinking at the glaring white sky.

Before I ate, before I even washed the stink of the place off of me, I went down to the wharves and asked every sailor I met if he'd ever heard of a ship called the *Bright Hope*.

No one had.

3

―――――

A VISION

DECEMBER 1660, London

"Lizzie, wake up." A boot prodded my ribs. Somewhere close by, a gull called forlornly.

I rolled over.

Penny's face hung above me, red hair falling around it. Behind her a coffin lid of white clouds pressed down.

"Everyone else is gone. Get up before you're robbed."

I sat up, cold and stiff after sleeping on the cobbles in the damp, and slipped my hand into my pocket. The two pennies I'd earned the day before were still there, and so was my glass luck piece. I fingered its rough edges before rising to my feet with a groan. I didn't need to dress; you never knew when you'd have to run for it. I simply stowed my blanket in the damp-stained barrel where we hid our things and was ready for the day.

"There's a merchantman from India. Should be enough for everyone. But *hurry*." Penny took off without waiting for me. No sense in losing her chance; she'd already done me a kindness by waking me before I'd gotten my throat slit.

Rubbing the sleep from my eyes, I stumbled out of the alley into the wider street beyond. Tall houses loomed out of the fog, their soot-stained plaster and rain-darkened timbers gloomy in the early light. My boots slipped on the wet cobbles as I picked my way down the hill. The sluggish brown river waited at the bottom of the hill, mist curling on its surface.

A forest of masts pressed against the sky, ships crowding close to the Custom House wharf. By the time I reached the river road beside it, my gut was cramping with hunger. *Soon,* I told myself, *soon.* Once I had the promise of work, I'd stop for bread and ale. I refused to spend my pennies till there were more to come.

I owed Penny for yet another kindness. Ever since Daniel had healed her leg and disappeared that night, she'd saved my neck more than once. I felt guilty. I'd done nothing to deserve her help, 'twas Daniel who saved her. But Penny argued Daniel would want it that way, and that was true.

I tried to walk quickly. There would be no sharing between rats from the takings from the merchantman. Every rat had to fend for herself.

The three-legged cranes on the Custom House wharf were already in motion, lifting nets of crates and bales from the holds of the ships, iron pulleys squealing as the ropes tightened with the weight.

A sailor waved me over. "This message needs to go to Threadneedle Street," he said. "Five pence if you go now, fast as you can." He recited the message and had me repeat it, twice. Then he handed me the coins.

I bobbed a curtsy and took off. Five pence was above the rate, *and* he paid up front.

On the way back, I stopped at the cook shop for a meat pasty. I hadn't tasted meat in months and had to stop myself from gobbling it down. I ate half and put the rest in my pocket for later.

At the Fish Street tavern on the corner, I stopped for a tankard. Ale would fill up the empty corners and dull the ache of my hunger.

I took my mug outside to sit on the bench by the door and watch the river traffic below. A watery sun broke through the clouds and I closed my eyes, enjoying the warmth on my face.

Shouts came from the road below. Two wagons had collided, blocking the way. Folk trying to get to work joined in, shouting insults at the drivers.

Ever since the ban against street performers and fairs had been lifted, the brightly colored clothing of the players, jugglers, and rope dancers was its own pleasure. They flooded across the bridge from Southwark every morning to coax pennies from the crowds in the better part of town. Two jugglers were setting up near the Custom House and a small crowd had gathered. Sober men of business, dressed in black with white lace, like good Puritans, stood cheek by jowl beside dandies, young men of fashion who imitated the king's long coats and petticoat trousers.

A boy Daniel's age passed me, holding his father's hand. His fair hair looked nothing like Daniel's dark curls, but when he smiled up at his father my chest ached. Three months had passed since Daniel had disappeared, with no word. I hadn't stopped asking new ships for news of him.

And now it was time for another child to disappear.

I counted my coins: four pence, enough for tomorrow, anyway. As I slipped 'em back into my pocket, the glass pricked my finger and I took it out, turning it back and forth in the sunlight. I'd found it in a rubbish tip the week before, picking over piles of rotting fruit and slimy vegetables for something to eat. Layers of light moved strangely in the depths, and the shifting shades of blue comforted me. I called it my lucky glass, and whether it was or no, I chose to believe it.

I'd lingered long enough. Time to check the new arrivals. Walking back toward Bear Quay and Penny's merchantman, I saw coopers delivering barrels and wharf men loading cargo onto carts. Two women with baskets on their heads sang ditties advertising their lemons and oranges.

I dodged a wagon laden with hogsheads and stopped suddenly, ignoring the bustle of shouting and cart wheels around me. There was a new ship, one that hadn't been there yesterday.

My boot heels made a hollow sound on the planks as I approached it, the ship tugging gently on its ropes on the slack tide. An ancient sailor with a blue kerchief wrapped 'round his head dozed on the deck. I hailed him.

He gave a snort and shook himself awake, clearing his throat. "And what would such a pretty lass want of me? 'Tis too early for swivin'." His grin revealed missing teeth. My dark blue skirt and V-shaped stomacher were of good linen and almost respectable. Still, only a sailor would call a freckled, skinny wharf rat of fourteen, with tangled brown hair, a "pretty lass."

"Please, sir, was my brother, Daniel Nelson, in your crew?" It was possible Daniel had been part of his cargo too, but I knew better than to ask. If he wanted to volunteer that, he could.

He shook his head. "Sorry, lass, no one by that name was aboard. What's your name? If I run across him, I'll tell him you're looking."

"His sister Lizzie, sir. Thank you."

He waved his hand to dismiss my thanks. "I wish ye luck."

Swallowing my disappointment, I turned away. A fine mist swept like a curtain down the wharf, beading my thin cloak. In the distance, the merchantman Penny had mentioned loomed at the end of Bear Quay.

At the near end of the wharf, a foreman I'd worked for the week before was directing three men loading barrels onto a cart. I stood behind him, waiting for the chance to ask for work. He watched as two men wrestled a barrel onto the cart bed with groans and curses.

Then I noticed Mattie on the other side of the cart, talking to a sailor.

The foreman waved her over and handed her a piece of paper. Benjamin stood beside her, the boy Daniel had healed, his shining round hair making him look like a tiny monk, or a roundhead.

He watched the men struggle to lift another barrel, but soon grew bored and wandered off, picking up a handful of stones and talking to himself. I tried to catch the foreman's eye but he ignored me. When I looked back, the stones were floating in the air around Benjamin's head. He laughed and clapped his hands. I must've exclaimed, for Mattie turned to look. She ran to him, swearing, then pulled him to his feet, shaking him. The stones dropped to the ground.

Unfortunately, I wasn't the only one who'd seen.

A man in a faded hat and shabby cloak approached, smiling. He bent down to say something to Benjamin. Mattie shouted at him to go away, dragging on Benjamin's hand. The man put his arms around the boy, as though to pick him up.

"No you don't!" Mattie shoved him. The shabby man went flying across the wharf as though he'd been tossed by a bull.

Mattie grabbed her brother's hand and pulled him away, plunging into the crowd of people and carts on the river road. Just before they disappeared, Benjamin glanced back at me, wide-eyed.

The men loading the cart were muttering. The foreman told them to get back to work. I decided not to linger and strode quickly down the wharf, my pulse beating in my throat.

Penny had explained why our group of wharf rats stayed together, while others left for better work. "Not every child will make it here," she'd said, "but some prefer to stay. It helps to be the right kind o' child. You'll see the other kinchin leave sooner or later: the boys go off to sea, boys and girls might become sweeps, or thieves, or doxies, or even respectable work. But if you're the right kind, and you're smart, you'll stay here."

"How will I know if I'm the right kind?"

"You'll know," she said, not meeting my eyes. She'd only said that much, I was sure, because of Daniel's gift.

Daniel was the right kind, I was certain. So was Mattie's brother Benjamin. But I still didn't see why anyone would stay here, at risk of agent kidnappings, if you had another choice. Whatever kind of child you might be.

The Indian merchantman was in the last berth on Bear Quay, fat-bellied and smug. I slowed my steps, considering our gang of wharf rats. They were a suspicious lot, and never spoke about themselves. Penny said once the best thing about living by the river was that the Quality never noticed us. She meant they wouldn't notice the gifted children hiding here.

When Da told me stories about the war and the Commonwealth, he'd mentioned gifted children. He said no one knew why gifts first appeared during the war and only in children, disappearing as the child grew older. Some said it was witchcraft, but the lords and ladies squashed such talk, saying it was a blessing instead. God, they argued, gave the children gifts to help them survive.

Da had laughed at that. He said being gifted was of no use to the children, not when it made them slaves. It wasn't long before those with money and power decided such gifts rightfully belonged to them. Hadn't God made them rich and powerful because they deserved to be so? They were following His divine plan by sending trackers to snatch these innocents to make more wealth, and acquire more power. That's how they justified it.

Then he said it was my job to watch over my brother and keep him safe. I didn't understand what he meant, not then. It was only after we'd come to live in London and he was dying that he came out and said that Daniel was gifted and that the trackers would be after him. Then he made me promise to keep him safe. A promise I didn't keep.

The mists blew away, as suddenly as they had come. The sun, free of the clouds, hung above the yardarm of the merchantman. I'd arrived at the foot of the ship's ramp.

"You girl, you here to work?" I nodded. "Can you read?"

"Yes, sir." I climbed the ramp and stood waiting.

"Good. I can't waste time explaining." The Quartermaster handed me a sheaf of papers.

For the rest of the day I visited chandlers, coopers, sailmakers and the like. It was the most work I'd ever had in one day, the most I'd ever earned. My luck had finally turned for the better. By suppertime I had a fistful of pennies and thought I well deserved another pie. I rubbed my fingers over the comforting glass in my pocket as I walked to the cook shop, imagining the taste of warm gravy and steaming pie crust.

I was but a few paces away, my mouth watering at the aroma of baking pies, when I felt a warmth in my pocket.

I reached into my pocket. The shard of glass was hot to the touch. I took it out and looked into its blue depths. Tall buildings blocked the failing light, yet the glass pulsed with a light of its own, and even as I watched, the light became a brightly lit scene. The same street appeared, in the flat light of noon. Seen from behind, a girl approached the cook shop. A cove in a brown coat and petticoat trousers was right behind her, his hat pulled low over his face. Across his back lay an empty sack, the kind hunters use for rabbits or birds. Just as the girl was about to enter the shop, the man lunged from behind, pulled the sack over her head, and threw her over his shoulder. Folk in the street cried out, but he drew his sword and slashed at anyone who came too close. He backed away, and then turned and ran, carrying the girl in the sack.

The image faded and the light went out, the glass now cool in my hand.

Heart pounding, I turned to look behind me. There was no man with a sack, just weary folk heading to the cook shop for their dinners after a hard day's work. It had been broad daylight in the vision, but the narrow patch of sky above the crowding houses was the misty blue of twilight.

Shaken, I bent over to catch my breath. My distorted reflection looked up at me from a puddle in the street. Then a ball of light appeared, and the same vision played out before me. There was the girl walking to the cook shop. There was the man with the sack. Only this time, the girl was facing me. She *was* me. I cried out as the man with the sword popped the sack over my head and carried me off.

Two men and a woman in an apron stopped in the street to look at me curiously, and then moved away quickly. Likely they thought me mad.

After a shaky breath or two, I walked away from the cook shop as fast as I could, almost running in my panic.

Either I *was* mad or I'd had a vision of the future, a foretelling. Whichever it was, I wasn't going near that cook shop again.

Evening shadows reached for me from the overhanging stories of the tall narrow houses. Any dark alley or passageway might hide footpads or trackers. If my vision proved true, a tracker would nick me in broad daylight on this very street. Would it happen no matter what, or could I escape it? I didn't believe I was mad; I was certain the vision was true.

Penny's words came back to me. Perhaps I was the 'right kind o' child' after all. If my vision *was* true, then I was like the others.

There was no safety for me anywhere.

I didn't eat that night. I hurried back to the alley, to curl up in my blue blanket, taking comfort in the presence of the other rats. I wondered if I would soon be joining Daniel, wherever he was. That might be some consolation. I'm not ashamed to admit I cried myself to sleep that night. Life had been hard enough as an orphan, with Daniel gone, and food and a living hard to come by. Now I was fair game, a treasure ripe for plucking. Any nob could steal me and keep me as a slave, with no one to stop them.

4

A WARNING

DECEMBER 1660, London

The next morning, I felt calmer.

Penny and the others had survived here with their gifts. I wasn't alone, and I wouldn't be nobbled without a fight. And if my vision were true, it didn't just affect me. It meant a tracker knew the cook shop was a good place to catch gifted children.

I imagined how I'd feel if someone else was nobbled—Penny, say, or Mattie—and beat down my fears. I warned every rat I saw to avoid the shop, saying I'd heard a rumor of a tracker loitering there. Mattie didn't reply but only stared at me. Despite her distrust, I saw she believed me. Most hurried away without a word.

Kat Jenkins, the wary dark-haired girl I'd long wanted to get to know, was tucking up her skirt, about to run a message on those long legs, when I touched her arm. She listened to my whispered warning, and nodded before she turned and strode away, her long dark braid swinging behind her.

Only to Penny did I say I'd actually *seen* a tracker lurking by the cook shop. I trusted her as much as I trusted anyone, but I couldn't tell her I'd seen myself nobbled *in a vision.* She'd know what that meant. Maybe she did anyway.

She gave me a hard look. "You saw a tracker there?"

I nodded. Her expression frightened me. She looked fierce, like one o' those Irish soldier women the ballads say fought in the war.

"Be careful who you tell. Never trust anyone who doesn't have a gift." She smiled and her eyes softened. "If you're one of us now, Lizzie, it's not as bad as you think." She surprised me by drawing me into a quick hug. She stepped back, apparently amused. "Jimmy and I had a bet on how long it would take you to find out. I won."

"Find out—?"

"You didn't know it usually runs in families?"

I shook my head, realized I'd just admitted it, and felt my face flush.

She laughed. "See you tonight. Remember, trust *no one* but our gang."

James Muldaur, the agent, was at his usual place by the Custom House stairs, his dark hair tied back with a silk ribbon, a coat of gleaming brocade over his breeches. Beside him, Cynthia, his doxy, fiddled with a pink muslin shawl, to make sure everyone noticed it. Penny said 'twas best to avoid them both, although she admitted she'd no proof he was a kidnapper.

Most of the rats mistrusted him not only because he was an agent, but also because he gave himself airs. For some reason he was always charming to me. He smiled at me when I approached, and we chatted about nothing for a few minutes.

Cynthia regarded me sourly and adjusted her shawl until finally I said how pretty it was. She smiled haughtily. "Of course, silk would be too good for the likes of you."

There's just no pleasing some people.

James winked. But I knew better than to be taken in by his charm. I didn't warn either of them.

When I left, James actually bowed. Cynthia made a huffing sound.

I couldn't risk telling the new boy, Thomas. He wasn't really one of us; he had a mother somewhere, but he'd run away from his apprenticeship because his brute of a master beat him. Jimmy brought him to sleep in our alley to hide from the bailiffs. Penny gave her brother a sour look, but she hadn't prevented it.

In any case, he looked like he could take care of himself. He still had the muscled shoulders and arms of a blacksmith, his former trade. If he hadn't guessed there were gifted kinchin in the alley by now, I wasn't going to give him ideas. Even a stupid man would figure it out at the mention of trackers, and Thomas wasn't stupid.

As luck would have it, I ran into him after I spoke with James. I was on Bear Quay, waiting for a merchant to finish his business so I could take his message to the Exchange.

He came over to where I waited by a gangplank, a pleased expression on his nut-brown face. "Lizzie! You'll be the first to know."

"Know what?" I asked, distracted. "Should you be in such a public place, Thomas?" If he was hiding from the bailiffs, he shouldn't be seen on the wharves in broad daylight.

A pink flush spread across his cheeks and he turned to watch the bustle of cargo being loaded onto waiting carts. "I'm running an errand for my *new* master." He tried to sound casual, but there was pride in his voice.

That was surprising. It wasn't often an apprentice was released from his contract. "What happened to the old one, then?"

"Master Sweets bought my contract. He said Perkins was a fool not to see what a good worker I am. I'm his apprentice now. He has a costermonger stall in the market." He beamed.

"Congratulations, then. Guess you won't need to hide from

the bailiffs anymore. The rats will be sorry to see you leave, but your mum will be happy to have you back."

"Will you?"

"Will I what?" I was watching the merchant; he'd said farewell to the ship's captain and was starting down the ramp. He'd expect me to be ready.

"Will you be sorry to see me go?"

"You'll still be around, won't you? But you'll be a respectable apprentice. You're well out of it." I laughed. "You won't miss that stinkin' alley."

"I'll miss some things," he said softly, his eyes on my face.

I didn't want to know what he meant by that, so I turned away, pretending I hadn't heard. But I felt a warm glow in my chest.

The merchant came toward me, with a wary glance at Thomas.

"Excuse me, Thomas." I stepped forward and curtsied, waiting to hear the merchant's errand.

No, there was no reason to warn Thomas.

Most rats stayed away from the cook shop for the next two weeks. I looked into my glass every now and then, whenever I felt worried or undecided, but the light never appeared again. I wondered if I'd imagined the whole thing.

It was Kat who told me what happened.

I was on the bench outside the Fish Street tavern, watching the ships sliding by on the river below, when she sat beside me. For a moment I was pleased she'd sought me out. Then I saw her expression.

"I thought you'd want to know," she said in a low voice. "Sairy was nobbled in broad daylight by the cook shop, under the nose of a dozen witnesses. Even the cook came out and threatened the tracker. But he just laughed, slashed at 'em with his sword, and threw Sairy over his shoulder. He got clean away."

A sense of guilt formed in my gut. My vision *was* true, but by staying away I'd changed what happened.

"Do you see, Lizzie? Even though you risked your neck to warn the others, it didn't make a bit o' difference." She spoke with gloomy certainty. "If you're not careful your kind-heartedness will get you nobbled." It took me a moment to see the contradiction in her words: she was warning me in turn.

"It wasn't kind-heartedness brought Sairy to the cook shop," I said, blinking back hot tears. "Just the opposite. nobody warned *her*. If we'd stuck together and trusted each other, no child would've gone near it. The rats are easy pickings because we *don't* help each other."

She shook her head. "You can't save them. Now the rats will wonder how you knew about the tracker. They'll suspect you knew he'd be there because of a gift."

Whatever she saw on my face was as good as an admission, for she nodded and said, "I won't tell, but others will figure it out. Watch yourself, Lizzie." She rose and walked away.

After she left, I sat staring at the river for a long time. Sairy was beyond my help, just as Daniel was. There was nothing I could do. No telling who'd nobbled her or where she'd end up.

And I might be joining her soon enough. By warning the others I might've revealed too much.

Three months after Sairy had been nobbled, the whispers began again. It was time, the rats said, for another child to disappear. And that's when I saw for myself what happened to a child who didn't keep his gift a secret.

I'd been delivering a message out in the countryside of Islington, returning to the city much later than I preferred. It was dark, with only a few torches on the main streets, and no one abroad but thieves, highwaymen and footpads. Or so my fears said.

I kept to the wider streets as much as I could, not wanting to discover what lay in wait in the narrow passages, but I knew better than to waste a coin on a linkboy's torch. Too many of them worked for the robbers.

I hurried toward the river road where there'd be respectable folk, even at that hour. Sailors returned late to their ships, and merchants came to the Custom House whenever the tide and a free berth allowed their ship to dock.

The moon was up, painting a quicksilver path across the water. At the end of it, the glow in the sky marked where the theaters and bear pits of Southwark lit up the sky. I stopped to listen to the waves lapping against the stone piers of the Custom House wharf, inhaling the river's breath of tar and mud. My eye was caught by the sudden appearance of a light on the water.

I moved closer to the edge to look.

Below me a lantern bobbed on the prow of a waterman's skiff, moored beside the stone steps of the Custom House stairs. A waterman was at the tiller, and a second man, directly below me, stood in the middle of the boat. He bent to throw a rope to someone on the stairs, and I saw a white scar on the back of his neck, as though someone had tried to cut off his head.

The man at the tiller hissed, "Be quick!"

A cloaked figure on the stairs leaned over the water and heaved a sack into the arms of the man with the scar. The boat dipped as the bundle thumped onto a seat, and the lantern's wildly swinging beams lit up the man on the stairs. A dark cloak muffled him from head to toe, with the hood pulled low over his face, but there was something familiar in the way he stood. He caught the purse tossed by the man with the scar, and tucked it beneath his cloak, revealing a flash of colorful brocade.

The sack squirmed and the top fell open, revealing the tear-streaked face of a child. It was Benjamin, who'd made stones dance in the air. He struggled but couldn't free himself. "Help me!

Help! Murder! They're stealing me!" His cries echoed off the stone steps.

"Quiet!" The man with the scar backhanded him, and he fell to the bottom of the boat. The waterman pushed off, and the bobbing light slid downriver until it disappeared.

I hadn't made a sound. I was shaking, the boy's cries still sounding in my ears.

They hadn't seen me. Then I realized the man on the stairs might come my way. I ran for the Custom House, gasping for breath when I arrived.

A few clerks were still scratching away at their desks. One of them glanced up and I caught his eye, desperate. He grimaced and turned back to his work. The two merchants standing before his desk ignored me completely. No help there, no one who would care about the fate of a wharf rat. Their presence reassured me all the same. Better to have witnesses, however indifferent, if the man on the stairs came looking for me.

My eyes stung. I rubbed them and found they were wet.

The sour taste of cowardice was in my mouth. I'd stood by and done nothing while Benjamin had been sold like a bag of flour. But there were three of them, I argued to myself. If I'd cried out the tracker would've had me too. I couldn't have saved him. There was nothing I could do. *Nothing I could do.*

Kat's warning rang in my head: *You can't save them.*

I'd heeded her warning, but my silence sickened me. When I finally headed for our alley, all I could see was Benjamin's tear-stained face and his look of hopelessness.

5

MAGS

LONDON, *September 5, 1661*

A year had passed since Daniel disappeared, and in all that time I'd heard nothing from him, nor found anyone who'd seen him. I'd asked at every ship, and stopped newly arrived sailors, for news of him. I demanded the glass show me where he was. All to no avail.

My lucky glass didn't respond to demands, I discovered. The only thing I really wanted to see, where Daniel was, it refused to show me. Of what use were visions if I couldn't see that? I couldn't even predict when it would show me a vision, or why it showed me what it did. It remained a lifeless, dull piece of blue glass until it turned warm in my hand and showed me a scene I rarely understood.

The glass, I guessed, showed me what would endanger *me*; it wouldn't warn me about the other rats, or Daniel. Sometimes I wondered whether I had imagined that first vision, and was not gifted at all. But Sairy had been kidnapped.

Penny's gang had no doubts. They'd decided I was one of them. All except Mattie, who hadn't forgiven me after I told her I'd seen her brother nobbled. I could hardly blame her, but at least she knew what happened; I wished someone would tell me what had happened to Daniel.

Once it was clear that Penny trusted me, the others whispered stories and offered advice: Stay by the river. Mingle with the crowds, become invisible, part of the background. Watch for folk who loiter on street corners or seem to be watching you. It became second nature, my skin prickling when anyone paid me too much attention. The riverbank became the only place I felt safe. Those who didn't belong stood out.

I'd changed over the last year, o' course, growing inches, my skirt a little too short for decency. The city had changed too. Soot-stained buildings that once seemed menacing had become old friends, and the three-legged cranes, once looked engines of Hell by torchlight, had become workaday machines of wood and rope. Everyone on the docks knew me, knew I belonged there. The dock men greeted me by name. Many sailors and some of the merchants would nod politely to me; I was someone they'd done business with, however faded my skirt.

The smell of the river, a blend of mud, pitch, and the sweet tang of hemp from the rigging, was the smell of home, like the fragrance of bread from the oven to me. Even the forlorn cries of the gulls sounded like home.

Thomas, on the other hand, said he couldn't wait to leave, to move out of the city to leave the smokes of town behind. He wanted to buy a market garden and live in the countryside. I told him I could never leave. Daniel would expect to find me here when he returned.

The sun, muffled white behind the clouds, rose above the cluster of masts and church spires on the other side of the river. Those who had to work on the Sabbath straggled down the river road, while those rich enough to be upright and God-fearing sat in church. Even the watermen had the day off. I missed their shouts and cheerful cursing as they plied their skiffs up and down the river. I had the day off too, and was lonely for someone to talk to.

By the Custom House sheds I stopped to watch the few dock men start their day. A sharp crack of thunder made me look up. Dark clouds were coming in from the sea.

The watermen's shed by the stairs wasn't far, and I ran, hoping to reach its shelter before the storm caught me.

Too late. The rain spattered around me, light at first but quickly becoming fat, heavy drops bouncing up from the road. I pulled up the hood of my cloak and ran. The shed was just ahead, beside the stairs where they moored their skiffs.

It was cold and cheerless inside, the bench cold even through my cloak. My view of the road was blurred by the rain. I suppose I should've braved the rain, looking for new ships and asking for news of Daniel, but my mood was as foul as the weather. I couldn't bear to hear "No" one more time.

For something to do, I took out my glass and waited, not expecting anything. But to my surprise, the glass grew warm and light appeared.

When the swirling light settled, there were the Custom House stairs, but on a fair, bright day. James Muldaur, the agent, was laughing with the little fair-haired boy who followed him around. What was his name? Potts, that was it. Potts had been with us in the alley and taken to Bridewell that day. He no longer slept with us in the alley, and I didn't know why, or where he'd gone.

I waited for something more, some sign of why I was seeing this, but the scene disappeared. Disappointed, I returned it to my pocket. A vision after all this time and it was another scene with no meaning, or none I understood.

A laugh sounded close by. I rose and went to the door to look. Two small figures were passing the shed, Potts with Mags, her bright-red cloak vivid against the rain dark cobbles.

Mags had only recently arrived on the wharves and was new

to our gang, about seven or eight, with brown skin and dark glossy curls tight against her head. Most kinchin never spoke of their past, and Mags didn't either. But she'd become friends with Potts, who seemed close to her age. Potts said he didn't know his age.

At times he seemed like a boy of six who was clever for his age, but when he played a trick on someone, he seemed older, meaner, only stunted from cold and hunger. His clothes had were stained and ragged when he'd arrived, so my guess was he escaped from the poorhouse. I never could decide whether he was touched in the head, or just oblivious to others' feelings, but he was too cocky for my taste. Once, after he'd stolen my glass and pretended he didn't know where it was, I'd asked Mags why she liked him. She said he made her laugh.

They passed me, invisible in the dark shed, chatting gaily. Potts waved at someone and I looked to see who else was out in the rain.

James stood in the sheltered lee of the Custom House, his hands in his pockets. He stepped from under the shelter of the overhanging roof and waved back.

And then right before my eyes, a man in a shabby cloak and faded hat stepped from the doorway of a nearby shed and fell in behind the children.

The rain fell harder, churning the dirt to mud.

My heart started to pound. There was little business at the Custom House on a Sunday, so pickings for thieves or beggars were slim. But trackers worked any time.

Mags and Potts were laughing, not paying attention to anything around them. The rain drowned out all other sounds. The tracker quickened his pace. Soon he'd be close enough to grab one. If I didn't do something, I'd see two more children nobbled before my eyes.

I yelled, but neither the children nor the tracker heard me. I took a deep breath, grabbed my skirts, and ran after them. The rain masked the sound of my boots on the cobbles. The tracker didn't even notice me until I'd passed him.

Skittering across wet cobbles, I grabbed for the children's hands.

"Run!" I shouted, pulling them along into a narrow side street, heading away from the Custom House.

For a moment all I could hear was the harsh sound of our breathing; then the sound of the tracker's boots grew loud behind us. Neither child turned to look. They struggled to keep up, short legs pumping. We'd made it through the alley and had circled back toward the river. I risked a glance behind. He was close, almost within arm's reach.

Then I looked ahead of us, where an alley doglegged up the hill. Jimmy stood in front of a plastered wall. "Jimmy! Help!"

Luckily for us he understood what was happening. He ran so fast he was a blur on the cobbles and slammed into the tracker. Something hit the cobbles, hard. We didn't stop. Only when we reached the alley across the road from Bear Quay did we slow down and stop. I leaned against the brick wall, hands on my knees, trying to catch my breath.

Cold rain ran down my face. I was trembling. I'd just thrown myself in the path of a tracker. So had Jimmy, I realized. "That was careless," I said, when I could speak. "You need to watch your back."

Mags took a shaky breath, her eyes frightened. "We'll be more careful, Lizzie, I promise." She turned to Potts and asked, "Won't we, Potty?"

If Potts was frightened, I couldn't tell. He grinned. "Thanks, Lizzie. Lucky for us you was there. Always lucky, is our Lizzie." He sauntered off with a casual wave. Nothing fazed Potts.

Ever since I'd warned the others about the cook shop, the rats had called me "Lucky Lizzie." No threat would make them stop. It was as if they *wanted* Fate to strike me down.

Mags watched Potts's retreating back, confusion on her face.

I leaned against the wall, my breath finally slowing.

"What about Jimmy?" she asked.

"He'll be all right. He moves too fast for a tracker." I wasn't breaking a confidence; she'd just seen his gift in action. I was shocked he'd revealed it to help us.

But right now my concern was Mags. Once she'd lived by the river a few months, caution would become second nature, but she had to survive that long first. The littlest often don't make it, either because they can't find food or a warm place to sleep, or because they're easiest to nobble. I'd given her another chance and it had cost me nothing. I was still free. "I'm ready for breakfast and a fire, Mags, how about you? Come and keep me company."

She frowned and took a step back, pride warring with hunger in her face. "I can find my own food."

I examined her critically. Her face was far too thin and pinched-looking, with dark shadows under her eyes beneath the warm brown skin. I'd wager she hadn't eaten enough in weeks. Maybe not since coming to the wharves.

"O' course you can," I said, smiling to hide my concern. "But friends share their good fortune. I can spare a few pennies for good company at breakfast. I'm starving, chilled to the bone, and you'd be doing me a favor to talk to me while I sup. Please?"

Her face cleared. "All right, then."

The tavern at the corner of Fish Street didn't mind serving wharf rats if we sat in the back or on the benches outside when they were busy. Sundays were slow, so I claimed one of the tables by the fire, ordering bread and ale for us both. We spread our cloaks on the bench to dry, the smell of wet wool mingling with tobacco smoke and the aroma of roasting meat.

When the ale and bread arrived, Mags tore into the bread.

I caught the maid's eye. "Bring us a plate of your ordinary too."

I could afford it, and Mags clearly hadn't had a proper meal in ages. I was ashamed I'd never thought to check how she fared. That's how it is with the little ones. No one pays attention and one day they're gone.

Mags continued to wolf down the bread. I ate mine more slowly, savoring the taste.

When the maid returned with a bowl of mutton swimming in a stew of peas and onions, I motioned for her to place it before Mags, who stared at me in surprise.

"I thought I wanted it, but I'm full now," I said, untruthfully.

Mags frowned and I thought she'd argue, but she only blinked several times, her eyes wet.

I looked away, embarrassed, and examined the Sunday morning customers, mostly workmen and apprentices, a sailor or two, and two maids eating together. I listened to scraps of conversation. Mags's spoon scraped across the bottom of her bowl; she was making short work of the stew. One man complained of tariffs, fondly recounting the days when smuggling was tolerated and sherry and tobacco were cheap. Another made a bawdy joke about Lady Castlemaine, the king's mistress, and everyone laughed. When I looked back, Mags was watching me. "Lizzie, how long have you been here?"

"By the river, you mean? Been a year now."

She glanced behind her and dropped her voice. "So maybe you can tell me. There's something I don't understand: Why doesn't he do something?"

"Who?"

"The king. Why doesn't he stop the trackers?"

God's teeth. I fiddled with the crumbs before me. "Are you finished?" I asked. She nodded. "Let's go outside."

We left the tavern and walked down Fish Street toward the river and the bridge. The rain had stopped, and the clean air, free of coal smoke if only for a moment, was pleasant after the fug of the tavern. At the bottom of the hill we left the bridge traffic and turned right, heading up the river road. I waited until we were past two men operating a crane before I said, "There really isn't anything to explain. The nobs do as they please and send the trackers."

"But why doesn't the king put the trackers in the Tower? I asked Mattie and she just laughed and said something about Cromwell. Is he a nob?"

I quickly hid my smile. "Not exactly."

She folded her arms. "Don't mock. How am I s'posed to know when no one will explain?"

She had a point. "All right, but promise me that after this you won't keep asking questions. It's dangerous. Keep your eyes and ears open. I'll answer you this once, but that's it, understand? Don't talk about the king — it'll just get you in trouble. You won't repeat what I say?"

She shook her head, waiting.

Barges and wherries glided by on the river, dodging the eel boats and lobstermen moored outside the river's main channel. A pale patch of blue sky hung above them, but the sun was hidden. Folk walked past us without a glance, their faces tired. Mags had already decided I was gifted, so I wasn't risking much. Someone had to tell her enough to keep her quiet. The question was how much to say. I gestured toward Botolph's wharf and we headed for it.

"You know there was a war, when the old king was on the throne?" She nodded. "When the old king lost the war, they cut off his head. Cromwell became Lord Protector, as good as king, and ran the Commonwealth. He protected gifted kinchin and there were laws to stop the kidnappings. We lived in a Republic then, and everyone had rights. But he died and everyone fought again, so with no king but the army, the nobs did as they pleased. That was the worst time, Da said. I remember some of that— there was rioting in the streets and everyone thought the army would attack London. That's why they invited *this* king, the son of the old one, to come back."

"So what about us?" Mags demanded. "Why doesn't the king protect us the way Cromwell did? Why doesn't he stop it?"

I sighed. "Don't say *us*, love. Informers are everywhere."

She flashed me a stubborn look, and we walked onto the wharf, our boots echoing on the wooden planks.

"Listen. *This* King Charles said let bygones be bygones, except for the men who'd sat in judgment at his father's trial. Their heads were cut off, and placed on pikes above Traitor's Gate. They had to dig up the Lord Protector's grave to put his head there with the others. To the king, Cromwell was a traitor and a murderer. He won't do as Cromwell did."

Mags squinted at the glare of the white sky. "So if Cromwell did it, he'll do the opposite, is that what you mean? Is that why he doesn't help us?"

Before I could think of a safe answer, she provided her own. "The king is on the side of the nobs and trackers."

That was too close to the truth. "You shouldn't speak of the king like that."

The sheds were in front of us. Three benches sat in a line, looking out over the road, wet after the rain. "Let's sit for a moment." I chose a bench and sat, heedless of the water soaking into my cloak. I turned my gaze up the road and saw no one close by. Across the road, rising up the hill, the streets of the city were quiet and empty.

Houses crowded up the hill, church spires interrupting the jagged line of stepped roofs. Chimneys spewed dark streamers of smoke, rising straight up until caught by the damp wind, then bending downriver. Coal smoke coated everything in its path, yellowing the plaster of every dark-timbered house, streaking everything with soot. Like our fear of trackers, the grimy film of smoke contaminated everything.

As they got nearer, two figures walking toward us became Jimmy and Penny, her flaming red hair easy to spot. Penny waved and Mags waved back. Were we being observed? I searched for any sign of movement, wondering if that tracker was nearby.

The wind dropped and smoke spread above us like a dark lid, trapping us.

Jimmy sat down beside Mags, his expression more serious than usual. Mags leaned over and patted his hand. "Thanks for your help. I'm glad you're all right."

He nodded. "We have news," he said quietly.

Penny stood in front of me. She glanced behind her and said, "Brandy was taken this morning, near the Exchange. Kat said she was talking to an agent."

"Then maybe it has naught to do with us," I said.

Jimmy shook his head. "We can't be sure o' that. Mattie says she thought she saw a girl being carried aboard a ship, but she isn't sure it was her."

I exhaled. "So perhaps it was just a spirit, after all."

"Makes no difference," Mags said. "The trackers work with the spirits."

We all stared at her in surprise.

"What do you mean?" I asked.

"There's nothing to stop an agent from selling a gifted kinchin to the nobs once they have them, is there? You don't know what happens after a ship leaves the wharf. It could stop anywhere and offload part of the cargo, 'specially if they'll get a better price."

"What've you heard?" Jimmy demanded.

"No one minds me, because I'm only small, right? They think I've no brains. But I overheard two coves talking: there's a ship offloads cargo down the river. It's always kinchin."

I had underestimated Mags. From the expression on their faces, I guessed Penny and Jimmy had too.

"We were due," Penny said. "Poor Brandy. It's *always* a gifted child, every three months. That means trackers. Or trackers and agents working together, like Mags says."

"Or she could've been nobbled by a spirit," I said softly. I was certain the man that had just chased us was a tracker. It would be foolish to assume the danger was past.

"Stands to reason they'd join forces," Jimmy pointed out. "Being in the same business, so to speak."

I thought of James standing beside a cart full of crying and grim-faced people, while he smugly pocketed his money. Brandy was seven, and agents *did* take children that young to work in the Colonies. "Do we know for sure she's gifted?" I asked. As far as I knew, all the rats in our alley were, including Mags.

Mags said simply, "I saw her fly. She's one of us."

"Maybe that will help her escape," I offered.

No one replied to that hopeful bit of fancy. Jimmy rose to his feet. "Pass the word along if you see anyone from our group," Penny said. "Mattie already knows."

I nodded. They set off toward the bridge and the Custom House.

"Your Da was wrong," Mags said with certainty, watching them go.

For a moment I didn't understand.

"*This* is the worst time. No one helps us. I owe you, Lizzie, for 'splaining things like Cromwell and such. I'll repay you, never fear."

I shook my head. "We're friends, Mags. You don't owe me a thing."

"Are we? Good. 'Cause friends help each other. You done me a good turn, and I'll do the same for you. I wager you need a friend; you always look sad."

My eyes dropped to the bare toes peeping from her boots where the toes had been hacked off so she could keep wearing them. She hadn't eaten properly in days, was barely keeping body and soul together, and she was worried about *me*. I shook my head. Living on the street hadn't knocked the good heart out of her yet. Kat would call both of us noddle-headed ninnies.

A loud crash sounded from down the wharf.

A crate had slipped from its sling and broken open, sending the pulley rope flying into the air and scattering cabbages over the wharf. Beyond the huddle of yelling wharfies, a golden ship gleamed in the sunlight. It hadn't been there yesterday.

"Will you wait a moment, Mags? I need to talk to someone."

She nodded.

A sailor stood at the bottom of the ship's ramp, a sheaf of papers in his hand, watching a net of hogsheads being lowered into a cart.

"Pardon, sir, was Daniel Nelson in your crew?"

He finished writing on the manifest before turning to me with an annoyed expression. "And what would you be wanting if he was? Jilted you, mebbe?"

"No, sir. He's my brother. It's been a year since I've seen him."

His expression changed, a smile flickering on his face before it resumed its creased contours. "Ah. Sorry lass, there was no Daniel aboard this trip."

I thanked him and turned to find Mags behind me. As we walked away, he called, "Good luck to 'ee." I glanced back and nodded. That's often how it goes. First the suspicion, then the grudging good will. Sailors don't see their families for long years at a time.

"Did your brother go to sea?" Mags asked. "Won't he look for you when he's back?"

Daniel was a subject too painful to share. Why should she care about my past troubles? She had her own. I shrugged. "I don't know. He might be at sea. He might be nobbled."

That was the first time I had said it aloud, and before I could stop them, tears rose in my eyes. Mags watched me, waiting. "So I ask new ships, just in case someone has seen him."

"Maybe I can help," she offered. "I could ask too."

I was about say she should look for work, when I saw my chance. "Would you? Let's make a bargain, then. Help me ask about Daniel in the mornings and then we can breakfast together before I go to work. What do you say?"

She'd never accept a regular meal otherwise. Daniel might be a slave in some country house, and all our asking for naught, but at least Mags would eat.

She reached out and shook my hand. "It's a bargain. Where do you want to meet?"

My thanks were drowned out by a cacophony of church bells ringing eight o'clock on both sides of the river, first one, then the next, a strangely beautiful sound.

"See you later," Mags said. "Tomorrow I'll start asking about Daniel. It feels good to finally trust someone, Lizzie."

I felt a stab of doubt. Those shining, trusting eyes frightened me. She was certain I wouldn't betray her.

"Remember—snug's the word," I cautioned.

She put a finger against her smiling lips, and then turned and walked up the road. A beam of sunlight fingered her cloak and the red wool glowed against the muddy street. I hoped I was doing right, meddling with her life.

6

THE FACTORY

LONDON, *September 6, 1661*

The next day it was back to work. Mags and I met and divided up the wharves, then ate breakfast, as promised. It was soon clear she could cover just as many wharves as I could. My hopes rose; maybe with two of us asking questions, I would finally learn what had happened. I was whistling cheerfully as I made my way up the hill to the shop.

No longer did I scrounge for a living on the wharves: I had a proper job working for Serena Hopkins, making hats and caps and running errands for her millinery shop. I'd fallen into luck one day, at the Royal Exchange, where I'd delivered a message. I was leaning against a pillar in the colonnade, waiting for a merchant's reply, watching folk shop, meet their friends, and make deals.

From behind me someone said in a lazy drawl, "Why, it's the revolutionary roundhead herself, consorting with the moneylenders in the temple."

I turned.

James Muldaur's dark eyes were laughing at me.

James had started out a wharf rat like the rest of us, but he claimed he was the son of a nob, and that someday he'd regain the family fortune. He said things would be put right now that we had a king on the throne again. No one really believed him, but no one gave him the lie, either. He had connections. And while no one could prove he kidnapped children, most of the kinchin were afraid of him. Besides, everyone needs a dream; who was I to say his was false, when no one told me I'd never see Daniel again? I know some thought it.

"And here's Your Lordship, consorting with riff-raff," I replied, making an exaggerated curtsy.

He bowed, his dark queue falling over his shoulder. There's wenches who giggle and flirt with James, because of his dark eyes and high cheekbones, but for me it would take more than good looks to forget what he does for a living.

"When I'm back where I belong, you'll have to address me as 'my lord.'"

My eyebrows lifted. "God made every man in his image, we're told. Why should some be treated better than others?"

He smiled, faintly, but his eyes were hard. "God appointed the king to rule us on his behalf, and the king raises up the nobility to order the laws and rule the counties."

"What if I don't believe God approves of your king? The kidnappings are worse now."

His face darkened. "You should be more careful what you say, Lizzie. A woman with a froward tongue is against the order of things. Know your place, lest someone call you a shrewish wench. Remain silent and listen to your betters."

It was true, I should've been more careful, speaking in public like that. But I thought he was only teasing. Then I saw his expression.

"Now *you* sound like a Puritan."

He bowed, but his eyes were still cold.

A woman who had her back to us now turned and inquired whether she could have a private word with me.

"Until next time, Lizzie dear." And James sauntered off.

I nodded, and glanced at the merchant, still busy with one of his clients.

"I am at your disposal, mistress."

She was between forty and fifty years of age, well-dressed, with a plain and sensible face. The bodice of her dove-grey dress was modestly covered with lace, but her new hat was velvet and in the latest mode.

She was sizing me up too, her shrewd glance apparently seeing more than I liked. "I've been looking for a girl just like you. Lizzie, is it?"

"Yes, mistress. Lizzie Nelson." Maybe she had another job for me.

"I'm Serena Hopkins. I run a millinery shop not far from here, and I need an assistant."

I stared, trying to guess her game. "But I've never...why me?"

"I like the way you told off that agent fellow. Oh yes, I know about him. And I know about the wharf rats too; that's why I'd like to do you a good turn. I can't pay much, I'm afraid, but there'll be two meals on weekdays, and one on Saturdays. And I'll find you some better clothes too. What do you say?"

What *could* I say? I couldn't pass up the chance to be warm and indoors during bad weather, or to eat regularly, or to be safely off the streets. Despite her strange explanation, I didn't immediately suspect her of working for a tracker. I don't know why. Perhaps it was because if she was trying to decoy me somewhere, there was no need for such an elaborate story.

"I'd be pleased to try and see if we suit, mistress. And I'm grateful. How do I find your shop?"

She gave me the address and told me to come the next morning before nine o'clock.

"Don't worry, Lizzie Nelson," she said with a knowing smile, "I'm not cozening you. I don't like trackers any more than you do, but I *do* like a girl who knows her own mind, and who doesn't believe all that nonsense about the king. But take my advice: only say such things to close friends. Don't announce your views at the Exchange."

And that's how I came to work for Serena. I've worked in her millinery shop ever since. I still didn't know how she knew about trackers, or wharf rats, but it seemed safer not to ask. Besides, the job was a godsend. For the first time in years, I had enough to eat. And enough coin to buy food for others as well.

The sun was breaking through the clouds as I neared the shop, the whitewash on the half-timbered houses glowing in the sunlight. I picked my way around the piles of refuse and offal in the gutters, hunting for dry cobbles. Watching my feet, I didn't see who was in the street waiting for me until I was almost on them.

The rats didn't know where I worked. I never told them, fearing they might let something slip to Serena, so when I arrived at the corner, I was surprised to see James and Cynthia waiting there beneath the painted sign for the shop.

James bowed. "Here she is, Cynthia. I told you she worked here."

Cynthia frowned, fluttering that bedamned pink shawl. She attempted a smile but it was not a success.

Cold fingers played down my spine. "How did you find me?"

"A little bird," James said. "I've always wanted to see where you work." His gaze flicked away, fastening on something behind me.

I followed his gaze. Thomas was coming up the street toward us.

"Why?"

"I'd like to see more of you," he said, "now that you're rising in the world. You don't have to associate with wharf rats or"—he glanced at Thomas with a grimace—"*grocers* anymore. You're educated. You were genteel folk once. You and I both belong to a higher station."

"Trying to borrow money, James?" Thomas asked pleasantly when he came up with us. "Why are you annoying Lizzie? I noticed you weren't around when the Mud Men came through this morning."

"Lizzie and I have affairs to discuss that you wouldn't understand, *costermonger*. Besides, I can't always be on the wharves," James said mildly, turning his attention back to me. "I have other business to attend to. But, well, *look* at you." He took a step back, shaking his head in mock astonishment. "I hear you've risen so high you have your *own* produce stall. Congratulations." His tone made it clear that both Thomas and grocers were far beneath him.

I gritted my teeth at his mockery. Why was he always riding Thomas?

"Thank you for your kind words, James. Covent Market has been an education for me, perhaps one you'll appreciate. In the market, we learn to separate what's good and wholesome from what's rotting. It's a useful skill in all parts of life. For example, there's altogether too much rotten hereabouts."

James smiled nastily. "Yes, I imagine it gets a bit foul there, doesn't it? Like working with offal, really."

"Folk earn an honest living in the market," Thomas said. "They don't sell desperate people into servitude. Or children into slavery."

"How dare you." James's face had flushed red. He stepped forward, fists clenched.

Cynthia put her hand on his arm and whispered something in his ear. She pointed her head down the street.

I turned to look.

A man in a shabby cloak stood near two men loading a cart, but I thought he was really watching us. His face was shadowed by the sweeping brim of his hat, but I swear he nodded at me when he noticed my gaze. My heart began to pound in slow, heavy strokes.

Thomas was looking at him too. "I think you'd best be off, James."

"Do you? Well, I don't want to risk the wrath of the Prince of Costermongers. Come, Cynthia." He held out his arm and she took it. He met my eyes. "Come find us at the Custom House steps, Lizzie. The clerks and merchants prefer to do business with *us*. You're well spoken; you could earn more coin than you've ever seen." He bowed, and he and his doxy set off down the street.

It pains me to admit I was flattered. But I'm not a complete clod-pate; there'd been fury in his eyes that day in the Exchange, when I'd spoken against the king and the nobs. Whatever smooth words came out of his mouth, James didn't like me. And that man down the street—it worried me that Cynthia had known he was there. As if it had been prearranged.

They strolled off toward the shabby man, ignoring him as they passed.

"How did you find me, Thomas?"

"I've been following James, ever since I saw him talking to that man in the market." He glanced down the street again. "Watch yourself. He's dangerous."

Thomas no longer lived in the alley, but we were still friends. He shared the market gossip and did us all a good turn now and then. From things he said, it was clear he knew the rats were gifted.

"Was there truly a Mud Men raid this morning?" I asked.

"Big raids all through the docks. Clamping down. Seems like somebody important is coming, so they're cleaning up the wharves." He stepped closer, dropping his voice. "There's something else." He glanced behind him. "I overheard Mistress Sweets talking to one of her friends. She says a new tracker's been seen hanging around the river. They say he works for Hazelton. All the rats need to know."

But that's what folk always say when they're frightened. The stories would be repeated to avid listeners. Children stolen for him were never seen again. Those whose gifts weren't useful to him became small corpses floating down the river. There were enough stories to make you wonder.

I nodded. "Thanks." I wouldn't risk saying more.

"Lizzie—" Thomas hesitated. "There's a new pleasure garden on the South Bank, New Springs Garden. It's like a fair, only more refined, with plays, and music, and the like. Would you like to go with me?"

God's teeth, he's finally asking me courting. I'd been dreading this moment, ignoring the hints that he wanted to be more than friends. As if such a thing were possible.

"Perhaps sometime, Thomas. But really, I must go."

His open face clouded. But if the man down the street was a tracker, I wanted to get away from the shop so he wouldn't guess where I worked.

"Who's minding your stall?" I prompted.

"Gaffer Sweets. Just wanted to make sure you were all right and to pass the word. Tell the others." He glanced up the street once more. "Be careful, Lizzie."

"Thanks for checking on me." I walked quickly to the end of the street and darted around the corner. I hurried down the mews and opened the gate to the kitchen garden. The kitchen door was never locked.

Inside, I crossed the empty shop, passing stands of hats and bonnets and a wooden counter, to enter the workroom. I hung up my cloak and bonnet and sat down at the baize-covered worktable. A bare hat waited on its stand, where it had dried overnight.

Serena came through the leather curtain, dressed in her usual dove-grey and white lace, grey curls arranged precisely on her forehead beneath her cap. She looked worried.

"Did you get away from the Mud Men, Lizzie? I heard there was a raid on the docks this morning."

"I just heard about it, but didn't see them."

"No?" Serena had a strange expression. "Did you warn the others?"

"I didn't know about it, mistress." *Why would she think I did?* A cold lump of worry formed in my stomach. She might have heard about my gift. Why else would she think I'd know about something before it happened?

She was about to say more, then shook her head. "Well, I'm glad you got away." She turned and pushed through the curtain.

I'd done nothing wrong, but I felt uneasy. No wharf rat would tell her I was "Lucky Lizzie," I was sure. Adults couldn't be trusted because they weren't gifted. But she might've heard some other way. And how did she know about the wharf rats, anyway? I shook my head at my fears. My proper mistress could have no idea how wharf rats lived.

At the end of the day, I had five hats trimmed and set to dry. Serena said I had good hands for the work, and I liked it. There was pleasure in choosing the colors and trimmings to tempt the wives and daughters of wealthy merchants or lawyers. I was careful not to waste even a scrap of ribbon or fabric. Serena was barely scraping by.

When it was time to close, she called me to supper. There was a thick turnip and nettle soup and a crusty loaf from the baker down the street.

"Esmeralda will be home tonight and we'll go to the procession together," Serena said. "Our nephew Harry will save us a place by the river. You'll like Esmeralda, Lizzie. I've told her all about you and the other wharf rats, and she wants to help. We both do, if you'd let us."

I hadn't really been listening. Now I froze, replaying the

words in my head. What had she done? The last thing we needed was some busybody do-gooder drawing attention to us. "But you've helped so much already!" I protested.

She saw the topic worried me and said no more. We finished the meal in silence. After dinner, Serena locked the door behind me, and I started toward the alley.

Two streets away, I noticed a man following me like a grimy shadow. Try as I might to see what he looked like, the hat and cloak defeated me.

I sprinted into a shortcut I hoped he didn't know, uphill, away from the river. I ran through every twisting passageway and alley I knew, following a circular path to the western-most gate of the city.

When I headed back to the warehouse district, there was no sign of him. I thought I'd lost him, but hid again, between a wall and a cart loaded with barrels. There was no sign of anyone else on that deserted street.

It was very late when I decided to sleep in any deserted place I could find. I picked my way into an alley between two old warehouses, clearly unused from the depth of rubbish that filled it. All was still and silent, and no lights showed. This district was a place for storing goods, not for spending the night.

The piles of rubbish were deep and treacherous. I stumbled and fell, falling into a pit, and for a moment I panicked, afraid I'd suffocate beneath mounds of trash. I dug through rotting sacks and old crates, then felt a corner of stone. Digging deeper, my hands found stone steps. Throwing garbage behind me, I dug until I found stairs, digging toward the bottom. A door had boards nailed across it, but some had warped. Wriggling through, I found myself in complete darkness that smelled of damp earth, most likely a cellar. I didn't dare move for fear of falling through a rotten floor, so I went back outside, grubbing through the piles until I found a bottle and some sacking.

Back inside, I stuffed the sacking into the bottle and lit it with my flint and steel. The sacking caught and burned brightly, sending black ashes into the air as I raised the bottle high.

Inches of dust coated every surface, and there were no footprints in the dust on the floor. The place had been abandoned a long time ago.

Two counters of brick stretched the length of the room, with mounds of broken glassware and sacks grey with dust on them. Jugs and barrels were tucked beneath them. They seemed to be supplies for whatever manufacturing had been done there. I found a box of tallow candles and lit one, blowing out the sacking. I winced as hot tallow fell on my hand, then began to explore.

A glimmer of grey light showed at the end of the cellar. I picked my way toward it cautiously, stepping over broken glass.

A flight of steps rose into the light. They were made of brick and quite sound.

At the top was an enormous factory floor, with shafts of moonlight falling from windows high under the roof, casting squares of light on the floor.

It was obvious the place had been a brick factory—there were stacks of them everywhere, with a forge for ironwork in a corner, and parked hod carriers. Three hearths with metal hoods formed a line across the floor. The soft sound of birds nesting in the rafters floated down, pigeons murmuring, disturbed by my light.

I couldn't believe my luck: a perfect hiding place, and no one was using it. Every wharf rat could live here with room to spare. With three hearths it would be toasty warm, and the smoke easily directed outside. With light from the high windows in daytime, and fresh air from the chimneys, it would be dry and comfortable. There was no sign of vermin except the pigeons, and we wouldn't mind them—they were practically wharf rats too. The windows were so high no one would see the firelight from the street. No one would know we were there.

I brought myself up short. If I shared this place with all the rats, I'd lose the safety it offered. All it would take would be one overheard word and it would be easy for the trackers to find us all, just like the alley I'd left. Why risk it?

Then I remembered Sairy. And Benjamin, stolen right under my nose. Maybe it was time we stopped thinking that way.

I sat down, cross-legged beside a cold hearth. A mean little voice in my head said, *the rats could betray you easy as spitting.*

Yes. But they can do that now, I told it. The mean little voice fell silent.

Everything the wharf rats did was driven by fear: fear of betrayal by strangers, friends, or family, and worst of all, fear that another rat would give us away. Trusting anyone was a risk. But if we had a place to hide, a place to defend, would that make betrayal too much of a risk for a possible informer? They would be at risk too.

I considered Penny's gang. We trusted each other, somewhat. We *did* help each other. Penny taught Daniel and me how to survive. I'd helped Mags and Potts, and Jimmy had helped us both. Kat warned me against helping them, but wasn't that done out of kindness too? If we risked more, we could protect each other. It was possible, at least.

It's happened before, the powerless coming together. Da told me about it, in his stories about the war and the Republic. Apprentices and journeymen, shop girls and butcher boys, all the common folk came together to make demands on the Quality and the mayor. They'd brought trade on the wharves to a halt and stopped the work of London for days. When the people came together it frightened the army's generals, for the soldiers wouldn't fight tradesmen and apprentices, nor women and children, and they'd given in to their demands. The wharf rats could join together, like the apprentices. We could have a Guild of our own. A Wharf Rat Guild.

Too risky. Go to sleep, said the mean little voice. *You'll be lucky if you're not nobbled at the shop, now that the tracker knows where you work.*

That was true. I might have to quit and go back to being hungry on the wharves again. But there was no safety there either.

As I fell asleep, lying on dusty sacks, the thought returned.

Why not? Why not fight back?

7

THE TRACKER

THE NEXT MORNING, the soft murmuring of pigeons woke me. Bands of gold and pink in the eastern windows announced the dawn. A fluttering sound made me glance toward one of the hearths in time to see two pigeons flutter up the chimney to start their day.

I pulled out my glass, hoping, as I always did, to see Daniel. It was warm and alive with light, and this time I understood what I saw. It showed me my tracker.

Three men stood in front of a booksellers' stall in Paternoster Row, the grey stone of Saint Paul's rising behind them. The first was my tracker in his shabby cloak. The other two were nobs. One wore a frizzy periwig of a peculiar yellow color, with a black patch on his face. Froths of white lace cascaded down the front of his canary-yellow coat. The other was dressed conservatively in russet and green, his periwig a dark brown, which went strangely with his pale eyes and paler eyebrows. He leaned in and whispered to the tracker. The only reason a nob would speak to such a man was to employ him.

The tracker nodded and left, and the two nobs strolled off together in a different direction.

A shadow detached itself from a nearby column. I inhaled sharply when I recognized Thomas. He followed the shabby man out of the Row, toward Saint Paul's.

The glass went dark.

What am I to do with that?

It was good news and bad. My tracker wasn't near the factory, but he wasn't that far away either, and Thomas was following him. I wondered how he'd found him.

Then I realized that if this was a foretelling, a vision of the *future*, my tracker might still be waiting outside.

At this time of the morning, Thomas should be at the market in his stall. Perhaps I'd check, to see if my vision was happening now. I admit I wasn't eager to go to the shop where the tracker might be waiting. He must be the same man who'd been watching us yesterday, or Thomas wouldn't be following him. He probably did know about the shop.

From Poultry Lane to Cheapside the crowds were so thick they blocked the carts and coaches trying to get across the city. The river road was faster, so I backtracked to Fish Street and threaded my way down the hill. Women with baskets on their arms were hurrying to Fishmonger's Hall for the morning's catch, while apprentices on errands headed for the shops on the bridge. The crowds included holiday-makers, gentry and middling folk in their best clothes, the country folk in funny-looking, out-of-date clothes. There were more street hawkers than usual, too, crying their wares of cherries, eels, or lemons. I had to crowd against the houses when a carriage, with some richly dressed nob inside, pushed through the street. Something was happening—a holiday I'd forgotten?

Passing the wharves, I glanced longingly at the ships, but if the Mud Men were still catching rats, better to stay away. I owed Mags a breakfast, and hoped she'd escaped. But most ships would be there tomorrow. Covent Square was safer for the likes of us.

I pulled a heel of stale bread from my pocket and nibbled as I walked.

In the Square, men and women were unlocking shed doors to remove barrows and carts stored for the night. A man waved and approached, a short stocky man with white hair and a square, reddish face, wearing a stained apron over his clothes. His blue eyes were friendly. "Hallo. You're that Lizzie girl Thomas talks about. Waiting for him, are ye?"

How did he know that? "Yes, sir." I bobbed a curtsy. "Is he here?"

"Not yet. Come along to our stall. My missus makes a fierce morning jollop."

I followed him inside a small wooden stall with a cozy fire burning in a firepit. A woman with a soft, good-natured face was stirring a pot hanging above it. The wisps of ginger hair escaping her cap were the same color as the ginger cat weaving between her legs.

"Look here, Sara, 'tis the wench Thomas talks about—Mistress Lizzie." He waved a hand as though he'd produced me from thin air. "This is Sara Sweets, my wife," he said. "I'm Gaffer Sweets. How about a bit of jollop for Miss Lizzie?"

So these two were the ones who'd rescued Thomas from his brutal master. I smiled and curtseyed. "'Tis an honor to meet you both. Thomas told me what you did for him."

Gaffer Sweets looked pleased, but shook his head. "Thomas is a clever, decent lad. He's earned what he has by his own hard work."

Sara Sweets turned away to beat an egg in a mug. She poured a ladle of steaming liquid into it and handed the foaming drink to me. It was hot, spicy, and delicious. After the first sip, I drank mouthfuls, and felt my blood sit up and start marching.

"Thank you, mistress, it's stingo."

She nodded. "What're you doing out and about so early? Looking for our Thomas? Have you two put up the banns for the wedding yet?"

I nearly spat the drink on the floor. My face grew hot. "Um, no," I mumbled. What on earth had he told them?

"Don't leave it too long, dear. Thomas needs a steady girl."

I took a deep breath and counted to ten, afraid I'd say something I'd regret. These were good-hearted folk, and Thomas's friends. But I'd be having a word with *him*. Banns indeed.

"Did Thomas know you'd be by?" Gaffer Sweets asked.

I shook my head. "Where is he?"

"Don't know, but he'll come. Just you bide here and wait, where you'll be out of the way."

In spite of the knowing looks they exchanged, I *was* glad to be sitting in their stall when the barrow men wheeled their heavily laden carts of fruits and vegetables down the lanes between the stalls, their iron-shod wheels rumbling like thunder. I sat beside the counter, sipping the jollop like a lady, and trying to decide if the tracker in my vision was the same man who'd almost nobbled Mags and Potts.

With that thought, my stomach wouldn't settle, despite the warm drink. I cradled the mug, warming my hands. If Thomas was following the shabby man at that very moment, then my vision was of the present. That was useful information: my visions weren't only of the future. But it didn't explain how Thomas had found the tracker in the first place. I wondered if he knew who the tracker worked for.

Someone shouted "Halloo!" right in my ear. I jumped.

A tall woman, dressed head to toe in green satin, had come up to the stall and was standing behind me. "Anyone about?" she called. She looked at me curiously. "Who're you?"

How very rude! I tilted my head back and gave her my most disdainful look.

Sara appeared. "Esmeralda! You're back!"

The two women embraced and Gaffer Sweets stepped forward to shake her hand. The three of them laughed and chatted like old friends. Esmeralda kept glancing at me. Finally she asked, "And who is this, Sara?"

"Oh, my manners! Ez, this is Lizzie Nelson, the one you've heard about. Lizzie, this is Esmeralda Hopkins. Fancy her coming while you're here!"

The one you've heard about?

"How do you do, Lizzie?" Esmeralda said. "I believe you work for my sister."

So this was the mysterious sister who was always traveling. At first glance, Esmeralda's rosy cheeks and greying curls gave her a comfortable, grandmotherly air, but those sharp blue eyes missed nothing as they raked me from head to toe.

She turned to say something to Gaffer Sweets and I examined her in turn. Those green shoes with the fashionable heels were not what a woman of the middling class would wear, and neither was that silk parasol. If she was a lady's companion, as her sister said, how could she afford satin and French heels? They weren't castoffs from her lady. That shade of green had been chosen by a woman whose name meant "Emerald." I couldn't imagine anyone who resembled Serena less. Esmeralda was the peacock to Serena's dove.

"What do you do," I asked, "for Lady Cheshire? That's who you work for, isn't it?"

Esmeralda's eyes narrowed. "Lady Cheshire investigates the treatment of servants and apprentices. I'm her eyes and ears, when she has to take cases to law. I travel a good deal."

"How interesting." I didn't believe the Quality gave a fig for servants or apprentices, but it would be rude to say so. "I'd like to hear more."

She smiled thinly. "Of course. But some other time." She whispered something to Sara Sweets.

"How do you know two each other?" I persisted.

Mistress Sweets smiled. "We're old friends, from long before you were born."

"You mean during the war?"

Esmeralda gave me a considering look.

Mistress Sweets said quickly, "Oh no, dear. We're even older than that. We were children in the same village, *years* before the war. Would you like more of the jollop? I don't mean to rush you, but we'll be opening soon."

I'm no clod-pate. She wanted to be rid of me so she could talk to Esmeralda. Whatever they were up to, I'd wager it didn't involve childhood reminiscences. I wondered what was so urgent, but after all, it was none of my business.

The church tower rang the quarter hour. If I didn't hurry, I'd be late for work. I bid the Sweets goodbye and told Esmeralda I was off to see her sister. She eyed me sharply. I was certain that Esmeralda and Mistress and Gaffer Sweets were involved in something havey-cavey. Maybe that was why Serena hardly ever mentioned her sister.

Gaffer Sweets didn't seem to notice the others' impatience; he told me to visit whenever I wanted, whether Thomas was there or no.

Halfway to the shop, busy rehearsing what I'd say to Thomas about our "betrothal," I realized I'd forgotten about my tracker.

I stopped and looked behind me.

My heart thudded in my chest. There he was, not twenty paces away, and we were but a street away from the shop. *Please God, don't let him know my destination.*

Pulse pounding, I ducked into a street that opened onto a warren of courts and alleyways with plenty of places to hide.

He followed much faster than I expected, down the alley filled with casks in front of a ships' chandlers, past barrels set out by the coopers. I ducked into a passageway where the door to a lean-to shed hung open, its padlock hanging loose. I slipped inside and closed the door behind me, hoping I'd been fast enough.

Dim light came from a knothole in the door. I put my eye

against it and nearly leaped back. The tracker stood but three feet away, his head turning this way and that. His face was still hidden by the sweeping brim of an old-fashioned, stained hat. All I could see were his thin lips smiling beneath a drooping mustache. He was staring straight at me and in spite of myself, I stepped back. He couldn't see me, but there was nowhere else to hide. He knew where I was.

The faded cloak suggested poverty; you'd find one like it on any ragged footpad or thief in the city. The boots, however, told a different story. They were well made, of beautiful leather. He stood, legs apart, balanced on his feet, ready to move. He was relaxed and easy—confident I couldn't escape him. He threw his cloak aside to take a clay pipe from a pouch and bent his head for a moment to light it, the flame illuminating his profile.

He straightened and exhaled smoke. Without the cloak, I could see his clothes and knew I'd been right. Above the beautiful boots, the dark coat and breeches were of expensive cloth. White lace flashed at his wrist. This wasn't a common footpad. He was a professional tracker, and he was after me.

I was trapped and he knew it. He stood as though he had all the time in the world for a pipe. He smiled and hummed a tune, satisfied his prey couldn't escape. I could fight, kicking him between the legs, as I'd done to drunken men who'd gotten too close, but I might not get the chance. A professional would expect that; he wouldn't be easy to fool.

"Aren't you tired of hiding yet?" he asked the empty air in a hoarse, raspy voice, as though continuing a conversation. "If you come along quietly now, you won't get hurt. Otherwise, I may have to use force, and I *will* cut you, milady, rather than risk getting hurt myself. Believe me."

Oh, I believed him. *Milady, indeed.* I shifted to put my other eye to the crack.

"Gifted kinchin are dangerous," he continued, "so I strike first.

You may not like what you look like afterwards. No telling what I'll damage. Best thing is to come out of your own accord."

I could see more of his face now. Pale face, thin lips, pale hair; only his eyebrows distinguished him, flaring upward, giving him a devilish look. He lived well and wore expensive clothes because he sold children into slavery. Some gifted children were dangerous, but I wasn't. My gift wouldn't help me. But his arrogance and casual threat of violence made me want to slap him. I was angry now. I wouldn't go without a fight, whatever he might do.

My eyes had adjusted to the dim light. A box of coal, stacks of firewood, and a row of buckets stood against the walls. The wood might make a club, but that meant getting close.

Next to the buckets were rags and jugs that smelled like turpentine. That could be useful. I bent to look into the buckets and straightened quickly, coughing from the pungent smell.

Pitch.

I fumbled in my pocket, pricking my finger on the sharp edge of my glass. I had my steel, and flint.

My hands were trembling and I had to take a breath to steady them. Using sailors' knots, I tied rags around a piece of firewood, and dunked the end of the improvised torch into the pitch until the rags were covered in it. I put my eye to a crack to check on my tracker. He hadn't moved. He was still smoking patiently, as though waiting for a friend. "You ready to come out yet, Lizzie?" he called.

God's teeth, he knows my name. My heart beat faster. *Now or never.* I crouched and struck flint against metal, holding them against the pitch-soaked rags.

Two tries before the spark caught hold. The blue flame quickened and spread over the rags. When the soaked rags were ablaze and the smoke was choking me, I burst out the door.

He was still puffing his pipe, caught off guard.

Yelling madly, I ran toward him, thrusting the flaming brand at his face. He backed away. I jabbed the torch beneath the hat once, twice, then beat at his chest with it before throwing it at him. He howled in pain, and I smelled burning hair and flesh. He tore off the hat, and I saw flames and rising from his head. He screamed.

I'd stayed too long. I ran for all I was worth, certain he'd kill me if he caught me.

I ducked into a lane that descended toward the river, then doubled back, running up a passageway that angled toward Covent Garden. Outside the market I paused for a moment, uncertain. Then I plunged into the crowds, hoping they would hide me. If Thomas were there I could hide in his stall. If I could find it. I'd never been there.

Once inside the market, I had to slow to a desperate walk, breathing hard, the cloying smell of rotting fruit in my nose. The lanes were crowded with shoppers. The Sweets' booth was too far away. Besides, they'd ask questions I couldn't answer.

There was no sign of my tracker, but I felt exposed in the crowd. Then, between one pyramid of fruit and another, I saw Thomas in his stall. Glancing once behind me, I headed for it.

"Hide me, Thomas!"

His smile of welcome disappeared. He quickly swung open the folded shutter that served as both door and counter. "In here."

Inside, there was just room enough for me to kneel at his feet, below the shutter, with shelves taking the rest of the space. From outside, all anyone could see were bunches of greens and stacks of gleaming vegetables and fruit.

"What's on earth is the matter?" he hissed softly.

Whispering, I told him what had happened.

He kept his eyes on the square. "I don't see anyone who looks like he's been set on fire, but your description would fit a hundred men any day of the week. London is full of shabby cloaks. But if he has good boots and no hat, or singe marks, I'll spot him, never fear. Are you all right? Are you burned yourself?" He looked down, his worried brown eyes searching mine.

"I'm fine, Thomas. A couple o' tiny burns, nothing to worry about." I tried to sound brave, but I was shaking. "I think it's the same one we saw yesterday. He may know about the shop."

His eyes never left the crowd. "If you don't know for sure— you'll have to risk it. You can't lose your job."

"There's something worse." I took a breath. "He knows my name."

He let out a low whistle. "The devil. How would he know that unless someone asked for you to be nobbled special?"

"That's just—"

"Hush." A shadow fell over the stall.

"Do you have any pears?" A man's voice.

"No, sir, not today. But these damsons are quite nice. Would you like to try one?" Thomas reached over the counter to hand a slice of fruit to the man. The knife stayed in his hand.

I made myself as small as I could, wrapping my arms around my knees with my head tucked.

"Mmm. I'll take a half pound." The voice didn't sound like my tracker's, but he could be an accomplice, sent to spy out the stalls. I held still while Thomas took the man's coppers and returned his basket full of plums.

"Thank you, sir," Thomas said pleasantly, "Do come find me again; I'm here most days."

The man's boots made a tapping sound as he walked away.

"Is he gone?" I whispered.

"Yes. No one is watching. Best get to the shop while you can."

I raised my head over the edge of the counter. No one was obviously watching the stall. I rose and faced him. "Thanks for hiding me. I—"

I almost asked him who my tracker worked for, but how would I explain that I'd seen him following my tracker?

"Yes?" He opened the door.

"Thanks again." Then I turned and plunged into the crowd, walking quickly, slipping between bodies without apology.

As I walked away, I wondered why Thomas hadn't volunteered who the tracker worked for. Perhaps he didn't know.

Then I laughed out loud. I still had to tell Thomas off for implying we were betrothed.

The laughter cleared my head.

The danger wasn't over, I knew that, but nonetheless I felt different. Stronger. I'd fought back against a tracker and gotten away; I *wasn't* powerless. But I'd also made an enemy. If my tracker wasn't too injured to come after me, he'd be angry.

Angry enough to do more than simply kidnap me.

8

A HOLIDAY

WHEN I FINALLY ARRIVED AT the shop, my luck held. No one waited in the street or in the mews behind the shop.

He wasn't in the shop, either, only Serena and a young woman dressed in the height of fashion, trying on a shawl before the looking glass. Serena saw the curtain move and frowned.

Straightening my cap, I took my place behind the counter, folding and tidying discarded shawls into their boxes while I decided what to tell Serena.

The rose-colored shawl of Indian muslin was paid for, and Serena curtsied and thanked the woman, opening the door for her as she left. Then she came over to me, her brown eyes troubled. "Where have you been all this time, Lizzie? You're not usually late. I had deliveries and no one to send."

I curtsied, my eyes lowered. "I'm sorry, mistress, but there was trouble this morning. A man tried to kidnap me and I had to hurt him to get away." I lifted my gaze, wondering if she'd believe me. Normally I'd never admit such a thing, but if the tracker came here, I'd have to run for it and she'd deserve an explanation. Odds were, she wouldn't want me in her shop now.

Her expression changed. "My poor Lizzie!" She came behind the counter and hugged me. After a moment, I pulled back, unused to such doings. "I feared it was something like that. *He that cannot fight let him run*," she quoted. She walked over to the chair we kept for customers and sat down heavily, her back to the looking glass. "Esmeralda said a known tracker was seen on the wharves yesterday, but I never dreamed he'd come after you." There was speculation in her eyes. "Where do you live now?"

How had Esmeralda heard about a tracker on the wharves if she worked at a grand lady's house? "I've a nice, dry place near the river." That at least was the truth. "By the way, I met Esmeralda this morning." *And if she's a lady's companion, I'm a nob.*

Serena sighed and began to rearrange hats on the stand on the counter. "I hope your new place hasn't upset someone. Or *was* it the tracker who came after you?"

Despite my intention to tell her something, I suddenly felt vulnerable. Exposed. "How do you know about trackers, mistress?"

"Hmph. Esmeralda and I know a great many things that might surprise you. The lords who hunt children now used to hunt other folk during the war. Lizzie—" She waited for me to meet her eyes. "I hope you know you can tell me anything. The Mud Men and trackers won't hear anything from either of us, you can be sure of that."

"Thank you, mistress." I had no intention of saying more. I trusted Serena more than most, but Esmeralda was another matter. I assumed Serena would share whatever I said with her sister.

"Well," she said, "let's get those deliveries out the door."

My stomach knotted. I didn't want to leave the safety of the shop, but I had to do it sometime. It was part of my job. I prayed the tracker was too injured to find me.

While we wrapped shawls and caps in brown paper, Serena

explained why the Mud Men had been scouring the wharves clean of beggars and wharf rats. There was to be a royal procession on the river the next day. A flotilla of boats, barges, and Royal Navy ships, would sail from Hampton Court to Whitehall Palace, to officially welcome Henrietta Maria, the king's mother, back to England. The Quality wanted to watch from the riverbank without seeing riffraff.

"The king has proclaimed tomorrow a half-holiday so everyone can watch the procession. Would you like to come with us?" Her voice rose in excitement. "Harry, my nephew, will save us a place on Bear Quay."

For all I knew my tracker was waiting just outside the door. Standing in a crowd where he could find me was no more of a risk. I was tempted. *Everyone* in London would be on holiday. Why should I be the only one skulking? Besides, I'd be hidden by the crowds.

Serena's excitement was contagious and I couldn't help it, I smiled back. "Thank you, mistress, I'd like to, but I'm not sure I should with this man about. Let me think about it."

"You'll be all right with us, Lizzie."

Why did they always think that? I busied myself arranging the packages in a basket to avoid replying. "I'm off, then." The bell on the door jangled, and I stepped into the street.

No sign of him.

Everyone in the street seemed excited, ready for a holiday. The streets felt safer with so many people, except there were likely more foists picking the pockets of the unwary. From the noise, the holiday had already begun for some.

Surrounded by smiling faces, my heart lightened. Perhaps I *would* go watch the procession.

Kat Jenkins was choosing a pasty in the street of bakers, her hair in a long braid down her back. She wore a dark cloak most of the time, so it was a shock to see her wearing a pale green dress that set off the red glints in her hair. She never wore white, no cap or shift of lawn beneath the bodice like other girls, usually a dark dress and a dark cloak, as though she wanted to disappear into the shadows.

A large fellow, built like a barrel, was waving his arms, lecturing her about something, but she ignored him. I smiled to myself. Kat was always a step ahead of the bailiffs and Mud Men; she wouldn't be impressed by this fellow's bluster. I'd long wanted to know her better, but she kept a chilly distance. I caught her eye and winked. She raised an eyebrow before the crowd came between us.

By the time I circled back to Covent Square to see if Thomas had seen my tracker, I had a few coppers jingling in my pocket from the tips I'd received. He said no burned man had appeared in the crowds of customers.

"I think I'll risk it," I said, after I told him about Serena's offer. "The crowds will make it hard to find anyone."

"*And* you deserve some fun, Lizzie, you're always working. I *was* going to ask you to go with me. If your friends don't mind, I'll meet you wherever you say."

"Somewhere on Bear Quay, is all I know."

He touched his cap in mock deference. "I'll see you there, mistress."

Maybe I shouldn't have agreed, but what was the harm, going with a group of people?

By the time I returned, the shop was closed and supper was ready.

Serena waited at the table. "We'll close the shop at noon tomorrow. There's always some who need something before the shops close. They'll be dying to spend their money. Let's help 'em by opening early. Can you be here by eight o'clock?"

I promised I would.

After supper, I stepped into the pearly light of an overcast evening, glad I'd worn my cloak as the mists thickened. I badly wanted to talk to Penny and the others, but they were probably in Bridewell. And that might be the safest place for them, with a burned tracker about.

On impulse, I decided to go to the Custom House to see if Kat Jenkins was there as she often was.

I found her in a shadowy corner, talking to an elderly gentleman with a cane. I waited for them to finish, and he actually bowed to me before he tapped his way slowly toward the door.

"Well, this is a surprise," Kat said, lifting an eyebrow. "What can I do for you, Lucky Lizzie?"

"I hoped you'd be here. I don't know if anyone is still here, but if you see any rats, warn them there's a tracker about. I burned him, so he's injured and angry."

"You burned him?" Kat sounded skeptical. "What do you mean?"

"He had me trapped, so I lit a torch and beat him with it until he caught fire. I've no doubt he wants to kill me now. But he might take it out on another rat instead, so the others should know."

"That was brave of you." She sounded as though she didn't believe me.

"No, it wasn't," I said. "There was naught else to do. Anyway, I thought you should know."

She raised an eyebrow. "Me? Why me?"

Her questions were getting on my nerves. Why couldn't she just believe I was trying to do her a good turn? "Because you always know more than you should, Kat Jenkins, and you have ways of passing information along. But mostly because I trust you not to be working with the tracker yourself. Do I need another reason? Good evening to you."

I turned on my heel and walked out the door without looking back. I no longer cared whether she told anyone or not.

Fuming, I muttered about the high and mighty Kat Jenkins all the way back to the factory. As far as I could tell, no one followed me.

9

THE RIVER PROCESSION

A DREAM of fire and my tracker's smiling face woke me in the grey dawn the next morning. I splashed my face with water I kept in a cracked basin I'd found, then braided my hair, pushing it beneath my cap.

Ready for the day, I took out my glass and sat in a shaft of sunlight, asking to see Daniel, or my tracker. But the glass remained cool in my hand, and no light appeared within.

At least it doesn't show my tracker. Maybe I'd burned him so badly he was dying. I felt reassured.

I left the factory, carefully examining both ends of the alley first, but no one else seemed to be there. The main streets were filled with people in their holiday best, ready for fun. Hawkers were selling pies, fruit, or cheap trinkets. Watch men were every-where. So were footpads, pickpockets in fancy dress, and all manner of shady rogues, weaving among the fruit and pasty sell-ers. The crowds would make it harder for a tracker to find me, but he'd be harder to spot, too.

The bells were ringing eight o'clock just as I arrived at the shop. Serena had been right: women were lined up, waiting to buy a new cap, new ribbons or lace, or "a little something to remember the holiday." We were busy until nearly noon, when Serena, looking harassed, said, "We'll have to close now or we'll never get to the river in time."

I shooed away a few stragglers and placed a sign on the shop door that read, "Closed for the Holiday." I felt a pang: was I telling the tracker where to find me? But I shook off my worries. We were on holiday. Besides, my glass told me I'd be safe.

Serena, her cloak and bonnet on, was waiting in the kitchen with a basket over her arm. She handed me a shawl. "You know how suddenly the river mist comes up."

We stepped outside and I laughed for no reason at all. I was on holiday. For the first time since my tracker had appeared, I relaxed. Serena locked the back door and I took her arm to lead the way to Bear Quay. She didn't know the back ways to the river the way I did, and this way we could avoid the crowds.

She objected only once, when I led her into a gloomy passage through a low arch, crowded with pallets of rotting vegetables and what smelled like an overflowing privy. "Are you sure this is the right way?" she asked, wrinkling her nose.

"We'll only be a moment." With my hand under her arm I guided her past crates and tumbled bricks. A crate of cabbages blocked the other end, and we stepped around it, out of the gloom into the clean daylight of a main street. A crowd engulfed us, walking in the same direction.

When we arrived at Bear Quay, Serena pointed to a huge fellow who towered above the crowd. We squirmed our way to where Harry, Serena's nephew, stood close to the edge, with nothing but a metal chain between him and a fall to the river below. There were grumbles when we pushed through, but they stopped when Harry turned to give them a warning look. He stood sideways, clearing a space for us by moving his massive shoulders and arms. Esmeralda was on his other side, nearly invisible behind his barrel-shaped chest.

"Well met, Mistress Lizzie," he boomed, smiling down at me.

Then he frowned at someone behind me. "Here you! What do you think you're doing?"

My heart in my mouth, I turned, afraid I'd see the burned face of my tracker. But it was only Thomas, struggling past the fat woman who'd locked arms with an old man wearing a helmet from the war, to stop him from getting through.

"Harry, he's with me," I called. Harry grabbed Thomas's arm and heaved him forward, nearly toppling Esmeralda into the river. Harry quickly yanked her back.

"Sweet heaven," she muttered, tucking her hair back under her cap.

"Are you all right, mistress?" I asked.

She peered around Harry. "Yes, thank you, Lizzie." She threw a dark look at Thomas.

I forgot about Esmeralda, because the crowd began to cheer.

The first barges passed. There were whistles and cheers from the watermen's boats below, and "Hurrahs!" from the crowd around us. Someone blew a trumpet. The old soldier, clearly deaf, yelled at his companion, "The watermen are making money hand over fist. They're charging double or triple, to watch from the water."

Two Royal Navy ships came around the bend. I craned my neck to see around Harry. Sailors on the decks stood at attention. From across the water came the piping of whistles.

I glanced at Thomas, who'd wanted to join the Navy when he was boy. He was smiling like an idiot.

Most of London had taken the afternoon off. The crowd was stifling, everyone hot and sweaty in the bright sun. Each time the crowd heaved forward I feared I'd be knocked down, or shoved over the chain and into the river. All too soon, I grew tired of watching the boats gliding past and turned to examine the crowd. With everyone pressed close, I had to stand on tiptoe and crane my neck to see much. Anyone doing the same might be a tracker —or a foist. In the small circle of faces near me, no one glanced my way except the old soldier, who prodded me resentfully with his elbow.

Another cheer went up, louder this time, and I looked back. The royal barge was sliding by. Gold leaf dazzled my eyes and music drifted across the water from a quartet under an awning. The Queen Mother, in a gilded chair, waved to the crowd. Her son, King Charles II, was beside her, his face dwarfed beneath the massive periwig of dark curls that must've been hot in the sun. He waved a languid hand and the crowd cheered again. There was no sign of his brother, the Duke of York, but the old soldier yelled that the duke was aboard his namesake ship, coming around the bend. Even at a distance, we heard the sails snapping in the wind as the warship approached. The watermen directly below invoked their ancient privilege and yelled a few insults at the king, but cheerfully; even they were mellowed by the sunny day and holiday mood.

"It's too bad the wharf rats are missing this," Thomas said. "The river's their home; it's only right they should have a front row seat."

"Well, *I'm* here, and I'll wager Kat's here somewhere. They didn't get all of us."

"And I'm glad you're here, Lizzie." Thomas smiled at me, his arm pressing into mine in the close quarters. "It wouldn't be a holiday without you."

My face and neck were suddenly too warm. "Uh…I'm glad you're here too," I said weakly. "Look." I pointed at the barge passing in front of us. "Who's that?"

He frowned but turned to look.

A new barge was passing. Surrounded by servants, a nobleman raised a golden cup to the crowd. The golden livery of the oarsmen flashed in the sun, blinding me for a moment. When I could see again, I saw some of the servants were children.

Garlands of flowers hung on the barge's sides, and live swans trailed in its wake, tethered by ropes to the stern. The swans were being dragged along, the barge traveling faster than they could swim. They trumpeted their protests, but the lord took no notice.

No one cheered or clapped. The crowd on the riverbank and the watermen below fell silent. The nob waved his hand, smiling all the same.

"Who's that?" I whispered again. But I had recognized him. I thought I knew.

The woman behind me said, "Hush, child. That's Lord Hazelton, or the Devil himself, take your pick." The barge slipped past the silent crowd, the swans flapping their wings, trying to stay above the water. As the barge passed, I saw the corpses of two swans already drowned, their tethered bodies tumbling in the wake.

He was the nob from my vision, one of the two who'd been with my tracker in Paternoster Row. Suddenly I felt ill. My stomach heaved from the stench of fish scales and unwashed bodies in the hot sun. I muttered, "Sorry. Have to go," and blindly pushed and pummeled my way past the woman and the soldier, tunneling through the crowd, until at last I reached the edges of it. Others were leaving too. The crowd was breaking up.

"Lizzie, wait!" Thomas called.

I barely heard him. I felt exposed and desperate to get away. What a fool I'd been! Still seeing the grinning face of Lord Hazelton and the tumbling dead swans, I dodged the remnants of the crowd, heading for that narrow passage that would take me back to the shop. I'd apologize to Serena later.

My boots slapped the cobbles as I ran, shaking off the smell of the overheated crowd. The crates of cabbages were directly ahead, blocking the entrance to the alley. I pushed past and was halfway down the passage before I saw who was at the other end, waiting for me.

A pleased smile spread below his mustache.

He doffed his hat and bowed like a courtier, his eyes never leaving mine, waiting for my reaction.

One side of his head was hairless, the skin burnt a livid red from the crown to the base of his neck. The other side was untouched; with his hat tilted at an angle he'd pass for normal. Without his hat, even in the dim light of the alley, he was hideous. He straightened, smiling, his eyes like chips of ice.

I'd marked him for life, and he was about to demand payment. Whatever he meant to do, I'd end up as hideous as he was.

If I lived.

10

KAT

THERE WAS nothing to do but run.

I sprinted back the way I'd come, dodging tired holiday-makers, weaving my way toward the river. His boots sounded close, and when I risked a look, the flash of his knife was only five or six paces behind. He made no effort to conceal the knife, and those who saw him coming quickly stepped aside. No one tried to stop him.

At the corner of Water Lane and Thames Street, a foundry and a cooper occupied a narrow lane, and beside them, two alleys snaked away. If I could get into one fast enough, he might waste time making a choice.

I ducked around the corner and headed for the first street on the right. Behind me, I heard him laugh.

"It won't work, Lizzie," he said.

I whirled around to face him. He stepped closer, smiling.

"You won't get away this time," he said softly in his raspy voice. "Lord Hazelton asked for you special, though he wouldn't say why. Can't say I see the appeal. I'm confident he doesn't want you for your beauty, though." He smirked. "That leaves me free to have a little fun with your face before I make delivery.

Just to settle our score, m'dear. I pay back every child who marks me."

My hands were on my knees, and I was gasping for breath. The cold wind chilled the sweat on my neck, and his words turned my blood as cold as river water.

He tossed the knife from hand to hand. "You have a choice. I can cut you with either hand. I'm more accurate with the right, so I won't accidentally cut your throat. The left might be easier to dodge, but I'll have less control over the result. Which would you prefer?"

I stared into those empty eyes and then ran for the alley, with the sound of his bootheels right behind me. "It doesn't matter, you can't escape now."

My mind seemed to have frozen, certain he was right. I fought the panic controlling my body, but it was winning. Instinct told me to run, run until he caught me.

Scarves of wet mist drifted across my path, making the cobbles slippery. The mists had rolled in just as Serena had predicted; I pulled her shawl tighter, and with the memory, I tried to think. The river. There might be help by the river.

I turned toward it, boots slipping on the wet stones. I could see the last of the crowd breaking up, leaving for warmer entertainments. They glanced at me, but moved away. There was no help there. I'd have to fight him at close quarters, and I'd get hurt.

There was the chain by the river, where I'd been with my friends only a few minutes before, happy with Thomas and Harry and the Hopkins sisters. I stopped and turned to face him.

He was on me, breathing hard, his eyes like slits, angry I'd eluded him so long. He moved toward me, arm lifted with the knife aimed at my face.

Then, out of nowhere, Kat Jenkins appeared. "Lizzie! Get down on your hands and knees! Now!"

I obeyed without thinking, hands and knees on the cobbles.

She came running, those long legs flashing below her skirt.

The tracker had turned to look, then turned back, amused, confident he'd deal with us both. "On your knees to me? It won't save you."

At the last moment, his eyes widened and he glanced back again, but it was too late. Kat, her arms held stiffly before her, ran into him full tilt, shoving him across my back. His neck lay on the chain, the rest of him across my back. He struggled to get up.

Kat bent, grabbed his ankles, and lifted. In a heartbeat, he was over the chain and falling toward the river and the pier jutting out below. He screamed once as he fell, then I heard a horrible crunching sound and a splash from the water below. I rose to my feet and looked over the chain. As I watched, his clothes darkened and dragged him under as the river took him. A dark shadow was carried downstream.

My breathing was still ragged. I turned to Kat and managed to croak, "Thanks."

A flicker of a smile. "You're welcome. A tracker?"

I nodded.

Her eyes narrowed. "He was going to cut you."

It was a question. I swallowed on a raw throat. "I told you. I set him on fire. He was going to pay me back."

"Good thing I was here then."

"Yes. Yes, it was. I can't thank you enough." My eyes fastened on her face. Why had she helped me?

Kat appeared to come to a decision. "Come with me. Looks like you could use a bite o' parkin and a safe place to rest." She put an arm around my shoulder and led me away, without even a glance over the chain.

The sky was clouding up, the clouds turning dark and a mist seeping over the riverbank. The sunny afternoon of an hour ago was turning damp and cold. I walked beside Kat, shivering, and the mist closed around us. We'd walked a quarter of an hour, heading away from the river, before I finally asked where we were going.

"To a house I use. I've food and a fire there."

My surprise must have shown. She said, "I'm not as unfriendly as some believe. I just pick my battles—and my friends—with care."

I nodded, uncertain whether she'd just called me a friend. I could think of no better word for someone who'd just saved my life.

Kat, who always kept her distance, had risked her life for me. Penny had taken me under her wing, Mags had offered to help me, and now Kat had stepped into harm's way to save me from a tracker. The rats weren't nearly as selfish as they pretended.

The sky was luminous with grey clouds, engulfing the road as well as the sky, when Kat stopped in front of what appeared to be a burnt-out house, its timbers and plaster blackened and smoke-stained. In the dim light it looked gloomy and abandoned.

"Here we are," she said, opening a gate in the wooden fence. She walked to a door hidden in the shadow of a vine and turned to see why I hadn't followed.

"Is this yours?"

"I stay here sometimes."

I closed the gate and followed her. The door opened into a kitchen, lit by the soft glow of a banked fire. To my right was an open hearth, big enough to stand inside. On the opposite wall stood a row of cupboards. Despite the derelict appearance outside, everything here was clean and well-ordered. There was even a cloth on the wooden table and the two wooden chairs had cushions.

"Sit," she ordered. "I'll find us some food." She stirred the fire before lighting a candle and bringing it to the table. I sat down, glad to rest. I lifted a hand to my eyes and saw it was shaking.

A braid of onions hung from a hook in the beam above me. Jugs sat on the sideboard opposite the door, beside a wheel of cheese under a glass bowl. Kat added kindling from a basket to the fire, prodding it with the poker until it caught and began to burn steadily. She swung an iron kettle over the fire and the smell of something savory filled the air. The room had become warm and cozy.

She placed two pewter plates on the table, with a knife, beside the bread and cheese, then poured ale into two mugs and handed one to me. "'Tis ale from the Blue Dog. Mistress Parker is the best brewer in London."

I nodded my thanks and drank in silence, before helping myself to the bread and cheese. I was ravenous.

When it was ready, Kat poured pease porridge into the waiting bowls and we ate in silence. After we'd finished, I finally asked, "How did you appear like that, out of nowhere?"

"You're no clod-pate, Lizzie Nelson. You know perfectly well how."

"Your gift is being invisible?" I'd never asked anyone about their gift before. It felt strange, impertinent.

"Not precisely. I can hide things from sight, including me. But I could hide you too, if I chose." She crossed her arms and rested them on the table, watching me closely.

"Oh." I didn't know what else to say.

"So what's yours, then?" She looked me in the eye. "Fair's fair. I told you my secret, now tell me yours."

In my entire life I'd never revealed my gift to anyone. Da was dead, and Daniel already gone when I'd found out. But she was right, it was only fair. "I don't completely understand it, but I see things. I see what will happen, or what's happening right now."

"A vision. A foretelling?" She spoke in a matter-of-fact voice.

"Yes. But I don't always know what it means, or when it will happen."

"Well, it *sounds* useful. Did you have a vision of your tracker before he found you?"

"No. Not this time."

"Not so useful, then."

"No. No, it's not." We were silent. I remembered the cry the tracker had made as he went over the chain, and the crunching sound of something striking the pier below. I shivered.

"Do you need a place to sleep?" Kat tilted her head to indicate the room around us. "I'm minding this for a friend, but I can stay here any time. You're welcome."

I was too exhausted to navigate back to the factory in the dark. And I was still afraid, in spite of seeing my tracker fall. "Thank you. I wouldn't mind biding till morning. There's something I'd like to talk to you about." On the way to her house, as my fears ebbed, the idea had taken hold and wouldn't let go. I felt strangely excited about telling her. She might call me a noddy and laugh, but she was the most cautious rat I knew and she'd risked her life for me. I thought she'd understand because *she* fought back. Maybe the others were ready too.

"I said you're welcome. And if you're going to stay—" She went to the cupboard again, and returned with a cloth-covered plate. She whisked the cloth away and I saw she'd spoken the truth, earlier. A beautiful round parkin, a gingerbread cake with a wedge missing, gleamed on the plate. The aroma of molasses and ginger made my mouth water.

I must've looked surprised, for Kat laughed. "I made it myself."

We each took a piece and I ate mine slowly, savoring the sweetness. The fire and the parkin made me feel safe, maybe too safe, but I felt compelled to share my idea.

While she washed the dishes in a basin, I sat on a cushion by the fire and ordered my arguments. Even if my tracker was dead, I had James threatening me, and any agent or tracker could nobble any one of us, at any time. We needed protection. If we watched each other's backs, and slept where no one could find us, we'd all be safer. The factory was too perfect to keep to myself. None of us would be alone anymore. But the important thing was to stop the kidnappings, and make the little ones safe from trackers and gangs.

How to explain it? Kat knew my gift and I knew hers. We

already held each other's lives in our hands. Besides, if she called me a looby, I'd survive.

"Kat, I'd like your opinion."

She took a cushion from a chair and sat down cross-legged on the other side of the hearth. The flames threw dancing shadows across her face. She didn't interrupt while I explained my idea, explained about using Haven, as I'd named it, as our hideaway. When I finished, she shook her head. "It'll never work. The littl'uns could never keep it quiet."

I took a deep breath. "We could keep the smallest kinchin inside, to keep 'em safe. We'd pool our money and share food. Once we're a Guild, we can set our rates, same as the other Guilds. We'll have more coin to pay anyone who finds out. Like the night soil men who collect from the privies, or the Mud Men."

"Huh." Kat cocked her head to one side. "Could end up costing more than we make."

"Lastly…" I hesitated a moment. "We should swear a blood oath to be true to each other."

Kat stifled a laugh. "An oath, is it? You're a dreamer, Lizzie. Words won't keep us safe. The only way to be safe is to have the *power* to defend yourself."

"Exactly. And we *have* the power, but we're afraid to use it. What if we used our gifts to help each other, to protect each other? That's why they nobble us: We *are* powerful."

She looked away, staring into the fire.

I waited.

"If it's such a good idea, why has no one tried it before?"

I examined her face for mockery, but saw only seriousness. "It could work," I repeated. "We're the ones with the power, if only we dare use it. All we need is a plan and a place we can defend."

"And the babies, the ones who don't understand about the danger? How will you keep them from leading the trackers to your door?"

"We keep them inside most of the time, until they do understand. We keep them safe. They can be taught."

"You're crazy." She said it gently, to take the sting from her words. "It's every man for himself by the river if you want to stay alive. You got away with helping the rats because you were lucky." She smiled ironically.

"Everyone *says* it's every man for himself. But it's not true: You just saved my life. Penny helped me, when I first came here. The rats *do* help each other—we just pretend we don't. I'm sick of standing by and watching trackers pick us off one by one. We're not powerless, we're simply *afraid.* I survived warning the others about the cook shop, and I survived helping Mags and Potts escape a tracker. You helped me and *you're still here.*

"I, for one, am tired of running. Even if we're nobbled, we should stand up for ourselves and each other. The others will follow, if we lead the way."

She looked thoughtful. "If they're threatened or blackmailed, the rats will betray you."

"Perhaps. But isn't that already true? You could've betrayed me after I warned everyone about the cook shop, but you didn't. You just saved my life today. Why did you take the risk?"

She was silent a long time, her brow furrowed, staring into the fire.

When she answered, her voice was low and fierce. "Because you needed help. Because I knew I could. Because I'm tired of being pushed around by the high and mighty—and the low and dirty. Every catchpoll, bailiff, and Mud Man thinks he has the right to bully and beat us, and to steal from us if he can. *We* have the gifts—why shouldn't we use them for what *we* want?"

She'd made my argument for me. "Maybe the lords and ladies are afraid that together we'd be more powerful than they are," I said. "For that to be true, we'd have to work together. I'd be honored to have you as the Guild's first member, Kat."

She laughed and her face relaxed. "You're hell-bent on saving these poor kinchin from the trackers, aren't you? Why? No one else cares about them."

"Because no one else *does* care. It's up to us." My eyes never left her face.

Her smile lingered. "Very well, Lizzie Nelson. I'll join your Guild. It will probably get us killed, but if we can fight the trackers and the Quality first, it might be worth it."

"Then let's take an oath together," I said. "I want to show you Haven and get your advice about what needs doing before we invite the others. But you must swear to protect the secret of its location. Put your right hand across your heart, like this, and repeat after me: 'As God is my witness, I swear I will protect the Guild, the members of the Guild and the secrets of the Guild, including its location, with my life. If anyone breaks this solemn vow, I will hunt them down for the Guild to punish. If I break this bond of loyalty, I shall pay with my life. If I betray, let me be betrayed also.'"

Kat smirked at the solemnity, but repeated the words exactly.

I held out my hand. "Congratulations. You're the first member of the Guild."

She didn't take it. "Now I want to hear *you* swear too."

I took a deep breath and repeated the oath.

"Good," she said. "Let's get down to Guild business."

11

THE WHARF RATS RETURN

I AWOKE beside Kat's hearth the next morning and checked the glass as I always did.

Warm in my hand, the glass was glowing. A vision appeared, and this time I feared the meaning was plain to see.

Thomas stood behind his counter, his market-seller's apron a blinding white in the sun. A cloaked man faced him, his back to me. I never saw his face, so I couldn't be sure, but the way the man stood reminded me of my tracker. I waited for him to turn, to see his face, but the glass went dark.

Was this the past or the future? It had to be the past; no one could've survived that fall. My tracker *must be* dead. But always before my visions were set in the present or the future, never the past. Either Thomas had spoken with my tracker *before* he'd found me by the river, or my tracker was still alive. I shook my head. The simpler explanation was that it was someone else.

Kat came into the kitchen, yawning. "Sleep well?"

I hurriedly put the glass in my pocket. "I did, thank you."

"If you'll get up, I'll make breakfast."

I folded the blanket I'd used and placed it on a chair, then went outside to find the privy. There was no reason to mention my vision to Kat, not until I was certain what it meant. She'd immediately suspect Thomas of being an informer. One could almost suppose he'd told the tracker where I'd be that day. I *didn't* want to suspect Thomas, but I wondered if I that made me a looby.

Once we'd eaten, we walked together toward the wharves. I stopped a moment to watch the wherries, schooners, and fat-bellied merchantmen gliding past us. A small skiff with three passengers moved directly into the path of a larger ship, in danger of being crushed. We heard the passengers shouting a warning. The waterman cursed and the skiff fell back.

Ships and boats constantly jockeyed for position, especially near the bridge, aiming for the narrow channels between the starlings, the barriers of wood and broken rock that guarded the pilings. If a boat lost that game of nerves, they had to back off and wait their turn, or risk being wrecked. Churning whitewater between the pilings could seize a boat and dash it against the starling, wrecking the boat and throwing the passengers into the water. They'd drown unless they were lucky enough to climb onto the starling to wait for rescue. It was a game of nerves that often drew spectators on the riverbank.

Kat prodded me with her elbow. "I thought you wanted to show me your hiding place?"

I came out of my reverie and smiled. I should be cheerful this morning. My tracker was dead and had floated downstream to be someone else's problem. But why had the glass shown me Thomas in a vision? For the second time.

Folk hurried past on their way to work. Maids and servants carried laden baskets, barrow boys pushed carts, and horses and wagons cut through the foot traffic. No one gave us a second glance.

As we approached Bear Quay, I recognized Penny from a distance, her long red hair loose from its braid. She sat on a crate, her head bent over something Mags was showing her. The wharf rats were back.

As we approached, Mags saw me and waved. Kat and I went to meet them.

"Told you Lizzie's still here," Mags said, her voice muffled by a mouthful of pie. "We heard you got nobbled," she said, "but I knew no tracker could catch Lucky Lizzie."

Kat and I exchanged a wry look. I gathered my skirts and sat on a crate beside her. News flowed along the wharves like piss in the gutters. "I'm still here," I agreed.

"What did we miss?" Penny asked. "I heard the procession for the Queen Mother was glorious. What did you see?"

"It was just boats on the river, Penny, though some of them were fine. We saw the king and the Queen Mother, dressed in all their finery. That was grand."

Kat snorted. "It was a stinking crowd of gawkers, middling folk, and footpads. The barges were pretty enough, but there was no work that day, except for the watermen. And Lord Hazelton went past in a gold-painted barge, bold as brass."

"Oh." Penny's smile faded for a moment. "Still, it would've been stingo to see that monster from a safe distance."

Mags leaned over and whispered into my ear, "I've asked about Daniel at all the new ships I saw this morning, Lizzie. That counts, right?" She searched my face anxiously. She didn't realize I'd feed her whether she asked or no.

"Of course. Here I was feeling bad 'cause I haven't asked today, and now you've done it for me." I slipped coins into her hand whispering, "Can you buy your own today? Here's some extra. I think I should pay in advance, just in case."

She frowned at me suspiciously. "Why?"

"I'm calling a meeting tonight for *all* the rats in our gang, Penny. Bring your dinners to the empty berth at the end of Bear Quay at sunset. Do *not* let James, Cynthia, or Potts find out."

The memory of jail would help. A safe place where trackers

and Mud Men couldn't find them would be all the more desirable after a night in Bridewell.

"Why can't I tell Potts?" Mags asked, sounding rebellious.

"Because for certain he'll tell James," I said, "and I don't want him to know."

"Oh." She looked thoughtful.

"Are you sure, Lizzie?" Penny asked. "It's dangerous for us all to be in one place." She lowered her voice. "A tracker's been seen near Saint Paul's."

"What did he look like?" I glanced at Kat. *It couldn't be him.*

"I don't know, I didn't see him," Penny said, looking at me curiously.

"Don't let anyone overhear when you talk about the meeting. We don't want others to know."

"We'll be there, won't we, Mags?" Penny said.

Mags had finished her pie and was licking her fingers. "Aye, we will. You always know when to stay away from a place, Lizzie. If you know it's safe, we'll be there."

My chest tightened at this tempting of fate. "Who says I'm lucky?" I tried to speak lightly.

Mags laid a finger against her nose. "Lot o' mites think you know what's going to happen. Everyone says so."

So much for hiding my gift. I took Kat's arm. "See you tonight then."

"See you, Lizzie," they chorused.

Kat waited until we were back on the road to say, "Not everyone will trust you the way Mags does, Lizzie. How are you going to keep one of 'em from informing on us? Just one frightened child, and the Mud Men will roust us out of your factory in no time."

"They have to understand that anyone who betrays us will pay. The blood oath is meant to demonstrate how serious this is," I said. "The same way the gangs repay disloyalty with death."

She stopped in the middle of the road. "Are you planning to kill a *child* if they make a mistake?"

"Of course not. But they don't know that. And loyalty *is* a matter of life and death. Once they see how much better off they are, they'll understand the oath keeps them safe. If they take it seriously, it will work."

We'd reached the Custom House, and weaved our way into the crowds of carts, horses, and people on foot coming from the bridge.

"Have you ever told anyone about your gift before?" I asked.

Kat frowned, watching those close to us. "Mum knew about it, before she died. She said not to reveal it to a living soul, and I haven't, until last night."

I wondered if she regretted that. Or rescuing me. "I've never told anyone before, either."

She shook her head. "I trust you more than most, Lizzie, but it makes me nervous all the same, someone knowing. It's the careless ones get nobbled first. If only we had a way to scare the youngest into silence, your idea could work. It's not just me—it will be hard for everyone to trust, having kept silent so long."

But that's not true, I argued silently. We simply don't notice the small acts of trust, when they happen. Most of us help the little ones when we know a tracker is around, keeping them out of sight, feeding them. They were easy pickings for the trackers, who saw them as bonuses—children they could sell to God-knows-who, whether they had a gift or not.

Carts and the gentry on horseback crowded past us. I recognized familiar faces in the crowd. London's parishes are like villages, and folk tended to stay in their village. I saw no more rats to invite to the meeting.

Halfway up Fish Street I turned into a curving street of warehouses, almost deserted except for a man pushing a cart and a woman with a basket of lemons on her head. No one worked or loitered where Haven sat, one of a row of blank-faced ware-houses. No one lived here. We were going to change that.

I strolled past the alley, while Kat waited on the corner. No one was in sight. I waved. Together we waded through the rubbish to find the stairwell. "Phew!" Kat said. "Where have you brought me?"

I squirmed through the warped boards and fumbled for the candle I'd left in the niche by the door. When it was lit, I held it up so Kat, coming in after me, could see.

Everything was just as I'd left it: empty rat-gnawed sacks scattered across on the floor and thick layers of dust on the counters. I picked my way through the broken glass to the stairs.

We climbed up into the pale daylight flooding the large main floor, and I blew out the candle. Particles of dust floated in the shafts of light falling from the windows. Haven was undisturbed, peaceful.

Kat walked to the center of the floor and turned in a circle. "It's large enough and the air seems sweet." She peered beneath the hood that hung over a fire pit. "And we can have as many fires as we want." She straightened. "It's a good place, Lizzie. But how do we come and go without attracting attention?"

I shrugged. "We could leave one by one, so's no one will notice. I haven't finished exploring. There may be a way in I haven't found."

"If we're noticed, you believe we can pay for silence, but I doubt it. The Mud Men might be satisfied with a few coppers, but others will want more than pennies." Kat crossed her arms and examined the room. "At least the place looks defensible, but we need another way out. I won't be trapped here." Her voice rose as she said that. She crouched down to examine the forge.

I hadn't thought about being trapped. She was seeing things I'd missed. "Were you ever trapped, Kat?"

She didn't reply immediately, taking a good long time with the forge. Finally she stood and said, "You've never been nobbled, have you Lizzie? Well, I have. For almost two years I was a slave for a family in Hampshire. I did their bidding, spied on their neighbors, stole for them too. Another girl was beaten to death while I was there. That's what it took for me to realize it would be my death one way or another if I stayed. When I saw my chance, I ran away. I've been by the river ever since."

For a moment I could think of nothing to say. "Then you understand why we have to do this."

"Of course I do! But banding together will make us *more* of a target. You need to be ready for that. We can't just hide from trackers. We have to think about fighting, weapons, and escape routes."

I stared in surprise. "You think we can fight grown men?"

"Sooner or later we'll have to. We can't hide forever, Lizzie." She cocked her head. "How did you end up by the river? I'll wager *you* were never in the poor house."

"We came close. After Ma died, we lost the farm, and Da was a masterless man. He only worked now and then, and Daniel and I were hungry all the time."

"Daniel?"

I looked away. "My brother."

"So that's who Mags was asking the sailors about. Did he run away?"

So I told her about Bridewell, and that I didn't know where he was.

She smiled grimly. "I was going to say you had it easy compared to some, but perhaps not. Penny says you can read and write. Is that true?"

I nodded, wondering why she wanted to know.

Kat was standing beneath a large pipe hanging from the ceiling. "Looks like water was piped in from above," Kat said. "Have you been on the roof?"

"No."

Kat picked up a pottery jug and frowned at the clouds of dust rising around it. After putting it down she turned to face me, fists planted on her hips. "I said I'd join your Guild, and I have. It's time for you to listen to *my* ideas now. Here's *my* proposition."

I waited, wondering what I'd gotten myself into.

"You're good at visions and ideals, Lizzie, but *I've* a knack for organizing and planning. Folk owe me favors. We need to fix this place up before you bring the rats here. I'll get you cooking pots, bedding, and coal for the fires. There's a helpful cove who'll bring it by for us, no questions asked, and he won't peach us. It would be a poor beginning if our first days were cold and cheerless."

I looked once more at empty space around us. She was right. There was no coal, no food, and little comfort to be had. The old sacks I'd used for bedding would hardly be enough for everyone.

"That's all very well," I said, "but what does your *helpful cove* want in return? When I make a bargain, I prefer to know who I'm making it with and what I'm agreeing to. This fellow could betray us if he knows where Haven is."

Kat was examining the shelves and not really listening. She said absently, "Don't worry. The only obligation is to me. Think of it as my gift to the Guild, to get it on its feet. I may ask a favor some day in return."

I met those dark eyes that gave nothing away and wondered what sort of bargain I'd already made by telling her so much. Did she plan to take over the Guild for her own reasons? I didn't know much about her. Only that she'd been a slave once and had saved my life. Perhaps that was enough.

She smiled, as though guessing my thoughts. "Don't worry, Lizzie. I'm much less trusting than you are, and will keep your secrets better than you do. You still expect the best in folk. But you *can* trust me, I promise. We're going to make this work."

I nodded and offered her my hand. She took it, covering it with both of hers. Her handshake was warm and firm. "That's settled," she said, surveying the room with satisfaction. "Kat

Jenkins will sort it for you. You go back to your visions and schemes to keep the trackers and Mud Men off our backs."

"Will you live here too?" I asked thinking of the burned house.

"Yes. But I'll have to visit my friend's house sometimes."

"I see," I said, although I didn't. She'd saved my life. If she brought supplies for the rats, I'd be even more indebted. I'd take the rest on trust. There was naught to stop me keeping an eye out for who owed Kat favors, and why.

I heard the church bells tolling the time, one after the other. I glanced at the eastern windows where the sun was above the roofs. "I have to go or I'll be late to work."

Kat was staring up at the pipe again. "You go on. I'm going to make a start here." She grinned. "It's a good place, Lizzie, close to the river, but far enough away there won't be prying eyes watching the alley. I'll work on a defense plan."

She came with me down the stairs. When I left, she was going through the cupboards in the cellar.

12

SECRETS

I DREADED GOING BACK to work and having to explain to Serena why I'd run away yesterday. She might be angry enough to fire me. How much would a respectable shopkeeper tolerate from a wharf rat? I took the long way to the shop, to postpone it as long as possible.

From the river road, I saw a ship had lost its sails and main-mast on Botolph's Quay, likely in a storm. Carpenters were hammering away on deck, while carts from sail-makers and chandlers unloaded supplies beside the gangplank. I saw no chil-dren among the groups of men. Everything looked normal enough. Sailors were a superstitious lot. If there was a tracker or other trouble on the wharves, they'd be jittery. Most ordinary seamen had been press-ganged at least once in their lives, forced to sea against their will. That was one reason some of them helped us. Kidnapped by His Majesty's Navy, and bullied by the Mud Men and bailiffs too, we shared a bond. Sometimes they'd even help us in a fight.

I heard a strange laugh and turned to look. Potts was laughing at a stranger I'd never seen before, standing with James and Cynthia beside the Custom House stairs. The stranger was dark-haired, with a broad, fleshy face, and large shoulders. He caught my gaze and smiled. Gooseflesh crawled up my arms and neck.

"Lizzie! Lizzie, wait!"

Someone was running behind me. I turned. It was Thomas, running until he caught up. He moved to embrace me, but remembering my vision, I stepped back.

"Thank God! Where've you been? When you ran away yesterday I thought…what's wrong?"

"I'm fine, Thomas. There was a tracker, but I got away." I spoke softly, glancing at the traffic passing us on the road. Folk were staring at us, their attention drawn by his yelling. That dark-haired man was watching, too.

Thomas ran his hand through his hair, nodding. "I knew it. Why did you suddenly bolt like that? I could have protected you."

I searched his face for signs of guilt. "Lower your voice, everyone's looking." I pointed to where some benches were screened by a row of sheds. I headed for one and sat down.

"I had to go. I felt trapped." I could hardly explain that I'd recognized Hazelton from a vision. A vision Thomas had been in as well.

He frowned. "Did anyone see you with the tracker? They'll suspect you have a gift."

As if I needed his advice about this. Nor was I best pleased by his easy assumption that he could discuss it with me. "Thomas, I know you mean well, but this is none of your business."

"I'm trying to *help*. Why do you hide things from me? You aren't sleeping in the alley anymore, so I don't know how to find you." He sounded reproachful. As if I owed him an explanation of where I slept.

My heart beat faster. He should know better. These were informer questions. After this morning's vision, I was no longer certain he wouldn't betray me. I had to know if my vision was true.

"Have you ever spoken with that tracker, Thomas?" The words were out of my mouth before I could stop them.

"What? What are you talking about? How would I even know?" He looked as though I'd slapped him.

But in that vision in Paternoster Row, I'd seen him following my tracker. Didn't that mean he'd recognize him? Why lie about it?

I shrugged. "The one we saw in the street by the shop. I thought I saw you talking to someone who looked like him in the market."

"Oh, him. No, I haven't spoken with him. For a moment I thought you were asking if I'd peached you to a tracker." He laughed grimly.

He'd been following the tracker in that first vision, so he must know more. Why wouldn't he tell me? Unless they were working together. I couldn't even ask him, not without revealing my gift.

"I'm sleep-addled," he said. "I couldn't sleep last night for worrying, wondering what had happened to you. I was certain that if you were alive, you'd come find me. But you didn't."

"Lord, Thomas, how could I? It was late by the time I got away, so I stayed with a friend. And now I should be at work."

"A *friend*. I see." His face was expressionless, but I knew he was hurt.

"Well," he said, rising to his feet. "I'm glad you're all right. I have work too," he said stiffly. He turned on his heel and walked back up the river road.

I felt badly, but told myself it was for the best. Thomas didn't *understand* about the gifted. *Never trust anyone who doesn't have a gift.* That's what Penny said, and she was right. Mayhap he'd learn from this. Whatever excuses I gave, I hadn't turned to him for help because I didn't think he could. His ignorance was danger-ous. And I wasn't certain he hadn't peached me to the tracker.

I rose and began to climb the hill, with tears leaking from my eyes. I wiped them away, scolding myself. I couldn't drag someone who wasn't gifted into my problems. Besides, the other rats wouldn't trust him. Better for him to find a normal girl. I'd only hurt him.

Folk stared at me curiously as I passed, so I stopped to wipe my face on my sleeve, and tucked up my plait before I stepped into the street outside the shop. No one was waiting there.

Of course not, you great looby, your tracker is dead.

Nevertheless, I walked around to the back door.

Serena was sitting at the table in the kitchen, a half-eaten piece of bread beside her empty bowl. Her eyes were red. Her normally honey-colored complexion was pale as the lace over her bodice.

Esmeralda sat across from her, with her back to me.

I stepped forward, hesitantly. "I'm sorry I ran away, mistress. Are you very angry with me?"

Esmeralda threw me an appraising look.

"Are you all right, Lizzie?" Serena asked, her voice husky.

I curtsied. "I'm fine, mistress. I'm sorry I ran away, when you'd been so kind. But I couldn't stand the—crowd any longer."

"Esmeralda heard you were chased by a man with a knife. Someone saw you running and then…no one knew where you were. I thought—" A tear ran down her face. "I thought you were dead in the river, Lizzie."

And she'd been mourning my death ever since. "I'm sorry, I didn't realize anyone had seen. I didn't mean for you to worry." *What else did someone see?*

Esmeralda smiled grimly. "I said she was clever, didn't I, Serena? What happened to the tracker? Will he come after you again?"

So they both knew. I took a deep breath. "I don't think so. I lost him, and spent the night with a friend." I made a show of straightening my hair under my cap.

The sisters exchanged a glance.

Serena said, "Have some of the porridge, Lizzie, before you start work."

Esmeralda scraped her chair back from the table and left the kitchen. Serena stood indecisively a moment longer, and then followed her.

I served myself from the kettle over the fire and sat down. The sound of whispering came from down the hall. When I'd finished eating, I went through to the workroom. An order of hats had to be ready for delivery on Monday. Serena was already seated on the stool next to mine, gluing blue ribbons on a crimson hat. To my surprise, Esmeralda came in too and perched on a stool in the corner, hands in her lap. Serena had told me once that Esmeralda found hat making too *finical*, preferring more active work. She made no move to help us, but seemed to be waiting for something.

Serena kept her eyes on her work. "Lizzie, I hope you don't think we're interfering, but Esmeralda and I would like to help you. You can trust us."

My heart beat faster. You *can't* trust adults, no matter what they say. I wanted to tell her to mind her own business, but I couldn't, I owed her too much. Besides, she already knew enough to make a good guess. "I don't understand—" I began stiffly.

"Serena, you can't expect her to admit it, just like that," Esmeralda said. "How long would she last on the streets if someone overheard her saying she has a gift?" She turned to me. "She expects you to trust her because she means well, but we can *show* you why you can."

Serena frowned at her sister. "You keep saying I don't understand what it's like for the kinchin on the wharves, as though we weren't both on the run ourselves a few years ago. *What's sauce for the goose is sauce for the gander.*"

"Things are different now," Esmeralda said. "In the old days we could run to the army or the network for help. But there's no help for these kinchin: neither the king nor Parliament cares what happens to them."

"Well, *I* care. Lizzie, you don't have to tell me about your gift, but I know you have one; that's why that man was chasing you. *'Tis an ill wind*, they say."

I frowned, trying to guess what they were after.

Esmeralda folded her arms across her ample bosom. "Tell her yours, then."

Serena's eyes widened. "What?"

"You expect her to reveal her gift. Why don't you go first?"

Adults don't have gifts.

Esmeralda nodded, looking at me. "That shut her gob, didn't it? Wants you to reveal yours, then clams up the moment I suggest she do the same. You wouldn't think it, would you, but we're both gifted. Ever since we were children."

"That's impossible," I croaked past a tight throat. "Adults grow out of their gifts. Everyone says so."

"Do they? Well, everyone's wrong. And how would they know, anyway? Do you think anyone who manages to survive that long would announce it?"

Esmeralda stood and pushed her stool under the work counter. She shook out her bright green skirts, and turned, smiling. It took a moment for me to realize she wasn't standing on the floor. The green shoes with the fashionable French heels were floating a few inches above it.

She rose in the air until her head gently bumped the ceiling.

"As you can see, Lizzie, I can levitate, quite easily. As long as there's no wind. Otherwise, I get a bit blown about."

I made a strangled sound and slid off my stool, staring up at the soles of Esmeralda's shoes above my head.

"Always a show-off," Serena muttered with narrowed eyes. "*All that glisters is not gold.*"

"Fie, you're only jealous because my gift's more of a crowd

pleaser than yours," Esmeralda said smugly. "You never received the applause *I* did, when we played the fairs."

Serena pushed her stool back to face her sister and stamp her foot. "Ha! You know perfectly well my singing was *very* well received. Why, Her Ladyship the Countess of—"

"Oh, here we go. The Countess of Marlborough again. Lord knows if I had a penny for every time you've dragged that poor woman into the conversation, I'd have retired in comfort ages ago. The fact is, Lizzie, my rope-dancing act was a headliner at *both* Saint James and Saint Bartholomew Fairs." Esmeralda peered down at me. "I had top billing and Serena knows it. *The Great Madame Esmeralda, Rope Dancer Extraordinaire.* Envy gets the better of her sometimes."

My hands were clammy. Nothing made sense. My proper mistress had performed at the *fairs*? Perhaps the dove and the peacock were more alike than I'd realized. "Mistress Serena, is singing your gift?" I asked faintly.

Serena snorted. "No, dear, that's a *talent*. I have a useful gift, but I'm not a brass-bound braggart like Esmeralda."

"The devil!" Esmeralda exclaimed. She folded her arms and stared pointedly at the ceiling, inches from her nose, one foot tapping the air.

"So, then…what's yours?" I asked. I didn't really want to know. What I *wanted* was for her to tell me they were joking. But Esmeralda was still up there. Floating.

"Just because my gift's not showy like Ezzie's …I got just as much applause for my singing as she did for her rope dancing, you know. She gets so puffed up. Some of us value modesty." She patted the lace tucker covering her bodice approvingly.

I waited for Esmeralda's reaction.

"Well?" she said. "Tell the poor girl. After all this dithering suspense she'll be disappointed."

Serena sniffed. "Lizzie, I don't blame you a bit, but I know you've been lying to me. I can tell when people are lying, you see.

That's my gift. Most of the time it's not much of a surprise; people tend not to be very good liars, as a rule. I suspected the first time I saw you in the Exchange that you were gifted."

Esmeralda floated down to land before me. "Serena's gift has saved our necks more than once, I have to admit. And no one can see it, or suspect it's a gift, so that's useful too. Still," she smiled complacently, "it's not quite the crowd pleaser mine is."

Beside me, Serena sighed.

"Why did you want to talk about my gift?" I turned away and sat down at the worktable, pretending to search through a dish of beads. My hands were shaking. The sisters knew my secret. They could sell me to a tracker in the next hour. But: *they* were gifted. Adults weren't supposed to be. It shifted everything in the world.

"We don't, really," Esmeralda said. "We just want to talk honestly about your situation. We can help. Who knows what gifted children need better than we do? We've survived that danger for more than thirty years."

I looked up to meet her gaze. "Help how?"

"A rumor is going 'round Covent Market that you're creating a Guild for the wharf rats. We think that's a good idea."

"Who told you?" I asked, distracted by a stab of anger that someone had betrayed us already. But who? Kat wouldn't. The Hopkins sisters knew far more than they should.

Serena smiled. "The point is, Lizzie, we'd like to join."

13

THE OATH

THE SUN SANK into red clouds behind a thicket of masts, setting the river on fire. A skiff passed me, torches lit, approaching the Tower. It overtook and passed a fat merchantman moving on the turning tide slowly out to sea.

I'd seen Esmeralda's gift with my own eyes, but wished I hadn't. I didn't *want* to know there were gifted adults. Esmeralda thought her demonstration would reassure me; instead, she had cut away the ground beneath my feet.

Every passing man or woman might be gifted. How would I know? The trackers who waited in the shadows to snatch us might be gifted. The faces passing me had become sinister in the shadowed torchlight.

The Quality assume wharf rats are pickpockets and robbers, but 'tisn't true of most of us. For one thing, kinchin in those trades don't last long; they either die in prison or, if they survive long enough, they're hanged or transported. Gifted rats live with a different set of risks. Most folk will never know why we prefer to live here. That's how we like it.

We never talk about it, so a new child either figures it out or they don't. Our small group of rats have survived because we're gifted.

After Penny took me under her wing, I kept my eyes open. Kat would suddenly appear and you'd no notion how or when she'd got there. When Mattie pushed a bully, he went sprawling twenty paces. The fact that a child had survived more than a year by the river was suspicious in itself.

Most rats knew, or at least suspected, who was gifted. A core group of us stayed by the river, even when we were offered better jobs. We knew we were safer with our own kind than we could be with distant relatives, or strangers who might peach us to a tracker. There were ungifted wharf rats, of course, but they kept to themselves, too. I'd only invited Penny's group, those I knew were gifted.

Sitting cross-legged on the planks at the end of Bear Quay, I waited for the others, after lighting the torches. Tiny wavelets slapped the hull of a ship moored nearby. The last berth was empty, so we wouldn't be overheard.

The rats began to arrive. I rose to greet them, brushing off my skirt.

Penny herded three little ones before her, and Jimmy, her older brother, came over to ask if I needed help, pushing the hair out of his blue eyes. Jimmy had shot up recently. At six feet he looked like a man, but his voice was still changing. He helped me move a crate for me to stand on.

Kat appeared at the edge of the circle, behind Mattie. Soon fifteen children stood in a group, laughing and chatting. The torches cast fitful shadows on their faces as the gusting wind snatched the flames. The rats sat in a semicircle around me, whispering, rustling paper as they ate their dinners.

If there were hidden watchers in the shadows, I couldn't tell. The wharf appeared deserted, but there were hiding places behind the barrels and crates ready for the next day's loading. I stood on the crate and spoke just loud enough for my voice to carry to the edge of the circle. "Welcome, wharf rats. 'Tis a weighty matter I want to discuss. I'll use no fair words or empty promises with you: you know the odds. Our lives are at the mercy of trackers, informers, and Mud Men. Nothing I say will change that. But we don't have to go like lambs to the slaughter. We aren't slaves already sold. I propose we form a Guild of our own, not only for protection and self-defense, but also for pride in our work." I waited a moment for the surprised exclamations to die down. "Pride, I say. We *should* be proud, not the way nobs are proud of the slaughter and greed of their ancestors, but because we're fighting for our rights. As a Guild, I propose we live in a place I've found, where no gangs or Mud Men will find us. Once we're pledged to each other we'll know who to trust, and who not to. Our lives will be better."

The rustling and whispering had ceased.

"The only way to live together is to trust each other. Once we've sworn the blood oath, to be true to the death, we'll use our gifts for defense. That means sooner or later, we have to reveal our gifts to each other. And a blood oath means that if you break it, you die."

A few heads nodded and all the faces were solemn; they knew this was how the gangs did it, and didn't expect anything different.

Mattie called from the back, "You're asking gifted children to use their gifts in public?"

"Once we swear the oath, we'll use our gifts to protect everyone."

"I don't want to be like no thievin' gentry," Mattie said.

"You won't be. We'll be protecting each other—not making one man rich and powerful. We won't steal or rob; we won't be a gang." I searched their faces to see if they understood. The young ones wouldn't know what I meant, but the older ones did. "We don't need our gifts to outwit the Mud Men, but the trackers are different. We'll use our gifts to protect our home and each other."

"You mean like a real home?" Mags asked, yearning in her voice. Willie and Deborah, the youngest toddlers, stared at me wide-eyed.

"Just like a real home."

Willie's lower lip trembled and his eyes filled with tears. Penny put her arm around him. He snuffled into her shoulder.

"Let me explain how this would work. If anyone betrays us, we'll know. One of us has a gift of knowing when someone lies. Anyone who betrays us can't hide—we'll find you. If you betray us, we'll know and so will God. You'll be an oath breaker and have that on your soul. Betrayal will bring judgement, and the penalty is death.

"I won't blame you if you decide not to join; it's a risk. But so is living on the streets with a tracker after you. Will you run the risk alone—or stand with the Guild under its protection?"

I scanned the upturned faces. Some looked frightened. Mags and Penny had hope in their eyes. "You must never reveal who belongs to the Guild, or where our home is. Anyone who breaks the oath must die. Do you understand?"

Willie, still wrapped in Penny's arms, began to sniffle when I said "die," but Penny shushed him and told him not to worry.

"Makes it *sound* like a gang, this talk o' killing," Mattie said. "I don't like it."

"I don't like it either," Kat said, "but I think she's right. Unless we protect each other, we have no defense against the trackers. I've already taken the oath."

Everyone turned to look at her in surprise. Penny stood up, with Willie in her arms. "It's harsh, but it's all our lives at stake. The gangs do the same. Maybe they're criminal, but we're not. We can earn our living without that. We're just protecting ourselves." She sat down again. Heads nodded, and the whispering grew louder.

"During the war, common folk learned they had rights and fought for them," I continued. "Parliament makes laws for all to obey, even the king and the Quality. The laws *should* protect everyone. But *we* aren't protected, because nobbling us makes men rich. So we have to protect ourselves."

"But why should we take your orders?" Mattie asked. "Who made you queen?" Heads turned to look at Mattie, then back, waiting for my answer.

"I'm no queen. But I found a safe place and decided to share it. Each of us runs the risk of being caught and enslaved by a nob, me the same as you. What should I do? Think only of myself? Keep Haven for myself alone? Or shall I share it and help the rats become a family?"

I heard, "Yes, Lizzie," and "Yes, let's be a family."

Kat called out, "Lizzie wants to help everyone. It makes sense to work together. That's what the apprentices did more than once, before and after the war. They brought London to its knees. Folk who are powerless alone are strong together. We can be too."

"Before you swear the oath, let me tell you the Guild's rules. The first rule is that we're one family. No matter where you came from, if you were poor or rich, Catholic, Protestant, or Dissenter, if you came from the parish workhouse or your parents were gentlefolk, we're all one family now. There'll be no airs and graces or pretending to be better than somebody else. The nobs and trackers don't care. We'll be Guild members, brothers and sisters. Remember that. The second rule is, we make decisions together, and everyone has a chance to speak. The third rule: you must swear the blood oath."

"If we're all to have a say, we should vote on it," Mattie said.

The rats were balanced on a hair. A distraction, a push either way, and I'd lose them. Expectant faces watched me, but no one spoke. Now was the time.

"Yes, let's vote. God made me gifted. I don't know why." There were gasps at this admission. "But I choose to use my gift to fight the trackers. You have a choice too."

"Raise your hands if you agree," Kat said, raising her own.

Every single child, even Mattie, raised their hands, eyes wide in the torchlight. "Anyone against?"

"We're with you, Lizzie," Jimmy said. "You warned us about the tracker. You're the one we trust."

I exhaled deeply. *It was going to work.* "Then let's take the oath to become brothers and sisters of the Wharf Rat Guild."

There was an expectant hush.

"Put your right hand over your heart and repeat after me: 'As God is my witness, I swear I'll protect the Guild, the members of the Guild, and the secrets of the Guild with my life.'"

I gave them each line and they repeated it after me, the littl'uns stumbling over the words. When it was done, I silently made a vow of my own, to keep them safe no matter what.

Jimmy's hand was in the air. "Yes, Jimmy?"

He came to stand beside me, facing the others. "Let's seal the bargain with a song." He began to sing the old Digger song from the war, the one with the refrain, "Stand up now!"

The others, recognizing it, joined in. It was a song of rebellion, one the apprentices still sang on Bonfire night, or whenever they felt restless. Folk angry at Parliament or the king would sing it in the streets, or in the taverns, wherever journeyman and apprentices gathered to get warm.

Jimmy changed the words from Diggers and Cavaliers to wharf rats and trackers, and the final line: *Stand up now, wharf rats all!*

And everyone did: they rose, and holding hands danced slowly in a circle, singing loud and free, not caring who heard them, eyes shining in the torch light. When it was over, everyone clapped, smiling. God bless Jimmy; he knew exactly what they needed.

"That's all for tonight, everyone. Be here tomorrow night at the same time with your things, and we'll go to Haven." The children chattered happily and left in twos and threes, to sleep in their usual places for the last time.

Kat appeared. "Well done, Lizzie. How do you feel?"

I rubbed my eyes. "How do I feel? Happy, excited, afraid. We've made a start. Now I want to go home and sleep."

"I'm worried about Cynthia and James. How do we keep this from them?"

"The oath. And even if they do hear about it somehow, they don't know where Haven is."

"Not yet," Kat said.

"No one's going to tell James anything. He's too mean."

"True. But the little ones like Cynthia because she gives them food. They might tell her. And Mags and Potts are friends. She doesn't understand that he can't be trusted."

"We've done what we can for tonight. The rest can wait till tomorrow."

"At least sleep at my friend's house tonight. If we go to Haven now, someone might follow. Let's not give away the secret at the last minute. Besides, I still have work to do. I want to surprise you tomorrow."

Too tired to argue, I let her take my arm. We spent the night at Kat's burned house. As far as I could see, no one followed us.

THE NEXT MORNING, I arrived at the shop early, to make up for worrying Serena. We were out of certain trimmings, so at midday I went to the Royal Exchange to buy more. I was paying for my basket of feathers when I saw Thomas on the other side of the square. I waved, but he disappeared into the crowd. I could've sworn he'd seen me.

Either he was still angry, or he hadn't seen me after all. I shrugged and pocketed my change, picked up my basket, and started back.

Now and again I looked over my shoulder, from habit. I truly thought my tracker was dead, but there was nothing to stop Hazelton from sending another one. Trouble was, London was full of footpads and any ragtag or draggle-tail cove might be one.

The bell rang as I entered the shop. Esmeralda popped through the curtain as though she'd been waiting for me. "Hello, Lizzie. I hear the rats took the oath last night. Serena and I are ready to join as soon as you give the word."

I ignored her and entered the workroom. She followed me.

"*How* did you hear about it?" I asked, trying to control my annoyance. I began to sort the feathers by color.

"That's not important. I'm trying to help."

I doubt it. She wanted something, that much was clear, and she heard things only the rats should know.

"Then the answer is *no*, Mistress Ropedancer. The rats decide things together and everyone has to agree first. You'll have to wait until the kinchin feel safe with each other before I spring gifted adults on them. If they agree, you'll both have to demonstrate your gifts and swear a blood oath." I met her eyes. "And you'll have to satisfy *me* as to how you hear things you shouldn't in the first place."

Her mouth quirked. "How do you plan to enforce a *blood* oath?"

"Serena offered to help, didn't she? She can tell us if we have a traitor. And there are other gifts we can use." I wasn't about to tell her more.

"Serena and I aren't a threat, Lizzie. Don't wait too long. You may need our help sooner than you think." With that, she left through the curtain, skirts rustling.

A FEW STARS pricked the indigo sky at the end of Bear Quay. The last berth was still empty. The barrels and crates from the day before were gone. Jimmy had lit the torches and found a crate for me to stand on before I arrived.

Many rats were already there, the last stragglers arriving as the others sat down. I gazed out over the expectant faces. It was low tide and the exposed foreshore filled the air with the stench of ancient mud and modern rubbish. Ships bumped against their fenders, and the rigging creaked. Every gifted rat I knew about was there. Except Kat.

Everyone waited, watching me.

I stepped onto the crate. "Good evening, brothers and sisters of the Guild. Tonight's the night we move into our new home. Did you all bring your things?"

Heads nodded. I looked toward the riverbank. Two men were loading a cart by the Custom House, and Kat was passing them, coming our way.

"Good. We'll go to Haven in four groups, so as not to attract attention. I'll take the first group now, Kat will lead the second, then we'll come back for the next two. Penny will stay at Haven to organize the sleeping areas. The fires are lit, so it will be toasty inside."

The children all began to speak at once, chattering like a flock of starlings. They slung bags or kerchiefs over their shoulders and Penny sorted them into groups.

"First group with me," I called.

Everyone made it to Haven without getting lost, and we saw no obvious footpads. By the time the last group arrived, Penny had settled the girls on one side of a canvas curtain, with the boys on the other, in beds of straw and canvas. Kat had worked all day setting up the beds and the kitchen, transforming the empty warehouse into a home. Large pots hung over two of the fires, and stoppered jugs of ale stood on the long table. Dishes were stacked in rows on the worktables. Fires burned brightly in the hearths and the large room was warm. There were even old chairs and stools around the fires. Haven felt cozy.

Stepping carefully between running and laughing children, I joined Kat by the fire. She poured water into a pot. "Everything seems to have gone well," she said, settling onto a three-legged stool.

I nodded and knelt before the fire, holding out my cold hands. "We've been lucky tonight anyway. Kat, don't take offense, but did you mention the Guild to anyone in Covent Market?"

Her eyebrows came together. "Of course not. Why would you ask?"

"Someone knew about the Guild ahead of time, and said they'd heard about it there. I suppose the rats could have been overheard."

Kat looked thoughtful. "Who told you this?"

"Esmeralda, Serena's sister. They both want to join."

"Most likely they heard a rumor and you just confirmed it. Do you think they're informers?"

I had my doubts about Esmeralda, but shook my head. I hadn't planned to tell her so soon, but I needed her advice. I whispered, "They still have their gifts."

Her eyebrows rose. "What? They're lying!"

I'd managed to surprise her for once. "I've seen Esmeralda's gift. Serena says they were hunted during the war and want to help us. I told them they had to wait, and we'd vote on it. But it worries me that Esmeralda knows things she shouldn't. I told her I can't trust her until she explains that."

The sound of giggling and whispers came from the sleeping areas. Penny scolded someone, trying to calm the children so they'd sleep.

Kat rose and took a mug from a shelf. She ladled broth from a pot into the mug and handed it to me. "I don't like this," she said. "If there are gifted adults, why haven't we heard about it before?"

I cradled the mug, warming my hands. "Well, what do we know for sure about gifts? Just the stories people tell. Everyone assumes the gift disappears as you grow older. If you grow older."

"No one stays here long enough for us to find out," Kat said thoughtfully.

"Or stays alive long enough." If we managed to survive with our gifts intact, perhaps there was a better future ahead of us than being killed or nobbled. But if *anyone* could be gifted, the danger was greater than we'd realized.

"I wonder who else knows," Kat said. "Does the king? Does he use gifted men and women the way the nobs use children? That tracker now—what if trackers are gifted?"

"Lower your voice."

She whispered fiercely, "What if that tracker was gifted? What if his gift saved him and he's still alive?"

Gooseflesh rose on my neck. I laughed nervously. "It's too soon to tell ghost stories beside the fire, Kat. I want to feel safe here first."

I'd never seen Kat afraid before, but she looked frightened now. "I mean it. Somehow I know he's not dead." She added quickly, "That fall should've killed him. But if he's gifted—"

My throat closed tight. She meant a gift that made him hard to kill, or impossible to kill. I shivered. That would make him a monster. Kat was uneasy, that was all, perhaps from a misplaced sense of guilt. He was dead.

Then I remembered my vision of Thomas in the market, talking to a man who looked like my tracker.

"Let's enjoy our first night here without letting a dead tracker spoil it." I yawned and stretched my arms, pretending not to care. "I'm for bed."

Kat's dark eyes were still troubled when we lay down to sleep. I felt her staring at the ceiling. Despite my brave words, the first thing I saw when I closed my eyes was the livid burn on my tracker's face.

14

FAMILY

Not all of the rats remembered having a home and a family, but I did. And that's what our first morning in Haven felt like.

Willie, the youngest, woke in the grey dawn and, finding himself in a strange place, began to wail. One of the older children got up to see what was the matter, and then Deborah and the other small ones woke and began to cry too.

From the warm nest of my blue blanket, I laughed. I couldn't help it.

Kat said grumpily, "What?"

"We even *sound* like a family now." I heard a snort and raised my head. Kat had buried her head beneath her pillow.

The crying continued. Someone said, "Hush now," which only made Willie cry harder. Penny, on the other side of me, got up and went to soothe him. I heard her take Willie and Deborah to the privies outside. Thank God for Penny. I drifted back to sleep.

When I woke again, pale sunlight fell from the high windows, although grey clouds loomed in the distance. Rain was coming. A savory smell came from the cooking pots. The older children were setting out bowls while Penny managed the cooking. I pulled my glass out of the bundle I'd used for a pillow. No one was near enough to see.

A pulse of light became Thomas in his market stall, arguing with a man in a cloak and hat. Thomas shook his head and pointed toward the river. The man had his back to me, but when he turned and walked away, the red burns on face and neck were visible. It was the same scene as before, but this time I was certain. This wasn't the past. My tracker was still alive.

My heart pounded. I put the glass in my pocket. He'd be looking for me, and Kat too. I didn't know how anyone could survive such a fall, but there he was. Talking to Thomas.

The little ones lined up to be served first, Penny and Jimmy ladling porridge into their bowls. They sat down on benches, on either side of a makeshift table, a plank set on casks, while the rest of us queued up.

Bowl in hand, I sat down between Kat and Penny at our own table.

"I've found a looking glass for the alley," Kat said between mouthfuls. Penny shot me a surprised glance and I shrugged. Looking glasses were expensive, but hung high up on the wall opposite the door, it would help us see if anyone lay in wait in the alley.

The older ones put their bowls in a wooden bucket and headed for the cellar. They'd count to twenty after the child in front of them left, so as not to attract attention.

I rinsed my bowl and set it on the work counter to dry. Seen in daylight, Kat's collection of dishes, pots, and piles of cutlery was astonishing, not to mention the canvas. Kat's 'friend' had been generous indeed. All these things would have cost a pretty penny, and whoever had paid for it would want something in return, assuming it wasn't stolen, or even if it was. What would our bargain cost?

"Lizzie, do you have a moment?" Behind me, Kat's face wore a mischievous expression. "I have something to show you."

I followed her down the stairs to the cellar, where the last children were waiting their turn to leave. Mags and Mattie whispered together apart from the others in the little alcove behind the door, but when she saw me, Mags came over to me. "I'll be asking at the ships today, Lizzie, never fear."

"Thank you, Mags, but you can stay inside too, if you want to."

We'd taken a vote the night before and agreed that those of us with work would share money and food, so the smallest rats could stay inside, safe from trackers and agents. Penny said she'd teach 'em their letters, too. Rats who could read and reckon would have a better chance when they were older.

"Naw, I like earning for myself." She smiled broadly. "I like talking to the sailors too. They tell me things."

"What sort of things?"

Before Mags could answer, Kat appeared beside me. "Bye, Mags. Be careful out there." She took my arm and led me to the other end of the cellar, to what I'd thought was simply a small, dark closet.

She opened the door and gestured inside.

There was nothing to see. Then she stepped inside and disappeared. "Follow me," she called. "It's quite safe. There's light at the top."

I took a deep breath and reluctantly stepped inside, almost tripping over the first step of a narrow staircase. I took the next step, both hands clutching the railing, praying it would hold my weight.

The darkness was suffocating. I've always hated small spaces, and I was about to turn back for a candle when I saw a square of daylight above me. I kept climbing and came out on the roof, the doors that covered the stairwell thrown open. The sky was filled with fat, dark clouds and the wind smelled of rain.

Kat waited beside an earthenware cistern nearly as tall as she was, covering half the roof. Standing on tiptoe, I peered over the side. It was open to the sky and full of rainwater. Leaves and a dead pigeon floated on the surface.

"I told you water was piped in from above," she said.

"You were right. Do we have to carry it downstairs?"

She walked to the edge of the roof and pointed down. I joined her, stepping carefully across the broken tiles. An earthenware pipe as thick as a man's thigh emerged from the side of the tank, angling down the side of the building where it disappeared into the wall.

I lifted my gaze to look at the city. The clouds cast swiftly moving shadows over London, the churches and houses alternately dark, then dappled golden. Smoke, twisted into strange shapes by the wind, rose from hundreds of chimneys.

"Once we clean out the rubbish we'll have fresh water," Kat said.

I returned my attention to the cistern. "The pipe will be cracked and broken by now, surely."

Kat raised her chin. "Why are you so gloomy? If we don't have to go outside to get water, we'll be safer. This will be cleaner than the river, and cheaper than ale."

I smiled, but the word "safer" spurred me to confess. "There's something I need to tell you."

She didn't even ask. She saw it in my face. "So he *is* alive."

I nodded. "I saw him talking to Thomas in a vision." I didn't want to mention Thomas, but it was both our lives now.

She frowned. "Why Thomas?"

"Someone probably told him we were friends."

Was that pity in her eyes?

"Remember, Lizzie, you must protect the Guild now, not only yourself."

As if I didn't know that.

We went back down the stairs, and I knew what she was thinking, what any of the rats would say if they heard: *Never trust anyone without a gift.*

On the main floor, Kat returned to the pipe above the stone tub by the forge. It looked the same as the pipe on the side of the building. Kat climbed into the tub and stared into it. "There's a stopcock to let the water come through."

She pulled on a lever on the outside of the pipe. Rusted metal gave way with a horrible screeching sound. Water trickled out, slowly at first, then increasing until a steady stream poured into the tub. Kat jumped clear. I covered my ears until she climbed up again to turn it to stop the flow, getting her skirts wet in the process.

"It seems to work. I don't see any leaks in the pipe, at least not inside."

Penny came over, holding Willie by the hand. "What's all the racket?"

"There's a cistern on the roof. I can show you where the stairs are. Could some of the kinchin clean it out today?" Kat asked.

Penny said doubtfully, "On the roof? I suppose so, if the rain holds off. They do need something to do—they'll be restless inside all day. They're not used to it."

"Good."

Church bells began to ring the hour, a cascade of different notes. It was time for me to leave. "I'll leave you to it," I said, heading for the stairs. Kat followed me.

"The tracker may know about the shop," she observed, as we descended into the cellar's gloom.

"I have to go to work, Kat."

"What if Thomas told the tracker where to find you?"

I turned to face her. "He won't. He knows I ran away from a burned man. Once he sees he's burned, he won't tell him anything." But I remembered that Thomas had appeared in the street outside the shop that first time I saw the tracker, after the tracker was already there. He'd said he was following James, but what if it had been *Thomas* who had told the tracker where I'd be? He could have timed his arrival to mislead me.

I was glad the cellar was dark and that Kat couldn't see my expression.

"All right," Kat said reasonably. "But what if the tracker hides his burns and tells a good tale? Thomas might think the questions harmless."

I bit my lip. "He's not stupid; he'd be suspicious of anyone who asked about me."

But I was thinking, *never trust anyone without a gift.*

"Does he know where this place is?" she asked.

"No," I said.

"So you trust him, but you aren't a fool. Good."

To hide my doubts, I peered through the cracks between the boards on the door.

Eight feet up on the opposite wall, Jimmy had one arm crooked around a ladder. With the other he hammered a nail into the brick wall. Propped against the wall near the ladder was a large looking glass, at the moment reflecting the pile of crates and sacks at the top of the stairwell. I turned to Kat. "How did you get it here so quickly? And with a ladder."

"What? Oh, the looking glass. That was a stroke of luck; someone I know just happened to have one. Should work nicely. Of course, it won't work at night, but it's better than nothing.

"I'm going to come with you," she said, as though she'd suddenly decided. "I want to see for myself that there's no one waiting for you. Besides, I have errands to run."

From the warehouse district, we made our way to a main street, walking side by side in the middle of it. There was no reason for me to be suspicious of Kat for coming with me, but I was. Maybe it was the looking glass, and the money it implied. I'd never believe she worked with trackers, but she was in the pay of *someone* wealthy. Why would such a person be interested in the rats if not to use their gifts?

My habit was to walk beneath the overhanging stories in the street, safe from chamber pots and rubbish dumped from the windows. But that meant being near the openings of alleys and passageways, where footpads lie in wait. The center of the street was safer if your dead tracker was alive, no matter what you stepped in.

We dodged wagons and men on horseback. An angry beggar kept following me, and when I wouldn't give him anything, he cursed me in words that made no sense. He finally wandered off, but not before he'd set my nerves on edge. I was glad Kat was with me, after all. If my tracker appeared, our chances were better together.

We turned the corner to the shop and someone *was* waiting beneath the sign of the lady's bonnet.

It was Thomas.

15

———

DOUBTING THOMAS

THOMAS WAS WEARING his market-seller's apron, twisting his cap in his hands with a worried expression. He smiled when he saw me, but one look at Kat's stony face and his smile disappeared.

"I have to go, Lizzie. Be careful." Kat frowned pointedly at Thomas.

He stepped back as she passed him, nodding stiffly.

"Lizzie, are you all right?"

"Why wouldn't I be?" There was a challenge in my voice.

"I came to warn you," he said in a low voice. "A man with a burned face was asking questions about you in the market. I told everyone snug's the word, but he heard I'm your friend somehow. He asked lots of questions before I finally got rid of him."

In the back of my mind I must've clung to the hope that my vision was of the past. With the confirmation that he was alive, my stomach dropped to my toes.

But Thomas *had* come to warn me. That meant he was innocent, didn't it? I looked up and down the busy street, checking doorways. "You didn't let him follow you, did you?"

"O' course not. I told him if he's looking for a wharf rat, perhaps he should look on the wharves. Furthermore, I said, I don't roll in the gutter with rats." He smiled at my outraged expression. "Then I told him to leave, so I could serve *real* customers. I waited to be sure he was gone before I came."

The details made it all too real. I dug my nails into my palms. "Thanks, Thomas. You only told him what he already knew. If he believes you don't care, maybe he'll leave you alone."

"It's odd for a tracker to waste time asking questions. Usually they pick someone off at random. Why is he targeting you?"

I nearly laughed. "It's about revenge now. He wants to hurt me. Kat, too."

"Because you burned him." I'd never told him that Kat had saved me from him, so he ignored the reference to Kat. Thank God.

Folk were glancing at us curiously as they passed. "Let's go behind the shop."

In single file, we threaded the narrow passageway to the mews behind the shop. I pushed through the gate and up the rock-bordered path to the back door. No one else was in sight.

"Lizzie," Thomas said, twisting his cap and dropping his eyes, "I don't know how to protect you. Have you thought about what I asked you before? About moving to the country?" He raised his eyes. "You'd be safer there. But here—"

I shook my head impatiently. "You're very kind, Thomas, but I can't, not now of all times."

He frowned, looking hurt. I rushed to explain. "Don't think I'm not grateful you want to help me—I am—but I can't leave, not yet. I've started something, Thomas, something important. I have the chance to keep the littl'uns safe and I have to do it. They need my help to make it work. This is about *all* the wharf rats, not just me. Do you understand?" I spoke quickly, hoping the rush of words would convince him.

His face flushed, and a muscle jumped in his jaw. "Grateful, is it? Well, I'm glad you're *grateful*. Perhaps a market grocer isn't fine enough for Mistress Lizzie of the wharf rats." His voice changed. "Tell me truly, Lizzie—don't you care about me, even a little?"

God's teeth. How could I make him see? Whatever I said could make things worse. So far I'd kept him from speaking about love and marriage so I wouldn't have to hurt him. But it was too late. I'd hurt his pride.

"Thomas, try to understand. The other rats need me and I need them. How do you think I'd feel if I was safe in a nice house but all my friends were nobbled, or hiding from the Mud Men, hungry and frightened? It isn't *right* the nobs hunt children. They deserve to be safe just as much as I do. We have to fight for our rights, same as the common folk did during the war. I wouldn't be safe without my friends anyway."

"I thought *I* was your friend," he said. "You're not a child anymore, Lizzie. Think about your future. There will always be kinchin living by the river. You can't save them. You can't even save yourself—I'm your best chance." His mouth hardened. "I went to find you in the alley where we used to sleep and no one was there. Where did everyone go, and what's this about secret meetings? You're hiding things from me. Are you afraid I'll peach you to a tracker?"

When he said that the children couldn't be saved, that I couldn't save myself, my face grew hot. Of course he thought that. The ungifted assumed our fates were sealed, that nothing could be done. It was easier for them that way; they needn't disturb themselves trying to change things.

Now he wanted me to tell him what he had no right to know. "You know perfectly well I won't answer that. You shouldn't even have asked, with a tracker about."

His eyes narrowed. "So there *is* someone else. I've seen the way James looks at you. Tell me the truth, Lizzie: are you playing me for a fool? That's what Cynthia says."

I was completely staggered for a moment. "What? Is *that* what this is about? Some nook-shotten lie of Cynthia's and you believed her? Cynthia's the one playing you for a fool. She's just jealous when James looks at any wench besides her. James doesn't give a fig for me, he just likes cozening her. And she's such a shallow-pate, she'd say the sky was purple to please James."

His face had gone hard and there was anger in his eyes. He didn't believe me.

"If you knew me at all, Thomas Oakapple, you'd know neither James nor Cynthia is a friend of mine."

"But if there isn't someone else, why won't you tell me—"

"And why, Master Oakapple," I said, my anger growing, "did you tell Gaffer and Mistress Sweets that we're betrothed, yet never said a word about it to me?"

His eyes widened. "They told you that?"

"They did. Sara asked me when we'd post the banns. Me! You've never said a word about marriage and now I'm being accused of leading you on. What've you been telling them?"

He ran his hand through his hair, loosening his queue. "Nothing! Leastways nothing about being betrothed." He had the grace to look away, blushing. "We were talking about plans for the future, and I let slip that I hoped someday to marry and live in a house and garden. So of course they asked who the girl was, and like a fool I told 'em you, Lizzie. But I never said we were betrothed. They must've assumed," he added lamely.

"They assumed! It's not respectable to talk about a girl that way if it's not true. *I'm* not responsible for your telling tales!" I took a breath. "If you wanted me to be your wife, Thomas, you haven't gone about it properly. And anyway, I'm not sure you even like me. I thought you were my friend, but you're asking too many questions. How can I trust you?"

He was breathing hard. He looked away, staring at the wooden gate. Finally he said, "Lizzie, I don't want to fight. But a fellow can only take so much waiting. I can't be any plainer. The fact is I care for you more than you do for me, isn't that it? Why do you need to have secrets from me? How can I protect you when you won't tell me what's going on?"

"You can't. You can be my *friend* by not asking so many questions." I felt badly for him, but he refused to understand. He thought a costermonger with good prospects could court me like a normal wench, and I'd recognize my luck because he'd have a farm someday. But I wasn't an ordinary girl; I was the leader of the Guild, and always at risk. Our dreams weren't the same. He had romantic fancies about me, thinking I'd fall into his arms. I knew better than to risk my life for a fairytale. I wouldn't abandon the Guild, just when it was beginning. Part of me wanted to tell him everything, but I pushed the traitorous thought aside.

His jealousy was a threat to all of us. If I said I didn't want to marry anyone it wouldn't help. He wouldn't believe it. Penny said the ungifted always turned on you in the end. He was asking where I lived, as if that was his business.

"Thomas, for both our sakes, we should stay away from each other. I don't want you to be hurt, but if you spy on me, you might be. Forget about me. Find a nice girl who doesn't worry about trackers. You deserve it."

"What do you mean, I'll get hurt? Are you threatening me with your gift? Anyway, I know what your gift is, and you can't hurt anyone with it. I came to warn you, remember? I've wondered where your loyalty lies, and you've made it clear it's not with me. You should know your tracker offered me ten gold guineas for you. Luckily, I *am* your friend. Too bad you don't recognize it."

Worse and worse. *Thomas knew my gift* and the tracker had offered him money. I wanted to cry and to strangle him, all at the same time.

"Lizzie, I'm asking now. Will you marry me?"

Tears sprang into my eyes. I shook my head.

"That's a 'no,' then, is it? Later, I hope you remember I tried to save you." He opened the gate and walked away, without looking back.

I couldn't move. I was crying hard, gasping for breath. I tried to stop, to steady myself, but the tears kept coming.

Finally, I wiped my eyes and stumbled into the empty kitchen to stand before the cold hearth, my eyes stinging and blurred. I *had* trusted Thomas, and losing his friendship hit me like a blow. Cynthia had confused him with her malicious lies, my tracker had tempted him with gold, and he was as angry as I'd ever seen him.

If he traded me for gold, he could buy the market garden he'd always dreamed of, and a house to boot. With a secure income, he'd easily find another girl to wed, maybe even Cynthia herself if that's what the cozening trull was after. Did he really even love me? What was friendship compared to security and a good living? He'd thought to play the hero and 'rescue' a wharf rat. Now he could console himself that I'd already betrayed him with someone else. That would justify selling me. Maybe he even hoped it was true, so he could take the money without guilt.

All this flashed through my mind in an instant. Before I'd seen the vision this morning, I'd have laughed at the idea that Thomas might betray me. I wasn't laughing now.

Church bells rang the half hour, down the street. *Work, Lizzie.*

I wiped my eyes on my sleeve, and tucked straying hairs beneath my cap. I needed advice. I couldn't guess what Thomas would do. Perhaps someone older and wiser, like Serena, could help me.

But when I entered the shop, Serena was busy with a customer. I pushed through into the workroom, where my tools waited on the work table.

Five hats had dried overnight and were ready for their final trimmings. While my hands were busy, I wondered what to tell the sisters about my tracker. I couldn't mention he worked for Hazelton. All London was afraid of Hazelton, not just the rats.

Serena wouldn't want to risk the shop being targeted by someone so powerful. She'd have to let me go.

I braided a ribbon through a slit in the felt for a hatband and held it out at arm's length to admire the crimson ribbon against the green felt. The colors would go well with chestnut hair, like Kat's. My tracker would be looking for Kat, too.

The hat back on its stand, I clasped my hands together, thinking hard. Thomas could betray *Kat* instead. The tracker would be after her too. Thomas could have his guineas, his garden, and me as well, if I never found out. Or did he think I wouldn't care?

Thomas knew what happened to the children the trackers sold. He couldn't live with that, I told myself. He wouldn't do such a thing. But the Thomas I'd just seen, with angry eyes in a cold face, wasn't the Thomas I thought I knew.

Esmeralda entered the workroom, smelling of cloves and oranges, her green muslin skirts rustling over petticoats. "Good, you're here. I've a question for you."

I braced myself. "Mistress?"

"It's about that friend you brought to the procession on the river. That day you ran away from us. What was his name?"

My stomach clenched. "Thomas Oakapple."

She pulled up a stool and sat down. "He stopped me in the street just now and asked if you were engaged to anyone. Why would he ask *me* such a thing?"

I swallowed hard. She had no reason to care about my troubles, and I didn't trust her, but this was nothing to do with the Guild. "Mistress, I need advice about Thomas. I'm afraid of what he might do."

"What do you mean?"

The words tumbled out in a rush. "He's spoken with my tracker, the one that chased me by the river. Another rat told him I'm in love with someone else and he believes it. Now he's jealous." I swallowed. "The tracker offered him ten gold guineas to hand me over. He came to warn me, but he's angry I won't marry him."

Esmeralda slowly shook her head. "This is bad, Lizzie. Even if he doesn't betray you, and he might, the tracker could find you by following him. I think you'd best leave London for a time. Put some distance between you and Thomas, as well as your tracker. Let him calm down. Serena can help with the Guild; they can get along without you for a while."

"But I've barely started—"

"And if the tracker follows you to your Haven, you'll have endangered everyone yourself." She smiled at me so gently I wondered if I was being foolish. And she was right. That tracker wouldn't give up. Sooner or later he'd find me, either here at the shop, or by trailing me to Haven.

The rats had survived without me before this. Now they had a home they could defend. "There's someone else involved," I said, choosing my words carefully. "Kat helped me get away from the tracker and he'll be after her too. I can't leave unless she comes with me."

"Oh yes, the tall, skinny one who can disappear."

I stared.

She laughed. "I saw her reappear once and I kept a lookout after that. She must know someone near my lady's house. I've seen her there from time to time."

That was interesting. What was Kat doing in a nob's neighborhood? Visiting whoever gave her the funds to buy pots, canvas, and looking glasses? "She saved my life. I can't leave her behind."

"Are you sure of her? Although I have to admit someone who can become invisible would be an asset where we're going."

"Hold on, I haven't agreed to go anywhere. And why should you go? You don't have anyone chasing you."

"How do you know?" she asked, her blue eyes disconcertingly sharp. "Besides, I'd bet some gold guineas myself that your tracker isn't working alone. That wouldn't be smart. If he's some lord's myrmidon, there will be others, mark my words."

My hands were shaking. I clasped them together. "You seem to know a lot about trackers."

"My dear, we've explained that. Serena and I have been hunted before, and believe it or not, under far worse conditions than you face now. You don't have to hide from bands of soldiers roving the countryside, looking for a quick sale."

"No, we have Lord Hazelton instead," I muttered.

"Granted, not a good situation, but one we can deal with by sharing information."

I folded my arms. "I don't understand."

"Is it Lord Hazelton who's after you? Do you know why? Have you told anyone outside the Guild about your gift?"

"Of course not."

"Could someone guess it? I had the impression the rats know your gift. They call you Lucky Lizzie, because you know when to avoid a certain place."

I dropped my eyes to the baize-covered counter.

"My guess is that Hazelton has heard about your gift and wants to know the future. Men like that think they can control it. We can use that."

"How?"

"Would you be willing to let him capture you?" Esmeralda asked, sounding curious.

Pushing the stool back, I rose to my feet. "You're mad! My tracker will cut me up before he delivers me to his master. He might even kill me."

She looked thoughtful. "If Hazelton has targeted you, he may even know where you work by now. If you can't trust Thomas, your enemy may know more than you want him to."

Even though I'd thought the same thing, hearing it said aloud made me feel sick. Both Thomas and James knew where the shop was, and either might inform on me. I told myself that even if

Thomas offered to betray me, I wasn't in any more danger than I'd been already. The important thing was that Haven was safe—as long as I didn't lead the tracker to it.

"If your only suggestion is to let myself be caught—"

"'Twas only a thought. I'll confer with Serena. I think you and I should go together." She raised an eyebrow. "I don't suppose you can sing, can you?"

Perhaps she really *was* mad, and Serena too ashamed to tell me. But the blue eyes were sharp enough. "I'm not a fair performer, Esmeralda. Nor am I going to leave London, where I know my way about. Why should I leave my home for a place where anyone could betray me? Besides, I can't leave Kat."

"On the contrary, once you're in the country, no one will suspect you're gifted. We'll be with people I know and trust."

"Just because *you* trust them—"

She stopped me with a gesture. "I know their secrets and they know mine. That makes them trustworthy. Traveling with them, we'll fade into the background. Lord Hazelton's men can't nobble you if they can't find you." She stood up and brushed her skirts in a way that indicated the discussion was over. "Both you and Kat will blend in with the troupe I have in mind." She smiled at some private thought.

God's teeth, the wench is bossy. She knew all my secrets and I knew only one of hers. I had no idea what she wanted from me, or why she had to leave town. She seemed to think she was giving the orders, too. Gifted or not, I didn't trust her.

Unfortunately, her arguments made sense. Maybe leaving town wasn't such a bad idea.

16

A MESSAGE

Esmeralda made plans to leave London. I pretended to agree, saying I had arrangements to make first, but I was hoping another solution would appear. Every now and again I'd come upon Esmeralda and Serena whispering, heads together, in the kitchen or shop. I asked Serena what they were discussing, but she just patted my arm and said cryptically, *"Never put all your eggs in one basket."*

Silently I recited my own proverb: *Never trust an adult.*

I avoided Covent Square.

Saturdays were always busy at the shop. My last delivery of gloves and a shawl had taken me a fair distance, and by the time I returned, it was well past the end of my workday and Serena wouldn't expect me back.

I stopped at the Royal Exchange, the best place in London to hear news and gossip. Folk of all sorts, from respectable matrons to wharf rats, crowded together beneath the covered arcades. Despite the heat and bright sun, men of business chatted in the open courtyard beneath the bell tower.

Those with coin in their pocket could visit the shops on the floors above—booksellers, haberdashers, goldsmiths, drapers—

whatever your heart desired. Ship captains and merchants met there to haggle and finish their deals, and to hire a wharf rat if they needed a message run, or to take a stroll with their wives. Some cut deals at the coffee houses, but we didn't go there. Women and kinchin weren't allowed inside.

It was crowded beneath the roofed colonnade, with everyone in search of shade. Beneath one of the arches, Kat was deep in conversation with two sailors. I leaned against a column to wait for her to finish. I assumed she was negotiating payment for herself, but she handed one of the sailors, a bandy-legged fellow with a kerchief over his head, a piece of paper.

That was odd. He should be giving her the message, not the other way 'round. The sailor tugged his forelock and bowed and I felt a chill down my back. Why treat a wharf rat with such respect? He and his companion left and a well-dressed gentleman in dark clothes moved forward to take his place. He and Kat strolled off together down the colonnade, talking intently. He leaned close, the plume of his hat brushing her shoulder. Kat frowned and shook her head. The man nodded, and then he too bowed with a flourish of his hat before walking away.

Kat was giving orders not only to a sailor, but to a *gentleman*.

She'd been honest with me, as far as I knew. She'd told me she had a patron. It was my own fault I hadn't insisted on knowing who he was, or what exactly she did for him. It didn't necessarily mean she was a threat. Neither man looked like a tracker. I couldn't believe Kat had anything to do with trackers, not with her history, but informing in some other way was possible. She could be keeping an eye on us for someone else.

Feeling uneasy, I slipped through the crowds and out into the street before she saw me.

The sun lingered two fingers' width above the rooftops, an hour before sunset. I slipped my hand into my pocket, searching for coins for dinner, and discovered my glass was warm.

The upper stories of a large inn across the street cast long shadows. I crossed the street to enter its courtyard, relying on the long shadows to make me inconspicuous. I sank down beside a wall out of the way, and pulled out my glass.

Inside the glass, light pulsed and became stacks of crates and barrels on a wharf. Mags crouched behind them, hidden in their shadow. She peered between the crates and then ducked down, hiding from someone. Sailors passed without seeing her.

Then, before I was certain what I was seeing, the scene shifted. There was Kat, at her usual place in the Custom House. A man in a velvet cloak stood with his back to me, his profile concealed by the ostrich plume on his hat. Cressets on the wall above smoked and flickered, sending the shadows dancing. The glass went dark.

I released the breath I'd been holding.

Mags was in hiding but the glass hadn't told me why, or even where. I thrust it angrily into my pocket. I considered going to look for her, but it was daylight and the vision had taken place at night. The scene at the Custom House had been at night too. I wondered if the man at the Custom House with the ostrich plume was Kat's patron. Only the wealthy could afford velvet and ostrich feathers.

Whatever the vision foretold, there was no guarantee it would happen tonight. I had time, I thought, to buy pies on the way back. The steam from the pies turned the paper bundle soggy and slippery in my hand long before I entered the warehouse district.

In the alley, more bricks and boards had been stacked to hide the entrance. Inside, the cellar had been cleaned from floor to ceiling, shelves gleaming in the dim light. The broken casks and petrified food were gone. In their place, jugs of ale, rolls of canvas, and dried cod that would last for years sat beside barrels of pickled beef on the shelves. If we had to stay inside to hide from trackers or Mud Men, we had ample supplies. *God's teeth, who paid for all this?* Whatever Kat's patron wanted in return, we were heavily indebted.

On the main floor, Penny was idly stirring a pot over a hearth in the middle of the floor. A group of kinchin played in the corner. I handed her the meat pies. "Where's Mags?"

"She's not back yet," Penny said. "Why?"

The light was fading in the sky framed by the windows.

At the sound of someone running in the cellar, Penny and I turned to watch the stairs.

Jimmy burst onto the floor and skidded to a halt beside me, trying to catch his breath. "Lizzie! I've just come from the docks. A sailor gave me a message: Your brother Daniel will meet you at sunset on Botolph's!"

"A message from Daniel?" I repeated idiotically. My first thought was that Mags must've found him. My second thought was to wonder why Mags hadn't come herself. Surely that would make more sense.

"Where on Botolph's?" I felt a strange reluctance. Part of me wanted to run out the door, but the other part didn't believe it. Something wasn't right. And there were my visions.

Jimmy shook his head. "That was all the sailor told me. He said a man gave him a coin and had him repeat those words to deliver to a wharf rat, but he knew no more than that."

I glanced up at the windows. The sky was dark enough now for stars to appear. "I'd better go, then. You didn't see Mags?"

Jimmy shook his head. He and Penny exchanged a look. "I should come with you."

Maybe Daniel was there and maybe he wasn't, but Mags was, I felt sure, and in hiding. If my visions all warned me about my safety, then *I* was the one at risk, but better not to risk anyone else. And if Daniel really were there…well, I needed no one else for that. "I'll be careful. Besides, it *could* be my brother. I haven't seen him in two years."

Penny moved to bar my way. "He might've changed in two years, Lizzie. Take Jimmy with you—or me."

I shook my head. "I'll be careful, I promise. Tell Kat where I've gone when she gets in. And if Mags comes home tell her to *stay here!*"

Despite my fears, I felt exhilarated as I half ran, half walked down Fish Street toward the river. The blue of dusk leached colors from buildings and clothes, until full dark made it hard to see. Torches were lit on some of the wharves, while others faded into invisibility. They were lit on Botolph's, where a merchantman was being unloaded at a feverish pace. A long line of carts and wagons extended to the road, waiting to take the cargo away. If there was something shifty about the message, at least there would be others about.

I steadied my breathing and tried to collect my thoughts, walking quickly.

I was torn between the hope that Daniel really was waiting for me, and the fear that someone else was.

17

THE TRAP

AT THE CUSTOM HOUSE, two men passed, one staggering a little. The other turned to watch me, saying something under his breath to his companion. They laughed. Being on the wharves on a Saturday night was risky. Sailors were often drunk, and workingmen went in search of whores and entertainment. After enough rum or ale, men weren't too particular, and became harder to evade. Then I realized what I was thinking and laughed out loud. If Daniel was waiting for me, I feared no sailor. And if a tracker was, sailors were the least of my worries.

A fine rain began, with the wind pushing it along. Thick clouds gathered above the river, dark against a luminous sky. Wet planks gleamed in the torchlight.

When I reached the benches and the row of sheds at the near end of Botolph's, I grew more cautious and slowed. The wind gusted fiercely, casting rain into my eyes and tugging open my cloak. Torches flickered and shadows lunged like reaching hands. Sensible folk were home, sitting by a fire, or in bed. The carts waiting for the merchantman were the only traffic on the road.

The wharf, however, bustled with motion. Sloops, frigates, and merchantmen crowded together, the tall masts swaying against the sky, their lanterns bobbing on the choppy water. Ships waited for days for a berth on the legal quays, to offload cargo, pay the excise men, and pay off their crews. Only then were they free to move up or down river to find a cheaper berth, releasing the crew until the next cargo was ready. Every minute they waited cost them money. That's why the dock men were still hard at it, in spite of the wind and rain, some stripped to the waist.

I stood still, searching for Daniel's slight figure and brown curls down the wharf, hoping to see him standing by one of the ships' ramps. He would've grown, of course, but surely I'd recognize him.

But someone else was examining the groups of men, and it was sheer luck I saw him before he saw me. Crouched behind a pile of meal sacks, he was slowly and methodically searching the wharf. He looked familiar: a broad, fleshy face, dark hair, and wide shoulders. I racked my memory for a moment, trying to recall where I'd seen him before. Then I remembered: he'd been talking to Cynthia, James, and Potts one day at the Custom House. And when I caught him watching me, it made me uneasy.

Mags had to be here, in hiding. I couldn't be certain my vision would happen tonight, but it was too much of a coincidence, the message and the vision. There were plenty of hiding places here, behind the sacks, crates, and barrels of ships stores stacked beneath tarpaulins.

First I had to know if Daniel was here. I hoped to see his slight figure beside a ramp, waiting for me to appear. But I didn't see him.

Lightning stabbed down, and thunder rumbled close by moments later. The world went white and strange and light flashed on a blade. The dark-haired man behind the sacks had risen to his feet and pulled a knife. In that moment, when all was brightly lit, I saw the second man, bent over a stack of crates as though looking for someone. He wore a sword on his hip.

Thunder rolled again. This time when the lightning stabbed down, the rain fell in sheets, dousing the torches. Covered lanterns on the ships, yellow eyes bobbing up and down, were the only source of light. The crane men shouted at each other to stop. They left nets and ropes dangling while they ran for the shelter of the sheds at the end of the wharf. That lightning had been too close.

I stared into the darkness, alert for movement, while my eyes adjusted. Rain thrummed on the wooden planks.

A torch flared to life in a shed doorway, a square of glowing orange that drew the eye. I quickly turned my back, to save my night vision. Another flare of light, this one closer. Someone had relit a torch and was coming toward me. The man with the sword.

When he was but a few feet away I recognized him. With an easy movement, he unsheathed his sword, the metal ringing. A wharf man standing nearby nudged his companion, nodding toward him. The brightness of the torch dazzled my eyes, making it hard to see.

He pointed at me with his sword. "See, Jeremiah? I told you she'd come." It was my tracker's raspy voice.

I didn't dare turn to look for Jeremiah, but kept my eyes on the sword. He moved closer, smiling, the sword pointed at my heart. That smile and the sword were all I saw.

"Come, Lizzie dear. 'Tis time."

With a loud yell, Mags ran at him, shoving him from behind. He stumbled, and dropped the torch. It went out. Mags came toward me, and only then did I turn to look for the other man.

He was close behind, the knife in his hand. "Give me the girl, or I'll hurt you." He lunged at Mags but I blocked him with an arm, and kicked the side of his knee. Down he went, holding it and cursing loudly. I grabbed Mags's hand.

Fire flamed across my ribs.

I cried out and leapt away. Behind me, my tracker crouched in a fighting stance, poised for another thrust, his blade red with my blood. He lunged, and I managed to dodge the blade.

Mags screamed, "Help! He's murdering her!"

He came on. Mags dragged me backwards. There was nothing to stop him from simply grabbing one of us and running.

Then I noticed the men coming up behind him. My tracker glanced over his shoulder, distracted, then at something behind me. I was afraid it was his partner, but I didn't turn to look, not with a sword a lunge away from my throat.

"Let her go!" someone called from behind me.

Wharf men stood behind him. They came closer, surrounding us. Orange torchlight reflected in their eyes as they moved past Mags and me to stand between us and the tracker, shielding us. Surrounded on all sides, the tracker spun in a circle, sword extended.

My breathing was ragged and my sodden clothes clung to me, making it hard to move. The rain pounded down. I leaned on Mags, her arm around my waist. "Thank you," I called hoarsely to the men closest to me. One nodded and said, "Wharf folk stick together."

"Let's go," Mags said.

I moved as quickly as I could, wincing at the pain in my side. Some of the wharf men drifted back to the shelter of the sheds and the tarpaulins, some back to the cranes, now that the lightning had passed. My tracker and Jeremiah were still there somewhere, in hiding. I knew it wasn't over. They'd come after us.

We made it as far as the next wharf, but I was struggling for breath. I stumbled and leaned against a barrel, the pain stabbing with every breath. If the trackers came now, I couldn't run, but Mags could. "You go on, Mags. Run to Haven and get help. I'll wait here."

I couldn't see clearly in the darkness but I felt her shake her head. "That's just leaving you for the trackers. I won't go."

I thought of my vision. "Kat's at the Custom House. Go tell

her I'm here, and she'll help me get home. But don't come back, Mags. Run to Haven. Promise me."

For an answer, she took off running.

Relieved, I sagged against the barrel, pressing the wadded-up folds of my cloak against my side. My numbed fingers became warm and sticky with blood. *He'll come now*, I thought. Each time I heard the splashing sound of someone walking toward me, I feared it was my tracker. The cold seeped into my bones.

Then hands took hold of me.

Kat put her shoulder under my arm on one side, and Esmeralda had her arm around my waist on the other. Mags was there too. Even while I struggled to breathe and walk, buffeted by the wind, I wondered why Esmeralda was there. Between them, they half carried me up the river road and then struggled up Fish Street, Mags scouting ahead. We'd almost made it to the corner of Haven's street. My sight was blurred by the rain. The streets were filled with dark, unrecognizable shapes.

Kat said in my ear, "Keep going, Lizzie. Nearly there."

A quiet fell once the buildings blocked the wind, and Esmeralda asked Mags, "What happened?"

"I asked every new ship if they'd heard o' Daniel, same as I always do, and no one had. Then I heard someone say, 'Daniel! That's it!' with a laugh. He looked like a tracker. Then he and another cove were whispering, but I heard Lizzie's name and I feared it was a trap. So I waited to warn her."

The rain was relentless, a cold, pounding force that churned the street into a river of fast-moving mud, sucking at our shoes. The weight of my soaked clothes dragged me down at every step. If a tracker appeared, none of us could run, hampered by our waterlogged skirts.

The pain in my side was so sharp I had to stop for a moment, gasping. The others waited.

"Who heard you asking about Daniel?" Kat asked. "Is that how they knew?"

"Anyone could've heard me asking," Mags said defensively.

Kat lifted me over a wooden spar floating down the road. "Nearly there, Lizzie, just a little further." She threw a worried glance at Esmeralda.

That's when I realized we'd led Esmeralda right to our door.

18

HAVEN

MAGS SCOUTED the alley while we waited. A stack of crates bulked menacingly, but no one waited behind it. Mags waved a come-ahead and we picked our way toward her. Garbage swirled past on a slow tide of water and mud. A floating board rammed my leg and Kat steadied me.

We picked our way down the wet, slippery stairs into the damp-smelling cellar. Climbing the stairs stretched my sword cut and I cried out. Mags ran past me.

At the top, a wave of warmth greeted us with the fragrance of mutton, wood smoke, and wet wool. Children ran across the floor, shrieking. Fires hissed and smoked in the open hearths. In a corner, Willie was crying again, but Penny was with him, soothing him with a bit of hardtack to suck on. The bedding was rolled up, stacked neatly against the walls, and the curtains pushed aside. The warm light of the fires bathed everything in a soft glow. Rain pounded on the roof, but all was warm and cozy inside.

I made it as far as the nearest fire, then sank onto a stool, spreading my skirts, water forming puddles on the bricks around me. Tears sprang into my eyes as feeling returned to my numbed fingers. I fumbled at my cloak until Esmeralda brushed my hand away and undid the knot. She lifted the heavy, steaming wool with ease, and hung it on a hook by the fire. I felt weak and remembered I hadn't eaten since breakfast.

Penny hurried over. "You're safe!" She was about to hug me when she saw Esmeralda and stopped. I was hunched over, favoring my side. The children gathered around Mags, questioning her softly.

Rain spattered down the chimney, hissing on the bricks of the hearth. Esmeralda knelt beside me to lift the hem of my bodice and examine my wound. "You were lucky. The cut is fairly shallow, but you've lost a lot of blood; your bodice is fair soaked. You may have cracked a rib. Your side should be cleaned and bandaged, and you'll need to rest."

I shrugged, wincing. "I'm all right. I'm grateful for your help, mistress, but how is it you were so ready to hand?"

Esmeralda's eyes flicked to Kat. "I had an errand at the Custom House. I saw Mags arrive and asked her what was going on."

It had been lucky for me she'd been there. But an errand at night at the Custom House didn't ring true; there was little business so late. If she was an informer, we'd brought her straight to Haven and delivered a treasure trove of gifted children into her hands. Her explanation told me nothing. "What sort of errand?"

She lowered herself onto the stool next to mine with a groan. "Arranging our trip out of town. You and I must leave."

"And now you know where we live," Kat said. She had been watching Esmeralda ever since we had made it as far as the fire, arms folded, not looking away even to hang up her cloak.

Esmeralda, for her part, ignored her. "Lizzie, what took you to the wharves tonight? The trackers were waiting for you. Is Thomas mixed up in this somehow?"

Kat jumped in. "How did *you* hear about the Guild, mistress? Seems to me, you were the one eager to learn where Haven is.

And now you have. Your presence at the Custom House was rather convenient. You might've planned this whole thing to get inside."

"Hmph." Esmeralda stared into the fire, ignoring her questions. "From everything you've said, Lizzie, Thomas is furious with you, and the tracker offered him gold. Does Thomas know you're looking for your brother?"

None of the others heard, thank God. I didn't think Esmeralda was working with the trackers, but I certainly regretted telling her about Thomas. Of course, the fool had accosted her with his jealous questions himself, the jobber knoll. And Kat was right, it *was* suspicious, her being ready to hand. "Mistress, we need a better explanation to trust you."

"Lizzie, why were *you* on the wharves tonight?" Kat asked, frowning and distracted in spite of herself.

"A message, pretending to be from my brother, saying to meet him there. It was a trick, o' course. My tracker was waiting—with an accomplice."

"Did Thomas know about your brother?" Esmeralda asked.

"Why do you keep bringing up Thomas?" Kat demanded. "You're the main suspect in all this, and Thomas would never hurt Lizzie, whatever other fool notions he may have."

Esmeralda folded her arms, mirroring Kat, and stared stubbornly back at her.

"Potts knew about Daniel too," Mags said, unexpectedly. "He kept following me every morning when I asked about him at the new ships. I didn't see any harm in it. I'm sorry, Lizzie."

"That might be it. I saw Potts talking to one of the trackers," I said, remembering. "The dark one called Jeremiah: Potts, James and Cynthia were chatting with him like old friends."

Shock, followed swiftly by a look of triumph, appeared on Esmeralda's face. I thought she'd recognized Jeremiah's name.

"Let's assume it was Potts who informed on you to the tracker," Kat said. "But that doesn't explain Esmeralda popping up like a jack-in-the-box. For all we know, she could be working with Jeremiah too."

Esmeralda began to cough as though she were choking, hand over her mouth. Was she laughing?

The children who had been watching us now huddled together, whispering.

I took off my boots and stockings and wiggled my toes near the fire. I badly wanted to crawl into bed and sleep for days, but this had to be resolved.

Kat stood beside the hearth, hands on hips, her gaze fixed on Esmeralda.

Mags knelt beside me and handed me a mug of spiced wine. "How are you feeling?" she asked. Then she glared at Esmeralda and Kat and said angrily, "Why don't you help her, instead of letting her bleed to death, you shallow-pated loobies? Get her some bandages!"

Kat seemed to come to herself. She rose and went to confer with Penny, who was putting the little ones to bed.

Penny bustled over. "Come along behind the curtain and we'll bandage you up."

I shook my head. "Not yet; not until we've settled whether Esmeralda can join the Guild."

Penny frowned as though I were being foolish. "In a minute, Penny, I promise."

Mags was hovering uncertainly, looking worried. I smiled at her. "Besides, I feel better already from the fire and the wine. I have to thank you, Mags. You saved my life tonight, when you shoved my tracker. You took a terrible risk."

She suddenly looked shy, ducking her head. "I wanted to help you, Lizzie, the way you helped me." Her lip trembled. "I was afraid he'd killed you, when I saw him go for you with the sword."

I smiled grimly. "Well, we're both still here, thanks to your quick thinking." She pecked my cheek and ran back to the others behind the curtain. I sipped the wine, feeling warmth spread through me.

"Now that you know where Haven is, what do *you* plan to do?" Kat was back beside me, eyeing Esmeralda like a terrier watching a rat.

"What do you mean? I came here to help," Esmeralda said. "I didn't expect bouquets and speeches, but you could at least say 'thank you.'"

"For all we know, 'twas you sent the message to Lizzie," Kat said. "Only those who took the oath should know about this place, yet here you are. Why are you really here?" Her hand moved to a dagger on her belt.

Esmeralda put her mug on the hearth and rose to stand only inches away from Kat. "I heard there was trouble on the wharf, and I stopped at the Custom House to find out more. By the time I heard about trackers, you and Mags were leaving."

"That sounds very well, mistress, but you might have set the whole thing up in the first place. Perhaps those trackers work for you. You could've planned to offer help if things didn't go the way you'd planned, so we'd trust you. The way Lizzie is trusting you right now. I don't know who you work for, but you know things you shouldn't." She turned to me. "She knew about the Guild, you said, and yet you never told her?"

I nodded. That was true. No one besides the wharf rats should have known.

"And now, mysteriously, you heard about 'trouble on the wharves.' Who sent you word?"

Some of the older children had gathered, watching Kat and Esmeralda with worried eyes. *Every* adult was a threat. And here one was, in our safe place.

Esmeralda gave an exasperated sigh. "My sister and I want to *join* the Guild, but Lizzie told us to wait until you felt safe. I'll take the oath right now, if that's what's worrying you."

"You didn't answer my question," Kat said. "How did you hear about the Guild?"

Esmeralda's face was expressionless. "I can't tell you."

"How can you join?" Mattie demanded, stepping forward. "You're not a wharf rat."

My need for sleep was growing stronger, but this had to be settled first. "Esmeralda and her sister want to join, Mattie, because they still have their gifts. They never outgrew them. They want to help."

"That can't be true!" Mattie looked stricken.

There was a horrified silence.

"It's true. I've seen Esmeralda's gift." I turned to Kat, "The sisters *could* help us. Serena can tell when someone is lying." I glanced at Esmeralda. "I don't know how she learns things, but if she takes the oath now, she'll either be one of us or die for it. That's if everyone agrees."

Kat's eyes were like flints. "She already knows where we are, so we have no choice. Maybe that was the plan all along."

I turned to the others. "Wharf rats, what do you say?"

The rats huddled together. After several minutes of whispers, Mattie announced, "No. Not unless she *shows* us her gift."

Esmeralda shrugged. "I don't mind."

It wasn't obvious at first, when she began to rise, but by the time she was over our heads, Mattie's mouth hung open and even Kat looked shocked.

I rose wearily to my feet as Esmeralda slowly drifted to the floor. "Place your right hand over your heart," I told her.

Esmeralda repeated each line of the oath after me, swearing to be true to the death. I sank back down onto the stool. "Good. Thank you for your help, Esmeralda. You can leave now if you like, or be welcome to spend the night."

Turning to Kat she said softly, "Now will you let this go?"

"Not until I know who you're working for," Kat said.

"What makes you think I'm working for anyone?"

Kat smiled grimly. "Thurloe."

Glancing from one to the other, I asked, "Who's Thurloe?"

Neither replied, or even glanced my way, their eyes locked on each other.

Esmeralda said she'd sleep at Haven. I didn't blame her; the rain was pounding on the roof like hail. All I wanted was to lie down and sleep for three days, but Kat said I had to wait, she had something to show me. "Then you'd best hurry, because I'm falling asleep where I sit."

"Give us a song, Mags," Mattie called. "The rain beats down so, it sounds like we're under attack by cannon."

Mags' black curls were plastered to her forehead, and her dress was still wet, but she looked pleased. She stood before the fire and curtsied, spreading her skirts. Her face grew serious. She folded her hands across her stomach and closed her eyes.

Then the sweetest sound came from those rosy lips, the first clear notes of *Barbara Allen.*

It was astonishing. Every one of us stared in amazement. I hadn't realized the strong voice I'd heard the night we sang the Diggers' song was hers. Others joined in, the thin high voices of the girls and young boys floating above Jimmy's cracking baritone. Soaring above them all was Mags' clear soprano.

When the song was over, she opened her eyes and curtsied, and everyone applauded.

Jimmy called, "That was marvelous, Mags. Give us another."

Mags began the wharf rats' version of the Diggers' song, with Jimmy's new words. Mattie clapped in time, and Jimmy grinned and joined in. Esmeralda clearly knew the song; she looked surprised, then pleased, and joined in as well.

Penny stood and clapped her hands. "Bed," she announced. There were groans, but the little ones were asleep where they sat. Penny led a group to the row of chamber pots in the corner.

My side hurt every time I moved and it must've shown, for when I got up to help her, Penny shooed me back to the fire and pushed the curtains closed to block the firelight.

I took Jimmy aside. "The trackers may know where we are. We'll need a guard on the door. Could you take the first watch? Wake me in two hours, and I'll wake Kat after that." He nodded, not at all surprised.

Kat appeared at my elbow. "You've put it off long enough. Time to clean your wound and see my surprise."

"No," I mumbled. "No more surprises. Tomorrow." My side hurt dreadfully now, no longer numbed by cold.

"Come." She gently put her arm around my waist and led me to the corner where a canvas sheet hung in front of the stone basin of the blacksmith's forge.

"What do you want me to see?"

"This." She swept aside the curtain to reveal the stone basin full of water, steam rising from the surface.

"What?" I asked stupidly.

"A bath, wharf rat. It will warm you up and clean out whatever muck got into the wound. In you get."

"You want me to get into the water when my clothes are just starting to dry?"

"You take your clothes off first," she said kindly, as though explaining to a pig-widgeon.

"Oh." I hesitated.

"Don't be a clunch-pate, Lizzie. Do you *want* a blood fever? Take off all your clothes right now. They'll be dry by the fire after you warm up and clean your wound in the bath."

I was too tired to argue. "Turn around then."

When she had, I dropped my bodice and skirt to the floor, but hesitated at my shift.

"All of it," she commanded, glancing over her shoulder.

First, I untied the strings of my pocket, with my glass inside it, and placed it carefully next to the tub. Uneasily, I dropped the shift too. Kat bundled everything into her arms.

"Don't look," I said.

"I won't if you get into the tub."

The water was hot, but not uncomfortably so. After a moment I decided I could sit down without parboiling myself, and lowered myself gingerly into the water.

"There's soap on the ledge there. Use it."

Good lord. The warm water felt like heaven on my back, the warmth relaxing muscles I hadn't known were clenched. My side, however, began to throb again. I checked the jagged edges of the wound; they were pale with no sign yet of angry infection below the skin. A lump of something green that smelled of rosemary sat on the edge of the tub. I rubbed it against the wound, gritting my teeth as it stung, and soaped myself all over, including my hair.

After I'd rinsed off, I lay back in the warmth and dozed, muscles relaxed, too tired to worry about trackers, or Esmeralda, even if she was in league with them. Allowing myself to hope that I might see Daniel had left sadness and exhaustion in its wake.

Kat had left a candle on the blacksmith's bench, and the flickering light danced on the water's surface. Eyes closing, I dozed off, slipping down into the tub. My chin touched the water and I jerked awake. Images moved on the surface of the water. I rubbed my eyes and sat up, but the images remained.

Jeremiah sat with his back to the fire in the common room of a public house. He lifted his knife to his mouth and bit off a hunk of mutton, chewing with a sullen expression. My tracker sat beside him, taking a long draught from his mug. "His Lordship won't be best pleased with this failure. But he doesn't need to know," he said. "So let's not tell him. We can make up some excuse about the ship."

"Stow it, Gilbert," Jeremiah said.

"Always so charming. You're too impatient. We'll think of

something else. She won't be cozened a second time, and I don't believe your precious informer even knows where the nest is. I think we should work on the rat boy. That fool of a chit trusts him. I'll wager *he* knows where the nest is. Then we can nobble 'em all and hold 'em until the price is right. His Lordship needn't know about it. There's enough we can sell a few on the side."

Jeremiah frowned at his plate. "We should've grabbed the chit. She knows folk's secrets, according to the rat boy. Hazelton would like that."

"She'll know yours too." Gilbert laughed at Jeremiah's expression. "Anyway, stop thinking like a small-time foist. Why shouldn't we nobble them all?" He drained his tankard. "And since the prophetess treasures the chit, they won't wish to be separated."

"We're past the deadline and the ship has sailed. How do we get them there?" Jeremiah said gloomily. "If we carry 'em ourselves, we risk hanging for kidnapping."

"Taking risks is what you're paid for. I've hired a coach. We can be there in less than a day. Once he has her, His Lordship won't give a fig about the ship."

The candle on the edge of the tub sputtered and went out. Faint light spilled around the edge of the curtain. Between the cooling water, the vision, and the sudden dark, I was fully awake. My skin was all over gooseflesh.

My tracker's name was Gilbert, and he and Jeremiah *didn't* know where we were. Not yet, anyway. If I was *the prophetess*, then *the chit* must be Mags. Who was their *precious informer*? That was the question. I was fairly certain Potts was the "rat boy." Mags trusted him too much. He'd known about Daniel and probably knew more than he should about the Guild.

Kat came through the curtain, carrying a piece of canvas, silhouetted against the firelight. "Stand up," she ordered, "and I'll wrap you in this."

I pulled the cloth around me. "This was a lot of work, Kat, thank you. But I don't need to be coddled."

"Too tough for a bath, eh? You have a sword cut in your side, Your Majesty. What do you think would happen to the Guild and the children if something happened to you? The kinchin trust *you*. Not me, not Jimmy, not even Penny has earned their trust the way you have. You have to remember that others need you now. Rub yourself all over with this and I'll bring your clothes."

Rubbing my hair, I stood dripping on the brick floor. The only sound was the wind hurling rain against the windows, and the fire hissing when the rain spattered down the chimney. Everyone else had gone to bed.

Only that morning I'd been worried about who Kat worked for. My suspicions seemed ridiculous now. For the first time, I wondered if my visions might be a curse, making me doubt my friends.

Kat returned and motioned for me to turn. I moved the canvas sheet while she wrapped a large cloth around my ribcage, winding it several times around and then tying it off.

"Did you enjoy your bath?" she asked, handing me clothes warm from the fire.

"It was glorious. Kat?"

"Yes?"

"I just saw our tracker in a vision. His name is Gilbert. His accomplice is Jeremiah."

She nodded, waiting, with no sign of surprise.

"I don't know for sure, but it's possible Potts knows where Haven is. They'll try to convince him to reveal our location. And they want to nobble Mags if they can't get me." I didn't tell them what Gilbert had said Mags' gift was. That was for her to reveal if she chose to. "We'll need guards on the door from now on."

"I'll take care of it. You are going to *bed*. We'll need you tomorrow." She took my arm and led me across the room to the sleeping area and my pallet.

Penny had placed a warm brick at the foot to warm it. I slipped beneath the blanket, wriggling my toes with pleasure. I was "Lucky Lizzie" after all, I thought—lucky in my friends. My eyes closed.

The trackers didn't know where Haven was. Not yet. But *we* didn't know who the informer was. James was most likely, or Potts. But I couldn't be sure of Thomas, or of Esmeralda for that matter, even if she was one of us now. She was up to something, but I couldn't believe Serena's sister would betray us to trackers.

I'd have to explain to Mags why being friends with Potts was too great a risk. We'd all have to convince her. I'd seen the doubt in her eyes when I said I'd seen Potts talking to Jeremiah.

There was only the sound of the rain on the roof, and of soft breathing around me.

Jeremiah and Gilbert had sprung their trap and failed, but they'd try again, and next time they'd be after Mags as well.

19

GIFTS

THE NEXT MORNING I was not the only one who slept late.

Finally awakened by the throbbing in my side, I stared up at the rafters and listened to the rain. Memory returned slowly. I considered the vision I'd seen in the bath. For whatever reason, Gilbert believed Potts knew our secrets. Whether he was the only informer, or was working with someone else, we needed a plan to protect ourselves.

The sound of crockery and the earthy smell of porridge came from the other side of the curtain. I sat up and reached for my pocket. When I removed the glass, it was already warm to the touch. I held it up to the light. A vision appeared immediately.

Jeremiah and a thin man, whose long nose made him look like a ferret, sat facing each other across a dirty table. A shaft of sunlight came through the open door where wagons and coaches waited in a courtyard. Men passed behind Jeremiah on their way to the door. One stopped and announced, "The coach for Barsington is leaving soon."

Jeremiah nodded. He waited until the man left before he said softly, "I know how you feel, Hawkins, but keep your bellyaching quiet at the manor. Hazelton's our master while his plan's underway. Don't let him see you angry. He'll be furious anyway, 'cause we missed our quota. Don't set him off."

"He makes me want to stick him," Hawkins said, his long nose hovering over his mug.

"I know, I know," Jeremiah said soothingly. "But it won't be for long. Lady Cheshire's party is coming up. Once His Lordship has done the deed, we don't need a *prophetess* to know what will happen to *him,* do we?" Hawkins grinned and both men chuckled, as though he'd said something clever. The glass went dark.

I'd already assumed Jeremiah worked for Hazelton. So he and this Hawkins fellow were going to Barsington. Wasn't that somewhere north of London? At least we didn't have to worry about Jeremiah on the wharves.

I stretched, yawning, and pulled on my skirt. No one had woken me for guard duty. Someone must've told Jimmy not to wake me. Who would ignore my orders? Picking my way over two sleeping girls, I parted the curtain.

Esmeralda sat at one of the tables, a bowl of porridge before her, children on either side. She smiled when she saw me. "Good, you're up. I've told everyone to stay inside today until we've decided what to do about the trackers. Besides, it's pouring buckets."

I frowned. She'd been here only a few hours and thought she could give orders? "Good morning to *you,* Mistress Esmeralda. May I remind you that *I'm* in charge?"

She shrugged and looked unrepentant.

Penny and Mattie were handing bowls of porridge to the children in line. I joined them, and once I had my own bowl, sat down across from Esmeralda and began to eat.

Kat sat beside me and whispered in my ear, "Potts can't be found. Jimmy and Mattie were out early this morning looking for him."

Possibly Potts had more brains than I thought. "Either Gilbert has nobbled him, or he's heard something. Either way, a confirmation he was involved."

Esmeralda said, "Potts, you mean?" In addition to her other annoying qualities, she apparently had excellent hearing. "Serena should question him."

It would be good to know whether Potts knew anything else that could threaten us, but we'd have to find him first.

I swallowed the last spoonful and carried my bowl to the soak bucket. When everyone had finished eating, I stood in the center of the floor and called, "Everyone, please gather 'round."

The rats made a circle, some on stools, some cross-legged on the floor. Willie and Deborah looked healthier already, their cheeks rosier and filled out. I saw it in the others too. Regular food and a warm place to sleep were making a difference.

"It's raining cats and dogs outside, so we're going to play games today," I said. The younger children's faces brightened. Mattie and Penny exchanged glances. "But first, we should talk about last night, about the trackers." The chattering ceased.

"Last night was the first test of the Guild. Someone tried to nobble one of us, and we fought back. If Mags hadn't risked her life to help me, I'd probably be nobbled, or worse."

Dead silence.

"There were two trackers waiting for me when I went to the wharves last night. Mags overheard them talking about me, so she hid to warn me when I arrived. A tracker came for me with his sword, but Mags pushed him and he fell. That time we were lucky: the wharf men helped us. Next time we might not be so lucky. Next time it might be one of you.

"Remember when I first spoke of the Guild? I said we'd demonstrate our gifts, so we can trust each other. Well, today's the day."

There were frightened faces, and heads bent together, whispering.

"The trackers may know more about us than we want them

to. That's scary, but *we* have the gifts. Please stand." There was rustling and whispers as everyone rose.

"Let's say the oath again, so we remember what we're fighting for."

Everyone repeated it after me.

Some of the rats who'd regarded Esmeralda with suspicion at breakfast seemed reassured when she recited it, hand over heart, with everyone else. But not all.

"Good. Now for the fun part." I smiled. "Showing off our gifts. I'll go first."

I carried a three-legged stool to the center of the circle and sat down. Like a conjuror performing a trick, I held up my glass so everyone could see it catch the light. "Some of you know my gift is foretelling. What you may not know is that I have no control over it. The vision shows me what it will, not what I ask to see. This is the glass I use to see the future."

Willie said, "Oh!" in a hushed, expectant voice.

I bent over the glass, calming my breathing, not certain the glass would cooperate. But it did. I waited for the swirling light to settle.

It was nighttime in the courtyard of an inn. A carriage pulled up to the door, the horses foam-flecked and blowing hard. Two men jumped down from the box and stretched their stiff limbs. The coach door opened and a third man stepped down. He leaned back inside and dragged out a sack. When he threw it over his shoulder, it squirmed and whimpered, and then the sack gave a high-pitched call for help. A child, then. A child about Mags' size.

The three men laughed as the sack wriggled again, and one struck it and told it to be quiet. They carried it into the inn. The paint on the sign above the door had faded, making it difficult to make out, but there was a circle and a thick line. Above them, in faded black letters, it proclaimed, *The Orb and Sceptre Inn.*

The glass went dark.

I'd never heard of that inn, but it had to be one of us in the sack, not some random stranger, else why show it to me? I raised my head, took a deep breath. The room came back into focus.

"What did you see, Lizzie?" Mags asked.

I pushed my hair out of my eyes, considering. "First, I should explain. Sometimes what I see is useful, but often it's not, because I don't know what it means. Just now I saw a small child bundled in a sack being carried up the steps of an inn, outside of London, I believe. But I don't know who the child is, except they're small and have a high voice."

Everyone looked at Mags.

"They haven't got us yet," Mags said. "Remember how Lizzie warned everyone to stay away from the cook shop?" Everyone nodded. "Well, we've been warned and I for one don't intend to be nobbled."

A few of the kinchin smiled, but most looked scared, as well they should. It could be any of the younger ones in that bag.

"Do you have to use the glass, Lizzie?" Mattie asked.

I hesitated, reluctant to reveal everything. But it was cowardly to hold back when I'd asked them to reveal their gifts. "No. I can see visions in water, or glass, but I prefer using my glass. It's saved my life more than once." I picked up the stool and returned to the circle.

"Right," Esmeralda said from the back. "Who's next?"

Those who had been asleep last night stared at her suspiciously. They hadn't seen her gift and didn't trust her, oath or not.

Esmeralda smiled. "Then it must be my turn. I love showing off my gift." She walked to the center, beaming as though a Master of Ceremonies had just announced her. She did love an audience.

This time, there were smiles and clapping by the time Esmeralda was a foot off the ground. Deborah's mouth hung open, her eyes wide, but then she, too, clapped in delight.

Esmeralda smiled graciously in midair and waved her arm with a flourish. She sank slowly to the floor and curtsied to each side of the circle. More clapping. She smiled complacently and resumed her place in the circle.

"Me next," said Kat. "Can I have a volunteer?"

Mattie joined her, with a knowing smile. Without a word, Kat put a hand on her shoulder and Mattie disappeared.

"Oh!" Willie said loudly.

"I can make anything invisible," Kat explained, "but I have to be near it, and I have to be able to concentrate. I can't do it if I'm too tired, or hurt."

Mattie reappeared. "Me next! I need Jimmy or someone else brave," she said, looking at our six-foot giant.

Jimmy stood up reluctantly. He knew what was coming. "Be gentle, gentle maid," he said, joining her in the center. That got a laugh. Most of us knew Mattie's gift.

She bent over to place her right hand on the floor, palm up. Jimmy placed his right foot on her hand and Mattie lifted him into the air above her head. Balancing on one foot, he teetered precariously, until Mattie put her other hand up for him to stand on. There he stood, like an acrobat over her head, grinning.

"What's your gift, Jimmy?" Willie called out.

Mattie bent down to let Jimmy jump to the floor. He examined the far wall doubtfully. "Not sure I can show it here," he said. "But I'll try."

He ran so swiftly he was a blur. He slammed into the far wall before he could stop. Rumor was he could run faster than a horse, and I thought 'twas true. He weaved unsteadily back to the circle and sat down.

One by one, the other rats demonstrated what they could do.

Penny waited until everyone else had gone, then walked slowly to the center of the circle, carrying a stool and leading Willie by the hand.

Surprisingly, our capable Penny turned red and mumbled.

She sat down, pulling Willie onto her lap. He squirmed, uneasy at being the center of attention. His lip trembled, tears spilled from his eyes, and I was sure he'd start bawling again. Penny murmured something and passed her hand over his face.

He instantly fell asleep. There was a hush while everyone digested this in silence. Then everyone began to clap and Mattie whistled loudly.

"You're in trouble now, Penny," Mattie called. "Every time one of 'em cries we'll beg you to put 'em to sleep." There were grins.

"I don't like to, it doesn't seem right," Penny said. "I just give a hint of it, to quiet them."

Willie was far too young to know whether he had a gift, but Penny said that despite his tottering walk and constant falls, he never had a scratch on him. Fast healer, she said. The other little ones were silent and wide-eyed, too young to be sure of their gift.

I returned to the center. "Thank you for sharing your gifts. I'm proud to be a wharf rat." I began to clap and everyone clapped back, smiling at each other. We'd revealed our gifts and no one had cried or bolted.

"Now let's have some fun," I said. "Esmeralda, Kat, and I will go around the room and put everyone in groups. We're going to practice using our gifts for defense. Which ones d'you think are the most useful?"

Someone called out, "Kat's," others said, "Jimmy" or "Mattie," the obvious ones, but Jimmy said thoughtfully, "Penny's is good too." I nodded. Most of them would be useful for defense. Mine was the only one that wasn't.

"Wait a minute," Mattie called. "What about Mags' gift?" Everyone fell silent.

"Mags? Don't you have a gift too?" Kat asked. "Why didn't you show it?"

Mags scowled at Mattie, but walked to the center of the circle.

"I don't like using it," she said. Her face was flushed and she kept her eyes on the floor. "I found out by accident. A boy stole my red cloak. I was angry at him, and yelled that he'd better show me where it was hidden. He was awfully surprised when he led me straight to the cellar where he'd hidden it behind some crates. After that, he ran away every time he saw me." She smiled grimly. "If I ask you to tell me something, you will. I don't like using it," she repeated.

Kat caught my eye. *Mags* could question Potts. If we ever found him.

"Does Potts know about your gift?" Esmeralda asked. Mags nodded.

"We'd only use your gift if we had to," I said. That was true of all of us. We'd survived by hiding our gifts, but to defend each other we'd have to use them where people could see. It had better be worth the risk.

I rose to my feet. "Let's practice!"

Esmeralda, Kat and I divided the children into three groups and the room descended into chaos.

20

THE WHARF RATS FIGHT BACK

WE SPENT the rest of the morning attacking each other.

Jimmy went after Mattie with a broom-handle sword that she easily twisted out of his grasp. Kat showed us how to move in close to our opponent, to use a wrestling hold to fight an armed man. A sword was useless, she explained, if you were inside their guard, making you too close for them to use it.

Esmeralda regarded her thoughtfully.

Willie and Deborah chased Penny around the floor, screaming with glee, until she stopped and, with a touch, sent them both to sleep, barely catching them in time. Esmeralda woke 'em up and gathered the other little ones to demonstrate tumbling tricks. Soon these apparently spineless creatures were leaping over obstacles and turning somersaults beneath make-believe swords and real knives.

"Where did you learn that?" I asked her.

"I told you. I was a headliner at the fairs. Fair folk know many a useful trick or two."

Kat came up from behind and made *me* invisible. She told me to stop breathing so loudly, and demonstrated to a laughing group gathered around me how to calm your breathing so no one could tell you were there. Then she explained how to stand so your shadow wouldn't give you away. It was fun.

When I crept up on Mags and tickled her, she leapt away squealing. Then the others had a turn and it was bedlam: invisible children pulled hair, tickled each other, and someone kissed Jimmy full on the mouth but wouldn't own up.

My side began to hurt again, so I stood with my back to the fire and watched. Rain still spattered the windows, but the fire popped and crackled with a comfortable sound, bathing our faces in a warm light. The kinchin raced across the floor happily, but what they were learning was deadly serious.

There were a few war wounds. Jimmy received a gash on his forehead when Mags took the broom-handle away from him. He was already bruised from running into the wall, so we told him he could retire from the field of battle with honor, to help Penny make lunch.

Mags began singing the wharf rats' song, "Stand up, stand up now!" and the others joined in, still fighting and laughing with each other.

By midday, everyone was worn out and hungry. We lined up for mutton and peas, the children boasting how they'd fight trackers when they got the chance, still flushed from their heroic victories. Putting their gifts to work had lessened their fear. I'd been afraid the fighting would upset them, but if anything they were too pleased with themselves. We'd have to practice when *not* to fight too.

After luncheon, Penny put Willie and Deborah down for their naps and confided she hurt all over and would join them. I think she hated using her gift, even in practice, and the reaction made her ill.

Mattie and Mags leaped over each other, practicing Esmeralda's somersaults, until Mags said she had to stop, her lunch was coming up.

Mattie sat down by the fire with a happy sigh and reached for the mending basket. Jimmy was washing the dishes.

Esmeralda and I sat a little apart at the second fire. She kept insisting we leave town. "If you're worried they're after Mags, she can come too, until the trackers lose the trail. The three of us should go soon," Esmeralda said.

I was about to ask her why she needed to leave town, when Kat sat down beside her. "What are you two whispering about?" she asked.

Esmeralda lifted her chin. "The best way to deal with the trackers. Lizzie, Mags, and I are going to leave town."

"Then Kat has to go too," I pointed out. "Gilbert's after both of us. If not for Kat, I wouldn't be here."

Esmeralda frowned, and pointedly turned to watch Mattie doing cartwheels.

Kat winked at me.

Three of the rats began to sing, "*Ring around the rosy, a pocket full of posies, ashes, ashes, all fall down.*" They danced in a circle, holding hands. At the last line, they dropped to the floor. Then they got up and did it again. And again. "*Ring around the rosy, a pocket full of posies, ashes, ashes, all fall down.*"

Kat said, "There's no reason to leave town. Mattie can defend the door, especially if she hides and surprises 'em. That's what I told her to do. We could hire guards for the alley, too, since we can't rely on the Watch or the Mud Men to help us."

Esmeralda's eyes narrowed. "Who exactly are you going to tell about Haven, so they can guard the door?"

Mags sang:

London Bridge is broken down, broken down, broken down,
London Bridge is broken down,
My fair Lady.

The rats formed two lines. With each verse they captured a child, their faces oddly serious, singing:

Set a man to watch all night,

Watch all night, watch all night.
Set a man to watch all night,
My fair Lady.
Suppose the man should fall asleep, fall asleep, fall asleep?

What could a watchman do if trackers came here? Nothing. Esmeralda was right. "No, Kat, we can't risk anyone knowing where we are."

The children sang, "*Give him a pipe to smoke all night,*" and I felt goosebumps on my neck, remembering my tracker lighting his pipe outside the shed, the flame illuminating his nose and eyebrows. Likely he was waiting for me on the wharves at that very moment, searching for Mags, too. Leaving London wasn't a bad idea. But where to go? The river was my home, my safety.

"I think—" I began, but my voice was too loud.

The room had gone quiet. Shocked faces stared at the stairs.

I turned to look. Potts stood there.

"Lizzie, come quick," he called, before darting down the stairs.

Had he brought the trackers with him? I turned to see Mags' reaction.

But Mags was gone.

21

BETRAYAL

I RAN FOR THE STAIRS.

Kat caught my arm. "Wait. It could be a trap. Let me go down first." She disappeared. My hands clenched into fists while I paced impatiently.

"I don't see anyone else," she called. I ran down the stairs.

Potts stood on the bottom step, his upturned face lit by the light in the stairwell. Kat had hold of his arm.

"Where is she, Potts?" I demanded. "What are you doing here? How did you find us? Who told you where we were?"

"Mags said she had to go out. I told her not to, but she wouldn't listen."

His face was partly shadowed, so it was difficult to read his expression, but his voice wasn't right. He didn't sound worried or upset, only excited.

"Did you bring trackers here?" I demanded. "Do they have Mags?"

He shook his head. "I came to *warn* Mags that they're looking for her. She just ran out the door!"

Kat's voice was harsh. "Don't act the fool. How did you find this place? Does James know where it is?"

"Did you see her go?" Esmeralda was coming down the stairs.

"I tried to try to stop her, but she pushed past me, out the door." His eyes shifted warily between the three of us.

I could imagine it: Potts standing at the top of the stairs, waving to Mags. She would come over to ask what he was doing here. That was all Potts had to do, if a tracker was waiting below.

Kat brought the candle from the niche and lit it. She raised it before his face. "I think you lured her to the cellar, where your accomplice waited, and he took her. Is he still outside? Waiting?"

Potts backed away, eyes darting between us. He ran to the cellar door and pulled it open. I followed him, afraid he'd get away. Dust motes danced in the light streaming between the boards. "Look for yourself," he said, "there's no one there. If we hurry, we can catch her." He turned to look up at me, where I hovered, ready to grab him.

"Why didn't *you* go after her, Potts?" Kat asked. "You did your part. Why are you still here?" She walked past us to kneel with the candle to examine the alcove behind the door.

He smiled uncertainly. "I…I didn't want to go alone."

I grabbed both of his arms and shook him. "Who's waiting outside? Who knows about this place?"

He pulled away. "No one." His voice cracked.

"You told the trackers where we are," I said flatly. "Didn't you?"

He laughed. "Trackers? No. Why would I? Anyway, you can see for yourself she's not here. I'm telling you, she just ran out the door."

"Mags isn't stupid. She wouldn't just run outside."

Esmeralda had come to stand beside him. He was surrounded. "Why did you betray her?" I asked. "For a reward? Or do you have a secret you thought she'd find out?"

Potts smiled desperately, shaking his head. He flinched when Kat rose to her feet behind him. He darted nervous glances at all of us.

"There are a man's boot prints in the dust in the alcove, too large for any of us," Kat said. "They weren't there yesterday. You were afraid Mags might reveal your secret, so you brought a tracker with you. Didn't you?"

"Is he waiting outside?" I said softly.

He finally looked afraid. "There's no tracker," he whined.

"Then who took her, Potts?" I demanded.

"'Tisn't no tracker. Mags won't be harmed. He promised."

Kat grabbed his other arm. "Who promised? You'd better tell us all of it. We won't let you leave now, to do more damage. You're our prisoner."

The look of surprise on his face would've been comical, if Mags' life hadn't been at stake. "No! She's safe, I tell you. James said it was just a lark. He'll keep Mags for an hour or so, and after everyone's upset and running around, he'll come laugh at you and your grand plans."

Kat bent down to look into his face. "James was here in the cellar?"

Potts nodded.

"If James was here, then none of us are safe. What do you think the rats will do to you, Potts, when they learn you're an informer? They'll be easier on you if you help us get Mags back." She was trying to persuade him to help, but the truth was, no matter what he did, the rats would never forgive him. Not if Mags was in the hands of Hazelton's men. James had boasted he'd restore his family fortunes when his plans came through. Maybe they had.

"Is James or anyone else waiting for us outside?" I asked.

He shook his head slowly, wide-eyed. This time I thought he told the truth.

"Was a tracker with him? Do the trackers know where Haven is?" Understanding finally appeared on his face. He hadn't imagined trackers coming here. Maybe he was simple after all.

"When did you arrange this?" Kat asked.

"Last night, on Botolph's. James laughed himself sick, watching Lizzie saunter up to the wharf expecting her brother. He said, 'Lizzie needs taking down a peg,' and asked me to help. He said it would be a lark." He shot me an uneasy glance.

"So, last night, when Lizzie and Mags were in danger, instead of helping them you plotted with James? You decided to help kidnap Mags *yourself?*" There was outrage in Kat's voice.

Potts shook his head. "No, it wasn't like that. Mags will be all right, 'coz James said the trackers want *Lizzie.*"

Potts' mixture of confidence and stupidity was baffling. I could almost understand his callousness toward me, but not toward Mags. I drew him over to the bottom step of the stairs, and sat down. "What happens next? Tell us the rest."

My calm tone reassured him. "After about an hour, once you've run around looking for her, I'm supposed to find Mags in a shed by the Custom House. When you turn up, James will appear and explain it was all a lark."

All a lark. But in an hour Mags could be on her way out of London by coach or wagon and we'd have no way to discover her destination, except I knew both Jeremiah and Gilbert worked for Hazelton. And Jeremiah was going to Barsington.

"Are you supposed to meet with James before you find Mags?" I asked.

His eyes shifted to Kat. "I'm not supposed to tell you."

Esmeralda laughed. "Great Saints! Kidnapping's a hanging offense, and you've already said enough to put a noose 'round your neck, never mind what the rats will do to you."

Potts shook his head stubbornly. "You don't understand."

"Where are you meeting him? The Custom House?"

His eyes widened in surprise, and I knew I was right. "Good. Kat, please ask Jimmy to come here."

She climbed the stairs. Potts watched me, no longer smiling. The candle cast his misshapen shadow on the wall.

"You'll stay here, Potts, until we've decided what to do with you. James knew we wouldn't let you leave. That was part of *his* plan."

Jimmy and Kat came down the stairs.

"Jimmy, Potts brought James inside Haven and it's James who took Mags. She's probably already sold to the trackers. We need to make sure Potts doesn't get away and cause more trouble. The trackers have figured out he knows Haven's location. Tie him up if you have to. We need guards on the door from now on."

The look in Jimmy's eyes didn't bode well for Potts. Soon every rat would know what Potts had done. "Don't worry, Lizzie. We know what to do with informers. Come with me, Potts." Jimmy pulled Potts to his feet and began to drag him up the stairs.

Potts hung back, whining, "Not true. 'Tisn't what happened."

I took a breath and let it out. What I did next had to be the right thing, or we'd lose both Mags and Haven. If we didn't go after her, the oath would be meaningless, so we had to. Besides, I was certain Gilbert would hurt her because of me.

But what about the rest of the rats?

I waited until Potts was out of earshot and said to Kat, "I'm going to look for Mags by the Custom House. Penny and Jimmy should be able to handle things here. If you have folk you trust to protect Haven, Kat, now's the time. Ask them to keep watch over the alley and stop any grown man from coming here."

She nodded. "I can send a message from the Custom House."

I spoke softly. "I can't let James get away with this. If the trackers have Mags, I'm going after her. Will either of you go with me?"

Esmeralda rolled her eyes. "I've been trying to get *you* to leave. I can be ready in an hour. I have to tell Serena where we're going —if you know."

"I believe I do. If Mags isn't at the Custom House, we're going to Barsington, to Lord Hazelton's estate. Meet us at the Custom House in an hour." Esmeralda nodded and squeezed through the door.

I turned to Kat. "What about you? Can you get away?"

A flicker of a smile. "Wouldn't miss it for the world."

22

THE CUSTOM HOUSE

Potts was shut away in the storeroom, with an iron bar through the hasp. He wouldn't be warning James today.

I threw on my cloak and gathered some things in a bundle tied beneath my skirt, next to the pocket holding my glass, my flint and steel, and a few coins. I was ready to leave the city.

But when I returned to the cellar, Mattie blocked the door, her arms folded. The rest of the rats stood around her.

"You're not going alone," she said. "We took the oath to help each other, yet at the first sign o' trouble you want us to hide. That's not right, and we're coming with you."

Heads nodded in the candlelight. Jimmy had followed me down the stairs. "She's right, Lizzie. All of us can fight the trackers, not just you. Isn't that what our practicing was for?"

I bit back what I'd been about to say, my thoughts in a jumble. I'd wanted the rats to defend themselves if trouble found them, but I'd never meant them to go looking for it.

Kat joined us, with her cloak on. "They're right. We'll find Mags more quickly with their help, if she's still here. They swore an oath to help her. We should all go."

Do they understand the danger? I wanted to say no, but they were right. "Very well," I said to the expectant faces. "But you have to agree to two things: First, you'll obey my orders without question. We can't have everyone running off and deciding what to do on their own. Second, if we don't find Mags and she's left London, everyone returns to Haven except Kat, Esmeralda, and me. We'll go after her. The rest of you will protect Haven and each other."

"But how will you know where to go, Lizzie?" Mattie asked.

They should know the worst. "I believe she's been nobbled by Hazelton. I saw the inn where they're taking her in a vision, remember?" Heads nodded. No one even looked surprised.

"But…she could still be here, if it was really a prank?" one of the girls asked.

"I hope so." I searched their faces. "Do you promise to return to protect Haven if we can't find her?"

"We promise," they chorused.

"Good. Penny, can you find us a bite to eat for the journey?"

"Already done." She handed me a cloth bag. "And we've enough food to stay inside for a while, too, thanks to Kat."

"Mattie and I made a guard schedule for the door," Jimmy said.

I nodded. "Sounds like you've thought of everything."

"If you go out to buy supplies," Kat said, "take a guard with you—Mattie, Jimmy, or Penny."

That was all the planning we could do. For the rest, I'd rely on Penny and Jimmy's good sense. "Let's leave in groups of three."

The rats lined up by the door, faces solemn.

After checking the mirror in the alley, Kat and I left first. Our cloaks were dripping by the time we reached Thames Street. Few people were out and no one approached us on our way to the Custom House. An hour had passed since Potts had beckoned to Mags from the stairs. If we saw James, we'd know one way or t'other whether this was a prank or he'd sold Mags to a tracker. But I didn't expect James or Mags to be there.

We trooped across the muddy yard, past the Custom House, to the sheds. No one else was out in the rain on a Sunday. I was about to open a door when Kat suggested we look for James inside the Custom House, while the others searched the sheds.

"Each group of three, pick a row, start at the end, and work your way back. If there's trouble, one can run to tell the others." They looked so serious and grim. Only an hour ago they'd been laughing and playing, proud of themselves. I hoped James *was* in the Custom House, so I could damage his poxy face.

The sheds stored ships' cargo before they were seen by Customs. The clerks would suspect us of thievery if they saw us entering the sheds, so it was a clever hiding place, if that's where they'd stashed Mags. We'd have to risk it.

Inside the Custom House, Kat and I walked slowly down the main aisle, past two clerks standing at their desks. The torches in wall cressets barely lightened the gloom, and our footsteps echoed in the cavernous building. A strong draught of cold air blew in from the door, defeating any hope of warmth from the tiny fire at the far end, spreading smoke throughout the building. It was a damp and cheerless place.

Women weren't often seen in the Custom House, and a well-dressed merchant stared as we passed. Another merchant, fat and well-dressed, followed me with his eyes, thoughtfully stroking his moustache. I quickened my pace.

I had a story ready, if we were challenged, saying I'd heard my father's ship had come in the night before. I stared hard into the shadows and made sure to look in every corner.

James wasn't there.

"Do you know what James' gift is?" Kat whispered in my ear.

"No, do you?"

Kat glanced over her shoulder. "Yes. In the market I once saw him swipe fruit from a costermonger's stall. A bailiff ran after him but when he caught up with him, he walked right past, as though he couldn't see him."

"But you could see him?"

"I wasn't the one he was hiding from. He can pass unseen when he wants to. He might be here and we'd never know."

"There's no sign of the trackers either. Let's help search the sheds. I'd hate to think Mags was still here and about to be taken away under our noses."

Kat said, "Wait for a me a moment?"

I nodded, mystified. She crossed the room to speak with a man I hadn't seen before, his grey clothing fading into the shadows of the room. Even before Kat returned to my side he had disappeared. "Ready," she said.

The rats were working their way from the far end, nearest the wharf, opening doors and calling Mags' name. I started from the other end, opening the door to the shed closest to the Custom House.

It smelled of damp earth. I lit the torch by the door and held it up. There was no hiding place behind the barrels and crates resting on wooden pallets. The spicy scent of pepper filled my nose and I sneezed, almost dropping the torch.

"Bless you," Kat said, looking past me.

"Nothing." I tugged the stiff door, swollen with the damp, until it shut.

The next one had crates and sacks, and strange, tall plants in a row of pots. I stepped inside to raise the torch, the flame flickering as the rain struck it. We examined each shed in the row methodically, one after the other, moving inside to check dark corners. None held a captive, or looked as though they ever had. The final door had a padlock upon it, so I pounded on the door and called her name, and put my ear to it. There was no sound.

The other rats were approaching our end. I was about to open the door of the next shed, when it burst open by itself.

Two men ran at us, swords drawn. One crowed, "Gilbert's

jade! Told ye we'd get her if we bided our time. You'll be a nice fat bonus for us, Prophetess!"

It was Hawkins, the man who'd wanted to 'stick Lord Hazelton' in my vision. He circled Kat, smiling.

Then she disappeared. So did his smile. He hacked at the air around him.

The man coming for me was a ginger-haired stranger. I stepped backwards, my eyes on his sword, and tripped over the hem of my cloak, falling into the mud. "Where's Mags?" I demanded, trying to rise. He smiled, the tip of his blade coming to rest on my breastbone.

Then the rats were on us, yelling bloody murder. Hawkins and Ginger turned to meet this new threat, but it was too late. Jimmy knocked the sword from Hawkins' hand and punched him, hard, in the face. When he tried to get up, Jimmy used his sword to indicate he should stay down.

Mattie tackled Ginger at the knees, but he wriggled away, and was able to grab one of the girls, pinning her arms behind her. With the tap of her finger, Penny sent him to sleep. He fell face down in the mud.

It had taken mere seconds for the wharf rats to disarm the trackers. They grinned at each other, well pleased with themselves, rattails of wet hair plastered on their faces.

Ginger was out cold and Hawkins sat in the mud watching us, his own sword at his throat.

For his benefit I said, "I supposed we'll have to kill them." His eyes widened in shock and he stopped watching Jimmy to look at me.

Then I realized I was seriously considering it. We didn't have Mags here to question them, and if they couldn't give us information, they were useless, although I considered letting Mattie break his arm to see if that would work. They were far too dangerous to let loose.

Kat reappeared. "Are there any more trackers besides these?"

"Not that we saw," Jimmy said. "Most of the sheds were empty."

My hands were shaking, my body only now reacting to the danger that had come and gone so quickly. I stood over Hawkins. "What have you done with Mags?"

He laughed. "Ye can't *make* me say anything, wharf rat. But it gives me the greatest pleasure to tell ye the little black girl is long gone, and you'll ne'er see her again. Or mebbe you will; Gilbert will be back for ye, I'd put money on that." He spat, just missing my boot.

Mattie kicked him in the ribs, none too gently.

The rogue was probably telling the truth. There'd been more than enough time to spirit Mags out of London, probably on her way to the *Orb and Sceptre*.

Kat said, "If Gilbert and Jeremiah have already left with Mags, then these two must not be that important. They probably don't know anything." Hawkins eyes glittered. His hand moved toward the knife on his belt.

Mattie kicked him again and pushed him down into the mud, her boot pressing firmly on his throat. He gasped, his hand still reaching for the knife. "Go ahead, try it," she coaxed. His hand dropped and she took the knife away.

"Their job was to catch whoever came after her," Kat continued. "I doubt James was here for long. Once he'd delivered Mags, his work was done."

Ginger woke up and moaned, loudly. He started to push himself up but Jimmy warned him, "Stay down or you'll get a beating." He lay down again, on his back, watching us with frightened eyes.

I drew Kat aside and whispered. "What can we do with them? If we let them go, they'll follow the rats home."

"I know what I'd like to do," she said, "but I won't ask it of the rats. Let's tie 'em up, and Penny can put them to sleep for a long time." I nodded.

I stood over Hawkins. "If you both swear you'll leave London and never bother us again, we'll let you go."

He laughed. "Your friend James said you were a great believer in words. We'll say whatever ye like, but just so ye knows, we don't pay much heed to God talk." Mattie applied pressure to his throat again and he waved a hand. "I swear I'll leave London, wench. But Lord Hazelton will know *all* your secrets soon enough. Then we'll clean out the lot of ye."

That was probably the truth, as he knew it. I took the sword from Jimmy and placed the tip on Ginger's neck, then pointed at a coil of rope. "How are your sailor's knots, Jimmy? Can you tie their hands and feet together?"

Jimmy smiled. "Soon done, Lizzie."

It was harder to convince Penny to put them to sleep, but she did it. We left them in an unlocked shed, so they'd be found eventually, their feet and hands trussed together like pigs in the market, snoring away.

"Let's get out of the wet." I pointed toward the watermen's hut by the Custom House stairs and led the way there. I waited until everyone was inside and quiet.

"I have two things to say. First: I'm proud of you all. You fought for Mags and the Guild and you brought those trackers down in seconds flat. Remember you can do that. These cowards are no match for us when we're quick and careful and work together. You were smart and brave."

Their eyes shone.

"The second is: we'll hold to the rules I laid down. Penny and Jimmy will be in charge at Haven. Go to them if you have problems or questions. Kat, Esmeralda, and I will go after Mags. We're going to Barsington, where Lord Hazelton lives. We'll get her back if we have to walk up and knock on the front door. Get back into your groups and head for home. Watch out for more trackers. If any try to follow you, remember what you just did. Remember you can fight—and *win.*"

We said our farewells. The rats were grim but determined. A few hours ago they'd been singing songs and playing games. Now they knew they could fight and win, but it had sobered them. They were soldiers taking orders, not children any longer. James, Potts, and the trackers had taken that away from them.

23

ON THE NORTH ROAD

THREE SHEDS REMAINED. I'd believed Hawkins when he said Mags was already gone, but I couldn't leave without checking. The first was empty. The second held only cobwebs shivering in the draft. I had my hand on the latch to the third when a voice said, "She's not there."

It was Thomas. "They've already left. Word in the market is, two trackers left an hour ago in a coach with a coat of arms on the door. They were carrying a sack and went out the Aldgate on the Cambridge Road."

Kat pushed her cloak away from her face. "Who told you?"

"The Sweets. They heard it from someone they trust, and I think 'tis true for I just saw James in the Saracen's Head. He was drunk as a lord and flashing gold coins, boasting that he's paid you back, Lizzie. He said he sold Mags for a purse full o' gold. He said if you hadn't been nobbled as well, I could find you by the Custom House, to ask how you liked his surprise." He wiped the rain out of his eyes. "Mags is gone. I'm sorry. Are you all right?"

I nodded. All I could think to say was, "You've been following James. Why?"

"I suspected he was working with trackers. Now I know for sure," he said.

"Do you still believe Cynthia's tale?" I asked.

He sighed deeply, shaking his head. "No. I've been a fool. Is there anything I can do?"

"Thanks for telling us about James, Thomas," Kat said, glancing at me. "The Wharf Rats Guild will decide what to do." She tucked my arm beneath hers and led me away.

I looked back. "Thanks for your help," I called.

He lifted a hand in farewell, looking sad.

"Come on, let's get out of the wet," Kat said.

We hurried inside the Custom House, shaking the rain off our cloaks. The sole remaining clerk shot us a nasty look. "'Tis closing time," he said, rattling his keys meaningfully.

Kat ignored him, steering me toward the far end of the room and its sputtering fire.

"Do you think James has been selling kinchin to the trackers all along?" I asked. She removed her cloak and held it before the grate. Steam rose from it.

"Probably," Kat said. "There's not much difference between an agent and someone who hands children over to trackers, in my book. So what's your plan when we get to Barsington? Will you march up to Hazelton's door and ask politely for him to return Mags?"

"Once we see the lay of the land, we'll think of something," I said, sounding more confident than I felt.

"I'd feel better if it was more definite," Kat muttered, swinging her cloak across her shoulders.

Clop, clop, clop. The sound of wooden pattens came toward us.

"Really, this is too much," the clerk objected.

A tall, cloaked figure approached, the clerk weaving from side to side in its wake, a small skiff trying to stop a merchantman. "Madam, we're closing. You shouldn't be here unescorted!"

"My good man, I shan't trouble you long." Esmeralda spoke in her haughtiest tones. "Would you deny an old woman a fire on such a terrible day?" She was wrapped head to toe in a cloak trimmed with white fur, a tapestry bag over her arm. A waxed paper parasol, green with red parrots painted on it, was angled over her head. She was the very image of a lady of fashion, balancing on wooden pattens to keep her pretty satin shoes from the muck. She bore down on us, a valiant, full-breasted galleon, with the clerk at her heels.

When she reached us, she asked, "Are you ready?"

"I must insist you leave," the clerk said shrilly.

Kat hid a smile behind her hand.

Esmeralda took each of us by the arm. Then, as one, we turned and proceeded sedately toward the door.

If the trackers were going to Barsington, they'd take the North Road, which began at the Aldgate. It would take them at least a day in a coach. We couldn't afford a coach, but if we were lucky, we could ask a passing carter or farmer for a ride on his wagon. On foot it would take us a couple of days to get there, and we'd be in no good state when we arrived. We wouldn't catch up with the kidnappers that way.

"By the way," Kat said casually, "I've hired a coach. The coachman will meet us in Saint Dunstan's courtyard." That was only a few streets away. I pushed my cloak aside to see her expression.

Esmeralda didn't appear surprised. "What an extravagance! Are you sure your master can afford it?" I'd expected her to object, but she looked pleased. I suppose she hadn't relished the idea of traveling in a farmer's wagon, and she wouldn't get far tottering on those pattens either.

"The trackers have a head start. We need to get as far north as we can today. The longer it rains, the greater the risk the road will become impassable. It's lucky for us Barsington is on the Cambridge road. That's in better repair than most," Kat said calmly.

How did she know that, and why was her patron supplying us with a coach? I tried and failed to imagine how our pursuit of Mags could benefit a nob. Unless *he* wanted to use her too.

We entered the grey stone courtyard of Saint Dunstan's to find the coach waiting as promised. It was beautiful, far too fine for middling folk, never mind wharf rats: a shiny black coach with yellow trim and wheels. The coachman let down the accordion stairs and we climbed inside. The rain beat heavily on the leather roof, and I was glad to be out of it. Rain dripped from the edges of the leather curtains covering the windows, but it was mostly dry inside and luxurious compared to a journey on foot in the wind and rain. We crowded together in the middle to avoid the drops that scattered across the coach when it bounced and jolted.

We drove north, lurching over the muddy, potholed road, until late in the evening. The bouncing made me grit my teeth, as it jarred the wound in my side. In the dark coach, with the rain pounding on the roof, I had ample time to reconsider what I thought I knew. If James helped trackers nobble children for Lord Hazelton, maybe that was what had happened to Daniel. Potts had seen Daniel heal Penny's leg that day in Bridewell. He could have gotten a message to James through that crooked jailer. Maybe when we arrived in Barsington we'd find not only Mags, but Daniel as well. If he was alive.

The rain slackened briefly, but by the time we stopped, long past the hour I wanted my supper, it beat down heavily once more.

Esmeralda and I climbed down in the courtyard of what turned out to be *The Robin Hood Inn* of Caxton, stiff and bruised, while Kat consulted the coachman.

Streams chuckled over the courtyard cobbles and gurgled down the rain spouts to splash over the edges of the rain barrels and pool in the courtyard. We had to wade through fast-moving water to reach the stairs.

The horses were lathered, their flanks shivering. They looked as exhausted as I felt. We'd been thrown and jostled against each other and the walls of the coach for hours. And the roads would only be worse tomorrow. The coachman said the horses could go no further tonight, Kat reported, then added she'd intended to stop here all along. Esmeralda gave her a sharp look.

It was clear now that Kat wasn't a wharf rat at all, or not only a wharf rat. With money and a coach at her beck and call, Kat was someone of importance. I still believed she was a friend of the Guild, but there was nothing I could do about it now if she wasn't.

Two stable boys with sacks over their heads darted from the shelter of the stable roof to unharness the horses. Picking our way carefully across the flooding courtyard, we climbed the stairs and entered the slate-paved entry hall, shaking the rain off boots and cloaks.

The common room was blissfully warm. The innkeeper, an older woman, appeared to recognize Kat when she stepped forward to greet us. While she and Kat conferred about a room, I moved to the wide hearth and its cheerful fire, rubbing my frozen hands. The door to the kitchen opened. A maid came in, carrying a laden tray, bringing appetizing smells in her wake.

Kat and Esmeralda joined me by the fire while we waited for our room to be made ready. I examined the other guests. They looked respectable enough. A few merchants traveling with their wives and local farmers sat at the polished wooden tables with tankards and their dinners. The landlady moved briskly here and there, giving orders to the maids. One brought me hot, spiced wine, and I wrapped my hands around the large mug and began to relax as the warmth spread through me. It was good wine too, and not too heavily spiced.

We were soon seated at the fire in our own room, a maidservant spreading our cloaks on the warming frame before it, and taking our soggy boots to be cleaned. A second maid came in with a tray. She laid a white cloth on the table, then plates and mugs, with a loaf of bread and a jug of ale. There was a knock on the door. When the maid opened it, a young man rolled in a trundle bed, arranging it at the foot of a four-poster hung with curtains.

"That must be for me," I said, walking over to test it. I was the smallest and glad indeed not to have to jockey for space with my two companions in the larger bedstead.

"Supper's on its way." The young man grinned cheekily and sketched a bow before closing the door.

I sat on the small bed, fingering the blue goose-feather quilt and the snowy linens beneath. They were clean, smelling of rosemary and lavender, with no sign of fleas. The *Robin Hood Inn* was clean and well run, and would be expensive. Kat's patron must be paying for this too. I was weary after a long day, and ready to climb into bed, not thinking clearly. But it was time to ask Kat about her patron. We were dependent on him now, on his coach and his money.

Another knock. A second maid balanced a dish of roast fowl, one of vegetables, and a second jug on a tray, then laid them on the table. Before she left she announced, "There'll be music in the common room, if you want to join the company later. A fiddler and a singer. And"—her eyes lit up with excitement—"if you're here tomorrow night, there's to be a play. A local troupe will present *The Roaring Girl* for three nights." Clearly it was a good place to work as well as to stay. Kat walked with the maid to the door and they held a whispered conversation. Kat pressed a coin into her hand.

Esmeralda sat down, shaking out a napkin. "What was that about?" she asked Kat, then placed a chicken breast on her plate. I sat down beside her. Kat sat across from me, pouring herself a tankard of ale.

"I asked if she'd seen two men with a sack arrive, and to ask the other servants without being overheard by her mistress."

Esmeralda tore off a wing of the chicken and took a bite.

"Why don't you want her mistress to hear?" I asked. Fragrant steam rose from the bread I'd torn apart, making my mouth water. I took a bite, and discovered I was ravenous.

"I want to hear her story for myself, so I can compare versions." Kat heaped her plate with food and began to eat. She didn't trust anyone, it seemed.

We were silent, giving our full attention to the food, which was excellent. Esmeralda kept glancing at Kat as though she were a question that needed answering. Finally, when there were more bones than chicken on our plates, Esmeralda refilled her tankard with ale from the jug and pushed her chair back.

She frowned pointedly at Kat, and I thought I knew what was coming. It was my fault I'd left it so long.

To forestall Esmeralda, I said, "I'm grateful for all your help, Kat, but I think it's time you explained who's paying for this. Who exactly do you work for and why would he help the wharf rats? What does he want in return?"

Kat rose and stood by the fire. She took the poker and pushed a log into the middle of the flames, gazing into it as though she'd find answers there. "Someone who doesn't like Lord Hazelton any more than we do," she said quietly. "And yes, he may find the wharf rats useful one day. Not," she said quickly, when she saw my expression, "not as slaves but as willing servants, paid and protected, if we aid him in his cause."

I studied her face. She met my eyes steadily, with no sign of uneasiness or deceit.

"And what exactly is this cause?" Esmeralda asked.

"The cause of a free England, free from foreign interference and ruled by the rightful king, not some upstart murderer who calls himself a lord," Kat said. "I can't reveal his name, but I'd wager Esmeralda's already guessed it. Would you care to tell Lizzie?" She lifted her chin defiantly.

"You're one of the Duke of York's spies," Esmeralda said heavily. "You work for those plaguey Stuarts, our old enemy from the war."

Kat laughed, dismissing the words with a flick of her hand. "The war happened years before I was born. He's not *my* enemy. Consider, Lizzie: he's the second man in the kingdom, the most powerful ally the wharf rats could have besides the king. He's trying to keep the king on the throne, and Lord Hazelton from kidnapping and murdering whomever he likes. Both worthy goals, if you ask me. The duke isn't interested in fighting the battles of the past. He can't. The king has no intention of making the same mistakes as his father."

Charles the First's mistakes had cost him his kingdom and his head. No, Charles the Second would need to be cannier than his father.

Esmeralda snorted and frowned at the fire.

"I don't understand," I said. "I know the Duke of York is the king's brother. But why would he have spies? Besides, the war's over. Who is there to spy on?"

"Every king has enemies, Lizzie," Kat explained. "Other kings. Men like Hazelton. Not everyone who opposed the monarchy during the war is happy it's returned." She glanced at Esmeralda. "People like Esmeralda. Or you." She smiled faintly.

I inhaled sharply. How had she learned that? I'd never said aught to Kat about the king. "I don't waste time plotting against kings, so you needn't worry about me. So let me understand: the Duke of York has been paying for all the things you brought to Haven? And you've been spying on us for him?"

Kat shook her head. "I'm not spying on the rats, Lizzie. At the moment, the duke has never heard of the wharf rats. Someday he will, because they could be useful to him. But yes, I'm using the funds he gives me, to spend as I see fit, to help the rats. I'm building his network in the city. You have to admit the wharf rats could be very useful to him—they can go anywhere without being noticed."

"Like Hazelton's estate, you mean?" I had the uncomfortable thought that the duke might be pleased one of us had been kidnapped. It gave him an excuse to find out more about what was going on inside Hazelton's estate. Kat seemed to know what I was thinking.

"He'll use us for his own ends," she said, nodding, "but so will we use him. Right now our enemy is the same. It would be foolish to reject help from the highest power in the land. Our enemy is almost as powerful as the king. With the duke's help, we have a chance, Lizzie."

"And why didn't you mention this before?" I asked, unfairly perhaps.

"Well, first, because you never asked, and second, because I was waiting for the right moment."

"And this is that moment?" Esmeralda said, coming out of her reverie. From her expression, her thoughts weren't pleasant.

"Yes. Both of you need to know how to get in touch with the network if anything happens to me. Tilda, the landlady here, is the safest person to send a message by. We have contacts here and in Barsington, but the closer we get to Hazelton's manor, the chancier those contacts are. His spies are just as good as ours, and some of *them* are gifted children." She looked grim and I wondered if she'd lost agents to Hazelton.

Kat being a spy for the duke worried me much less than other possibilities. It made sense she was after political information, not looking for children to sell. My worst fear had been that her patron was a nob like Hazelton. It was almost a relief to know she worked for the king's brother.

There was a knock on the door.

In a heartbeat, Kat disappeared. Esmeralda moved to the door and I picked up the poker from the hearth. I stood ready, cursing the maid who had our boots. "Come in," I called.

The landlady entered, smiling. Esmeralda closed the door. "Is everything to your satisfaction? Can we get you anything else?

Bessie will be up shortly with your cleaned boots." She glanced around the room. "I thought there were three of you?"

Kat reappeared behind her and tapped her on the shoulder. She started. "Mistress! You gave me a turn."

"You have something to report about the trackers?" She gestured at us. "You may speak freely."

The landlady took a moment to gaze at Esmeralda and myself in turn, as though she were memorizing our faces. "Yes, there were three men, counting the coachman. They stopped here to eat. I never saw what was in the sack, but it was a child, right enough, from the sounds it made. I heard it when I went in to check on the room. The men yelled at me to get out, but not before I heard whimpering. Those evil-faced coves were ready to cut my throat."

"When was this?" I asked.

"About half past one."

"They'll be in Barsington tonight then," said Kat. "Well, we won't catch up with them, but at least we know we're going in the right direction. I'll have messages to send on the morrow."

Tilda curtsied and headed for the door, but turned before she opened it. "I near forgot. There's a cove asking for news of a woman named Esmeralda." She glanced at her. "I thought I'd warn you, in case you thought to hear the fiddler."

"Good work, finding out about the child. I won't forget."

The landlady curtsied again and glanced at Esmeralda curiously before she left.

I waited until the door had closed before turning to her. "Is this something we should know about?"

Esmeralda smiled and said smugly. "I can have secrets too." Then she laughed at our expressions. "Oh, pish. I told you, Lizzie —I sent word to friends that I was looking for work at the fairs, long before Mags was kidnapped. That was my plan to get you out of London and away from your tracker. It will probably be a message saying someone's found me work."

"But how did this friend know you'd be in Caxton tonight, and at this inn?" Kat said sharply. I wondered that too. *I hadn't known we'd be stopping here.*

She shrugged, but her lips thinned to a line. "Caxton is the logical place to stop, and this is the best inn in Caxton. Is that so mysterious?"

"You were part of Thurloe's network during the war," Kat said. It was a statement.

Esmeralda took the poker from my hand and turned to prod the fire with it. The silence drew out. "I've no idea what you're talking about."

"Thurloe's network?" I asked.

"Thurloe was Cromwell's spy master during the Commonwealth," Kat said, watching Esmeralda. "Which could be a problem if she's currently working against the king. If you are, we'll find out soon enough. Thurloe works *for* the king now. He values his skin."

Esmeralda replaced the poker in its stand, her face expressionless. "Hmph. As if we don't have more pressing matters to worry about."

"Once you got a job at the fair, what did you think Kat and I would do?" I couldn't imagine us fitting in easily among jugglers, clowns, and ropedancers.

"Oh, someone always needs help. You'd blend in well enough. Fair folk are rightfully proud of their skills, but they welcome anyone ready to lend a hand."

I yawned. I couldn't worry about it tonight; I was too tired. "I'm for bed. Anyone else?"

Kat said casually, "There's a fair held every year near Hazelton's manor, I believe. Barsington Fair. Would you know anyone there, perhaps?"

"You *are* well informed," Esmeralda said.

"Working at the fair would be a good cover story for why we're there," Kat said.

Esmeralda's eyes were flinty. "I'll agree to that if you promise not to spy on the fair folk. I'll not bring a sneak into their company."

"I'm not interested in the doings of mountebanks, jack-puddings, and tumblers."

"Promise me, then."

Kat grimaced. "Very well, I promise. I'm only interested in Hazelton and his men."

Esmeralda rose to her feet. "Then I'd better find that fellow in the common room. You needn't wait up. Good night."

Once the door closed, I swiftly shed my skirt and bodice, placing them at the foot of the bed. I crawled between the fragrant sheets and murmured, "Kat, I don't care if she's working for the king of France, I've got to sleep. Anyway," I yawned, "if I'm surrounded by spies, how much safer could I be?"

Kat didn't answer. I heard the boards creak as she padded softly to the door in her stocking feet, and the sound of the door opening and closing.

BARSINGTON FAIR

Lord Hazelton sat in a dark room, his face illuminated by two white candles. Within their pool of light, a crystal ball cast a prism of light on a square of blue velvet. Behind him, the wall seemed to billow and collapse like sails in the wind. Wisps of white smoke drifted into Hazelton's face. He coughed, but continued to stare at the woman across from him.

A scarf covered her hair, and when she adjusted her shawl of brightly patterned silk, her headdress of pierced coins tinkled softly. The face beneath the headscarf was shadowed, and her dark, deep-set eyes never blinked. It was her stillness, more than the wrinkled folds at the corners of her eyes and mouth, which gave the impression of great age.

She unwrapped the velvet square, revealing a deck of cards painted in garish colors. She shuffled them, eyes shut, muttering, then slapped them on the table. She tapped the top of the deck. "You must cut. Three times."

He leaned forward and cut the deck with his right hand, then again and again. The woman took the stacks and placed the last on top of the other, then dealt two cards face up in front of her.

"You have great wealth and great power." She tapped the card with a picture of a man holding a sword. "Many people do your will. What you ask for happens. You've done terrible things and overcome great obstacles." She pointed to a card with a crudely drawn picture of a man on a throne with a crown on his head and the word *Rex* written above it. "You have almost reached your heart's desire."

She laid another card across the Emperor and tapped it. It showed a picture of a child riding a horse, the sun rising behind her, with the word *Sol* written above. "But there are forces crossing you; to save yourself you will need extraordinary luck. Children will try to stop you; they will be your downfall, unless you use your power wisely."

"But surely the Sun is good luck," Lord Hazelton protested in a strangely shrill voice. "I know that much. It should be a *good* omen."

"You know the cards better than Maglena?" She laughed, revealing gaps in her teeth. "The cards *speak* to me. They tell me what to say. Children will fight you." She placed several more cards on the table, until she had formed a cross. "Unless you stop them, they will be your death."

Lord Hazelton appeared stricken, his face pale. He chewed his lip and said, "God's blood! What must I do? How can I prevent it?"

She grinned. "Maglena can help. I have a blessed charm, sanctified with the blood of martyrs, and bathed in powerful herbs only the gypsies know. But I have only one left. I don't know if I can sell it."

"I will pay whatever you ask," Lord Hazelton said urgently. "I must have it. Nothing must go wrong. I'm too close!"

"Very well." She reached below the table into her skirts and placed a glass bottle filled with amber-colored liquid on the table. "I will tell you how to use it. But first you must cross my palm with silver again." Her smile never reached her hooded eyes.

The glass went dark. I blinked, and the sunlit room came into focus. The pale square of sunlight on the wall hadn't moved since I'd taken out my glass.

In the large bedstead behind me, there was only one lump under the blankets, and the sound of gentle breathing. I reached for my clothes and began to dress.

Lord Hazelton had believed every word the fortune-teller said. If we knew what his heart's desire was, perhaps we could use it against him. Maglena's talent might be real—after all, mine was. The children she warned him against must be his collection of gifted children. That gave me hope. Maybe he couldn't control them completely. And his obvious belief in fortune telling explained why he needed me to be his "prophetess."

I went to the eastern window and pushed the curtain aside. The courtyard below was still, and a mist floated in the far fields. Not even birdsong broke the early morning stillness.

Kat sat up in the bed. "'Morning, Lizzie," she said with a yawn. She glanced around the room. "Where's Esmeralda?"

"I don't know. What happened between you two after I went to bed?"

Kat began to curse steadily and fluently, throwing aside the bedclothes. She ran to the door in her shift and yelled loudly down the hall for the maid, then turned to me.

"Her things are gone. She's left without us."

When a sleepy-eyed maid appeared, we learned Esmeralda had hired a horse a few hours before and ridden off. The maid didn't know where she'd gone, but her mistress might. She went to find her. Kat was calling herself names. "I should've expected this. I was getting too close to finding out why she's here."

In less than half an hour we had breakfasted and were ready to leave. Kat spoke with Tilda, while I waited inside the coach. I wasn't looking forward to another bruising journey, but every moment we delayed made it more likely that Mags would be a prisoner in Hazelton's manor before we could reach her. I couldn't guess what Esmeralda was up to. I leaned out the coach window to catch Kat's eye, impatient to be off.

"'Tis a pity about the little girl. They were none too kind to her," Tilda was saying. "But it's more than my life's worth to interfere with Hazelton's men. They come through here about once a fortnight, throwing money around. I keep an eye on 'em and pass the word just as you said. I only hope one of these days someone will put a stop to it. I suppose the king's too busy with his dogs and his mistresses." It seemed even those who worked for the king were impatient with his weaknesses.

"Keep sending word. Something will be done," Kat said. She climbed inside and rapped the ceiling. The coachman started off, the sound of the horses loud on the cobbles in the early morning stillness. As we left Caxton, I told Kat about my vision.

"Perhaps we could use that," Kat said. "If we knew more about it. But for certain, he'll want more predictions of the future."

"And here I am, you mean? If we don't catch up with the trackers before they reach the manor, I could let myself be captured. If Hazelton comes to rely on my visions, I'd be too valuable for Gilbert to hurt. Maybe he'd even do what I advise him to do. And we'd find Mags." *And perhaps Daniel.*

Kat shook her head. "That is *not* what I meant. Mags might not even be there. Letting yourself be nobbled isn't a plan, it's giving up. A bloodthirsty rogue like Hazelton won't care if Gilbert slices you up. We can't predict what he'll do, visions or no. Why hasn't even one gifted child escaped? There's too much we don't know: how Hazelton controls the children, or what he uses them for. We should be cautious."

"So what's *your* plan?"

"First, gather information in the village and at the fair. Second, find Esmeralda." She rolled her eyes. "If she's even there. I think she will be; she's probably gone to talk to her contacts at the fair. They may know something useful, and I have someone in the village."

"How did Esmeralda's contact know she'd be in Caxton?"

Kat sighed heavily. "I don't know. Seems there's a lot we don't know about our Mistress Esmeralda."

Once we arrived in Barsington, surely we'd hear rumors of Mags or Daniel. If all else failed, I'd find Hazelton's men and let them capture me. I'd prefer that Kat agree to the plan, so she could follow me, or come with me, invisible, but I'd do it anyway. It was the best way to get inside. "When we arrive, let's find the *Orb and Sceptre*. We know Mags was there—maybe she still is."

Kat nodded absently.

With the leather curtains open, the scents of a warm day flooded in, mown hay and flowers in the hedgerows. We bounced along the rutted road for three hours, making good time in the clear weather.

Then we came over a hill, and the village appeared in the distance. The coach overtook a long train of brightly painted wagons, with people walking behind them.

"Fair folk," Kat said.

We passed them quickly, and entered the village itself, half-timbered houses with thatched roofs set around the commons. It was ten o'clock of a hot sunny morning when we stepped down at the village green, our cloaks over our arms. I rubbed my sore hip, happy to be out of the coach. I felt a hostile gaze on my back and turned. The leader of a flock of geese took a step toward me, hissing.

Kat said a few words to the coachman and waved him off. "He has to return to London." I watched my last tie to the river and my home clatter off in a cloud of dust. "How will we get home?"

"Let's worry about finding Mags first."

The sound of creaking carts and jingling harness grew louder, and the caravan of wagons came into view. Some were small cottages on wheels, elaborately painted and gilded, like fairy cottages moving through the countryside, with wheels of yellow or red. Some had signs painted on them. The sign on the green cart proclaimed "the finest players in the kingdom, performing *The Roaring Girl* and *The Brazen Head*." Then a blue wagon passed, bearing a hand covered in occult symbols. I stopped to watch it go past.

Maglena the fortune-teller sat on the driving bench with two raggedy children beside her. The boy saw me staring and made a face, sticking out his tongue. He was perhaps eight, with a dirty face and raggedly chopped brown hair. The little girl beside him, her probably-blonde hair matted and dirty, stared vacantly ahead. Didn't Maglena know Barsington wasn't a good place for children?

"Egyptians, too, I see," Kat said thoughtfully. "You'll have competition for your fortune telling."

"Ha."

Once the final wagon passed, we joined the line behind them. I introduced myself to the woman next to me and said I'd come to work the fair.

Heads turned. Not all of the expressions were friendly. I quickly added that we were apprentices to the Great Esmeralda, Rope Dancer extraordinaire, hoping she was actually there. "And we're happy to help anyone who needs it," Kat added. Folk smiled then.

I chatted with two women who ran a booth for games of skill. Kat asked questions about the different acts. A man next to her said, "Everyone talks about Saint Bartholomew's Fair, but once you're out of London, most folk have never seen these plays before. They'll come more than once, too, if they've coin to spare. Good takings." No one said a word about Hazelton, but the only kinchin I saw were the two on Maglena's wagon.

The line slowed as the carts climbed a steep hill. The yellow caravan directly in front of us creaked loudly as the tired horse slowed. At the top, Kat and I stood aside, letting folk pass.

Below us, ropes enclosed a large field, with separate areas

marked off for wagons and horses. Smoke rose from the cooking fires beside wagons already parked, but no children played beside them.

Brightly dressed people were working hard, setting up tents and booths in the main fairway. They called to each other, working quickly, while others unloaded canvas and rope and wooden stalls. Booths for gingerbread and roasted apples were already doing a brisk business, while the local tavern had tapped a barrel of ale and set out tables and benches. Curious locals wandered the lanes, servants slacking from work, or young men looking for excitement.

Two jugglers in harlequin costumes tossed clubs back and forth. A woman wrapped in shawls of every color walked past them to speak to a man wearing pink stockings and a short silvery cape, with no sign of breeches below it. It was difficult not to stare.

"Halloo! Halloo! There you are!" Esmeralda climbed down from the yellow caravan and hurried toward us. "How clever of you to arrive on time!" she said cheerfully. "I told everyone about you and you're expected." She smiled and pulled me into a tight hug. "Play along or you'll land us all in it," she whispered fiercely in my ear.

"It's good to see you again," I said awkwardly.

Kat looked amused. "Well, Esmeralda, how've you been keeping since we saw you last?"

"Oh, pretty well, pretty well. Come, let's talk." She hooked her arms through ours, and we followed the caravan down the hill.

She spoke rapidly, in a soft voice. "Word in the village is that it's impossible to get into the estate. No one gets in, and no one's ever escaped. The few who tried to rescue a child were never seen again."

Grim news, but no worse than we'd expected. "Do they know how Hazelton controls the gifted kinchin?"

She shook her head. "No one knows."

"Why did you leave without us?" I demanded.

"Had to. Message from a friend. Besides, arriving in a coach would arouse suspicions."

"A message you couldn't tell us about?" Kat asked innocently.

"Nothing to do with you."

"Why *are* you here, Esmeralda?" Kat asked.

Esmeralda took a breath and let it out. "I'm searching for a man. He works for Hazelton. Nothing to concern you two, but I *will* be busy with the act and with this—other matter. It won't interfere with looking for Mags."

Kat and I exchanged glances. *Nothing to concern us?*

"But Esmeralda—" I began.

"One thing more," Esmeralda interrupted, "don't tell any of the fair folk the real reason we're here. Hazelton has a spy among them. Now I must go: I have a rehearsal. Don't look so gloomy and *try to fit in.*" She let go of our arms and walked off to greet someone.

I was upset. Esmeralda wasn't here to find Mags at all. Kat wouldn't agree to my plan, yet had none of her own. I was on my own.

Once Esmeralda was busy with her performance and Kat was looking for her contact, I'd be free to do some spying of my own. Hazelton's men were bound to be here; Mags might be with them. If I got into trouble, I trusted Kat to help. I wasn't so sure about Esmeralda.

The moment I'd seen Maglena on her cart, I knew Hazelton would come to the fair to have his fortune told. Why a man of wealth and power would trust a wandering vagabond to advise him was beyond me, but all I needed to do was stick close to Maglena and wait. I was bound to learn something.

We walked down the hill, each lost in our own thoughts.

The fare gate was up and people were paying, but once we said we were with Esmeralda the fare taker waved us through.

Performers and booth owners waved and called greetings to each other as more carts arrived.

Kat and I passed a stage, the curtain already in place. A placard proclaimed *The History of Friar Bungay and Friar Bacon and their Brazen Head; with the Merry Conceits of their Man Miles*. I'd seen the play at Saint Bartholomew's Fair, and been pleasantly frightened by the spooky head of brass, created to predict the future. It was a crowd favorite. Fortune-tellers used a picture of the Brazen Head on their signs. That's how I hoped to find Maglena.

"It's all very well for Esmeralda to say we should try to fit in," Kat said, "but how exactly? All this hugging and kissing. Help me find the tavern: that's where my contact should be." Even as we passed, booths sprang up like jack-in-the-boxes, men and women straining at the ropes.

"You look for the tavern, I'll ask for the *Orb and Sceptre*."

"We don't even know for sure it's in Barsington," Kat pointed out.

"We could ask more people if we split up," I said, impatient to be on my own.

"How will I find you again?"

"Let's meet at the food booths at noon."

She nodded and headed toward the stand with the cask of ale.

My intention was to look for Maglena's booth, but I was distracted by the attractions. Fair folk who'd heard Kat's offer stopped me to ask for help, so I pulled on ropes and fitted wooden frames together for the stalls. After I helped set up the ring toss, I took three tries, and spectacularly missed every one. The owner had never heard of the *Orb and Sceptre*.

A young apprentice took a swing at the *Try Your Strength* hammer. He reminded me a bit of Thomas, being brown and muscular, except he was gap-toothed and laughed idiotically when the bobbin rose only to the level of *Weakling*. He looked proud of himself anyway, so I doubted he could read. Thomas wouldn't laugh idiotically.

"You're one of the wenches with Esmeralda, aren't ye? Care to try it?" The man asking the question had a black mustache and was wearing a wide red leather belt and short breeches to show off his muscles, which were considerable.

I looked at the painting on the canvas behind him. "Are you Mr. Morpurgo, the Amazing Strong Man?"

He grinned and said, "That I am, lass. Have a go. No charge."

"Ta, then." I smiled and picked up the hammer, which weighed several pounds.

I swung the hammer as hard as I could, but the little bobbin barely rose to *"Death's door."* Mr. Morpurgo smiled and slapped me on the shoulder. "Nice try, lass. Come back when you're a lad." He laughed at his brilliant joke. I was too disgusted to ask about the inn.

I stopped at a booth selling ale to ask if they were from the *Orb and Sceptre.*

"What, you've come here to insult us?" the barmaid asked.

"No, I just want directions—"

"Their ale is horse piss compared to ours. You going to order or not?"

"Where's your ale from, then?"

"Green Bush tavern. What'll you have?"

"Can you give me directions to the inn? I'm meeting someone there."

"Too bad. If you're not a customer, be off." There was a hard gleam in her eye and I left. If she was Kat's contact, I doubted she'd be much help.

I had yet to see any sign with a Brazen Head on it, or Maglena, but I spotted Esmeralda and a man in a shimmering purple cloak with white paint on his face. They were discussing business, to judge by Esmeralda's steely expression. The man spoke loudly and pretended to pull out his hair before finally throwing up his hands.

"Esmeralda, do you have a moment?" I'd come up from behind her.

"I'll see you later, Malcolm," Esmeralda said. "Thirty percent, mind." Malcolm glared but nodded with a defeated sigh.

"You haven't forgotten why we're here, have you?" I asked.

She looked down her long nose. "Of course not. But if I say I'm looking for work I can hardly refuse it when it's offered. And in case you hadn't noticed, my performing makes it easier for the fair people to accept you. They think you're trustworthy because I said so. Since we don't know who the informer is, we should act like we're here to work."

During my search for Maglena's booth, I'd stopped to watch a magician rehearse when another reason for the fair folk's suspicion of outsiders came to me. I leaned close to Esmeralda and whispered, "This would be a safe place for gifted adults. They could hide their talents in plain sight. The public would naturally assume their abilities were illusions or trickery."

Esmeralda stared over my shoulder. "I'm sure I'd never ask such a *personal* question."

So I was right. "Have you heard anything more about the kinchin?"

She shook her head. "I have to get ready for my performance. Where's Kat?"

"Looking for her contact."

"And what will you be doing?" she asked. "Don't do anything stupid, Lizzie. You and Kat should stick together, not go wandering about alone. I'll come find you after the performance. Watch out for Hazelton's men. They're bound to be here."

I nodded, smiling vaguely. She headed for the attiring rooms at the main stage, carrying her bag and parasol.

At that moment, the two children I'd seen on Maglena's cart

ran past, yelling with glee. A portly gentleman, in proper Puritan black, chased them. "My purse! Stop them! Thieves!"

It was wicked of me to laugh, but I couldn't help it; he looked like an outraged rooster. The girl wiggled her fingers insultingly at him before disappearing into the crowd.

She might be running to Maglena's booth. I dived into the crowd after them, hoping they'd lead me to the fortune-teller.

25

JEREMIAH'S SECRET

THE TWO CHILDREN disappeared into the grassy lane between rows of red-striped booths, their blue and red pennants snapping in the breeze. I turned into it and stopped dead.

Jeremiah and Hawkins were directly ahead, standing beside a placard painted with the Brazen Head. Both had their backs to me. Hawkins must've ridden all night to be here before us. Jeremiah was warned we were coming.

I'd found Maglena's booth. Hazelton could be inside at that very moment.

I darted between the booths on the other side, into the narrow gap between them, stumbling over ropes strung like mooring lines. I looked back, breathing hard. They hadn't seen me.

A narrow footpath ran behind the booths and I stumbled down it, wanting to keep an eye on them from a safe distance. When I peered out to check, Hawkins was gone. A nob in a bright yellow periwig had Jeremiah by the arm and they were walking toward me. My heart beat faster, but it wasn't Hazelton. It was the foppish fellow I'd seen in my vision of Gilbert in Paternoster Row. It was easy to recognize him; he wore the same canary-yellow coat. They stopped before reaching me, pushing aside a canvas flap to enter a palm reader's booth.

A woman hurried out, stuffing coins into her belt purse. Making sure I was unobserved, I crossed the grassy aisle, into the gap between tents, and hurried behind the palm reader's booth. The back was nothing but canvas panels loosely laced, like a woman's bodice. I leaned in and put my eye to one of the gaps.

The two men faced each other warily on the grassy floor, ignoring the chairs and table. Daylight came from the door flap, left open.

The man in the periwig wrinkled his nose, and regarded Jeremiah with distaste. He lifted a yellow shoe to examine it, tapping the heel with his ebony cane in evident satisfaction. He spoke to the shoe. "I don't like your insolence, Jeremiah," he said, not raising his eyes. "His Lordship's instructions are very particular. He wants me to do this carefully, so that I don't draw attention by asking questions like an arrogant cock-a-whoop. I must be careful not to arouse suspicion." His voice carried clearly, but he wasn't English and his accent was hard to understand.

"That's all very well, Montmorency," Jeremiah said, "but you're taking too long. I need to know more about the house and grounds."

Montmorency looked up, narrowing his eyes. "You will address me as 'my lord' or I shall inform Lord Hazelton of your insolence." Then he sighed and waved his hand. "You're making excuses. I've given you every detail of the dock, the mews, and the house. You control half the gifted children in the kingdom. What more do you need? Could it be that now that the test has finally come, you're simply afraid? Even a plaguey whoreson like you, Jeremiah, might fear God's punishment for killing a king. Perhaps you're a true *Englishman* after all." He spoke the word *Englishman* with contempt.

Kill the king? I moved closer. Jeremiah's face was turning red and sweating. I thought he might strike the other man. But

Montmorency ignored him, or pretended to, pulling an orange from his pocket and holding it to his nose.

"*Lord* Montmorency," Jeremiah said thickly, "you risk your life, taunting me this way. No other man would dare. Any *Englishman*," he said, his voice rising, "could tell you the army saved the country by killing a king last time." He laughed. "Free Englishmen don't *need* kings."

Montmorency shrugged, but his eyes flickered uneasily. "And you should remember that without me, His Majesty's trusted confidante, you won't get near the king."

Jeremiah smiled, his eyes hard and flat. That smile made gooseflesh creep up my neck and arms. He said softly, "And without me, Lord Hazelton's kinchin are worthless. Only I can control them. Perhaps you should remember *that*."

I inhaled sharply.

"Enough. Lord Hazelton is expecting me," Montmorency said, pushing a panel aside.

When they had both left, heading in opposite directions, I merged with the passing crowd of fairgoers in the lane. No one was outside Maglena's booth.

Perhaps I should have followed Jeremiah, so he could capture me, but I didn't. Kat and Esmeralda had to know what I'd discovered. But I was afraid, too; if Jeremiah could control the gifted kinchin, he'd be able to control me. I'd be trapped at Hazelton's manor with the rest.

The sun beat down. The aroma of roasting meat and wood smoke drifted from the food booths, drawing me toward the roasting spits and kettles over the fires. Villagers were eating their nuncheon at the tables. I spotted Kat coming toward me and waited for her, trying to decide what to tell her. Once she knew of the plot against the king, we'd lose her and all her help. She'd leave for London immediately, to warn the duke.

Without her, Daniel and Mags had no chance to escape. They

were *my* priority. The king had an army to protect him. He could take his chances.

"There you are." Kat looked worried. "I've been looking for you everywhere. Did you find the inn?"

"No, the fair folk don't know it."

"Then let's eat here, I'm starving. And I have news." She gazed longingly at a pig roasting over an open fire. My mouth watered too. But we hadn't come here to eat, and any innkeeper would be more willing to talk to us if we were customers. "No," I said. "We should eat at the inn. Mags might still be there."

"My God, can't you smell the meat? I think your *Orb and Sceptre* might be imaginary anyway."

The children from Maglena's cart ran past us. "Those are the first children I've seen all day," Kat said.

"Let's ask them."

Kat laughed. "I doubt they've ever been inside an inn."

"They might know where it is, all the same." I ran after them and grabbed the girl's arm.

"Sam! Sam!" She screamed at the top of her lungs and raised her fists. I let go, raising my hands to show I meant no harm.

"What'cha want?"

"Do you know if there's an inn called the *Orb and Sceptre* here?"

She looked me up and down skeptically. "They charge dear for a room at the *Orb and Sceptre*."

Sam moved to stand in front of her. "They bothering ye, Rosie?"

"Naw." Rosie couldn't have been more than six, but she had a calculating look in her eye. "If I show you the inn, will you give me sixpence?"

Kat had joined us. "No, but I'll give you tuppence."

Rosie considered, then nodded. "This way."

They led us up the hill, back to the village. At the village green, we turned down a dirt lane on the left, running between high hedges, which ended at a large courtyard. The sign above the steps leading to the large oak door read *The Orb and Sceptre*. We'd found the place where the trackers had brought Mags.

Kat handed Rosie the pennies. She quickly embraced Kat, who looked startled, then Rosie curtsied, smiling. Sam laughed and the two of them ran off.

After the bright sunlight, the entryway seemed dark and gloomy, but wood and brass gleamed in the common room and there were clean white cloths on the orderly rows of tables. I walked up to the serving counter. A sleepy-looking girl told me the ordinary lunch was pease pottage with mutton and onion. It smelled wonderful. I brought two tankards of ale back to the table where Kat waited.

She rummaged in her pocket, then looked at me. "Those thievin' sneaks cut my purse!"

That hug. I should've remembered the man chasing them. I shook my head, and dug into my pocket to see how many coins I had left. Not many.

We retraced our steps to search for the purse, but I knew she was right. Rosie had cut the strings to her purse and taken it.

Without money, where could we sleep? Sleeping outdoors wasn't safe with Hazelton's men about; I wanted a door with a lock. Esmeralda might find us a bed with her friends, but I suspected she'd be too proud to ask for help. She was enjoying the role of Great Performer returning to the boards. To go from that to asking for a place to sleep would hurt her pride. Besides, I'd seen Mags arrive here. She might be here still.

The landlady was setting out the food when we returned to the table. "Mistress, I can pay for our meal." I held out the coins from my pocket. "But my friend's purse was just stolen by those Egyptian children, and we can't pay for a room. Might we bed down in the stable? I can afford that, if you're agreeable."

To my surprise, she believed me. "They're a terrible plague hereabouts, the stealing kinchin. You'd think being so close to

Barsington Manor the parents wouldn't bring them here, but they do, and we're so hungry for sight of a child—" She broke off, afraid. "Anyway, you're welcome. I'll tell Robbie to give you a stall. How does thruppence sound?"

"Very well, mistress. Thank you." I handed her the coins. There weren't many left. I could pay for meals today, but we'd go hungry tomorrow.

The landlady glanced behind her, then sat down next to Kat. "I don't normally interfere in my customers' business," she said, "but you two are so young. Has anyone warned you this neighborhood isn't healthy for children? I don't want to sound inhospitable, but the sooner you're out of Barsington, the safer you'll be. I'd feel better returning your pence and seeing you on your way."

I didn't know what to think. Ever since my vision had shown trackers using the inn, I'd assumed the innkeeper was in league with Lord Hazelton, yet here she was, warning us. Maybe it was a trick, to get us to trust her, but her concern seemed genuine. "Thank you, mistress. It's kind of you to warn us, but we can't leave yet. We've come to find a friend. Maybe you've seen her? We think two men brought her here last night." I didn't say we were afraid she'd been nobbled by Lord Hazelton. I didn't have to.

She pressed her lips together as though trying to stop herself from saying anything. She shook her head and said, "Only one thing I can say 'bout that. No one returns once *he's* got ahold of them. You'd best get away and save yourself. Your friend is gone."

Kat put down her mug. "Why doesn't he nobble the traveling children?"

"That's just it," the landlady said, glancing nervously behind her again. "We don't know, unless it's that they're not gifted. It's my belief they're working *for* him, and that's why he leaves them alone. They go everywhere and see everything, spying on the rest of us. That's one reason I keep 'em out of my inn; the other's the thievin'. I expect *that's* just to keep their hand in. We've complained to the constable but he does nothing. He's in the lord's pocket, too."

She rose. "Take my advice and leave. Your friend is beyond help."

Kat and I exchanged worried looks. If Rosie and Sam were spies, Lord Hazelton's men might know where we were at that very moment. I glanced toward the serving hatch before I whispered, "I overheard a conversation between Jeremiah and another cove, a lord. Jeremiah boasted he's the one who controls the gifted kinchin."

"Did he say how?"

I shook my head.

She began to eat. "I can't believe I fell for that foist's trick! My penny-pinching master won't be pleased. We'll just have to make this trip worth it."

Once she knew about the plot against the king, she'd have all the justification she needed. But I couldn't tell her, not until Daniel and Mags were free. Besides, I told myself, for the information to be of any use, we had to know more.

"Bad news," she continued. "My contacts have all disappeared. Every single one. That shouldn't be possible, not without someone noticing. Folk look at me like I've got the plague and walk away when they realize what I'm asking."

That was bad. I'd hoped Kat's network would help us if we got in trouble. "What do you think happened?"

She shook her head. "You know as much as I do. I'd guess Hazelton's men nobbled them, or worse."

We finished the meal in silence. I was mopping up the gravy with my bread when Kat whispered, "I didn't want to say anything while you spoke with the landlady, but I don't think it's safe to stay here, not if those two kinchin are spies for Hazelton. Why don't we stay with the fair folk? They'll at least have a fire. Maybe they know something useful."

"We can ask Esmeralda, but we need to search *here*. The land-lady and her staff will be less suspicious if we're sleeping here. Besides, there's an informer—"

"Among the fair folk," Kat finished. She sighed. "No fire, no bed, informers everywhere, and it's going to rain again. I always enjoy my trips to the country."

26

THE ROPE DANCER

ROBBIE SHOWED us an empty stall where we could sleep that night. It was clean, smelling of hay and horses. I stopped to stroke the nose of the bay in the next stall and he snuffled into my neck. It wouldn't be so bad; the hay would keep us warm and the horses could warn us of intruders in the night. I'd slept in many worse places.

After Robbie left, we agreed I'd search the outbuildings, while an invisible Kat searched for Mags inside.

But we didn't find her, not even a trace.

"Hazelton has her by now," Kat said gloomily when we met again in the stable.

I took my glass from my pocket while Kat watched, willing it to show something useful. It refused to be commanded. It remained cold in my hand, lifeless. I shook my head.

"Perhaps we already know what we need to. Now we just have to find Hazelton's manor. That's bound to be where the kinchin are," she said.

"If I let them capture me—" I began.

"We aren't that desperate," she said quickly.

"I'll be safe enough if you come along, invisible."

"Safe? What about locked doors, armed guards, or Gilbert killing you on sight? Being invisible doesn't solve everything, Lizzie."

"Hazelton needs a prophetess. Gilbert can't kill me."

"Wait and talk to Esmeralda," Kat said. "That is, if she remembers who we are."

The sun beat down fiercely on the walk back, but haze on the distant horizon promised rain. The fair was in full swing when we returned, crowded and noisy. Afternoon sunlight lay on the meadow grass, gilding the booths and making the red and blue colors of the pennants flying over the booths glow. Folk surged up and down the aisles, with long queues at the popular booths.

We tried to find Esmeralda. The rude serving maid from the tavern approached Kat and whispered something.

"I have to go," she said. "Where will you be?"

"Finding Esmeralda."

"Don't do anything foolish, Lizzie."

Who's to say what's foolish?

I headed toward the attiring rooms where I thought she'd be, and was lucky; she was leaving, dressed in tights and a cape.

"Not now, Lizzie," she said. "I'm on in a few minutes."

"This will take but a moment."

She shook her head, but waited, tapping her foot.

A man passed, crying, "Fifteen minutes until show time! The *Great Esmeralda* will *defy death* for your entertainment on a rope suspended fifteen feet in the air! Witness *amazing feats* of daring never before seen in England!"

"I've learned something I can't tell Kat, but someone has to know besides me. But I can't trust you if you won't tell me why you're here."

Curiosity struggled with caution in her face. Then she shrugged. "I have my own score to settle with Jeremiah Sawyer," she said quickly. "And I don't want you or Kat interfering in my personal business." She glanced at the man waiting to announce her act.

"We're supposed to be here for Mags on Guild business, not a private feud."

"And I've already helped a great deal by agreeing to perform. Without me, the fair folk would've stuck a knife in your back by now."

"What did Jeremiah do to you?" I asked.

"That's not your concern." Esmeralda's face had gone blank. *Something really bad, then.*

"Will you wait until Mags is free before getting revenge?"

She pressed her lips together, considering, then shook her head. "I can't promise. Who would notice if he disappeared? Lord Hazelton would simply think he'd run off. He won't suspect us. We'll find Mags, no matter what happens to Jeremiah."

I didn't think she'd lift a finger to stop the king from being assassinated, so I told her about Jeremiah's boast that he was the one who controlled the children. Her eyebrows rose but all she said was, "I have to go." She walked quickly toward the roped-off area where she was to perform.

Esmeralda had given us another deadline: find Mags and the other kinchin, and get them away before Esmeralda took her revenge on Jeremiah. I knew I should allow myself to be captured, the fastest way to find the kinchin. But I wasn't ready. Truth be told, I was still too afraid to risk it. I thought Gilbert might kill me.

Late afternoon sun gilded the green hill that hid the village. The crowd engulfed me, chattering with excitement and carrying me along until we arrived at a roped-off enclosure, a tightrope strung high above it between two poles. So many people were jammed together that soon I couldn't move, trapped between a man who smelled of pigs and a woman whose hat threatened my eye every time she turned her head. Across from me, Rosie and her brother had wormed their way to the front. Rosie saw me and stuck out her tongue.

Esmeralda appeared at the bottom of a ladder, wearing silver-spangled pink tights with green silk pantaloons. There was scattered clapping. She bowed and removed a silver cape, handing it to someone I couldn't see. A trumpet brayed loudly and a drummer played a tattoo as Esmeralda, shod in leather slippers, climbed the rope ladder until she reached a platform high above us. From below, someone handed her a long pole.

In the hush, with all eyes craning upward, I spared a glance for Rosie and her brother. Their faces were tilted up, but I'd wager Kat's lost purse their hands were in someone's pocket.

Esmeralda crossed the rope, holding the pole in front of her. One slipper-clad foot slipped, and she swayed from side to side.

The crowd gasped. I was glad I knew her gift and could enjoy the performance without worrying. A fall from that height would certainly kill her, and the crowd was getting their money's worth of delightful shivers.

Rosie and her brother had both disappeared. What was more interesting than a ropedancer? I scanned the crowd for them.

Polite clapping. I looked up. Esmeralda was across the rope. She picked up her parasol from the other platform, its green and red parrots lit up by the afternoon sun. She stepped delicately onto the rope, with one leg in the air. Balancing on one foot, using the parasol for balance, she began to hop across.

Esmeralda was not a willowy maid. Each time her full weight landed, the rope dropped several inches. The crowd was entranced, gasping with fear and delight. She made it all the way across, then curtsied on the tiny platform. The crowd cheered and clapped enthusiastically. Someone cried, "That's more like it!"

Rosie was in the crowd, moving behind Jeremiah. I hadn't noticed him before.

"Ladies and gentlemen! Make no sound! The Great Esmeralda

needs all her concentration for the *ultimate* feat of daring! A forward somersault!"

Esmeralda placed a small board, no wider than a few inches, on the rope. She straightened, both arms in the air, and bent over, with a hand on either side of the board. Falling into a forward roll, head on the board, body on the rope, she rolled to her feet and lifted her arms gracefully.

"Hurrah! Hurrah!" The crowd clapped enthusiastically. There were whistles, and the rackety sound of a wooden noisemaker. Esmeralda strolled casually to the other platform.

I looked back. Sam and Rosie were gone. Jeremiah hadn't moved. Had he seen me?

Esmeralda did a forward flip onto the platform. She curtsied, sketching a salute with her hand, drinking in the applause, and I had to smile.

While she was climbing down the ladder, I headed toward where I'd last seen Jeremiah.

He was gone. I cursed, calling myself a coward for waiting. There had to be another chance.

I followed Esmeralda to the attiring rooms. Outside, actors were fixing their makeup and gossiping, waiting for their entrances, and mumbling their lines. Esmeralda soon emerged in her green dress, her bag and cloak over her arm.

"Where's Kat?" she asked. "I'm starved."

Rosie and her brother ran past, disappearing into the crowd. The scream that came from that direction sounded like Rosie. I broke into a run.

An audience was gathering. I pushed through.

Jeremiah held Rosie with one hand; with the other he held off Sam, who was trying to hit him, but he was too far out of reach. Rosie had picked one pocket too many; she struggled to pull free. Jeremiah knocked Sam to the ground and took both of her arms. "Stop squirming," he growled. "I'm going to teach you not to steal from your betters."

No one moved. This was my chance. "Help her, you hollow-hearted cowards! Hey! Greedy-guts! Over here!" I shoved a man out of my way.

"She's getting what's coming to her," someone yelled. "Let her see what happens to kinchin who steal."

As I approached Jeremiah from behind, I could smell his sweat.

From somewhere in the crowd Kat yelled, "Lizzie, no!"

I grabbed Jeremiah's arm and pulled him around to face me. His look of surprise turned to satisfaction. "Ah, Prophetess! Can't stay away from me, eh?"

"Run, Rosie!" My eyes were on Jeremiah.

He reached for me, and I darted away. It mustn't look too easy. He grabbed my arm and I kicked out, catching his leg. He swore and pulled his knife. Before I could move, Hawkins had my arms pinned behind me. I went limp, ready to be taken, when something sailed through the air, toppling Hawkins to the ground.

It was Esmeralda. As she fell, Jeremiah had raised his knife, slicing a deep, jagged gash down her leg. A dark stain began to spread across the green dress. The crowd's mood shifted. Men yelled and ran toward Hawkins and Jeremiah, but they had already taken to their heels.

I kneeled beside her. "Oh, Esmeralda, there was no need. I would've been all right." I tore strips from my petticoat to bandage her leg.

A spasm of pain contorted her face. "That's our Lizzie," she said hoarsely, "single-handedly defeating murderous cutthroats. Kat and I needn't have come."

Where was Kat? I thought she'd been at the edge of the crowd. A moment later she was beside me, holding a blanket that smelled of horse.

The crowd was breaking up, with muttered oaths and dark

looks, as though the attack were our fault. No one wanted to cross Hazelton's men.

"Here," Kat said, "shift yourself onto this and we'll carry you to the inn."

"Are you mad?" I protested. "We can't carry her—she weighs twelve stone if she—"

Kat interrupted, kneeling beside Esmeralda, "You'll have to help us, Esmeralda. Concentrate on floating just a bit. Make yourself lighter. Then we'll take you where we can tend your wound. Can you do that?" Esmeralda nodded, her face contorted.

She groaned when we rolled her onto the horse blanket. Kat took the blanket at her head with me at her feet. We lifted the blanket and headed away from the fair, with Kat walking backwards and glancing awkwardly over her shoulder. We began to climb the hill to the village with Esmeralda floating the barest fraction above the blanket.

27

AT THE ORB AND SCEPTRE

Not only had my plan failed, Esmeralda was injured and her leg wouldn't stop bleeding. She whimpered from the pain.

I was in hardly better shape, the sword cut in my side throbbing with the strain of carrying her. Then the rain began, and our misery was complete. The water worked its way inside my cloak and soaked my boots, until I was chilled to the bone. Every time we stumbled, Esmeralda moaned pitifully. If I was shivering, despite the effort of carrying her, she had to be dangerously cold. Water pooled in the center of the blanket and began to drip.

It was growing dark, the rain clouds obscuring the sun. Somehow we made it to the courtyard of *The Orb and Sceptre*.

We stumbled toward the stables. Robbie had put out fresh hay for us and I un-baled even more to cover Esmeralda once we laid her down. Now we truly needed a room. Without a fire, Esmeralda might die. She was too pale, her lips blue, and her eyes wide and dark. Murmuring an apology to the bay in the next stall, I stole his blanket and tucked it over the straw around her.

I kneeled beside her, my back to the door. Kat was across from me, retying my petticoat bandage. One thing was clear: Esmeralda had just risked her life to help me. Not knowing what else to do, I took out my glass. Nothing. The smooth surface was cold.

I heard a sound behind me and looked up. Kat had disappeared.

Behind me, Jeremiah and Hawkins were in the doorway.

"Don't make a sound if you want your friend to live." Jeremiah said, nodding at Esmeralda. "Lord Hazelton wants to see you."

My mind felt as numb as my fingers. I nodded and began to gather our things. Had he seen Kat?

It was up to me to keep them from killing Esmeralda. I hoisted our bags over my shoulder and said, "My friend is hurt, thanks to you. If she doesn't get care soon, she's going to bleed to death. Then *you'll* be wanted for murder, Jeremiah. Get us a room with a fire here. We can eat something while her wound is dressed. I could do with a mug of ale to wet my throat. I've heard the landlady here is one of the best brewers in the kingdom."

Jeremiah shook his head.

I said quickly, "Your lord will be angry if she dies before he can question her."

Hawkins liked my suggestion about food and ale: he grinned and licked his lips, and I suspected Jeremiah also wanted a mug of ale before setting out in the windy, rain-drenched weather. Jeremiah exchanged a look with Hawkins. He was weakening.

Hawkins said, "A meal won't take long."

Jeremiah nodded. "Very well. We'll stop to sup while the ostlers finish tending the horses. Order a private room, with food and ale. Then ask for someone to tend the old lady."

Hawkins left, smiling.

I bobbed a curtsy, my eyes lowered. "Thank you."

He waved away my thanks and squatted on his haunches in the doorway. "I have my eye on both of you. Whatever your gift may be, I can take it away. Resting here gives me time to make certain of that."

I shivered. That had always been the flaw in my plan. If he

could take away my gift, what else could he do? Was he gifted as well?

He came toward me. I stumbled backwards, but he bent over and threw Esmeralda over his shoulder as though she were a sack of flour. She cried out.

"Now, none of that," Jeremiah warned. "We're getting you help. No complaining."

He grinned at me, and pulled the knife from his belt. He used it to point at the door. "Lead the way, Prophetess. Don't do anything to make me use this on your friend."

In the entryway, we waited for a room to be made ready, dripping on the flagstones. Finally, the maid I'd seen earlier beckoned for us to follow her.

We entered a comfortable room, with a fire on the hearth. Beeswax candles on the table scented the air with the smell of honey. Past the table and chairs was a bed. Courage seeped back into me. We were in a civilized place. There was help here, if I could wake my wits.

Everything had gone wrong. I'd assumed Kat and Esmeralda would be free when I was captured. I hadn't considered what we'd do if they were captured too. Who would help us? Not the landlady, she was too frightened. Not Esmeralda's friends. They were too far away, and I doubted they'd risk it anyway.

Jeremiah dumped Esmeralda on the bed. He didn't seem to recognize her. I kneeled beside her, placing a pillow beneath her head, and covered her with a blanket. Esmeralda's face was pale and sweat gleamed on her forehead. How could I face Serena if I allowed Jeremiah to cause her sister's death?

Serena.

Jeremiah whispered something to Hawkins who glanced at me and left.

"Sir," I appealed to Jeremiah in my sweetest voice, "would you permit me to write a note to my sister? She knows I've traveled to Barsington to find my friend, Kat. If she doesn't hear from me, she'll worry, and might come to find out why."

Esmeralda watched me from the pillow, her eyes shadowed with pain.

Jeremiah laughed. "I care *that*," he snapped his fingers, "for your sister and her worries."

"But my sister works for Lady Cheshire," I said, my thoughts leaping. "Her Ladyship is interested in servants and has the ear of the king. If Serena tells her I'm missing, Lady Cheshire might come here to find me. She can be quite persistent." I let the threat hang in the air. Even a brute who worked for Hazelton might've heard of Lady Cheshire.

He must have heard something, for at the sound of her name his face paled. He asked hoarsely, "You know Lady Cheshire? Is that why you're here?"

What did he mean? I shook my head. "No, sir. I'm here to find my friend, Kat, who's missing. We heard she might be in Barsington. But if I disappear too, my sister will ask Lady Cheshire for help."

He didn't know whether to believe me, but I saw fear in his eyes. "Explain to me, wench, why a great lady would care about you and yours?"

"She champions servants' rights. She'd help my sister look for me—and for Kat too. Especially if she's being held against her will."

He chewed his lip. For all he knew, Kat was one of the gifted children imprisoned at Lord Hazelton's estate. He didn't want a nob asking questions about that.

"Old busybody, is she?" His face had a calculating expression. "And what would you write to your sister to keep Lady Cheshire happy?"

I took a breath. "I'd write that we think we've found Kat, but that my friend here is too ill to move, so we have to stay until she's better. That will keep her from worrying—or coming here."

I was careful not to use Esmeralda's name in case it jogged his memory.

"Hmm." He stared as though trying to guess my thoughts.

Esmeralda spoke up, her voice hoarse. "She's right. Lady Cheshire can be quite interfering if she thinks there's a wrong to be righted. You don't want her to become curious about what's happened to us." She was breathing fast, her face too pale, but her mind was working.

"Know her well, do you?" He sneered. "I suppose you take chocolate with her on Sunday afternoons?"

"No," Esmeralda said calmly, though her voice was faint. "I don't like chocolate. But sometimes we ride together in the park."

Jeremiah laughed. Esmeralda stared haughtily at him and I saw him hesitate. He examined her clothes. She spoke like a nob and even flat on her back, maybe bleeding to death, she had the air of someone who might go riding with a lady. His gaze shifted uneasily to me.

There was a knock on the door. The landlady came in, carrying a tray, followed by the maid with jugs of ale and loaves of bread in a basket. She put the tray down on the table and laid out mutton and roasted vegetables, and a set of plates and cutlery.

She looked at Esmeralda and frowned, turning to Jeremiah. "This woman is injured?"

"Yes." He waved his hand. "Get a clean bandage on her. We'll be leaving as soon as we've eaten."

She curtsied. "Yes, sir." She nodded at the serving girl who went out the door.

Before the landlady reached the door, I said quickly, "May I have paper, pen and ink? I need to write a letter."

She stopped in surprise, and that's when she recognized me. She glanced at Jeremiah.

"Bring it," he said.

She curtsied again and went out, shutting the door behind her.

Jeremiah stood over my chair. "I can read, girl, though I'm surprised you can. I'll read what you write." He smiled unpleasantly. "If you say anything you shouldn't, there'll be no letter and I'll tell His Lordship what you tried."

I nodded, dropping my eyes.

Jeremiah served himself a plate of food and dragged a chair nearer the fire, placing himself between us and the door. He waved toward the table. "Go ahead and eat."

Propping two pillows behind her, I helped Esmeralda sit up. "How are you?" I asked.

She whispered, "Be careful, that man's a murderer. He killed our sister."

"Shut it!" Jeremiah said. "No talking to each other."

I took a plate, filled it with food and brought it to her. Then I returned with a cup of ale and a napkin. She drank the ale thirstily. I filled my own plate and sat down. I took no ale; I wanted my wits clear.

The maid returned with a jug, and a basket full of sewing things. She gently peeled the bandage away from the leg and bathed it with something from the jug. Esmeralda gasped, but then pressed her lips together. The maid worked quickly, wrapping a piece of linen around the leg several times before she fastened it with stitches. She stood, gathered her things, and curtsied before she left. What did she think of it all? I wondered.

The landlady returned with ink, paper, and quill, and set them down on the table before me, with no sign of recognition. She returned to the door and stood waiting.

Jeremiah nodded to her. "Thank you. That's all."

As she was leaving, Hawkins entered. He crossed to the table and helped himself.

I rose to take Esmeralda's empty plate and cup. Her eyes were closed. "Sleep now," I said. I moved the pillows flat and eased her down.

Pulling my chair closer to the table, I picked up the inkbottle, swirling it to check the ink, then took up the quill. I wrote slowly, for fear of blots. In the middle of the sheet I wrote: *Serena Hopkins, in care of Lady Cheshire at Cheshire House, Chelsea*

I waited for that to dry, then, beginning at the top of the other side:

September 14, 1661

Dearest sister,

I write so you won't worry. E and I have arrived safely at the Orb and Sceptre near Barsington Manor, Lord Hazelton's estate.

We have heard my friend Kat may be at Lord Hazelton's manor. Some of the lord's men have promised us an escort to the manor to seek her out. I know Lady Cheshire was concerned also. Be sure to inform her that we think we shall be joining Kat shortly.

I fear I must relate that E was hurt at Barsington Fair. She is too ill to be moved. We pray for her recovery. The landlady and staff here have treated us most kindly.

Things are proceeding much as expected.

Your loving sister,

Lizzie

I waited for the ink to dry, then folded the letter and handed it to Jeremiah, hoping he wouldn't notice Serena's name on the other side. He read it and glanced up. "Do you think I'm a simpleton? You can't mention Lord Hazelton."

"But she knows that's where we've gone," I said. "If I *don't* mention him, she'll know we've been nobbled. This has to fit what she knows."

"Hmm." He growled but read the letter again and shrugged. "Hawkins." He handed him the letter. "Here's a penny. Take it to the landlady and tell her to put it on the mail coach." Hawkins raised an eyebrow. "Do as I say, clunch-pate."

Hawkins bowed stiffly and left.

I exhaled slowly. There was no guarantee the letter would arrive, but at least I'd tried.

Jeremiah smiled at me. "Time for *my* fun."

He went to stand over Esmeralda, who gave no sign she was aware of him, and I almost rose to stop whatever he would do.

But once satisfied she was asleep, he carried his chair over to me and sat down, much too close. "I'm going to show you how we welcome gifted children to Hazelton's manor, Lizzie."

I shrank back. But he pushed his chair closer, until our knees touched. He stared at me and I stared back. Was he using a gift? My hands were clammy with fear.

He leaned forward and touched my forehead. Then he spoke slowly, rhythmically, in a cadence that made me sleepy. "Lizzie girl, Lizzie dear, listen to my words. Nothing in the world but your master, Jeremiah. Nothing in the world but serving your master. You have no gift, you remember no gift, you're an ordinary girl, Lizzie dear. No gift, and no memory of a gift. Listen to my words, Lizzie girl. Nothing in the world but serving your master. But when I say, 'Cromwell,' you will remember your gift, and you will serve *me*, your master, Jeremiah." He leaned forward and touched my forehead again.

My mind was strangely cloudy. I dimly heard him talking but the words made no sense. By the time he was done, I wasn't certain whether I was awake or asleep.

I tried to shake my head to clear it, but it was heavy, like my thoughts. I couldn't remember. What had he done?

28

BARSINGTON MANOR

WE WAITED for Hazelton's coach in *The Orb and Sceptre's* court-yard, the rain now a fine mist beaded our cloaks. The cold and wet cleared my mind, although my memory had gaps. The land-lady watched us sadly from the open door.

Jeremiah concealed a pistol in the folds of his cloak, aimed at me, but he needn't have bothered. Esmeralda could barely stand without my support, and I wouldn't leave her.

The coach rattled up, with Hawkins driving. I helped Esmer-alda inside and eased her down the length of one seat. I hoped Kat was nearby, and knew we were leaving. Jeremiah climbed inside, the cocked pistol in his hand, and we were off.

Every time the coach bounced or shook I held my breath, waiting for that pistol to go off. I pressed into the far corner, as far away from Jeremiah as I could get. A lantern swung above his head, casting frightening shadows on his face.

I feared the journey would kill Esmeralda. Whenever the coach bounced or jolted on the rutted road, she groaned, and no threat from Jeremiah would make her stop. The road was no more than a pitted track of mud, full of gullies and potholes carved by the rain. There was a danger the coach might sink in the mud so deeply we'd be unable to free it. But even after several pints of ale, Hawkins kept the horses to a slow, even pace. We stuck fast twice, but he managed to free us, cursing and whipping the horses.

Whatever Jeremiah had done to me, I couldn't remember it. His words echoed in my head, muddling my thoughts. I felt empty and strange, as though my body were someone else's. We were going to Hazelton's manor because… something to do with Daniel? And Mags. That was it: my tracker, Gilbert, had Mags.

A shard of indigo glass appeared in my mind, shining with light. Something about—

The sound of the wheels changed. Gravel spattered against the underside of the coach. "We're on Lord Hazelton's land," Jeremiah said, grinning. "No one can help you now."

I stared at the leather curtain beside me to avoid Jeremiah's leering grin. In the moving shadows, Jeremiah appeared monstrous. Why did he smile so?

Some things I remembered clearly. Kat was free, and I'd sent a letter to Lady Cheshire, for all the good it might do. The thought that someone would know our destination gave me hope. The lantern swung wildly, shifting my corner from darkness to light, and back. Without moving my head I slid my eyes toward Jeremiah. That disturbing smile was still there.

I leaned back and closed my eyes, pretending to sleep. I longed to slide my blue glass out of my pocket, for reassurance. It was lucky; it would comfort me, and would—I couldn't remember. But I couldn't reach for it; Jeremiah watched me too closely. I'd wait until he glanced away or became drowsy. If only Hawkins had been inside with us. He'd drunk so much ale he was probably half-asleep by now and we'd be lucky not to end up in a ditch. Jeremiah showed no sign of weariness. I feared he'd try to touch me, or worse, before we arrived. There was no help for me if he did.

Esmeralda stirred, moaning softly. While his attention was on

Esmeralda, I slid the glass from my pocket, watching him from beneath lowered lids. My hand lay between the folds of my skirt and the side of the coach. I squinted at my hand. The glass was dark in the shadows. I felt a stinging disappointment. What more had I expected? It was just a piece of glass.

I glanced at Jeremiah. He smiled as though he knew what I was thinking. Slowly, I edged the glass back into my pocket.

The coach turned onto a gravel drive, a great half circle before a large stone house. Cressets on iron stands flickered in the wind. Footmen in gold and red livery formed a double line to the door. We were expected. It was only when Esmeralda and I stumbled past them that I saw they held staves or nets in their hands. One held a glass jar of dark powder. Clearly they'd welcomed gifted children before. I tried to notice all I could. Selfishly, I hoped Kat was with us.

A tall man, his cloak falling from broad shoulders, stood silhouetted in the doorway. A wide-brimmed hat obscured his face. My heart thudded painfully, as I waited to see if Gilbert would kill me where I stood. Then he stepped forward into the light, and I saw I'd been mistaken. Lord Hazelton himself waited to greet us.

He addressed Jeremiah. "Is this all of them? I thought there were three." The nasal voice was surprisingly high for such a large man.

Jeremiah's arrogance had disappeared. He bowed low and spoke with deference. "There was no sign of another, despite what the informants said. The travelling children confirmed they'd only seen two."

"Or perhaps one of 'em played you for a fool by using her gift, eh, Jeremiah? Could your control be slipping? Why bring the old one? You should've killed her."

Jeremiah straightened, his resentment barely concealed. "My lord, my control worked perfectly on this one." He gestured toward me. "She's made no attempt to escape. As for the other one," he glanced at Esmeralda, then drew close to Lord Hazelton to whisper something.

Esmeralda leaned against me, one arm draped over my shoulder. I couldn't tell if she knew what was happening.

"Very well. But we can't risk a mistake, now of all times."

"No, my lord." Jeremiah's expression was stony. He turned to me. "Inside! Don't keep my lord waiting." He shoved me, almost knocking us both to the ground. I thought it strange they pushed us toward the front door, as though we were nobs ourselves.

We were led across a wide hall of white stone into a small anteroom, and the reason for our grand entry became clear. Inside, the red velvet and gilded chairs were adorned with chains and padlocks.

Long red curtains shut out the night, but the hearth was empty and cold. Two candles burned on the mantelpiece, their reflection in the mirror behind them making the shadows darker. A man in gold livery pushed Esmeralda into a chair, then me. Another came swiftly behind, fastening an iron collar around my neck before I had a chance to resist. Esmeralda sagged under the weight of her collar and blinked, staring in confusion at the comfortless room.

"Lady Cheshire? How? How could they know? *Someone* has talked." Lord Hazelton spoke outside the door. I didn't hear Jeremiah's reply, but His Lordship's voice was loud and shrill. "If it was Montmorency, I'll send him back to France in a trunk."

Jeremiah murmured, "Not here, my lord. We are overheard."

Lord Hazelton looked at me and I quickly dropped my eyes. When I raised them again, he was gone.

Once we were securely padlocked to the chairs, the servants left. I guessed they were waiting for evidence of a gift not under Jeremiah's control. That was what the chains were for.

"Esmeralda," I whispered. "Are you awake? Do you know where we are?"

"Yes," she said, without opening her eyes.

My eyes were closing, too. We spent the night there, padlocked to our chairs.

"I AM SO pleased you accepted my invitation," that high-pitched, nasal voice said.

Lord Hazelton stood before us. Morning light the color of dried blood came through the red curtains. Esmeralda regarded him as though he were a poisonous snake crawling toward her. I took a deep breath and gathered my wits. "We never meant to impose on your hospitality, my lord."

He ignored this. "Gilbert wanted us to meet, Lizzie. That's quite an honor for you; I don't normally extend a personal greeting to my children, but Gilbert insisted. He wants me to make an example of you, since you marked him so dramatically."

My heart pounded under my sore ribs and my hands were cold. I took a deep breath and examined our captor. He wore his fair hair in a queue. His eyebrows were pale to the point of invisibility, arched over prominent blue eyes, with a long nose and fleshy lips. I thought he seemed like any other nob, until I realized the cold blue eyes hadn't blinked in a long while.

Lord Hazelton frowned. "Where is Gilbert? He should be here for this." He turned his head slightly. "Hawkins?"

"My lord." I hadn't noticed Hawkins standing in the shadows by the door.

"Ask Gilbert to attend me here."

"But my lord—"

"Don't worry, Hawkins," Lord Hazelton said testily, "I can be alone with a padlocked child for a few minutes. Jeremiah said she's safe. And bring the little girl."

"Yes, my lord." Hawkins bowed and left.

We were alone with Lord Hazelton, not that it mattered. He'd do whatever he wanted, witnesses or not.

He smiled. "They worry about my safety. I am fortunate to have such loyal servants."

Something brushed my ear but I didn't turn, just slid my eyes to look. An insect? I felt it again—like someone blowing in my ear.

Kat. I kept my eyes on Hazelton, my spirits rising.

The door opened and Gilbert came in. He bowed low, with a sweep of his hat. The burned skin was healing, fading to a raw pink, but it was still disturbing to see. I almost didn't blame him for wanting revenge. Then again, no one had forced him to make a living by selling children into slavery. He straightened, watching me.

"So, my lord," Esmeralda said, in a conversational tone. "I believe you wanted Lizzie to become your prophetess, to foretell the future. Do you no longer need to know your fate?"

Lord Hazelton was taken aback, as though a piece of furniture had spoken. "I beg your pardon, did you address me?"

"I did, my lord. Pardon me for speaking to you without being formally introduced. My name's Esmeralda. I'm a friend of Lizzie here, and I know all about her gift. It's a useful one for any man to have—especially a man of ambition. I've heard you're such a man, my lord. Don't you want to know the outcome of your plans? There will be obstacles ahead. Wouldn't it be better to know them in advance to avoid them? I'm curious," she said, cocking her head to one side, "why you'd give up such power to please a servant. Surely this man should take orders, not give them."

Gilbert shot Esmeralda a look of pure hatred and moved toward her.

Lord Hazelton put out his arm, blocking his way. "I see what you're trying to do, beldam. It's true, when I heard about the girl, I thought she'd be useful. That's why I gave Gilbert her contract. But poor Gilbert," he said with a smirk, "has had such a difficult time bringing her in, I'd all but given up. He's been damaged before, but not this badly. I don't mind doing him a favor. And no," he added coldly, "I don't take orders from any man. You'd like me to spare your friend's life. I understand. Sadly, we can't all have what we want. Gilbert, for instance," he glanced at the man, "would like to cut the girl limb from limb, while she's still alive." He smiled when he saw me flinch. "But as you say, Lizzie could be quite useful. So we'll do this my way."

He spoke gently. "You will prophesy at my command, Prophetess. If your prophecy fails to come true, or to warn me of danger, Gilbert will cut your face with his knife. Isn't that clever?" He smiled with satisfaction. "Serve me well, or make my most useful servant happy. Your choice. Make *me* happy, and you could live a long time." He asked Gilbert, "What say you?"

Gilbert bowed again, his eyes never leaving my face. "I'm most grateful, my lord."

The hatred in his eyes made me shudder. No doubt he was imagining my face when he was through with it. I felt light-headed. Once Lord Hazelton discovered I had no gift, Gilbert could do as he pleased with me.

29

PRISONERS

Hawkins entered the room, dragging an unwilling Mags behind him. Her eyes widened when she saw us.

"I believe you two know each other?" Hazelton asked. "Gilbert said our dearest Margaret was the best way to get you here, without his having to lift a finger. Apparently he was right. She has a knack for learning secrets. What's yours, I wonder?"

I frowned, hoping Mags would pretend not to know us.

"Margaret, dear," Hazelton said, "please ask this annoying wench why she's here."

Mags shook her head. Instantly Hawkins struck her across the face. A trail of fresh bruises covered both her arms.

"It's all right. Do what he says." I didn't use her name. The last thing I wanted was to confirm what Gilbert had said.

"Ask her what she's doing here," Hazelton said again.

Mags was smart; she pretended not to know me. "Mistress, why did you come here?"

I was about to repeat the story I'd told Jeremiah, about looking for Kat. Instead I said, "We came to rescue you, Mags. And my brother, if he's here."

Her mouth trembled and her eyes filled with tears, but she wiped them away angrily.

"There, you see? That wasn't difficult at all," Hazelton said. "I'm pleased to hear you value the mort. All you need do to keep her safe is make sure your prophecies are true. Now what's this about a brother?" He looked at Gilbert.

"She thinks he's one of your children."

Hazelton arched an eyebrow. "And is he?"

"No, my lord." He waited for my reaction with a malicious smirk.

Gilbert had no reason to lie, not when he could use Daniel against me. Disappointment hit me like a blow.

"I shall test your gift presently," Lord Hazelton said, "after I deal with more urgent matters. Hawkins, come with me and bring Margaret. Gilbert, see that these two are taken to the stables, unharmed please, then wait for me in the hall."

"Yes, my lord."

Gilbert waited until the others were gone. "Before they take you away, Lizzie dear, I want you to know how much fun I've had getting acquainted with Mags." He laughed at my expression. "Poor Mags. You weren't lucky for *her*, were you? She told me about Daniel, too. He must've been the smart one in your family. Smart enough to run away before he starved. So you had to find other victims for your lofty phrases. Playing house, swearing oaths, singing songs. Your friend James was laughing at you."

"James is no friend of mine."

"No, perhaps not. But thanks to you, all the rats are in one trap. That will make it so much easier to catch them."

My breath caught. I struggled to control my face. If they didn't already know where Haven was, they soon would. Potts or James would tell them. Eventually.

Gilbert seemed pleased with his sport. "I must take my leave. Do think of me, while you're waiting for your chance to prophesy."

He swept off his hat in a mocking bow. As he did, I noticed the thin white scar on the back of his neck, as though someone had tried to cut off his head.

He left and two men entered. The first had a badly set broken nose. After unlocking my padlock and dropping the chains, he threaded a chain through my collar, and then Esmeralda's. He yanked us to our feet and pulled us down a hallway and out a back door. The second man followed us. Outside, we passed a cook roasting a pig over an open fire. He never even looked up as we went by.

Esmeralda's color was better after a night's sleep, but she winced with every step. She stumbled, nearly pulling me down with her.

I steadied her and yelled at the broken-nosed man, "Be careful! Can't you see she's ill?"

"Shut your gob." He yanked the chain so hard we grabbed each other to keep from falling. Esmeralda scowled, nostrils flaring, but said nothing.

First he led us to the privy, then back past the kitchen again to a stone building that looked like a stable. The second man lifted an iron bar and opened the heavy oak doors, gesturing for us to go inside.

Row upon row of children sat on wooden benches. The broken-nosed man led us to an empty one, threading our chain through a hasp in the floor, then locking it. Then the two men left, closing the door, and we heard the iron bar fall into place. I pulled on the chain but it wouldn't shift. I'd become one of Hazelton's stable of children.

Pale, thin faces turned to look at us. Every child was chained to another, except for a small redheaded girl who sat alone. There was no fire, no sign of food or water, and from the smell, infrequent access to a privy. Some kinchin stared at us with dull eyes. Others stared listlessly at nothing.

I recognized a few I'd known in London, blank-eyed, and thin as starving dogs, but alive. Sairy was there, a year older and chained to another girl I didn't know. Benjamin, the boy who'd made stones dance in the air, was there too. Somehow, I was responsible for both of them being there, but I couldn't remember why. I felt ashamed.

"Lizzie, dear," Esmeralda said quietly, "what did Jeremiah do to you while I was asleep? You look different. Are you all right?"

I leaned over and said in her ear. "He said some hocus pocus words that made my head all muzzy and confused."

"Have you looked into your glass?"

"What do you mean?"

"Take out your glass and look into it. Tell me what you see."

How very nonsensical. But I did it anyway, first checking that no one was looking; I didn't want my pretty glass stolen. "I don't see anything," I said finally. "It's just a shiny piece of glass. Did you think it was magic?"

She sighed heavily. "I see. I wish I'd been able to stay awake to see how he did it. But it might not have made any difference."

Jeremiah's mumbo jumbo hadn't harmed me, that I could tell. But then, I couldn't remember. I whispered, "Kat's here somewhere."

Mags and Daniel. That's why we were here. Gilbert said he wasn't here, and I didn't see him in the stable. Still, there were empty seats. I wouldn't let go of hope, not completely. "Does anyone know if a boy named Daniel was ever here? He looked a bit like me, but with dark curly hair."

Shaking heads.

"I'm sorry, Lizzie," Esmeralda said softly. Then she leaned forward and tapped the shoulder of the boy in front of her. When he turned, his mouth fell open. "It's an old lady!" he exclaimed. "What're you doing here?"

"Never mind that," she said. "Is everyone here gifted?"

The boy next to him turned. "Yeah, o' course we know about the gifted ones. But they all deny they have one, even though we seen 'em. They's all liars. Not that I blame 'em, but I'm the only one here without one."

"Ach, Sean, there you go again," the first boy said, exasperated. "I've *seen* you use yours. *I'm* the only one who doesn't have a gift."

This was said loud enough for everyone to hear, and more heads turned. Someone sitting near us laughed. Someone else said, "Here we go again." Several children began to argue, each claiming they had no gift, while others said they did.

It was obvious that no one in the stable thought they were gifted, although they could see everyone else was. I wondered how they could be so foolish as to miss the obvious. They wouldn't be here if they didn't have a gift. It was basic common sense. Everyone here was gifted. Everyone except me.

"Can you tell me what everyone's gifts are?" Esmeralda asked in a friendly voice. "It might help us escape."

That set off a storm of explanations and accusations. Everyone agreed on each child's gift—everyone except the child. One boy could melt stone or metal. The girl in the red shawl could freeze people or animals, just like a game of statues. Alf could lift things into the air. Jenny, an older girl with dark blonde hair and a worried expression, sang a song that put you to sleep. If she didn't sing again, they said, you'd never wake.

But no matter what the others said, each child was convinced they had no gift.

"Don't you see," Esmeralda said, "Jeremiah has convinced you of this? It's not true."

They stared at her, confused. They didn't see.

I nodded wisely. What she said made perfect sense.

We sat there for hours, Esmeralda patiently extracting information, but I barely paid attention. I felt hopeless. Daniel had never been there, and now that Gilbert knew about Mags, she was in horrible danger. And Gilbert's words nagged at me. Had Daniel left to get away from me, to save himself? Perhaps Mags would be free and happy if I hadn't meddled. Who was I to think

I could change anything? Maybe the wharf rats were being rounded up and sold off, even as we sat there.

Near midday, the bar on the door was lifted. Mags was escorted inside, and chained to the little redheaded girl. Then the servants unchained a boy with a shaven head and a little girl in a grubby apron and took them outside. Clean daylight streamed in from the door, a welcome sight.

Something touched me gently in the center of my forehead. A voice whispered, "Cromwell." Then, "Lizzie, my love, you always had a gift, you always will have a gift and you'll never forget that. You'll never obey Jeremiah no matter what he says. You're free of him. Do you understand, Lizzie?"

The cloud that had settled over my mind lifted and I remembered. Jeremiah had convinced me I was helpless, that I had no gift. But I wasn't helpless. I remembered what my glass could do. "Kat?" I whispered.

A soft voice murmured, "Cromwell," to the boy in front of me.

I pulled the glass from my pocket and stared into it hungrily. The light appeared.

Hazelton and Gilbert were in the entrance hall, talking quietly. "It's time to ask the girl for a prophecy," Lord Hazelton said. "I know you'll be pleased. Everything is in place. Once we're certain the king will come, we can leave for London."

"We should bring little Margaret too," Gilbert said. "We might need her at the house."

Lord Hazelton nodded, "'Tis a pity we'll have to kill her afterwards. She's invaluable."

Gilbert nodded, smiling. "Perhaps, my lord…please don't think me presumptuous, but perhaps when you're through with her, you could give her to me? That way she'd no longer be yours, and no longer a threat. Or only to me. I have my own plans for her, you see."

Hazelton laughed. "Still trying to pay the prophetess back? I understand you very well, Gilbert. I don't see why not. Still, it's a shame to lose such a useful gift."

"That reminds me, my lord. Little Mags knows the location of the den of these gifted children. They live together near the river. Find them, and you may replenish your stock, once these are safely disposed of. Once the king is dead, I'm sure that would be safe."

Lord Hazelton slapped him on the shoulder. "Capital notion, Gilbert. Bring her."

Even after the glass went dark, I continued to stare at it. Thinking.

It was all clear now: the plot against the king, and Maglena's warning that children would be his downfall. That's why Hazelton was afraid of them. Of course the simple-minded rogue would kill them all. And Gilbert had plans of his own. Even after I was dead, his revenge would go on—on Mags, and on the others in the Guild.

Around me, freed from Jeremiah's control, kinchin were trying out their gifts for the first time in months. But they could still die today, when Hazelton sent his men to kill them.

Voices outside the door announced the servants had returned. The children quickly fell silent, staring at the floor. The men unchained another pair and led them away.

I whispered in Esmeralda's ear, "Hazelton is going to kill every child here because of a poxy fortune-teller. We have to free the children before he leaves."

"Shh. They're coming back."

The broken-nosed man came toward me, keys in hand.

I spoke loudly, so the whole room could hear. "We need to do it within the next hour, do you understand?" I looked at Esmeralda desperately. "Or it will be too late."

"Shut your gob," the man said, unlocking my padlock. Unthreading the chain from my collar, he gestured for me to stand. "Yer wanted at the house." He relocked Esmeralda to the bench. At the door I stopped and looked back. Esmeralda nodded.

Impatient, the man yanked me outside by my braid.

We returned to the room with the red velvet chairs, where I was wrapped in chains and padlocked to the chair again. Free of Jeremiah's control, I realized the padlock was a sign not of powerlessness, but of our power. Hazelton had to chain us up to be in the same room. He was afraid of us.

It was possible Esmeralda and Kat could free the others in time, but I doubted it. I had to convince Hazelton to change his mind, give him a reason to keep the children alive. That was worth risking Gilbert's knife.

Hazelton took a wide stance before the empty hearth. Gilbert and Hawkins were by the door. Jeremiah moved to stand behind me. He stank of fear.

Hazelton smiled. "Well, Lizzie, time to prove yourself. Jeremiah?" He waved his hand.

Jeremiah touched my forehead and whispered, "Cromwell." He straightened and said loudly, "Use your gift for your master."

I shook my head from side to side and blinked my eyes, feigning confusion. "Yes, master?"

Lord Hazelton loomed over me. "Will the king be at the party, Lizzie? Will he be there?"

I blinked. *A party?* The king would have to be a bufflehead to accept an invitation from Hazelton, if he knew the man wanted his throne.

"I need a bowl of water," I said. "And a table to put it on." My hand was in my pocket, holding my glass for reassurance, but I wouldn't risk using it; they might take it from me.

Hawkins opened the door and spoke to someone. Soon, a servant dragged a table before me, while a second brought a bowl of water, placing it before me.

I stared at my reflection, but nothing happened. "Open the curtains. There isn't enough light."

Instead of being irritated, Lord Hazelton appeared impressed by my requests. He stood with folded arms, watching me intently. The curtains were thrown open.

I bent over the bowl, waiting. The ball of light spun, then the scene formed. A wide, paved street ended at an arched gateway of stone. A black coach drove through it, stopping at the steps to a grand, four-story house. Servants in green livery spilled out the door to welcome the guests. A coat of arms, brightly painted and gilded, was carved on the door. It grew larger before my eyes. Lions, a unicorn, a harp; they were the coat of arms of the kings of England.

A footman opened the door and lowered the steps. A man in a dark periwig, dressed in white satin with crimson slashes, stepped down from the coach, and began to climb the steps to the front door. It was the king; I recognized him from the river procession. The man who stepped down after the king resembled him, especially his long nose. He wore a chestnut periwig, a green velvet cloak, and a sour expression.

The king entered a grand entrance hall, the walls and floor of pinkish marble, with tapestries on the walls. A grey-haired woman in a pale-colored dress, her bodice too modest for current fashion, curtsied deeply. Then the vision shrank and disappeared.

I took a deep breath and sat back, wondering what it meant.

Lord Hazelton demanded, "What did you see?"

Time to lie. This must be about his plan to kill the king. But normally the visions I saw warned me of something that would threaten *me*. How could I be threatened by the king's arrival?

Racking my brains, I tried to imagine what would play on Hazelton's fears. Even the truth might work.

"My lord, I see danger for you. Someone close to you, a dark-haired man, threatens your life. But what you need to defend yourself is at hand. Your children could save you." Jeremiah inhaled sharply.

Hazelton raised a skeptical eyebrow. "Really?" He flicked a glance at Jeremiah, who flushed. "I don't suppose *you're* one of those children who will save me? Really, my dear, if you're going to tell such an obvious lie, I'm afraid Gilbert—"

I interrupted quickly. "I saw the king's coach pull up to the steps of a grand house. The king was greeted in the entrance hall by a woman with grey hair. The floor was pink marble and there were red and green tapestries on the walls. Another man accompanied him, with a chestnut periwig, but I didn't know him. He looked like the king, so 'twas probably his brother."

Lord Hazelton smiled happily, my warning apparently forgotten. "You see, Gilbert? The king will come. She saw him arrive at the house."

Jeremiah put his hands on the table and leaned over me. "Ask her who the lady was." His eyes glittered with anger. He'd pay me back for that warning.

Lord Hazelton raised his eyebrows. "Well?"

"I don't know, my lord. I've never seen her before."

Jeremiah backhanded me across the face. "Liar!"

When I straightened, eyes tearing from anger and humiliation, Gilbert was smiling broadly. Jeremiah leaned over me and I shrank back. He pointed, his finger inches from my eyes. "You wrote to Lady Cheshire and you expect my lord to believe you've never seen her?"

"Is that who it was? My sister works for her, but I've never met her. How would I know a great lady?"

Jeremiah raised his hand again but looked uncertain.

Hazelton said dismissively, "Of course Lady Cheshire wouldn't associate with a servant's sister. Don't damage my prophetess again, Jeremiah. I'm sure she's telling the truth—she described the house perfectly. *She saw the king arrive.* Do you understand? We don't need to change our plans. Everything will happen just as we thought. We should leave soon, to be in London in good time." He glanced at Gilbert. "Cheer up, man, this is the best news we could hope for. In a few days, when you're living in Whitehall Palace with the king's ear, you won't care about this dirty ragtag."

He walked to the door. "Take care of her, Jeremiah. I may need her again before we leave. Gilbert? Come with me."

Gilbert threw a longing glance in my direction but followed him. I braced myself for what was to come.

Jeremiah touched the center of my forehead, saying, "Cromwell. I'll pay you back, jade. No one crosses me and lives."

I fought the muzzy feeling that swept over me, and repeated silently: *Cromwell, Cromwell, I have a gift, Cromwell, Cromwell, I have a gift,* repeating it over and over, to block Jeremiah's words.

Then the man with the broken nose was unlocking the padlock and pulling on the chain. I ignored him, repeating the words, *I have a gift, I have a gift,* until Jeremiah was gone.

I was jerked to my feet and led down the hallway.

I'd failed. Hazelton would still order the death of every child in the stable before he left.

30

FREEDOM

JEREMIAH WAS GONE. The broken-nosed servant was leading me down the hallway.

Standing by the front door, Hazelton and Gilbert conferred in low voices. Hazelton noticed the servant and beckoned. The man dropped my chain and obeyed. Then the three of them walked out the door, closing it behind them. I was alone in the hallway.

With trembling hands, I pulled out my glass, afraid my gift was gone. When the ball of light appeared, I sank to the floor in relief.

The vision showed that same entrance hall, but with bright sunlight streaming through an open door. Footmen were carrying trunks and boxes outside to where a coach was being loaded.

Hazelton spoke quietly with Gilbert. "You want power, just as I do, Gilbert. That's how I know I can trust you," Hazelton said. "Jeremiah will show his hand at the party. He wants to bring back the old days of marauding with the army, with no law but himself. He wants civil war." He laughed grimly. "I had the girl question Hawkins. He told me everything. Jeremiah plans to kill me, once the king is dead. The prophetess' warning was true."

"What if Hawkins warns *him*?"

Lord Hazelton brushed a speck from his sleeve. "Hawkins won't be warning anyone. Jeremiah thinks I sent him to London on an errand."

"Then why not take care of Jeremiah too? Why wait?" Gilbert said.

Lord Hazelton gave him a fond look. "It would be more sensible, wouldn't it? But I need him to control the children. Keeping them alive is risky enough. That fortune-teller has been right about everything else, and the children *are* a threat, whatever Jeremiah says. Once he's killed the king for me, I'll take care of him. If anything goes wrong, it'll be him that's drawn and quartered. Once all the children are dead, I'll be safe. And I'll be king."

"And if Jeremiah refuses?"

"Then he's given himself away and I expect you to deal with him. Will you do that for me, Gilbert?"

Gilbert bowed. "Of course, my lord. I'm honored by your confidence."

The glass went dark.

Hazelton and his men would be leaving soon. We had to get away, before Hazelton's men arrived at the stable to kill us.

"Lizzie!" a whisper startled me out of my thoughts. No one was there. "Kat?"

She appeared in front of me. "We can go to London with them," she said breathlessly. "I can hide you in the boot of the coach, and I'll ride up top. We can free Mags on the road."

I shook my head. "We can't just leave the children."

"Lizzie, *Mags* is why we're here."

"Hazelton has ordered that every child is to be killed. Whatever you choose to do, I have to stay and free them."

For a moment she looked surprised, and then that faint smile appeared. "You think I'd leave you behind? Of course I'll stay. Just one condition: we keep Esmeralda chained up."

I laughed. I'd been certain Kat wouldn't let me down. "My guard has disappeared. Let's go."

At the reminder, she disappeared too. I heard her say beside me, "I don't understand any of this. What's in London?"

"A party at Lady Cheshire's house."

"You're joking."

I'd have to tell her the rest soon, but not yet. And when I did, she might never speak to me again. Assuming we lived that long.

The hallway was empty and the outdoor kitchen deserted. All the servants must be helping prepare for the journey. And the massacre. But why wasn't anyone guarding me? The answer came all too readily: *because my gift is no threat.*

We made it to the door of the stables without meeting a soul. It was a hot sunny morning, birds chittering in the surrounding trees. Together, Kat and I lifted the bar on the door.

Dust motes danced in the light from the door. Everything looked the same. The children sat chained together in pairs, staring dully at the walls or floor. I left the door open behind me. Heads turned as I approached Esmeralda.

"She's back," a boy announced, grinning broadly. "Can we start now?"

"Indeed we can," Esmeralda said.

He rose, hunched over because of the chain, and screwed his eyes shut. His chain dripped, slowly at first, then melted completely, like butter in the sun. The children clapped.

"Shh." Esmeralda said. "Don't make noise or they'll check on us. Let's be quick and quiet. Save your cheering for when we're away from here."

The children nodded, their faces solemn. Some were still trying out their gifts, as though they couldn't believe their luck.

"Well, Lizzie? What's to do?" Esmeralda asked.

I said, loud enough for all to hear, "Hazelton is leaving with Gilbert and Jeremiah. That's the good news. Here's the bad: he's given orders to his men that we're all to be killed once they're away. We have to escape *now*."

It was a risk, telling them the truth. They might panic, but they had to know how serious this was. Some cried out, but others looked defiant. David, a child of great strength, ripped a chain from its hasp, freeing the girl in the red shawl. The boy who could melt metal was concentrating on the padlocks now; it took too long for the chains to melt.

A shadow passed across the door. The children shrank down into their seats, heads down, but there was no one there. Then Kat was standing beside me, a key in her hand. "The loobies left it on a hook by the door. Let's get those chains off," she said.

She moved up and down the rows, unlocking the padlocks. It seemed to take forever, but at long last the hated chains and collars came off. The kinchin who'd been there the longest had raw wounds around their necks.

Kat asked loudly, "Does Jeremiah have a gift?"

A boy replied, "Grown-ups don't have gifts."

"I'm afraid some do," I said. "It's possible Jeremiah used more than words to control us. We have to avoid him at all costs." I looked at the empty seats on the benches. Mags was missing. "Who isn't here?"

"Jenny's not here," a girl called.

"Alf's gone too," someone said. Alf was the one who could lift objects into the air.

"They took them after you," the girl said. "Gilbert came and took your friend, said he wanted to take special care of her."

Fear rose like bile in my throat. Gilbert knew I cared about Mags and I had no doubt he'd take his anger out on her. If Hazelton already had the children he needed, the killers might already be on their way. "Is everyone free?" Heads nodded. "Then let's go."

No one was in sight at the back of the house. The children filed out silently, blinking in the bright sunlight. Some were limping, after being chained so long. We set out in a straggling line, reaching the thin woods without being seen.

I stopped in a clearing and asked softly, "Does anyone know how to get to the road?"

Jane, the little girl with the red shawl, raised her hand. "We weren't always locked up, see. Sometimes the lord took us for walks, like we was pets or something. We'd come out here to welcome visitors. He showed us off like we was his *menage-ary*."

Thank God for the man's vanity. "Lead the way."

We trudged slowly through the woods, and we weren't quiet; children who haven't had exercise or proper sleep for months can't be expected to walk without stumbling or making noise.

That's why the men who came after us found us easily.

They carried nets and staves, but they hadn't reckoned on the children having regained their gifts. They'd bullied and beaten these children before, and they weren't remotely cautious. A man raised his stave to hit a cowering boy, only to find himself frozen in that position.

Another man threatened a child with a knife. It flew up into the air, then dived back to wound him.

All the nets and staves rose into the air and stayed there, until some of the staves floated toward the men and began to beat them on the head. They cowered down, afraid to run.

Jane turned some into statues.

One little girl lifted every man in her reach and set him astride a tree branch. They sat in the trees looking stunned, afraid to call for help.

The children laughed and congratulated each other until Kat reminded them we were still on Lord Hazelton's land, saying that more men would come. They lowered their voices, but the smiles remained. I heard whispered boasts. We set off again, following Jane through the woods.

I feared an ambush with swords or pistols, but we made it to the road without interference. No other men came. The wrought-iron gates swung open noiselessly when Kat pushed them, and we stumbled through, across the road, and into the thicker woods beyond.

We'd left Hazelton's land. But how would we get back to London with twenty-odd children, starving, ragged, and injured?

Kat, Esmeralda, and I each led a group. We herded them along, a stone's throw to the left of the road, scrambling through thickets of blackberry and hemlock, ready to scatter and hide if we saw anyone coming.

I told my group to stay together, and then ran to catch up with Kat. Gathering my courage, I touched her arm. "I have something to tell you."

Her eyes were examining the undergrowth as though expecting an ambush. "What's that?" she asked absently.

"Hazelton and his men are going to a party at Lady Cheshire's house, I think tonight. The king will be there. I saw him arrive in a vision. Hazelton plans to kill the king."

"*What?*" Kat stopped. The children stopped too, watching us nervously. "Why didn't you tell me before?"

"Well, first because we had other things to think about, and second, after Jeremiah caught us I couldn't—"

Her eyes flashed. "You could have, Lizzie, and you know it."

"And then what? You'd have gone straight to London, and we'd all still be locked in the stable. None of the children would know they were gifted, including me. We needed you, Kat."

She was furious: her face pale, her lips pressed in a thin line. She walked away from me without a word.

I've just lost a friend. Maybe she'd never trust me again, but I couldn't have done anything else. No one helped *us*. The plaguey king left us to fend for ourselves—let him do the same. At least he had an army.

I returned to my group. Half an hour had passed since we left the gate behind, when we heard horses coming toward us on the road.

"Everyone hide," Esmeralda called. The children scattered behind bushes and trees. I ran to the opposite side of the road. If a decoy was needed, I'd be ready.

There was the rattle of harness and then four horses came into view, pulling not a coach but a wagon. And *Thomas* was on the driver's bench. Beside him were the two travelling children, Rosie and Sam.

I ran out into the road, waving my arms above my head. "Thomas!"

He pulled hard on the reins. The horses, sweating hard, stopped barely a few feet away. Thomas jumped down and pulled me into a tight embrace. When he released me, he looked me up and down critically. "Are you all right?"

"I'm fine. What're you doing here?"

"Serena sent me." He grinned at my expression. So Serena had gotten my letter. And done something about it.

"Are you sure you're all right? Who else is with you?"

"I'm fine, Thomas. But Esmeralda's been hurt, and some of the children from Hazelton's stable are in sad shape, but we're all ready to leave." I called out to the woods. "He's a friend."

Rosie and Sam climbed down and Rosie ran over to give me a hug. I took hold of my pocket and held on tight before embracing her. "Why are you here, Rosie?"

"Rosie told me you'd been captured and offered to show me the way here," Thomas said.

"You saved me from them cutthroats," Rosie said seriously. "An' I told my folks we had to save you."

Sam said, "That's right. We always pay debts o' honor."

Surprised, all I could think to say was, "Thank you."

Rosie turned to her brother. "See? I told you she'd believe me." Sam punched her lightly in the arm, grinning.

The children came out of their hiding places slowly, afraid it was a trick.

"It's all right," I said, speaking mostly to Kat and Esmeralda. "Serena sent him. I'll explain later."

With Kat and Esmeralda assuring their groups it was safe, everyone climbed aboard the wagon and settled in the wagon bed. The children were so relieved they didn't have to walk that soon they were talking loudly, all caution forgotten.

I sat on the driving bench between Thomas and Rosie. Thomas coaxed the horses to back and turn the wagon. "How did you know to bring a wagon, Thomas? A horse would have been faster."

"Serena told me about the Guild." He stole a glance sideways. "I do understand, Lizzie. I knew you wouldn't leave without the kinchin. The wagon is to take everyone home."

Warmth spread through me. Likely I was smiling like a looby. Thomas had never betrayed me. And to come all this way—he must care about me. The moment I saw him on the wagon, I felt so happy. I decided I cared for him, too.

But the rats still needed me. I took a breath. "We'll need fresh horses soon."

"I know," he said. "But I've spent all the money. I don't know how we'll get them. And these need to be returned to the mail post."

"I've an idea." I climbed into the back and kneeled beside Kat to explain the situation. She listened, at least.

"If we can convince the postmaster at Caxton to exchange these for fresh horses, we can make it." Then she said loudly, "It's too bad I lost my purse. There's a letter in it that would get us fresh horses." She stared meaningfully at Rosie.

Rosie reached into her pocket and pulled out the purse, handing it to Kat, not the least bit embarrassed. "Will that help, mistress?"

Kat opened it and removed a folded piece of parchment with a red seal dangling from it. "Yes."

Rosie looked pleased.

In the end, we stopped at the fair to borrow four horses from Rosie's uncle, since ours were nearly spent, with the promise to send the children back with them from Caxton. I was amazed they agreed. Rosie must have described her rescue in glowing terms. They even refused the reward Kat offered. Of course, most of the coins in Kat's purse had already disappeared. Leading the exhausted post horses behind the wagon, we arrived in Caxton in good time.

Our luck held in Caxton. Fresh post horses were available in exchange for the ones Thomas had brought, and Kat's letter worked a charm. The postmaster bowed and surrendered them to her.

Before we sent Rosie and Sam back to Barsington, I hugged Rosie goodbye, hand firmly on my pocket. They rode off, leading the extra horses.

Everyone was hungry, so we stopped at the *Robin Hood Inn* to gather news and have a quick bite in the courtyard. Esmeralda paid for it out of her fair earnings. While the children wolfed down bread and cheese, Kat gave Tilda a letter to send to the duke by express messenger.

If Kat's warning arrived before we did, the king might not go to the party, but that wouldn't save Mags or the other children. I wanted the king to go to the party. If Hazelton was caught in the act of trying to kill him, the king would have to arrest him. And if we were the ones who stopped him, wouldn't the king help us?

Esmeralda came over to me, munching on bread and cheese. "That bloody-handed rogue Jeremiah has escaped me again," she muttered. "We have to catch them, Lizzie. We must arrive before the king."

"Now you're worried about Charles Stuart's safety?"

"Ha! A pox on all Stuarts. We have to get there in time, or Jeremiah will escape me again."

I shivered at the thought of Hazelton or Jeremiah free to come after us again. "Everyone, let's go!"

Back in the wagon, I claimed the seat beside Thomas again.

"How long before we reach London?" I asked, raising my voice to be heard over the sound of the horses' hooves.

"By nightfall if we're lucky. God knows I'm going to try." His expression was grim and determined.

"I didn't know you cared so much about the king."

He glanced at me in surprise. "The king? I wouldn't give a clipped farthing for the king."

"Then why—"

"Don't you understand, Lizzie? Those men kidnapped you. They could've killed you, not to mention the kinchin." He spoke slowly, measuring each word. "I'm going to make sure Hazelton's head ends up on a pike above Traitor's Gate."

31

LADY CHESHIRE'S PARTY

With fresh horses and a dry road we made good time, passing through the Aldgate at sunset.

After my absence, the city felt different. The tall houses stooped menacingly over streets darkened by rain and coal smoke. The twisting lanes and alleys were a trap for the unwary. Beneath the choking ceiling of smoke, mismatched buildings crowded near the river, fighting to breathe. Not until a last finger of sunlight gleamed across the brown water did I feel I'd come home.

I was torn; I wanted to save Mags and the others before harm came to them, and to expose Hazelton as a traitor, but the children in the wagon had been through enough. If we brought them to Lady Cheshire's, they'd be within Hazelton's reach again. "Esmeralda, will you take the children to Haven?"

"No," she said simply. "And you know why. I wager they won't go, either." She turned and asked them in a loud voice.

She was right. The children shook their heads. Pale, sick, and frightened though they were, they wanted to make sure Hazelton was stopped. "Besides," Sairy said, "he has Jenny, Alf, and Mags. We can't abandon them."

Dusk fell. Torches flared on the main streets. Following Esmeralda's directions, we passed empty fields until we reached Chelsea and the imposing house I'd seen in my vision. It sat but a stone's throw from the river, with boats bobbing on the evening tide at its dock. The smell of reeds and brackish water greeted me like an old friend.

Judging by the coaches parked in the mews, the party was well underway. The royal coach wasn't there, but other fancy coaches were lined up, their white-gloved footmen and drivers in groups, talking quietly. They looked startled when Thomas parked the wagon beside them and jumped down to help us climb down. Esmeralda led the way into the kitchen. The cook and serving maids nodded to her, but were too busy loading trays and preparing food to ask questions.

"Everyone," Esmeralda called out, and they looked up. "Help any ragged child who asks for it, and don't interfere with them. They're here on Lady's Cheshire's orders, to help the king." There were disbelieving looks at that, but no one contradicted her. The servants knew Esmeralda had Lady Cheshire's confidence.

Esmeralda murmured to Kat and me, "Lady Cheshire's folk are sensible. They'll believe me. The difficulty will be the servants hired for the night."

She was right; we looked like beggars, our clothes torn and dirty. We'd be lucky not to be thrown out. The children counted off into three groups, with Kat, Thomas, and Esmeralda each leading one. I would run between them.

"There may be guards around the king who'll stop us from getting close," Esmeralda said. "Kat, go to the duke and warn him of the danger. He'll trust you."

I smiled to myself. Cromwell's former spy had changed her tune.

Thomas called, "My group, with me, to the cellar." They headed down the servants' hallway.

Esmeralda and her group headed for the boathouse. Kat's

group would search the first floor, but Kat came with me to look for the duke in the ballroom. Esmeralda said it was on the first floor, the one above where we'd entered.

"I hear music," Kat said. White-gloved servants passed us carrying trays of food; one of them frowned at me as though I were a stain on the carpet. We followed them—at a safe distance—through a wide doorway.

A crowd of nobs and merchants, dressed in their finest, stood beneath crystal chandeliers, the trembling pendants sending rainbows across the walls. Long tables held every kind of fish, fowl, and fruit. My stomach rumbled and I swiped a handful of grapes and ate them, my back turned, hoping no one noticed.

A viola and harpsichord played in the corner, but loud voices drowned them out. Silks of apricot and lime flashed against satins of cherry and lemon while gold jewelry and precious gems winked in the candlelight. Merchants, their black attire relieved only by white lace at the wrist and throat, stood in a corner by themselves. Flowers sat beside bowls of punch, with bottles of wine and sack. The opulence of the room made me feel even more conspicuous and dirty in my faded, travel-stained clothes.

Across the room, uncurtained windows stretched from floor to ceiling, framing the deep blue sky of summer. Montmorency was admiring his reflection in one, while chatting with a woman powdered and tinted to the height of fashion. At least one of the conspirators was already here.

I guessed Hazelton would be hiding with the children until Montmorency lured the king within reach. Of course, if he'd been invited, he might simply walk in like any other guest.

Kat completed a circuit of the room and joined me by the door. "I don't see him. Do we know whether the king has arrived?"

I shook my head. "The safest thing would be to get him to leave," I whispered.

"I'd rather catch Hazelton in the act, wouldn't you?"

I nodded, surprised she felt the same way. After all, there was a risk Hazelton's plan might succeed. Whatever his faults, Charles the Second seemed a good-natured cove. He was probably a better king than his sour-faced brother would be. Rumor said James, the Duke of York, was still a practicing Catholic, and a Catholic on the throne would start another civil war as surely as Jeremiah's plan.

A well-dressed couple entered and stopped dead, staring at us with shocked expressions. We were too conspicuous. I tapped Kat's arm and nodded toward a corner where a footman held a tray. We moved behind him.

A loud *thump* startled me. A man in wine-colored satin with a powdered peruke stood in the doorway, rapping the floor with his staff. He called loudly, "Ladies and gentlemen, lords and ladies, I give you His Royal Highness, King Charles the Second, Ruler of Great Britain, France and Hibernia, and James, Duke of York."

Everyone turned to look. The majordomo (Kat whispered that's who he was) stepped aside, bowing, and the king entered, followed by his brother.

Lady Cheshire stepped forward and curtsied, saying, "Welcome, Your Majesty." This wasn't how it had happened in my vision. Maybe that was a good sign.

Lord Montmorency's heels clicked across the floor. He pushed forward to bow with a flourish. "Your Majesty," he said, "there's someone I'd like you to meet." *Here it comes. This is how they'll do it.*

But Lady Cheshire smoothly interrupted. "Forgive me, Lord Montmorency, but as hostess, it is *my* duty to introduce my guests. There are many important people here tonight." She smiled at Montmorency with a look that would curdle milk. He bowed and moved out of her way.

Well done, Lady Cheshire. I peered around the footman at the king's guards. Two young gentlemen in extravagant clothes, wearing dress swords, followed the king and his brother. The perfume trailing them would choke a horse. I didn't think they'd be much use in a fight.

I turned to speak to Kat, but she'd disappeared, probably to warn the duke.

The footman gave me a sour look. "If you leave now without causing a fuss, I won't summon the grooms to give you a working over. Stay and the fellows will be happy to give you a beating."

I gave him the evil eye right back. "If you interfere with me or any of the other kinchin, you'll be sorry. Lady Cheshire knows why we're here and approves."

He laughed. "Pull the other one. Now, out or I'll toss you out."

I scowled but edged toward the door. There was no reason to stay anyway—Hazelton wasn't here. Mags, Jenny, and Alf would be with him, and they were my main concern now. The king had Kat and his perfumed gentleman to protect him.

In the hall, I waited for a couple to pass before I grabbed a lit candelabrum from a table. Opening a door down the hall at random, I entered an empty bedroom with no curtains and the mattress rolled up. I put down the candlestick, sat on the floor, and reached for my glass.

The swirling light became a sitting room with a fire burning on the hearth and candles flickering in the breeze from an open window. Lord Hazelton sat at his ease in a red wing chair, fiddling with a pistol. Gilbert stood beside him, arms folded, staring at nothing. Mags, Jenny, and Alf were on stools on the other side of him; they looked sleepy and confused. Through the window, the masts of a ship slid down river against the evening sky. Lord Hazelton was already here, but on the ground floor in a room facing the river. I was on the wrong floor.

Hazelton turned his head. "Find out what's keeping Jeremiah."

Gilbert bowed and left the room.

The scene changed. Thomas walked past a wall of undressed

stone to stand behind a circle of children. And in the center was Jeremiah.

He drew a knife, but dropped it quickly, sucking his hand as though he'd been burned. His eyes showed white, like a frightened horse.

The expression on Thomas's face in the shadows was unreadable.

Jeremiah kept turning, trying to keep all the children in sight. I thought he was grinning, until I realized his lips were contorted in a grimace. He muttered over and over, "Cromwell, my dears, Cromwell. I'm your master. Do what your master says. Go to sleep now. Go to sleep."

The children stared at him without pity. The redheaded girl rose in the air and hovered over Jeremiah's head, pretending to reach for him or kick him, although she never touched him. Jeremiah stumbled, trying to keep her in sight.

It was a bear baiting, with Jeremiah as the bear. It wouldn't be long before the threatened blows became real. Traitor or not, if they killed him the children would be hanged. Why didn't Thomas stop it?

I shoved the glass into my pocket and blew out the candles. I ran down the stairs to the hallway I guessed led to the cellar. Opening a heavy door, I saw stone steps descending, torches burning above them. I went down cautiously.

The scene from my vision was laid out before me.

Jeremiah, desperate to protect himself, was muttering, "Cromwell," to no avail. He froze, then tried to run, desperate, until he was frozen again. Soon he'd hurt a child, trying to break free. The children's faces were calm and intent. Much as I hated Jeremiah, I couldn't let them kill him. That would be Hazelton's final crime against them. There was a better way, one that wouldn't risk a child hanging.

"It's too late," I called loudly. "Let him go. The king is dead."

The children gasped. Thomas stepped forward and met my eyes. I shook my head the tiniest fraction.

"She's right. Let him go. We should find Alf, Jenny, and Mags. It was a good try and now it's over. But Jeremiah—" Thomas moved forward. "Come near these children again and I'll shoot you like a dog." He raised a flintlock. *Where had that come from?*

Jeremiah nodded, relieved. It was easy to guess his thoughts: part of his plan was already accomplished. All he had to do now was kill Hazelton and the good old days would return.

He hurried up the stairs. After the door closed, I said quietly. "Everyone, go to the kitchen and wait. Thomas, will you stay with them?" He swallowed a protest and nodded.

I intended to follow Jeremiah to the room where Hazelton waited.

I ran up the stairs and down the servants' hallway, following the sound of Jeremiah's footsteps. When I reached the marble entrance, he was out of sight. The footman who stood beside the front door stared at me open-mouthed, but made no move to stop me.

I crossed to the hall opposite. The first door on the right slammed. Before I could reach it, I heard the sound of a pistol shot.

I ran to the door and threw it open.

Jeremiah's body lay on the floor. Hazelton stood over him, a pistol dangling from his hand. Blue smoke hung in the air, and with it the smell of gunpowder.

Mags was on her feet, staring down at Jeremiah with a mixture of triumph and disgust on her face. Jenny and Alf had moved behind chairs, and now peered around them.

The smoke made me cough. At the sound, Hazelton threw down the flintlock to draw his sword. Before I could move, the tip was against my throat. "What are you doing here, Prophetess?" he hissed. "You should be dead."

For the second time, Mags saved my life. She darted beneath

his arm and stomped his foot before leaping away. Hazelton swore and turned, slicing the air where she'd been moments before. Alf shoved him from behind. He stumbled and nearly fell, his face turning crimson. He whipped around, cursing, ready to skewer any child in reach.

"No!" I yelled. "Face me, you coward!"

He turned back and raised the tip of his sword once more to my throat. "Gladly."

I heard the door open and footsteps behind me, but I didn't turn, my eyes on Hazelton, waiting for him to slit my throat. A cloud of perfume enveloped me, and a man stepped between us, his sword aimed at Hazelton's heart.

Hazelton took a step back. Then another.

It was one of the king's perfumed gentlemen, dressed in petticoat trousers of green silk.

The second gentleman stepped forward to slam Hazelton's wrist with the butt of his knife. The sword fell to the floor. The first gentleman had his arm around Hazelton's neck. He said to me, "Your pardon, mistress, if I brushed against you." He looked behind me. "We have him, Your Majesty."

I turned and gasped. The king stood behind me.

"Caught in the act, Hazelton," he said, "with a body warm on the floor. Thank you for making this so easy. These gentlemen will escort you to the Tower."

"For what?" Hazelton drew himself up. "It was self-defense."

"The charge is treason. Your title is hereby abolished. But we can speak at leisure once you've gone down the river. Gentlemen, if you will?"

For a moment I thought Hazelton would try to escape, but he went limp, muttering, "Not possible!" He looked at me with horror. "It was *you*, you and the other children, just as the gipsy said. I should've killed you when I had the chance."

The first gentleman pushed Hazelton toward the door, while the other retrieved the sword and pistol. The king considered me a moment, raising an eyebrow, then he nodded and left. It had all happened so fast I hadn't the wits to curtsy.

Mags and I simply looked at each other. Alf and Jenny came forward with dazed expressions. Jeremiah was dead and Hazelton had been arrested by the king himself.

It was difficult to take in. Staring at Jeremiah's body on the red Turkey carpet, all I felt was emptiness. I wondered if Esmeralda would feel cheated.

Mags touched my arm. "I knew you'd come. What now?"

Suddenly I was so tired I couldn't think. "First of all, Mags, *Cromwell*." I touched her forehead. "You're free to use your gift and no one can ever take it away again." When I'd done the same for Jenny and Alf, we left the room, stepping over Jeremiah's body.

"Go to the kitchen, down that hallway." I pointed. "I'll be there in a minute." I went back down the hall, opening doors. I found an empty room with a fire and sat down beside it, hugging myself to stop trembling. I took the glass from my pocket and rubbed my fingers over its warm surface. Then I held it up and asked to see where Gilbert was.

The river appeared, in daylight. Above it, ranks of dark clouds moved swiftly across the sky and there were whitecaps on the waves. Small boats had snapped their moorings and were racing down river, out of control. Some had already smashed against the starlings beneath the bridge, the wreckage spinning in eddies around them.

A great storm was blowing down the Thames. Skiffs, wherries, and ships battled the rising tide, struggling toward shelter. Those already wrecked, dashed against a pier or hitting each other at their moorings, were a hazard. Merchantmen headed downriver, to safer anchorage at sea, while the watermen tied up their boats and left them, abandoning them to the storm. There was no sign of Gilbert.

Of what use is this? Where's Daniel, then? I asked angrily. As if in reply, the glass went dark.

Anger cleared my wits. I hurried down the hall. A crowd of servants prevented me from reaching the entrance hall. I tried to push through but a footman pulled me back. "Stay here, wench! The king is leaving." I wriggled out of his grasp and edged to the front.

Lady Cheshire had dropped into a curtsy, her skirts spread around her. The king and his brother were saying goodbye.

"We thank you," said the king, "for your help in thwarting this man's plan to assassinate us and to throw our kingdom into chaos. We are deeply in your debt." He inclined his head and Lady Cheshire bent hers.

Just what I'd expect from a king. He thanked the nob and ignored us completely. Yes, Lady Cheshire helped us escape by sending Thomas, and she'd given us the run of her house, but what about us, the kinchin and the wharf rats? We'd helped save his life, too.

Kat told me later she'd warned the Duke of York that Hazelton was there, waiting to assassinate the king. The duke tried to persuade his brother to leave, but the king had insisted on looking for Hazelton himself.

After the king and his brother had left, taking Montmorency and Hazelton with him, the party continued. None of the guests seemed to notice anything amiss until it was time to leave and they gathered to say farewell to Lady Cheshire, and to collect their cloaks in the entry hall.

"I suppose it's some crank of Lady Cheshire's," I heard a well-upholstered woman mutter to her husband, as she eyed the dirty, ragged kinchin.

The children handed the guests their coats and wraps, smiling and bowing and bidding them good night.

"Thank heavens those ragamuffins didn't find their way into the party!"

32

REUNION

IN THE KITCHEN, a second party was underway.

Beside the great hearth, the children sat around a long table, eating and drinking their fill. Their eyes sparkled and they laughed easily, free from fear at last.

In a low voice, I told Kat Gilbert had gotten away. She frowned. "Well, we can't chase him tonight."

Then I took Esmeralda aside and told her Jeremiah was dead. "Where is he?" she asked fiercely. "I have to see for myself." So I led her to the door of the room where his body lay and left her there. We never spoke of it again.

It was late, so Lady Cheshire let us stay the night, two or three kinchin sharing a bed. I was practically asleep where I stood and don't remember how I got to bed. I woke in the hours before dawn, panic gripping me. Mags was asleep beside me, with Jane on the other side. Memory returned gradually: Jeremiah was dead and Hazelton was arrested and in the Tower. But Gilbert was still free. I slid out of the bed onto cold floorboards, trying not to wake the others. I sat beside the hearth, using the faint ember light to look at my glass.

Boats bobbed beneath me on the river: I was looking down like a gull hovering in flight. An empty cargo net floated vertically, driven by the wind. Bits of rope, straw, and empty sacks scudded down a wharf, tumbling over men and equipment. The cranes had been abandoned and the wharf men were taking cover from the storm.

The glass went dark. Another poxy mystery. It seemed the glass refused to show me what I most needed to know, whether it was about my brother, or Gilbert. There was nothing I could do about a storm on the river. I climbed back into bed and fell asleep.

We breakfasted with Lady Cheshire, and Quality or no, she seemed pleased to have us as guests, even after a party for the king.

The party helped. There was so much food left over she said it was a mercy we could help her eat it before it all went bad. We tried delicacies none of us had ever seen before. Tiny birds in aspic jelly, tarts and pastries made with butter and filled with jam or savories, larks' tongues, venison, lobster. The freed kinchin celebrated their new lives with a feast, but I felt gloomy. Now that these children were safe, my disappointment at not finding my brother returned. And I was impatient to return to Haven, to learn whether the wharf rats were safe.

Lady Cheshire sat at the long, grand table chatting happily with all the kinchin, and I decided she was simply a good person and forgot she was a nob. She took me aside and said when she'd received my letter from Barsington she'd given Serena the money to send someone. I thanked her again and again, saying we wouldn't have made it back in time without her help.

The children were stuffing themselves full of pastries when Serena rushed in. She curtsied to Her Ladyship, then embraced Esmeralda, crying in relief. They whispered a moment and Serena nodded with grim satisfaction. Then she came and pulled me into a hug. "I'm so glad to see you safe, Lizzie! I feared I'd never see you again. *All's well that ends well.*" I smiled and said nothing. I couldn't shake my sadness. Besides, I knew it wasn't over for me. Gilbert was out there somewhere.

Lady Cheshire's housekeeper began to clean and bandage the kinchin's wounds, but when she saw how serious some of the cases were, she insisted we all had to have a bath, to make sure the wounds didn't fester. There was quite a to-do of housemaids carrying buckets of hot water and one boy protesting loudly that it made no sense to risk dying from an ague, after all they'd been through. Besides the raw sores on their necks, one lad had maggots in a wound on his leg, and Emily had an infected foot. After the baths, the housekeeper cleaned and bandaged their wounds, and when she was finished, they both appeared happier.

When I emerged, raw and dripping from a housemaid's scrubbing, I sat with the other kinchin in the warm kitchen beside the hearth, wrapped in a sheet and rubbing my hair with a towel. They'd taken our clothes away, but I'd snatched my pocket back.

Lady Cheshire and Esmeralda bustled in, their arms full of clothes. "I hope you can use some of these. My nieces and nephews grew out of them long ago. They're not the latest fashion, but I hope you won't mind." We exchanged glances. No one could object to the fine silks and muslins she'd found. Such clothes would fetch a good price, even if they didn't fit.

But nearly everyone found some that did. Thomas said he couldn't take charity, but when Lady Cheshire explained she'd have to sell the clothes anyway, he took hold of his pride and accepted a cream-colored, nettle-cloth shirt, new smallclothes, and a pair of faded but sound breeches of green linen. He got his old clothes back too. Many didn't. Some had been wearing rags.

For me there was a blue suit of nettle-cloth, which lasts forever, the skirt happily longer than my old one. A new shift of lawn and new petticoats made me feel quite beautiful, but when Serena handed me a cap of the whitest lawn, I felt like a princess. "We'll get some ribbons on that, to match the blue," she promised.

Mags danced over wearing a fancy dress of purple satin. "See my new tackle?"

"That won't last long on the street," Kat said. Mags grinned and pranced away. She would outgrow it long before she'd wear it out, and could pass it on. Kat was quite stylish herself, in a dark green brocade that set off her hair.

When everyone was dressed in their new clothes, the old ones drying on the rosemary hedges in the kitchen garden, we gathered in the kitchen to discuss next steps. Some had parents to find. Others knew a trade. Some were orphans like the wharf rats, and I said they could join the Guild if they took the oath.

"My dears," Lady Cheshire said, "you're all welcome to stay here until you've made plans. Send a message to your family and bide here until you have an answer." That was a relief.

We settled in the kitchen. Mags hovered in the doorway, the center of attention of a group of younger kinchin. She told them about the Guild and the oath and how we'd learned to fight. She boasted she'd lead them to Haven herself. Just then, Lady Cheshire asked me a question and I turned away. When I looked back, Mags and her group were gone.

I ran outside to call them back, but a footman said the children had already left.

"They'll be all right, Lizzie," Esmeralda called. "Mags knows her way around."

Kat joined me. "Mags left?" I nodded and our eyes met. She understood. Neither of us could forget that Gilbert was still free.

"Well, *I'm* not walking home," Esmeralda said. "My leg hurts like anything, and I've been jostled, bounced, stabbed and threatened enough. I deserve to go home sitting quietly, like a lady."

Kat held up a purse and shook it. It made a lovely, full sound.

The duke must have rewarded her. "Then let's go by the river. Maybe we'll beat them home."

We said goodbye to Lady Cheshire, with more words of gratitude, and Thomas, Kat, the Hopkins sisters and I left together. The rest of the children stayed behind. The Chelsea docks were a regular stop for the watermen, so being in the money, we hired a two-oared wherry to take us to the Custom House stairs. As we moved downriver, dark clouds were piling up behind the Tower, and I hoped we'd make it home before the storm broke. Barges and high-masted ships cut through the water near us, rocking the wherry in their wake.

What would Gilbert do, with his master in the Tower? I didn't think he'd leave London without paying me back. Then I remembered Gilbert saying Mags would lead him to the "den of gifted kinchin." If he found Mags, he'd use her to find Haven.

I called to the nearest waterman. "Can we go faster? Our friend is dangerously ill. She might die before we can get there." I feared it was the truth.

Thomas and Esmeralda stared at me as though I'd lost my mind. Kat bit her lip.

The waterman shrugged and called to his partner. They increased their stroke and the boat bounced on the choppy water. The wind blew harder and the waves grew steeper.

We landed at the Custom House stairs. Black clouds loomed above us. I was about to run to Haven, when Esmeralda pulled me into a hug.

"I'll be back to Haven soon," she said. "But Serena wants me home now." I almost asked her to come with us, but she was limping and had earned a rest.

Serena hugged me too. "I'm so glad you're all right, Lizzie," she said, kissing me on the cheek. "Don't come back to work until you're ready." The sisters headed up the Fish Street hill.

Seeing his chance, Thomas leaned in and hugged me too, with a quick kiss on the cheek. "I've got to get back to my stall. The

Sweets are doing double duty. Come find me later, Lizzie." For a moment I thought of asking him to come with us, but what could he do against Gilbert's sword?

Kat and I ran up the hill with an eye on the alleys and courts where Gilbert could be hiding. By the time we reached the alley outside Haven, we were both breathing hard.

The crates blocking the door looked just the same. Inside, everything seemed peaceful and quiet: the bedding rolled away, the pots and dishes clean and lined up on the counters. *Please God, let me be wrong.*

Then I saw the children. They sat in a circle by the fire furthest from the stairs. Willie was crying. When she saw us, Penny took Deborah off her lap and rose to her feet. The children Mags had led there huddled in a group by themselves, their faces stained with tears.

Mags wasn't there.

Sairy came and took my hand. "We tried to fight him, Lizzie, but he was too quick. We were in the alley an' he just sort of appeared behind us. He said, 'Mags,' an' picked her up an' carried her away. David ran after him, but he couldn't find him. We wanted to fight for her, like the oath says, Lizzie, but they was gone."

I didn't dare cry. "It's all right. There was nothing you could do," I said.

"It was Hazelton's tracker, Gilbert," Sairy said. "An' he said: 'Tell Lizzie Mags' life will be a living hell. Tell her that exactly.' I'm sorry, Lizzie."

I took a deep breath and said, loud enough for all to hear, "Don't blame yourselves. He planned this before they left for London—for Mags to lead him to Haven. He's a professional."

Kat had come up behind me, and took in the scene. "So he has her. Does he know about Haven?"

"Yes." We'd lost our home, as well as Mags.

I tried to guess what he'd do next. I couldn't ask the rats to look for him; he was too dangerous. And wasn't this my fight alone? Mine and Kat's. He'd be happy to take his revenge on Mags, but wouldn't he rather have me instead? Wouldn't he *want* me to find him? He might let her go in exchange for me.

"I think I know where he'll go," I said. "Everyone stay here!"

GILBERT AND THE RIVER

MY VISIONS HAD WARNED ME, but I hadn't understood.

I ran down the hill toward the river. I'd search every wharf until I found him.

At the Custom House I slowed, watching the river. I'd never seen it like this. The tide was racing, whipped by the lash of the wind. Darkness had spread across the sky. The wind blew so hard I staggered, turning onto the river road, beating against it like a ship under sail.

Wharf men pointed at the rising water, shouting. Some boats were already swamped, and two small skiffs were sinking, smashed like eggs against the jetty. A wherry broke its painter and was swept away, bobbing between white-capped waves.

Men ran past, heading for shelter. Others were tying down what they could, while sailors clung to the ratlines high above the decks, taking in more sail. Some ships were leaving the wharves for safer running room at sea.

Thunder boomed and the rain came down steadily. Halfway down the Custom House wharf, someone called my name. I turned and Cynthia caught up with me, smiling.

That was so strange I stopped. "What do you want?"

"You'll want to hear my news, Lizzie Nelson."

I shook my head impatiently. "Have you seen Mags—or Gilbert, your tracker?"

She scowled. "Not mine. I had nothing to do with that. Or at least not until today. I *have* made a bargain with Gilbert, but it's one you'll approve."

"What do you mean? Where's James?"

She laughed. "I sold him to Gilbert."

I stared at her in disbelief. "Why? I thought you were in love with him."

"Love, ha!" She spat. "I thought he'd make me a lady, more fool me. Believe me or not, as you will, I didn't know where the money came from. He was selling children. He sold Potts!" Her voice rose shrilly. "He said the jobber knoll had no brains at all and could testify against him as a kidnapper. So he 'rescued' Potts from your lot, only to sell him to a captain bound for Barbados to get him out of the way. The cozening bastard thought I'd say naught. But I knew I'd be next, so I told Gilbert where to find him, once he was drunk. Now he's off to Barbados himself, and I've the coin in *my* pocket. Let him see what it's like." She pointed. "Come with me. 'Tis a sight worth seeing." She headed down the wharf and I followed, blinking against the rain. She stopped beside a cart holding a group of people huddled together against the rain.

James stood with the others, his wrists tied to the railing. They were waiting to be taken aboard the ship behind them, as cargo. James was getting a taste of what it was like to be on the other side of his business. Whoever had bought their contracts was giving them no chance to run away.

James saw Cynthia and cried out, "Help me! I'm being spirited!"

"No, James, dear. Gilbert wouldn't like it."

Surprise became anger. "He paid you."

"Perhaps." Cynthia adjusted her shawl. "*He* keeps his word."

"I'll pay you back, you faithless jade!" he yelled furiously.

"Why blame me? 'Twas Gilbert got you to sign," she said sweetly.

"By getting me drunk and lying to the captain."

People passing by stared at him. "Help! Someone! Tell a magistrate I'm being spirited!"

Then he saw me and his swagger returned. "Well, Lizzie, found your brother yet?"

I inhaled sharply. "What do you know about it?"

"You haven't figured it out? I suppose it wouldn't be fair for you to be both lucky *and* clever. I sold him to a captain headed for Virginia. For a nice tidy sum, too."

For a moment I thought I'd misheard. "You sold him across the water? You didn't nobble him because he was gifted?" I asked.

"What?" His surprise seemed genuine.

"Potts didn't tell you he was gifted?"

James face flushed red, then pale. He could've gotten far more for a gifted child. Potts had fooled him. Both his followers had paid him back for his bullying and betrayals.

"You sold Daniel to the planters," I said slowly. "And now Gilbert has done the same to you. Perhaps God is just." Daniel might even be safer in the colonies. At least such contracts were supposed to end someday. "Where *is* Gilbert?"

"That cozening whelp of the Devil—" he trailed off, his eyes on something behind me. I turned, and forgot all about James.

Gilbert had his back to me, standing in the doorway of the watermen's shelter. Clamped against his side, a small figure kicked and squirmed.

I started walking toward them.

Gilbert was shouting. As I drew closer, I recognized the waterman inside, shaking his head. Surely Gilbert didn't think he could hire a boat during a storm?

But he did. I saw him hold up a gold coin. The man hesitated, then grabbed it before Gilbert could change his mind. He led the way down the steps to where his boat was tied, bobbing violently on the swells. Gilbert pushed Mags in front of him, gesturing for her to get in.

She looked at him, then back at the waves. With an angry shove he pushed her down the stairs, then he picked her up and dropped her in the boat before climbing in himself.

"What can I do?" In my desperation, I'd spoken aloud.

"Nothing." Kat had come up beside me, breathing hard.

We stood at the edge of the wharf. The waterman stepped into the rocking boat and pulled the canvas cover forward as far as it would go, lashing it to the frame. Gilbert and Mags were now hidden from view. He cast off. In an instant, the boat was taken by the racing tide, bobbing like a cork on monstrous waves.

No other craft were out, only a couple of heavy barges trying to head upriver. Kat and I ran to the end of the wharf, keeping the boat in sight as it rose and fell, climbing each wave to topple and plunge down sickeningly, disappearing in the trough. Each time I was certain it had capsized for good.

"She'll be killed." I had to yell to be heard above the wind.

"Better that than live as Gilbert's slave," Kat said.

I shook my head. "We could take a boat—"

"No, Lizzie, we can't. No one can. We have to wait."

"Wait for what?"

She pointed. The boat was approaching the starlings beneath the bridge, the piles of rock, rubble, and wood that guarded each stone pier. White water raced in the narrow channels, and broken boats and flotsam churned around them, piled high by the storm. If the waterman's boat wasn't thrown against the starlings by the current, it might be wrecked in the whirlpool of debris.

I glanced at her. "You think they'll have to abandon the boat? On the starling?"

"Wouldn't you, if you were out there? They won't make it past the bridge piers."

My eyes never left the boat. I prayed the waterman would realize the mistake he'd made. Dead men don't spend gold. Would Gilbert agree to abandon the boat? He wanted out of London at any cost, but this was madness.

Kat and I watched, our skirts whipping around us, hands steepled over our eyes to protect them from the rain.

The boat drew near one of the channels beneath the bridge, and the waterman lost control. The boat fishtailed and swerved, heading stern first for the port starling. It swung athwart the channel, blocking it, in danger of being battered by the flotsam jostling there. Then the canvas cover flew off down the river. In a moment, the boat drifted toward the other starling. The stern would hit it if the waterman didn't regain control.

He didn't. Faster than I could see, the stern cracked and broke apart. Three people huddled in the bow, the water rising fast.

The waterman still had his oar. He stuck it into the starling closest to the bow and pulled the broken shell closer to the pile of rocks. He leapt and was safe. Then he reached for Mags. Gilbert shoved her aside to take her place.

She leapt, scrabbling at the slimy rocks, sliding down into the water until only her head was above the waves. Still she held on, the relentless current tugging at her.

The waterman reached down and pulled her out by one arm. She huddled on the rocks, soaked and shivering. But she was out of the river.

The boat had disappeared beneath the swirling brown water. Mags and the waterman sat on the starling, buffeted by the wind and threatened by the rising tide, but alive. Kat and I waited, watching the brown water for who knows how long. Of Gilbert there was no sign.

That evening after supper, I took Mags behind the curtain on the girls' side. We sat on the rolled-up bedding.

"You know 'twas Potts who betrayed you, don't you?"

She nodded. "He's an informer." She took a breath and began to cry. I put my arms around her and held her. Two of the children peeked through the curtain to see what the matter was. They walked away, whispering.

I didn't say a word, just held her. After all that had happened, she had every right to cry. When she finally pushed away, wiping her eyes with both hands, she said, "I'm still here. He'll get what's coming to him."

I nodded. "Did anyone tell you where he went?"

She raised her tear-stained face, shaking her head.

"James sold him to Barbados. We might not see him again, at least not anytime soon." Life on the plantations was harsh; many didn't survive. I thought of Daniel and felt like crying myself.

"Good," Mags said. "I hope he's marooned on an island of cannibals and they eat him."

I smiled. She probably still cared about him, whatever she said, but she was young enough to recover quickly. She wiped her face on her sleeve and returned to the children sitting around the fire to whisper in Sairy's ear. They went a little apart, speaking quietly. Mags would be all right.

I, on the other hand, was far from all right. I found a stool by the fire, feeling hopeless. I knew what had happened to Daniel, but he was beyond my help. My search was over, unless I signed a contract to go over the sea myself. But there was no guarantee I'd survive the journey, or that I'd end up anywhere near him. He could be anywhere from Virginia to Jamaica. I hoped his master or mistress would recognize the value of his gift and treat him well. There seemed nothing more I could do.

Kat came up the stairs and crossed the floor, her cloak wet. "You'll never guess what a messenger just handed to me."

"Who knows our address, Kat?"

"Don't be silly. I was at the Custom House."

She pulled a stiff piece of paper from her pocket and handed it to me. It had been folded and sealed with wax. The address said *The Wharf Rats c/o Kat Jenkins.* I slid my index finger beneath the wax seal. It had a heraldic crest with a unicorn and a lion—

I read aloud, "His Royal Majesty, King Charles the Second, Ruler of—" I stopped and raised my eyes to Kat's. The children around us had fallen silent.

"I think you can skip that part," Kat said, taking it from me. She read silently for a moment and then spoke loud enough for all to hear. "Requests the presence of five representatives of the wharf rats to attend upon him at Whitehall Palace, in the king's study on September 18, 1661. Present this letter to the king's gentlemen at two o'clock in the afternoon. Signed Carolus Rex, etc."

Kat smiled mischievously. "The king wants to see us, Lizzie. Are you ready to ask him to make the Guild official?"

34

THE KING

Esmeralda came up the stairs while we were rolling out the bedding. She said she wanted to be sure we were all safe and sound, but I believe she missed us. Kat told her Gilbert was likely drowned, that James had sold my brother *and* Potts as indentured labor across the sea, and having seen where the wind was blowing, Cynthia had done the same to him.

Esmeralda was silent a moment. "So that's over."

Before we went to bed, we voted on who should meet with the king. In the end it was agreed that Kat, Esmeralda, Mags, and I should go. Esmeralda, however, declined the honor, saying that if the king never knew she existed, that would be fine with her. I guessed Cromwell's spy didn't want the attention. The children chose Penny to replace her and there was one spot left.

Sairy suggested Thomas, even though he wasn't a rat, because he'd helped us escape and helped save the king by disarming Jeremiah. Everyone agreed, so I wrote to ask him to meet us the next day at noon by the Custom House stairs, wearing his best clothes. Jimmy volunteered to take it to Thomas's house. I told him to warn Thomas the meeting was with the king, since Kat said we shouldn't put that in writing. She also said we must go to Whitehall Palace by the river to avoid getting mud all over our clothes. The rain still thrummed on the roof and heavy grey clouds filled the windows. No matter how we traveled tomorrow, we'd get wet.

INDEED, the rain beat down the next morning, churning the river to a boiling brown. We wore the clothes Lady Cheshire had given us, and Esmeralda brought Penny one of her green dresses to wear for the occasion. We pooled the few respectable cloaks among us and left Haven, trying to keep our skirts and cloaks out of the mud.

Thomas was waiting for us at the Custom House stairs. Then we all waited miserably in the rain for twenty minutes before we found a wherry to take us to the Palace stairs. We'd left early, though, so we arrived in good time. I'd been afraid we'd lose ourselves in Whitehall's maze of rooms, but Kat seemed to know her way about. The footmen recognized her too, more evidence of just how important Kat was. I suspected the invitation was her doing.

A footman ushered us into a small sitting room, beautifully appointed. Tapestries of red, green, and blue depicted a hunting scene on one wall, with something mythological involving nymphs and satyrs on the other. The legs of the table and chairs were carved with vines and flowers, the seat cushions embroidered with flowers and fruit. A bright fire burned on the hearth, more than welcome, for the Palace was damp and cold. We hung our cloaks on the fire screen to dry.

After a quarter of an hour the footman returned to announce His Majesty would soon be with us. "Would you care for refreshments while you wait?" he asked. Everyone nodded and he came back with a silver tray of cakes and ale. We ate hungrily; most of us had been too nervous to eat before. Warmed by the ale, I was almost ready for what was to come.

With no warning, the king entered the room, followed by two spaniel puppies that wagged their tails excitedly at visitors, licked our hands, then peed on the beautiful carpet. I tried to conceal my shock. We all curtsied and bowed, Thomas doffing his cap with a flourish.

The king sat and waved for us to be seated. "We wished to personally thank you for ridding us of that man, Hazelton. He's been a threat to our kingdom for too long. We are most grateful. May I know your names?"

One by one we introduced ourselves.

"And who is your leader?"

Before I could speak, Kat glanced at me. "Lizzie is. The Wharf Rat Guild was her idea."

I shot her a look of gratitude.

"Well, then," said the king, "let me say informally that my brother and I are most grateful for your help in ridding my kingdom of that pestilential man." He regarded us thoughtfully. "Given his most barbarous treatment of you and other gifted children, we thought you'd be pleased to know that Hazelton and his man Jeremiah were tried and found guilty of treason. Hazelton's title is abolished and his estates are forfeit. As of yesterday, Hazelton's head adorns Traitor's Gate, beside that of Jeremiah Sawyer."

I stole a glance at Thomas. He'd gotten his wish.

"On another matter," he began but stopped, for Mags had walked over to stand in front of him.

"Mags!" Penny hissed. "Come back!"

"Yes, my child?"

"Will you stop the agents and trackers, Your Majesty? Stop them from kidnapping us?"

He frowned. "Unfortunately, that is not a simple request. There are many surplus workers, and the planters and merchants need their labor in the colonies. Besides, catching trackers is difficult. 'Tis even more difficult to control the nobility."

"But you're the king!" Mags said, frowning. "Can't you do anything you want?"

Charles the Second gave a rueful laugh. "No, child, not anything. The nobles are powerful too." He leaned forward to pat Mags on the cheek and smiled. "Please be seated. We have more to say. And you may know that my brother has one or two ideas about dealing with trackers."

Mags frowned, but returned to her seat, with arms folded.

"We've heard your request," he glanced at Kat, "to be allowed to form a Guild, but that cannot be. The ancient Guilds of the City of London guard their privileges jealously. It would cause no end of trouble and they won't accept you. Children, especially *girls*, cannot be free citizens of London. The Lord Mayor and Aldermen would be furious."

Penny and Mags looked disappointed. We'd known it wasn't likely, but I felt let down. We'd done the king a service—he'd just said so. I didn't know about the politics. But I noticed Kat looked smug.

The king raised his hand. "However, we *are* grateful and we recognize our obligation to you. Lady Cheshire proposed another idea. Perhaps a better one." The corners of his mouth twitched.

"The merchants of the City will one day be as powerful as the nobility, perhaps not in a year, but certainly in twenty. Trade runs the City, the City runs London, and London runs the country." He paused, staring into the fire. "You children are important to the shipping that creates the wealth of London and my kingdom. It is only fitting, we think, that you become a chartered *Company* to reflect this importance. Therefore," the king said, "we have decided to grant you a Charter to form the Royal Company of Wharf Rats." The king held up a long document affixed with red seals and ribbons.

"This is the Charter. We suggest you put it in a safe place. Lord Montagu can help you with that." He glanced toward the door where a gentleman who had entered with the king stood waiting. He looked imposing, with a large brooch glittering with diamonds on his blue sash. He came forward and took the Charter from the king to hand it to me.

Flustered, I nodded when I should have curtsied.

"Here"—the king drew out another piece of paper—"is a letter to my banker, if you would like to avail yourselves of his services. He can keep your funds safe for you. Also, please accept this, um, more substantial, token of our gratitude." He nodded at Lord Montagu, who stepped forward to place the letter and a small but heavy leather bag in my hand.

Everyone watched me expectantly.

I stood and curtsied. "Thank you, Your Majesty, you are most generous." I glanced at the others. I didn't know what else I should say.

"Now, you'd probably like to know what that means, being a Royal Chartered Company?" the king asked, his eyes crinkling at the corners.

"Yes, Your Majesty," I said.

"Well, in this case, it means we have drawn up articles of incorporation that outline your duties as king's messengers. We have also issued a Royal Decree, directing the Custom House clerks and Excise men to deal *exclusively* with The Royal Chartered Company of Wharf Rats. Every time they send messages or contracts to the wharves, to the Exchange, or to clerks in Whitehall, they must hire you first, at set rates."

"You mean the clerks at the Custom House *have* to hire us?" I thought of the prune-faced clerk who'd tried to chase us out. "And so will the ship captains? And the merchants?"

The king smiled. "That's it exactly, Mistress Nelson. We believe you are living in a building whose owner was arrested for smuggling, was he not, Montagu?"

Lord Montagu bent his head in agreement.

"Since his goods were forfeit to the Crown when he was convicted, I shall grant the building to you. You now own—what did you call it?"

I stared at him in disbelief. "Haven, Your Majesty."

He sat back, folding his hands across his stomach. "Haven. Very appropriate." He gazed at us with a mischievous expression. "We've also taken the liberty of directing the College of Heralds to devise a seal for your company. All royal companies have one."

Mags blinked. "You mean the pictures on the stamps, right? We see 'em on the casks and crates."

The king nodded. "Precisely." He reached behind him to remove a sheet of parchment from a folio on the table. He looked at it for a moment, eyes crinkling, then held it up. "Here's your seal. As you can see, it has two rats rampant above a bridge, representing London Bridge, over azure waves for the river (the heralds prefer to see the world in its ideal state). Here's my name in Latin, required to make it official, I'm afraid, '*Carolus Secondus, Regis Magnae Brittaniae, Francia et Hibernia*'—anyway, rats, the bridge, and the Thames. What could be better, eh? I hope you like it."

We stared. Mags giggled nervously and Thomas burst out laughing. The king joined him and we all laughed at the picture of rats dancing above the river. We were a Royal Chartered Company, with rights, privileges, and obligations to the king.

AFTERWARDS, we decided a celebration was in order. Thomas begged off, saying he had to be back at his stall before supper. Since we'd pass it on the way, we walked to Covent Square with him. By the time we reached the square it was raining so hard most of the stalls had closed. We took shelter inside the Sweets' shop, and when Thomas told them where we'd been, they insisted we start our celebration there. They handed 'round gingerbread and spiced wine to keep out the chill, and I unwrapped the seal carefully from the oilskin cloth the king's Secretary had wrapped it in, to show it off.

"That's a proper king then, if we have to have one," Gaffer Sweets said, handing the parchment back. "Not like his father. His father hadn't a sense of humor to save his life."

His wife cleared her throat and Gaffer Sweets realized he'd said too much. "Still, it's odd for a king to put rats on a seal, isn't it?" he said.

"Well, no one will dispute them the privilege," Thomas said.

We waited for the rain to slacken before trudging back to Haven, our finery bedraggled and damp. Patches of blue sky appeared in the west. The clouds were breaking up, though it was still drizzling when we arrived home. All the rats crowded 'round to hear what had happened. I let Kat and Penny tell the tale, while Mags boasted to Sairy of her talk with the king. I put the seal on a high shelf where all could see it, but it would come to no harm.

Then I pulled off my wet dress, wrapped myself in my blue blanket, and lay down. I wanted to be quiet and rest. In spite of the good news, I felt lonely and sad. Whatever happened for the rats, I'd still failed Daniel. It looked as though I'd never see my brother again. I muffled my face in the pillow, cried a little, quietly, and fell asleep.

AFTER SUPPER, the children gathered around the fire and asked Penny to tell the story again.

I drew Kat aside. "What did the king mean about the duke having 'one or two ideas' about stopping trackers?"

She led me away from the chattering children into a corner. "Don't tell Esmeralda, but the duke will hire anyone willing to use their gift to work with us. We catch trackers, smugglers, and

Catholic plotters. It's interesting work, and the duke is a fair man."

I glared at her. It was dangerous work, was what it was, and why did she think I'd keep secrets from Esmeralda? "I don't like it. Did you help free the children from Lord Hazelton just so they could become spies for your duke? Besides, I'm supposed to be running a messenger service. How will I do that if you take my messengers away from me?"

"Only a few, Lizzie, the ones that have a gift useful for the work, and only volunteers. I didn't think you'd be stubborn about this."

"You want to use them as cannon fodder in the duke's plots." My voice broke with the threat of tears. I didn't know why I was so upset. Heads turned to look.

Kat's eyes flashed. "No, I want them to catch trackers and stop plots against the king, like *you* just did. I'll be training them personally. It's no more dangerous than being on the wharves with trackers looking for you. Maybe less. We're always on the lookout for gifted children. We might hear news of Daniel."

One more false hope; was she trying to lead me by the nose? "Hmph. Why should I keep this secret from Esmeralda? Don't you trust her?"

"Oh, Lizzie." Kat sounded exasperated. "Of course I trust her —up to a point. I'm not asking you to lie. I just don't want to hear more of her ranting Cromwellian nonsense."

That at least was probably true. "So where do your loyalties lie, Kat? Are you using us to win favor with your duke? Would you betray us if he decides we'd be more useful as slaves? Or do you trust nobs and kings completely now?"

"I was wondering when you'd finally ask that."

I crossed my arms. "Do you have an answer?"

"Yes. I work for the duke, Lizzie, because no one should be held against their will, not wharf rats, nor Dissenters, nor Quakers, nor servants, nor Africans—no one. We're supposed to be free Englishmen. As long as the duke supports that, I support him."

"And when he doesn't?"

A flicker of a smile. "I'm a wharf rat with a gift, in as much danger as anyone else. I know who my friends are. The duke is always suspicious. How much do you think he trusts someone who can become invisible?"

"Then why work for him?"

"Because he values my gift and his power helps me defend myself. It's a bargain of mutual advantage. As you say, he could change his mind, but so far he's never done anything to make me doubt him."

I nodded, still upset. Kat would do as she would, Royal Chartered Company or no. And she was right: keeping the good will of both the king and the duke was insurance for the future. "Let's talk about it later. The children will be messengers for the company until I'm convinced otherwise. For one thing, it's safer. For another, I'm not about to explain to the king why we rejected his generous offer."

"We're still on the same side, Lizzie." She smiled and added gently, "And if I can help you find Daniel, I will."

That finally undid me. I hurried away to cry in the cellar.

35

AFTER THE DELUGE

THE DAY we met the king was the beginning of the worst rain-storm any of us had ever seen; it lasted for weeks. We stayed inside, sending a few brave volunteers out for supplies. There was no work on the wharves since no ships would risk the fierce winds. The Thames flooded its banks, sending the muck of the river into the streets and warehouses near it. We were lucky Haven was on a hill. When the rain finally stopped, the feeble sun revealed a stinking mess of water in the low-lying streets, with mud and garbage everywhere. Once the river dropped below its banks, Mud Men appeared to clear the wreckage. Perhaps they'd find Gilbert's body.

Inside Haven, we played games, practiced self-defense, and talked over all that had happened. The younger children easily accepted Hazelton's death and the king's favor. For them, every-thing was new and change was easy. But nothing lifted my sadness. That there was nothing I could do about Daniel, it dragged on me. The good fortune of the Guild felt hollow.

We divided up the reward money, giving some to Thomas and Esmeralda, using the rest to make Haven more comfortable, with real bedding, more kitchen things and shoes for everyone. Mags finally had boots that covered her toes.

The biggest change was in the rats. Confident they could defend themselves, they were cautious, but not afraid. For the first time, they made plans for the future. Mattie, Penny, and Jimmy sewed blue armbands with a white badge painted with our seal, to identify members of the company. Mags and Sairy modeled them for me, strutting around Haven with their heads held high.

One morning Jimmy woke us early, saying the alley was blocked. He'd gone to buy food only to return muddy and frightened. "There are Mud Men at both ends of our alley. I had to go next door to their roof to jump to ours." It took me a moment to understand him. The two buildings weren't that close, but Jimmy's speed had sent him flying across the gap, at the risk of a long fall to the street below. I shivered. Had the king changed his mind and decided to sell us?

Kat saw my expression and shook her head. "I don't think they're here to nobble us. But let's find out." She was down the cellar steps before I could stop her. I ran to the door and watched her in the mirror above the alley. The others crowded about me, whispering.

"She's walking up to one. God's teeth! He just bowed to her. He seems polite enough. Now he's gesturing at the alley. I have no—she's coming back." I moved away from the door.

Back inside, Kat stood on the bottom step of the stairs and turned to face us. "We can remove the boards on the door," she said, brushing off her sleeves. "The Mud Men are here to guard us against trackers, at the request of the king. We can tell people where to find us, Lizzie. It'll be good for business. We'll need a guard inside though, and a table for messages."

The rats looked at each other in silence. If we didn't have to hide, things would be different. With the Mud Men on guard, no tracker would wait for us in the alley. We had a powerful protector, and folk would know it. I could give the sailors my address, in hopes that when Daniel returned, he would find me. I had to believe he'd return.

When the city began to reopen for business, we made handbills advertising our messenger service. Kat took a stack to the Custom House, and I carried mine to the Royal Exchange.

On buff paper the black lettering said: *By Appointment to His Majesty, Rex Carolus II, the Wharf Rats are designated Royal Messengers for trade upon the wharves. Inquire at the Custom House or Royal Exchange.* At the top was our seal; Sairy had drawn a fair copy and Jimmy's friend at the printers had cut the die. It was quite handsome.

The Exchange was crowded with folk shopping for goods from all over the world. I wandered through the arcades, looking for customers. When I found a likely one, I smiled, curtseyed, and gave him a handbill. Most laughed when they saw the seal, but I was pleased to see they tucked it away in their pockets. Even if they kept it simply to share the joke with their wives or friends at the tavern, they'd remember us. Word would spread.

Returning by the river road, I met Thomas carrying a large package under his arm. He was as pleased as I'd ever seen him. With his share of the reward money he'd bought his market garden. Three other grocers had already promised to buy from him. He was on his way.

"And," he said, holding out the package with a flourish, "there was enough left over to buy you a present. I hope you like it."

"Thomas, that's wonderful. You've worked so hard, you deserve it. But you didn't have to get me anything…" I trailed off. I heard the caution in my voice, and so did he.

He burst out laughing. "You should see your face. Don't worry, I'm not going to hound you to marry me. You don't have to avoid the lovesick noddy. Just open it, will you?" He handed me the package. It was heavy, wrapped in brown paper and tied with string.

"You'll have to hold it." I undid the knots and pulled off the paper, but I couldn't tell what it was until Thomas stepped back and I saw it properly.

It was a signboard, like those all over London, marking the address of shops or homes with a picture. Painted in bright colors on a piece of heavy oak was the seal of our company. Picked out in red were the words, *The Wharf Rat Company.*

"It's beautiful!" I said. It truly was.

"I'll help you hang it over the door. Can't have a business without a sign."

I tilted it to see the colors gleam. "It's perfect, but you shouldn't have spent your money on us. You'll need it for your market garden."

"Consider it my investment in your company. I expect dividends, mind." His eyes laughed in a way I found appealing. "I'll carry it back for you."

"Thomas, about that lovesick noddy. I want him to know—" I felt my face turning red and stopped uncertainly. "Well, that I feel the same way. But I can't leave the rats, not yet."

He didn't smile, he just put the signboard down and pulled me into an embrace, and we kissed for the first time. "But someday," he said when we stood apart.

After that, we were comfortable together. I knew he understood about the rats.

The number of customers on our first day was astonishing. Stranger still, not one of them haggled over the fees. We'd printed 'em on a sign posted on the desks at the Exchange and Custom House. Customers simply accepted them. We could well afford to keep the little ones inside now.

At the end of that first week of business, I was at the Custom House, tired and out of sorts from arguing with the prune-faced clerk about the location of our desk, when Mags came running up to me. "Lizzie, come quick!"

"What's the matter?"

She pulled on my arm. "Trouble at Haven. Kat says you have to come."

I escaped from the clerk with relief. Mags and I ran up the hill, arriving hot and out of breath. The Mud Men waved cheerfully. No sign of trouble there.

Climbing the cellar stairs, I smelled lamb and nettle stew, my favorite, and something else. Flowers?

At the top of the stairs, I stopped.

Streamers hung from the windows, and a centerpiece of roses sat between covered dishes on a white tablecloth.

Serena, Esmeralda, Kat, and Thomas stood beside the table, the kinchin gathered around them. Penny glanced up from where she was pouring something into bowls.

"Happy birthday, Lizzie!" everyone shouted. I was too surprised to move until Mags led me to the table. That was when I saw the presents. There were so many, I felt a moment of panic at what they must have cost. We couldn't afford extravagance, not when the children kept growing out of their clothes.

Serena stepped forward. "Lizzie, dear, we wish you a very happy birthday. Your family decided you deserved a party. And we have a Guild matter to discuss too." Serena had taken the oath after we'd returned. I helped in the shop now and then, but she'd hired a new rat to take my place.

My family? Yes, that was what they were.

Mattie stepped forward, hand in hand with Benjamin, and said with great seriousness, "Thank you, Lizzie, for the Guild, for stopping Hazelton, for bringing my brother home, and for making our lives better. Without you, none of this"—she gestured at the room—"would exist. Because we trusted you, we learned to trust each other."

They clapped and looked at me expectantly.

I took a deep breath and shook my head. "We did this together. You all took the risk and believed in each other. Be proud of yourselves."

Thomas shouted, "Three cheers for the Royal Company of Wharf Rats! Hip, hip, hooray!"

They cheered three times. I wiped tears away, hoping no one saw.

Then Kat raised her hands and said, "We decided to give you a better present than sweetmeats or new clobber. Mags?"

I waited, mystified, while Mags came forward. "We know you blame yourself that Daniel was taken away," she said. "But that's being a clunch-pate." Heads nodded vigorously.

"But," I began, "you don't understand—"

"Actually, we do," Mattie said, slipping her arm over Mags's shoulder. "Benjamin was nobbled too, remember? And I was there in Bridewell that night he helped Penny. I saw what happened. There was nothing you could have done. The jailer could've taken him any time, for any reason. Daniel was excited and happy to get a ship. He thought he'd learn a trade, have adventures. You let him have hope, even if it wasn't true. Aren't you glad he wasn't at Hazelton's, where he could've been starved or killed?"

I bit my lip. "I should've stopped him from helping—" I stopped, realizing what I was about to say. I glanced at Penny and flushed with shame.

Mattie grinned. "It's all right, Lizzie. We know. Who knows better than we do, what it's like? But you have to stop flogging yourself. It wasn't your fault. We aren't responsible for trackers. It wasn't your fault then, and it's not your fault now. Daniel saved Penny's life. You helped all the rats. What is there to feel guilty about?"

I was in mortal danger of crying. I gave her a wobbly smile. "Thanks."

Jimmy saved me by loudly singing the first lines of the *Wharf Rats* song. Mags joined in, and then everyone did. When it was over the rats clapped loudly, hugging each other. I wiped my eyes.

"Food's ready!" Penny announced. While Emily and Sairy served the others, Penny led me to the end of the table and whipped off a cloth, revealing a large cake. I took her hand and said quietly, "I wouldn't have survived a day on the wharves without you. Thank you."

She shrugged. "You taught me a few things too, Lucky Lizzie." She went back to help hand out the food.

Everyone ate while I opened the presents. I got a new blue stomacher that matched my skirt, from Serena and Esmeralda, but most of 'em turned out to be useful items for sharing, like cloaks for the little ones, so someone had known what I'd really like, Penny probably. Thomas had already given me the signboard; he caught my eye and winked.

I sat beside the hearth, watching the faces of the children in the warm light of the fire. Some had fallen asleep. Esmeralda brought a mug of ale and joined me. "You know, I like it here," she said with a sigh. "Reminds me of the old days." She dropped her voice. "I'll be off traveling, Lizzie. Don't tell Kat. Not even Serena knows where I'm really going. She's not as young as she used to be, and I don't want to worry her. I've written a contact down for you, in case you need to get in touch with me, but Kat must never know."

It sounded dangerous. "Do you have to go? I wish you and Kat weren't—"

"But we are. It's not a problem for us. We just have to be mindful not to interfere with each other's business. Here." She handed me a slip of paper, sealed with a dab of wax. "That's the name and address of a cove who can get a message to me. If Kat knew about it, she'd do her duty, even if she didn't want to."

I sighed. "All right. If I'm to keep secrets, can I know what it's about?"

"Better if you don't."

I pocketed the paper, hoping she wasn't involved in a conspiracy against the king. "I'll keep it safe."

"There's something else I wanted to say," she continued. "'Tis a good moment to remind you of your good fortune, with all of us here together. When you consider it, most of us should be dead in the river or starving in some nob's cellar. Instead, here's a family of good-hearted souls you can trust, a thriving business, and kinchin to look after. Not a bad life."

She'd surprised me. "I've never heard you talk like this before."

"Well, you probably won't again, my chick, so don't get used to it. We all need to be reminded, sometimes, how lucky we are. Don't pine for what you don't have. Don't let worrying about Daniel cause you to miss what's good right now. For all you know, he's having a fine time. Wherever he is, punishing yourself won't help him."

First the kinchin telling me I wasn't to blame, and now Esmeralda giving advice. Everyone had noticed my sadness about Daniel. She was right. It was time to focus on the family I did have, right there.

"You may be right," I said softly.

It was the best birthday I ever had. I would say it was the best day of my life, even including the visit with the king, except that two weeks later, something strange and wonderful happened.

I was on Botolph's Quay, waiting for the reply to a merchant's message, when a sailor approached me.

"You that Lizzie Nelson who goes around asking for her brother?"

I couldn't breathe for a moment. "I am."

The sailor bowed, looking up at me with a grin before he straightened. "Here's something you'll like, then." He handed me a letter sealed with wax. My name was written on the outside and the handwriting was familiar.

I opened it then and there, forgetting all about the sailor.

Dear Lizzie,

I'm writing to let you know I was sold to Virginia, but the Captain changed his mind and kept me as his cabin boy after all. I am fine.

Captain says two more voyages up and down the coast here and we'll be back to England. Captain changed his mind about selling me when he saw my gift. I know you've been worrying away all this time and please stop. I'll be home in a year or so, with coin in my pocket. I hope you're safe and well and the rats are taking care of you. Stay away from James. He's a hollow-hearted rogue.

Love, Daniel

Believe me, I tipped the sailor generously after I read that. He'd brought me happiness from over the sea.

The day I received that letter was the best day of my life. Or it will be, until Daniel comes home. Thomas still wants to marry, but he's willing to wait. And meanwhile, I'll be running the messenger service.

It seems I'm *Lucky Lizzie* after all.

The End

<<<<>>>>

GLOSSARY

bailiff. Enforces laws, especially against debtors or renters. One charged with public administrative authority in a certain district.

beldam. An aged woman, a matron of advanced years.

bufflehead. A fool, blockhead, stupid fellow.

catchpoll. Thief taker. A petty officer of justice; a sheriff's officer or sergeant, esp. a warrant officer who arrests for debt, a bum-bailiff.

chit. Young girl.

clobber. Clothes.

clod-pate. Foolish fellow

clunch-pate. Stupid fellow.

costermonger. Green grocer

cove. Man

cozen. To cheat, defraud by deceit.

doxy. Unmarried mistress of a rogue.

foist. Pickpocket.

footpad. Robber, highwayman who robs on foot.

gob. Mouth.

jobber knoll. Blockhead, foolish person who talks too much.

jack-pudding. A buffoon, clown, or merry-andrew, esp. one attending on a mountebank.

jade. Demeaning term for a woman (originally used for horses).

kinchin. Children.

linkboy. A boy employed to carry a link (torch) to light passengers along the streets.

looby. A lazy hulking fellow; a lout; an awkward, stupid, clownish person.

mort. Girl or woman.

mountebank. An itinerant quack who from an elevated platform appealed to his audience by means of stories, tricks, juggling, and the like, in which he was often assisted by a professional clown or fool.

Mud Men. Bum bailiffs sent to do the dirty jobs.

Myrmidon. A faithful follower or servant (17th-Century slang). Otherwise a soldier or bodyguard.

nob. Member of the nobility.

noddle-headed. Foolish.

noddy. A fool, simpleton, noodle.

nook-shotten. Awkward corners and angles, a hodge-podge

parkin. Gingerbread made with oatmeal.

peach. To inform on. To give incriminating evidence against.

periwig. A massive wig of long curled hair, usually artificial; a sign of wealth, status and fashion

peruke. A smaller more natural-looking wig. Or referring to natural hair in a queue.

pig-widgeon. A simpleton, contemptible, insignificant or petty person,

poxy. Disease-ridden. Infected with pox; spotty; figurative meaning, trashy, worthless. Also a general term of abuse.

Quality. A person of rank, upper classes, *see* nob.

ragtag. The ragged, disreputable portion of the community; the riffraff or rabble.

rogue. Dishonest fellow, criminal.

Rope-dancer. Tightrope walker. One who 'dances' or balances on a rope suspended at some height above the ground; a funambulist.

shallow-pate. Stupid fellow.

spirits. Agents who kidnap adults and children to sell as labor overseas.

tackle. Clothes, esp. of sailors

tracker. Men hired to find and kidnap gifted children for the nobility

trull. Dishonest woman, criminal, prostitute.

wench. Woman.

AFTERWORD

The attentive reader may recall that there was nothing about gifted children in their history books. That is, of course, because that part of the wharf rats' adventures is made up, as are all the main characters with the exception of King Charles II and the Duke of York.

Agents kidnapping children and shipping them overseas, however, is entirely accurate for this time period, a practice lasting well over a hundred years. Children as young as six were taken, although the usual targets were adults or teens. The fate of all of these "servants" was often grim, especially in struggling colonies like Virginia where the population couldn't feed itself in the early days. Some servants starved to death. There was no guarantee that the master or mistress who bought a child's contract would bother to feed or clothe them, although the contracts stated they had that responsibility.

Orphaned children and men without jobs were considered a burden on the Kingdom (by the nobs and the merchants). These "surplus" people were supposed to be fed in the parish poor-houses. Charles II was all too happy to have this "burden" shipped overseas to take its chances, and to provide relatively cheap labor to the upper class planters. The King was *not*, as far as we know, sympathetic to the plight of children kidnapped in this way.

It was only after a public outcry, driven by parents of kidnapped children, that Parliament passed a law against such kidnappings; the citation for that is at the beginning of the first chapter. This is when and how the word "kidnapping" entered the English language.

Many of the earliest English immigrants to this country were shipped here against their will, or came because they were desperate for work. That part of the wharf rats' story is all too true.

About alcohol

Yes, children drank ale, beer, and wine. Access to clean water in London was chancy, and most people knew it was safer to drink ale or beer, however weak, rather than risk the water from the river. The Thames received industrial waste as well as rubbish from households and was a reliable source of disease.

ABOUT THE AUTHOR

Elizabeth Forest is a former librarian who lives in Northern California, where she writes speculative and historical fiction for all ages.

If you liked this book, please leave a review at your favorite bookseller!

Also by Elizabeth Forest:

The Third Kind of Magic — *Book One in the Crow Magic series*
The Cursed Amulet — *Book Two in the Crow Magic series*
Sign up for Elizabeth's newsletter, with giveaways and the latest releases, here:
https://www.elizabethsforest.com/newsletter
Find Elizabeth Forest's other books on her website at:
https://www.elizabethsforest.com
or chat with her at:
twitter.com/@elizasforest

www.ingramcontent.com/pod-product-compliance
Lightning Source LLC
Chambersburg PA
CBHW021641110726

47902CB00007B/1778